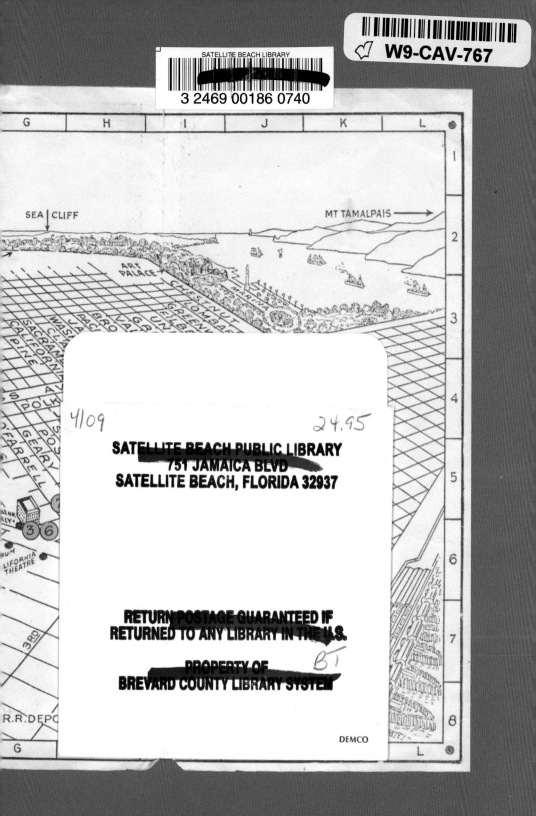

DEVIL'S
GARDEN

DEVIL'S
GARDEN

ACE ATKINS

G. P. PUTNAM'S SONS
NEW YORK

PUTNAM

G. P. PUTNAM'S SONS
Publishers Since 1838
Published by the Penguin Group
Penguin Group (USA) Inc., 375 Hudson Street, New York, New York 10014, USA • Penguin Group (Canada),
90 Eglinton Avenue East, Suite 700, Toronto, Ontario M4P 2Y3, Canada (a division of Pearson Canada Inc.) •
Penguin Books Ltd, 80 Strand, London WC2R 0RL, England • Penguin Ireland, 25 St Stephen's Green, Dublin 2,
Ireland (a division of Penguin Books Ltd) • Penguin Group (Australia), 250 Camberwell Road, Camberwell,
Victoria 3124, Australia (a division of Pearson Australia Group Pty Ltd) • Penguin Books India Pvt Ltd,
11 Community Centre, Panchsheel Park, New Delhi–110 017, India • Penguin Group (NZ), 67 Apollo Drive,
Rosedale, North Shore 0632, New Zealand (a division of Pearson New Zealand Ltd) • Penguin Books
(South Africa) (Pty) Ltd, 24 Sturdee Avenue, Rosebank, Johannesburg 2196, South Africa

Penguin Books Ltd, Registered Offices: 80 Strand, London WC2R 0RL, England

Library of Congress Cataloging-in-Publication Data

Atkins, Ace.
    Devil's garden / Ace Atkins.
        p.   cm.
    ISBN 978-0-399-15536-9
    1. Arbuckle, Roscoe, 1887–1933—Fiction.   2. Rappe, Virginia, 1895–1921—Fiction.   3. Hammett, Dashiell,
1894–1961—Fiction.   4. Motion picture actors and actresses—Fiction.   5. Private investigators—Fiction.
6. Trials (Murder)—California—Fiction.   I. Title.
    PS3551.T49D48   2009   2008046361
    813'.54—dc22

Printed in the United States of America
10 9 8 7 6 5 4 3 2 1

BOOK DESIGN BY MEIGHAN CAVANAUGH

This is a work of fiction. Names, characters, places, and incidents either are the product of the author's imagination
or are used fictitiously. Except for the author's fictional use of the actual death of Virginia Rappe and the subsequent
trial and media coverage, any resemblance to actual persons, living or dead, businesses, companies, events, or locales
is entirely coincidental.

While the author has made every effort to provide accurate telephone numbers and Internet addresses at the time of
publication, neither the publisher nor the author assumes any responsibility for errors, or for changes that occur after
publication. Further, the publisher does not have any control over and does not assume any responsibility for author
or third-party websites or their content.

To Angel

The American public is ardent in its hero worship and quite as ruthless in destroying its idols in any walk of life. It elevates a man more quickly than any nation in the world, and casts him down more quickly—quite often on surmise or a mere hunch.

—ROSCOE ARBUCKLE, 1922

The Arbuckle case was the funniest case I ever worked on. In trying to convict him, everyone framed everybody else.

—DASHIELL HAMMETT, *New York Herald Tribune*, 1933

DEVIL'S
GARDEN

July 31, 1917

Anaconda, Montana

H*e'd shadowed Frank Little for weeks, from El Paso to Butte to Bisbee, and for days now along the wooden sidewalks of the old mining town, built at the base of bleak hills where dusty workers made their way up a crooked path to the foundry and deep down into the earth. They'd started work on the furnace then, and half of the brick phallus rose from the city, towering above the buildings and hills, and would soon smelt the copper they'd sell for twenty-six cents a pound to make pots and newspaper presses.*

The town smelled of acrid metal and burnt meat.

Anaconda was open all night. There were saloons and whorehouses and one good hotel and dozens of bad ones, rooming houses where Sam had taken a bed. In the off-hours, when Little would wobble up the staircase and get an hour or two of sleep, Sam would lay on the narrow bed and read the Butte newspapers about a possible war with Germany and a ragged copy of Dangerous Ground, *a novel about a Pinkerton he'd had since he was a boy.*

It used to be an adventure. Now it was just a reminder.

He'd asked for the room two doors down from Little, where he'd loosened a plank by the stairs so he'd hear a squeak when the union leader went on his rounds. Sam had heard most of the speeches before, Little talking mainly about the country only having two classes, one exploiting the other, and how International Workers of the World wanted to make the fat cats pay for strong backs.

Little said he'd once been arrested for reading the Declaration of Independence on a street corner.

He talked about that mining disaster in Butte in June and how the boys in Anaconda worked under even worse conditions. He called the furnace chimney another ivory tower where the wealthy burned up the common man.

The Pinkerton's client was supposed to be kept under wraps, but Sam knew it was the Hearst outfit, which owned a piece of pretty much every mine in the country. He was told to tail Little, make notes on the speeches, type out a neat report, and send it back to Baltimore. It was a basic assignment that didn't need much thought.

The food wasn't bad. Now and then he could sneak a whiskey at the bars. And two nights ago he'd found a fine, full redheaded whore named Sally who worked overtime off the clock.

Sam heard a creak, put down the copy of Dangerous Ground, noting the Pinkerton standing on the hill shining a beacon of light down on a hooved red devil leading a virtuous woman away, and he followed Little down the stairs through the narrow lobby and out onto Main Street. There were horses and wagons and an automobile or two, the gas lamps burning all the way past the Montana Hotel, down to City Hall and to the dead end of mountain and mine.

Little was up on some wooden crates, talking again, waving his hands wildly to men in overalls and women holding up hand-painted signs. The women looked determined; the men looked scared.

The light was just going down in Anaconda, the shadows on the hills showing purple and black with bright yellow patches. As Sam jotted down some of what Little said, really just repeating a speech he'd heard two weeks ago in Bisbee about those miners shipped off to die in boxcars, he felt a soft hand on his shoulder and turned to see a man dressed in a three-piece black suit holding a gold timepiece in his hand.

"Has a lot of wind, doesn't he, friend?"

Sam nodded.

The man clicked the gold watch closed and removed a pouch of tobacco from his vest pocket.

"He's gonna keep going. How 'bout a drink?"

Sam thanked him but said no.

"You're the Pinkerton, aren't you? One of them anyway."

Sam turned back. The man grinned and spit brown tobacco juice on the ground. "Let's have that drink."

They found a saloon called Kate's just off Main Street filled with miners and whores and a back table where a sweaty Chinaman cooked T-bone steaks on an open grill. Sam Hammett, just an edge over twenty but nearly white-headed, leaned back in his seat and put a match to a Fatima cigarette.

The man removed the wad of tobacco from his cheek and tossed it below the table.

Men in the front room had gathered around a piano. A whore was singing "Buffalo Gals," and the men yelled and thumped their boots on the wooden floors, and in all the action and laughter, Sam and the man were alone.

"I won't waste time," he said. "I have a deal to make."

Sam nodded.

"I'll put up five hundred dollars over your Pinkerton pay to shut Little's mouth."

Sam burned down the cigarette, nearly coughing on the smoke. He watched the man but didn't say a word.

"That's not my job."

"The money all comes from the same place."

"Hearst?" Sam said, smiling, confident he was right.

"I'm not at liberty."

"But you are at liberty to hire me out like a goon."

"Not a goon."

"Go hire some palooka," Sam said. "This isn't my line."

He stood. The man grabbed his arm, trying to stop him, and tried to crush great wide green bills into Sam's hand. "I'm not talking about a beating."

*Sam looked down at him, at his jug ears and iron-gray hair and dark com-
plexion, and walked away into the crowd, brushing by a fat whore who grabbed
his pecker through his trousers the way some shake hands.*

*He could breathe on the street, and he walked the wooden planks southward,
back toward the emerging smokestack of the mine, and found Little there talking to a dispersing crowd more about the boys in New Mexico, Mexes and Indians and negroes all carted off like animals with no food or water, some of them
dying in the boxcars, and then let loose in the desert.*

Sam checked his watch.

He made a note.

*He followed Little to another bar, where the man drank until the early
morning with two burly miners. The man never seeing him. Sam remembering everything he'd learned from his mentor in Baltimore: not to worry about a
suspect's face. Tricks of carriage, ways of wearing clothes, general outline, indi-
vidual mannerisms—all as seen from the rear—were much more important to
the shadow than faces.*

*But then, outside, he made contact with Little's eyes and the man noticed him
and walked away from two men he was talking to, crossing Main Street, and
came over to Sam and simply said, "Don't I know you, brother?"*

Sam shook his head, embarrassed, admonishing himself for being caught.

*Little thrust out his hand, well-calloused and warm, and told Sam that it was
damn good to meet him, pumping his hand up and down, and left him with a
fresh pamphlet from the International Workers of the World asking,* WHERE DO
YOU STAND?

*The men broke up their party in the blackness of a deep night, smoke and
steam pumping from the foundries, passing men in leather aprons on the way
to work. Tired, pinch-faced women washed laundry in tin buckets while skinny,
pasty children played in dry ditches.*

*Little headed back to the rooming house and Sam followed, waiting five min-
utes until the man disappeared up the stairs, and then returned to bed.*

*An hour later, he didn't hear the creak of the board—what woke him was
the muffled cursing and the thundering boots on the landing. Sam pulled on his*

pants, slapped his suspenders over his bony shoulders, and ran out into the hall, but they were gone, running down the stairs and into the street, where he spotted four men in burlap hoods, one holding a torch, throwing Frank Little onto the bed of a wagon and whipping the two lead horses away.

Sam followed them on foot, but returned back to the rooming house at daybreak. He shaved, dressed in fresh clothes, and packed his saddlebag. He had an hour till Western Union opened its doors. He would cable Baltimore for instructions.

He waited on the porch of the offices, the sun rising over the hills and covering crevices in white, hot light. He smoked a cigarette and was nearly done as the sound of horses approached, and he saw the sheriff and some of his men as they gathered and whipped their bridles to and fro, and skinny young Sam ran out to meet them to ask what was going on.

They were headed to the train trestle outside town and Sam followed, riding in the back of a Model T flatbed with a newspaperman at the wheel. The little truck jostled and threw him and he held on tight for fear he'd be tossed out on the road.

A crowd had already gathered under the trestle and there was pointing and shouting and a couple boys standing under a twisting body covered by a white hood and swaying back and forth from a twenty-foot hemp rope.

FIRST AND LAST WARNING had been painted in white across Little's chest.

A big black camera snapped. The sheriff yelled for someone to get up there and cut the damn man down. One of the boys boasted he'd found part of an ear in the dirt and said Little hadn't gone down without a fight.

Sam searched his pocket for his notebook but instead found the IWW pamphlet. When he pulled it out, the fresh ink bled on his fingers.

1

San Francisco
September 1921

W ith his two best buddies and his movie star dog, Roscoe Arbuckle
drove north in a twenty-five-thousand-dollar Pierce-Arrow that
came equipped with a cocktail bar and a backseat toilet. Roscoe
was a big man, not as fat as he appeared in those two-reel comedies that
had made him famous in which he wore pants twice his size, but portly
nonetheless. His eyes were a pale light blue, the transparent color of a new-
born, and his soft, hairless face often reminded moviegoers of a child. A
two-hundred-and-sixty-pound child stuck in all kinds of bad situations
where "Fatty" Arbuckle, as he was known to America, would dress up like
a woman, nearly drown, or sometimes get shot in the ass.

As they hugged the rocky, sunny coast of northern California, Roscoe
had sweet thoughts of his new three-million-dollar Paramount contract and
a weekend with ever-flowing Scotch and endless warm pussy.

His dog, Luke, who now earned three hundred a week, hung his head
out the window and soon sniffed the fetid air off San Francisco Bay, while
in back, Roscoe's buddies Lowell and Freddie smoked cigars, played cards,
and poured more whiskey for the chauffeur, who hadn't touched the wheel

since Los Angeles. And soon that big Pierce-Arrow glided down Market Street, passing cable cars on the way up the hill, and toward the Ferry Building, before curving with a light touch of the brakes into Union Square and the St. Francis Hotel.

Roscoe pulled up under a portico, honking the horn and tossing the keys to the doorman, and heard whispers of "Fatty" and "Fatty Arbuckle," and he smiled and winked and took a few pictures with Luke for the newspapers before doffing his chauffeur's cap and checking into the twelfth floor.

"Luke's hungry," Roscoe said, relaxing with a plop into a red velvet sofa. "Order up a steak."

"For a dog?" Fred asked.

"For me and the dog. Make it two."

"What about gin?"

"Use the telephone, have 'em send up whatever you like. And a Victrola. We got to have a Victrola."

Crates and crates of bootleg gin and Scotch whiskey appeared in the suite as if by magic, carried in on the strong backs of bellhops, and Roscoe peeled off great gobs of money and placed it into their palms. The men ordered ice and table fans and opened up the windows as pitchers of fresh-squeezed orange juice arrived for gin blossoms. The Victrola was wheeled in on a dolly with a crate of 78s and Fatty selected James Reese Europe and the 369th U.S. Infantry "Hell Fighters" Band playing "St. Louis Blues." And the music came out tinny and loud and patriotic and festive at the same time and Roscoe sweated a bit as he moved with it. He cracked open another window looking down upon Union Square, feeling a breeze off the San Francisco Bay, hearing the sounds of the cable cars clanging, and spotting a crowd gathered down on Geary.

They were looking up at the perfect blue sky, hands shielding their eyes from the sun, and for a moment Roscoe thought the word must've spread he'd come to town. But he heard a noise from a roof, a motor, and one of the bellhops, now wheeling in a cart filled with silver platters of steaks—Luke licking his chops as he sat in a velvet chair—said there was a circus man about to ride his motorcycle over a tightrope.

Roscoe smiled and took his drink up to the roof just as the man, dressed in leather, with helmet and goggles, a woman beside him in a sidecar, revved off on a line of ridiculously narrow wire crossing over the people on the street, the paper hawkers and the newsboys and the dishwashers and the cooks, and the crowd whistled and clapped and yelled, their hearts about to explode from the excitement.

And Roscoe took a big swig of Scotch and clapped and applauded and yelled down to the crowd, the newsboys taking a shot of the famous film star cheering on the acrobat.

Roscoe walked to the hotel's ledge and peered down, pretending to test the line and pantomiming a test walk, and then waved his hands off from the wire, and everyone yelled. All the dishwashers and maids and raggedy kids on the street. And that made Roscoe Arbuckle feel good, as he returned to room 1220 and asked his friend Fred to fetch up some women.

He twisted himself into a pair of striped pajamas and put on a silk robe and knew this was going to be a fine vacation, not planning on leaving the room till they carried him out. He cranked up the Victrola as far as it would go, playing his new favorite, Marion Harris singing "A Good Man Is Hard to Find."

As he waited for the party to come to him, Roscoe cut up Luke's steak and placed the silver tray on the floor, rubbing the nubbed ears of his old friend.

SAM HAMMETT HAD CASED the old slump-backed roadhouse for two nights, following up on a forty-dollar payoff to a San Quentin snitch named Pinto about the whereabouts of "Gloomy" Gus Schaefer. A few weeks back, Schaefer's boys had knocked off a jewelry store in St. Paul, and the Old Man had sent him out to this beaten, nowhere crossroads just outside Vallejo to make sure the information they got was good. It was night, a full moon, and from the protective shadow of a eucalyptus tree Sam watched the sequined girls with painted lips and their rich daddies in double-breasted suits. They stumbled out onto the old porch and to their Model Ts and Cadillacs, while poor men in overalls would wander back down the crooked road.

Two of the Schaefers' black Fords sat close to the rear porch, his gang upstairs laughing and playing cards, their images wobbly through the glass panes. Schaefer himself had appeared twenty minutes ago, Sam knowing instantly it was him, with the hangdog face and droopy eyes, leaning out an upstairs window, checking out the moon and stars, before taking off his jacket and resuming his place at the card table.

Sam craned his head up to the window and shook his head.

He found a foothold under the second-story porch and climbed, careful not to rip a suit he couldn't afford in a month's pay, and shimmied up a drainpipe, finding purchase on the rail, and hoisted himself over the banister with a thud.

He breathed slow, trying to catch his breath and feeling that wet cough deep in his throat. He tried to silence the hacking with a bloodied handkerchief.

Lying close to the windowsill, he could see the figures and hear them now, every word, as they talked about everything but the heist. Mainly about a batch of hooch loaded up in one of the Fords for a delivery to a tong in Chinatown named Mickey Wu.

One of the boys had a girl in a short skirt on his knee and bounced her up and down like a child. She clapped and laughed as the boy wiggled a poker chip over his knuckles.

Sam coughed again and bit into the handkerchief to silence himself. His hands shook as he righted himself on the railing, sitting there for ages, maybe an hour, before the conversation turned to another meeting, somewhere in Oakland, and a trade with Gloomy Gus's wife.

Sam leaned in and listened, thinking about who the hell would've married a fella like Gloomy Gus, and then there was a small crack. The slightest splitting of wood that sounded like warming ice.

Sam held his breath, unsure what had happened, and reached for the railing.

Then he heard a larger crack, and within seconds the entire porch fell away from the roadhouse. Sam tried to hold on to the drainpipe, keeping the entire rickety affair up in the air for a few moments, enough that he steadied himself and got some air back in his lungs, but then the porch leaned far away and crumbled like a tired fighter into a solid, violent mess.

The Schaefer gang was on him before he could get to his feet. They extended their revolvers down as he lay on his back. The air had gone out of him like a burst balloon.

Four of them, including Gus, stared down at him. He tried to catch a breath.

"Hello, Gus."

"Shut up," Gus said.

"Sure thing."

"You the cops?"

"I have some business."

"What business?"

"Diamonds," Sam said, two men pulling him to his feet as he dusted off the pin-striped suit. He tried to look annoyed at the dirt on his elbows while two of the boys poked guns into his ribs, another frisking him and finding the little .32.

Someone had hit the headlights on a Model T and Sam turned his head and squinted. Schaefer nodded thoughtfully, checking out Sam, with the shock of white hair and the young face and the wiry, rail-thin frame.

"In times like these," Sam said, coughing, "a man can't be too careful."

Schaefer's droopy eyes lightened. He smiled.

Sam smiled back. A crowd started to form on the roadhouse's porch. The tinny sounds of the piano player started again.

"Somebody shoot this bastard," Schaefer said.

"Now, Gus."

"Don't make a mess," Schaefer said. "Put down a blanket or something first. We'll dump him in the bay."

They brought Sam upstairs, tied him to a ladder-back chair, stuck a handkerchief in his mouth, and locked him in a broom closet. He heard the men walk away and waited until he heard laughter and poker chips again to try to work his hands from the knots.

————

HER NAME WAS Bambina Del Monte.

Her name was Maude Delmont.

Her name was Bambina Maude Delmont Montgomery. Hopper-Woods, if you count the last two.

Her last husband, Cassius Clay Woods, was a real screw. He hadn't known she was still married to the Hopper fella and was still sending her sap letters about eternal love and even little poems he'd written, really horrible ones about her eyes being like the sky and her skin the color of milk. Her eyes were black, her hair was black, and she had her father's dark Italian skin. Who was this guy trying to fool? But that's what happened to a man who'd slipped a vise on your finger and still didn't get into your drawers.

It was after hours at Tait's Café, a speakeasy on O'Farrell, and as usual Al was late. Paddle fans worked away the smoke that rose from marble-topped tables where couples sat in little wiry chairs. There was a big stage, but the stage was bare except for a placard announcing A SPRIGHTLY AND DIVERTING ENTERTAINMENT INTERSPERSED WITH GUEST DANCING.

She ate ice cream and drank bourbon, mixing the two a bit, and hadn't a clue on how she was going to be paying if Al didn't show up with some cash. He was the one who drove her from Los Angeles along with the girl, the whole way bragging how they'd soon be dining in Paris on a king's budget.

But Al Semnacher didn't look much like a king when he walked through the alley door of the speakeasy. He looked more like a goddamn rube, with his graying hair, low hairline, and horn-rimmed glasses. A guy who'd stutter if his hand touched your tit.

"Anyone ever tell you that you look like a rube?" she asked. "Why don't you clean your glasses now and again?"

"He's here."

"Who?"

"The mark."

Maude rolled her eyes. "Just pay the tab and let's fly. 'The mark'? You never worked a con in your life."

"What's that?"

"Bourbon and ice cream."

He wrinkled his nose, making him look like a spoiled-rotten kid smelling something he didn't like.

"It's good. Want some?"

"It's gone."

"So it is," said Maude. "Say, your girl doesn't exactly look like her pictures."

"The nightie shots or the one from *Punch of the Irish*?"

"Both," Maude said. "She's gotten fat."

Al Semnacher leaned back into the chair and drummed his little fingers. He readjusted his thick, dirty glasses and leaned in, speaking in his little voice: "She needs money and we need her."

"And she'll stick with the script?"

"A variation on the Engineer's Daughter. But it's a long con."

"I'm glad you listen," Maude said, thumping her fist on the table. "But, Al?"

"Yeah."

"Let me do the thinkin' in this relationship."

Al fiddled with the long spoon, dabbing out just a teaspoon of the melted ice cream. He winked before he slipped the spoon into his mouth and said, "I like your hair."

"Do you, now? You don't think I look like a boy?"

"With those knockers that'd be kind of tough."

Maude reached down and hefted those big boobs on her skinny frame and asked, "She'll get us in?"

"She's been knowin' ole Fatty for years now. His pecker will get hard just hearin' her name. Trust me."

Maude met Al's eyes and she smiled, keeping the contact.

"You have balls, Al. No brains. But a big set of 'em."

am had knocked over the chair and was working the ropes on a rusty pipe when the door opened and rough hands gripped him by the arms and jerked him into a room where the gang played poker. Gloomy Gus glanced over at Sam as he counted out some cash, tossing a wad to the center of the table, and said to one of his boys, "Thought I told you to kill the bastard."

"Thought we'd wait 'cause of the mess."

"Are you trying to say something?" Gus asked. One of the gang stooped down and pulled the handkerchief from Sam's mouth.

"I came with an offer."

"You came to us as a copper or a bank dick. Look at you, the way you're dressed, you look like a copper from a mile away."

"Can I explain my offer?"

"Explain, my ass."

The boys laughed, Gus laughed, chomping down on an unlit cigar. His right incisor made of gold.

Sam was jerked to his feet by two men. His legs felt strange, tingling and light.

"I can give you five grand for it all."

"Who sent you?"

"I can't tell you that."

One of the boys punched him hard in the stomach. He doubled over and, as the wind came back to him, spat blood.

"Five grand. Is this a joke?"

"How 'bout I sit in for a hand?" Sam asked. "Then you can get to killing me."

Gus looked up from the cards that he'd begun to deal. He glanced over at the boys and shrugged, one of 'em just a kid, with jet-black hair parted down hard with drugstore grease.

Gus picked the cards off the table. He shuffled. He relit the old cigar, the tip glowing red-hot.

He stomped his feet in time with the music below them.

Sam wandered to the table, took a chair, and said, "Stud?"

"I call the fucking game," Gus said. "So, Mr. Big Shot, you got ten dollars for the pot?"

Sam reached into his coat pocket and, having left his wallet with Haultain, smiled and said, "You stake me, Gus?"

Gus cut his eyes up from the deck in hand, and then just as slow and lazy, began to deal around the table.

They played until dawn, and Sam's stomach felt hollowed out from the cheap gin they drank from fruit jars. Someone brought in some coffee and he drank that and smoked two more Fatima cigarettes and played two more hands and was feeling pretty good with the situation and was just about to bring up the diamonds again until one of Gus's boys thundered up the steps, threw open the door, and yelled that someone had just set fire to their cars.

Gus's dark eyes turned right toward Sam.

LABOR DAY MORNING.

Virginia was in the hotel bathroom, naked as a jaybird, door wide-open, powdering her face and big fat boobs before checking her red lips and pulling herself into a slip. Still no panties, mind you, just the slip, as she played and combed her mousy brown hair and danced a little fox-trot before flushing the commode and adding makeup under her eyes.

Maude Delmont watched from the edge of the bed, legs crossed, dressed in a cute little black dress and smoking a thin brown cigarette. She studied herself in the mirror on back of the door. Her black hair was bobbed, as every girl who read a magazine knew to do, and she'd painted her eyes up like some kind of Oriental.

She liked it. She didn't look half bad.

Virginia must've been a hell of a looker based on those photographs of Al's. But somewhere down the line, she'd developed an ass the size of a zeppelin and looked just plain tuckered-out. She'd been sleeping pretty much since they'd gotten to San Francisco.

Virginia Rappe. She pronounced it Rap-*pay*, telling people she'd learned that in France. But from the boring stories Maude heard on the drive, the only thing Virginia had learned in France was how to pick pockets of rich, dumb Americans and dance in her underwear.

Al was a lousy con man.

Virginia was a lousy whore.

But Al wanted to believe she was an actress, a star of tomorrow, and had told Maude a half dozen times about how six years ago Virginia's face appeared on the sheet music to "Let Me Call You Sweetheart." And Al would say it all serious, like a man in love, and that would make Maude laugh even more. "Let Me Call You Sweetheart." She couldn't believe he didn't see the humor in talking about a tired broad like Virginia as if the girl was some kind of kid virgin.

Virginia walked through the shabby little hotel room drinking some gin, still wearing a slip up top but no dress. When she turned to Maude, Maude noticed a sizable patch of fur between her white thighs, like a French poodle being strangled, and she motioned to it with the burning end of her cigarette and coughed.

"Oh, shit," Virginia said.

"You sure you're up for this?"

"You asked me that ten times."

"So, how do you know ole Fatty?"

"I worked for Sennett when he was there."

"You really in the pictures?"

"I was in a restaurant scene. Fatty was throwing pies."

"Did you get a pie?"

"Not a crumb."

"I always wanted to be in pictures," Maude said and recrossed her legs. "You sure you're okay? You look a little peaked."

"Just nerves."

Maude watched the girl's hand's shake as she combed her hair some more and tugged on her stockings and dress. Her face looked drained, and even with the makeup black circles rimmed her eyes as she turned back from the dressing table.

"After this is done, can I have dinner?" Virginia asked.

"Sure, sweetie."

"With dessert?"

"With dessert."

"Please excuse me."

Virginia went back to the bathroom, where Maude heard gagging and vomiting and then the toilet flush. When she returned, Virginia asked, "Isn't this the cutest little hat?"

It was a straw panama with a blue bow.

Maude ticked off the ash of her cigarette. "You might want to take off the price tag, honey."

SAM FELT A LOAD of bricks against his neck and tumbled to his knees. There were fists and feet and cursing and spit, and a lot of blood after that. He heard a thud on the floor—half of an old brick had landed beside his head—and he tried to make his way on all fours as another gleaming shoe knocked him in the stomach and against the wall, and soon it felt like he was underwater trying to find the right way up, searching for air. He covered his face the way he'd seen fighters do and curled up into a ball, as there was more shouting but then less kicking, and for a few seconds he was left alone, until a final blow came to the ribs like an exclamation point to it all.

He could not breathe.

It felt like minutes passed until a sliver of air worked into his diseased lungs and he saw some light flat across the wooden floor and heard feet up and down the staircase, stumbling and bumbling like the Keystone Kops. He tried to sit but only fell flat to the ground.

Someone called his name and he opened the only eye he could.

The hands were more gentle this time but no less strong, and Sam felt himself standing through no fault of his own. His arm was draped around a man, maybe a head taller than him, and they were walking across the room in a crazy, jumbled dance, down the stairs and out to the back of the roadhouse, where the early-morning light split Sam's skull.

He was flopped into a rumble seat and the ignition was pressed and they were off down the bumpy, curving road without a word.

"How you doin' back there, buddy?"

Sam crossed a forearm over his eyes. "Why'd you have to go and do that?"

"What?"

"Distract 'em," Sam said. "Don't you know I had that son of a bitch right where I wanted him?"

"You think Gus will be more upset about his Fords or the hooch I used to start the fire?"

"Good question, Phil. Ask it to me again when we reach The City."

ROSCOE WOKE UP Monday morning on the couch, a watery glass of Scotch in his lap, hearing the sounds of Powell Street below. He glanced over at Freddie, tall, dark, athletic Freddie, who'd snuggled up with the singer he'd met at Tait's Café last night as Lowell walked into the bedroom shaved and showered, a fresh drink in his hand, wanting to know what everyone wanted for breakfast. His girl, a skinny redhead who wore knickers like a boy, appeared from one of the two adjoining bedrooms, trying to straighten the flower in her hat. And Roscoe said he'd love some eggs and toast and coffee. And then he told Lowell, who was on the telephone to room service, to skip that coffee and have another case of gin sent up. He was feeling like gin blossoms this morning.

"Don't you want to go out?" Freddie asked, slipping his broad shoulders into a navy blazer. He futzed with his thick Romanian eyebrows in a window's reflection. "See the city?"

"Why'd I want to do a fool thing like that?"

Roscoe walked over to the window facing Powell Street and looked down at the rooftops of cars lined up for the valet. Freddie's gal joined him and pinched his waist.

"You aren't so fat, Mr. Arbuckle."

"Thanks, girlie," he said. "Hey, you wanna jump? I will if you will. You think any of 'em would care?"

She narrowed her eyes a bit but then caught his smile. She smiled back.

"You mind signing something for my kid sis?"

He turned and smiled at her. "You're not leaving, are you? The party's just started. Go ahead and crank up that Victrola."

The girl found the "Wang Wang Blues" and "On the 'Gin 'Gin 'Ginny Shore," and she and Roscoe were making a beautiful duet as the boys wheeled in the breakfast, Freddie on the phone to some showgirls he'd met at Tait's last night.

About the time they'd finished eating, the mixing of gin blossoms in fine form now, the telephone rang, the telephone having rung nonstop since they'd all arrived, and Freddie said, "Come on up."

"Who's that?" Roscoe asked.

"You remember that big-eyed girl of Henry Lehrman's? She was at Keystone a few years back."

"Sure, sure. She comin' up?"

"She's here."

"What's her name?"

"Virginia Rappe."

"A virgin what?"

By the time Virginia walked into the party, Roscoe was on his third blossom of the morning and greeted the woman with a slight bow. "I *do* know you."

She winked at him.

She was indeed a big-eyed girl with a scandalous little bob and good arms and shoulders. She cocked her hip as she talked, a bit meatier in the bust and butt since he'd known her but still looking luscious and sensual. Dynamite smile. A sharp dresser, with clothes that looked straight out of a French fashion magazine. Smelled just like a plucked rose.

"I like your hat," he said.

"Knew you would," she said.

She smiled and stuck it on the fat man's head—way too small—and Roscoe made a straight face, walking back to the bathroom for another gin blossom, in pajamas and robe and that ridiculous little hat.

"You mind if I invite a friend up?" Virginia Rappe asked.

"Send her up. Send them all up. All girls welcome. Didn't you see our sign?"

He pressed a gin blossom in Virginia's hand as she sat in a green chair, crossed her legs, and dialed the house phone. The Victrola played "Second Hand Rose," one of Roscoe's favorites, and he clutched old Freddie near and sang to him as if he were a fine ole gal under a paper moon.

PHIL HAULTAIN DROVE to Eddy Street and helped Sam up to the third floor and the one-bedroom apartment he shared with his new wife, Jose. She pronounced her name like *Joe* with an *s* on the end. Sam knew she'd be waiting up for him, probably walking the floor with worry, and that perhaps would be worse than the beating.

"What happened?" she asked, unlatching the door chain and helping Phil get Sam into the room and then to the bedroom, where they set Sam down.

"I tried to kiss a tiger," Sam said.

"Who are you?" she asked Phil.

"The new Pinkerton man," he said. "Your husband is training me."

"Lesson four," Sam said. "Remove head from oncoming bricks."

"Someone hit him with a brick?" Jose asked. She had a rosary in her hand.

"He took a pretty beatin' this morning, ma'am. But he didn't want to go to no hospital, only wanted me to stop by a speak and then drop him here. I seen him cough up a pool of blood, though."

Jose shook her head and told the young partner that was another matter. She tucked a pillow up under Sam's head, now feeling the same way as he had up at Cushman's sanitarium in Tacoma, and she went to the bath, returned with a cool towel, wiped his face, and made him turn his head. He felt those goose eggs right quick and let out a few choice words.

"Be still. I'm just trying to help."

"Are you trying to play nurse again?" Sam said. "Phil, my wife's crazy. She loves blood."

"Apparently you do, too," Jose said.

"I'll be goin', ma'am."

"What your name?"

"Phil. Phil Haultain. I see you're expecting, too. You mind me asking when?"

Out the good eye, Sam watched Jose smile at the big fella.

Jose was a woman of healthy proportions with bright blue eyes and brown hair and nice little sprinkling of freckles across her nose. She'd been so damn cute back at Cushman's that he hadn't been able to keep his hands off of her. And she didn't seem to mind him being a lunger.

A few months after a long rainy day at a little hotel, he'd gotten a letter down in San Diego. Apparently, he'd left something with her.

He heard Phil and Jose talking in the main room of the apartment and then the door closing. She returned to the room and closed the drapes.

"I was worried."

"I figured."

"But I knew you'd be back."

"Like a bad penny."

"That's my man."

Sam winked at her.

It hurt to wink when only one eye worked.

———

THE SHOWGIRLS ARRIVED at the St. Francis a short time later. One was an absolute doll, with brown eyes and soft lips, and the other had bulging blue eyes and crooked teeth. But she had big tits, and nice legs, too, and Roscoe wasn't in a picky mood, opening the door wide. Freddie took an instant liking to the pretty one, Alice, while the other one, calling herself Zey, wanted to sit on the love seat next to Roscoe and run down all the tunes she could sing. She had very cute knees.

But her singing wasn't much better than her face, and Luke howled when she hit the high notes. *How he loved that dog.*

"Do you sing, Mr. Arbuckle?" she asked.

"Caruso once called me a beautiful songbird."

"Who's that?"

"He sings. Well, he sang. He just passed."

Roscoe studied her to make sure she wasn't joking and caught the eye of Virginia, who was now standing next to the window, the curtains flowing in the hot afternoon air, most of the folks in the room now sweating, and he smiled.

She smiled back, and he noticed the dark circles and the sad black eyes.

Roscoe went back into the bathroom, where they'd set up the bar, and found more ice in the sink and a fresh bottle of Scotch. The gin blossoms were starting to hurt his throat a little and he thought the Scotch would calm it all down.

He looked at himself in the mirror, adjusting the collar of his silk robe along his sizable neck. He plugged a cigar in the corner of his mouth, bit off the end, and winked back at his own reflection.

And then he thought more about it, straightened his pajama collar, and blew himself a kiss. His eyes were bloodshot, his skin a bright pink.

In room 1220, Virginia's friend Maude was dancing on the fireplace hearth. She was wearing Roscoe's pajamas, the striped material swallowing her body, this weird-looking fella who claimed he was in the movie biz egging her on as she went through a whole routine, sweating in the tent of clothes, her black hair matted to her face, not once losing a drop of the alcohol from her glass.

She was a fine little gal, too. And Roscoe was glad to add her to the collection.

He watched her, standing back from a small crowd, and as the song ended Maude took a polite bow. The big record needle caught on the sea of dead space and swam and swam, all eyes turning back to Roscoe. He narrowed his eyes at Maude, friend of that bit-part chippie from Los Angeles. His pajama top loose and raggedly buttoned on her, split nearly down to her navel.

That straight face slowly cracked into a grin and then into an all-out laugh, and everyone laughed with him, and the Victrola was reloaded and Roscoe guzzled down the Scotch, now thinking of Kentucky bourbon, and he rocked and danced, the space between the ice in the bathroom and the big chair where he held court seeming to stretch and spin and grow with life.

He wiped his face and took off his robe. The breath and laughter and people in the room had brought in so much heat, and Lowell came by and introduced a pretty green-eyed girl with a pert nose and Roscoe was thinking, This was the one. Yes, Daddy, this was the one. Her name was Mae, and he'd promised to take her for a ride in the Pierce. He remembered.

"Want to get married?" Roscoe asked.

Lowell laughed at his drunken leer and said the girl was already married and to keep his paws off, and, on top of it all, Roscoe would never guess in a million years who her father-in-law was.

"Kaiser Wilhelm."

"Billy Sunday."

Roscoe laughed and laughed.

"No, I'm serious."

"What would Reverend Sunday say about this party?" Roscoe asked the girl.

"He'd say his little sweetie would like another drink," she said.

"I knew I liked that guy."

"You'll take me for a ride?"

"I'll let you drive."

Up on the hearth, Maude tossed her sweaty black hair from side to side and swung around, doing high kicks with that Semnacher fella until she couldn't breathe, and then she told everyone to step back and they did. And the dark girl with the nice build removed the pajama top and showed off her fine, sweating breasts.

Roscoe licked his lips and stood and shuffled over to her, moving Semnacher away and trying to dance with this girl Maude, tugging at the pajama bottoms she had tied into a knot.

And Maude pushed him away and played like she was going to slap his face. One of the new girls—the showgirls—joined her up on the hearth stage, removing her top, saying her figure was much better, Maude saying she didn't stand a chance.

Maude tried to bump the girl from the hearth with her hips and butt.

The girl got down to her brassiere, the jazz and the room so damn hot. Everyone dancing and carrying on, and there was knock at the door from the hotel dick and Lowell sent him away with a twenty-dollar bill before he could peep into the room.

Roscoe joined the showgirls—Alice and Zey, that was their names—and they took to singing every other chorus of a new record called "I Found a Rose in the Devil's Garden." And that ugly Zey girl could really sing now, Roscoe telling her that after they'd sung the record five times, him nearly tripping over a couple rolling around the floor in an impromptu petting party.

Maude tore at the brassiere of the showgirl and ripped it from her chest and the girl gave a pleasant little shriek, modestly covering her breasts, but then breaking away and opening her arms wide in display. The girl so proud that her breasts were twice the size of Maude's. Her nipples so long and rubbery that Roscoe licked his lips again.

They shook and shimmied together, both showing off in fine form. Roscoe changed records and danced with Alice Blake. He kept dancing with her, her nude back hot and wet and wonderful, and then stumbled toward the bathroom.

"Aren't we going for a ride?" asked Mae.

"Freddie's got the car," he said. "He's taking Miss Whosit to Tait's. I need to freshen up, my daisy. Get dressed."

"You promised," she said. "Who is that girl?"

Roscoe winked back at her.

When he walked back into the adjoining room, room 1219, he found Virginia splayed out on his bed, eyes glassy and face as white as a boiled shirt. Roscoe looked at the girl and tilted his head. He got to his knee and smoothed back the bobbed hair from her big black eyes and she turned a big look up at him.

The stare startled him.

"Hello there, snuggle pup," she said.

Roscoe walked back to the door and closed it with a light click. The music was muffled and the laughter coming from a million miles away.

He wet his lips, hearing the girls still singing and men egging them on.

Sometime later, Roscoe would be jostled awake, hearing hard banging on the door and that girl Maude screaming for him to open the door. More pounding and that Maude woman yelling, wanting to know why the girl had screamed.

"Is someone hurt?"

Roscoe got to his feet and ran his hand over his sweaty face. He opened and shut his eyes, adjusting to the thin light coming through the breaking white curtains. His pajamas were soaked.

Another voice yelled, a man's voice, after the pounding, this time announcing it was the hotel detective and to open the goddamn door.

M aude Delmont screamed for everyone to back the hell up and let the poor girl breathe. Roscoe just snorted at her, looking down at both of them huddled on the single bed like they were some kind of pathetic pair. And then the fat man had the nerve to walk right past the hotel dick and into the bathroom to refill his Scotch glass. Maude cradled the girl's head in her lap and felt her forehead and told the dick to run find a doctor, rocking Virginia like you would a small child and breathing her drunk breath into her ear, "There, there, it will all be all right." Virginia looked truly terrible, her green dress wringing wet, skin clammy, and eyes half closed.

"What s'matter with her?" the hotel dick asked.

"It's a complex medical situation, sport," Lowell Sherman said. "She's plastered."

"I better call the doc."

"You want a drink first?" Lowell asked. Sherman already wearing a fresh pin-striped suit, hair pressed and neat, after Maude had let him have his way in the bathroom in room 1221.

The dick looked down at the sweating and moaning girl and shrugged. "Maybe she'll sober up."

Zey Prevon popped into the room and then came the other bobbed tart, her better-looking twin, that dark-eyed showgirl, Alice Blake. Alice said that her rehearsal at Tait's Café had been canceled, but it didn't matter because she could sing and dance the number in her sleep and didn't care that much for the song anyway. "That's why I try to mix it up a little bit in my mind. No one likes to hear a song when they know where the notes hit."

"I like the standards," Roscoe said, coming from the bath with a tall Scotch, Virginia's little straw hat with long ribbon still cocked on his head. "I used to sing them for seventeen bucks a week at the Portola Theater. 'By the light of the silvery moon.'"

"'By the light. By the light.'" Alice perked up and copied his soft-shoe move, tap for tap.

Maude held Virginia, feeling her shaking body, and thinking how Virginia sure was a good egg. And she whispered to her, so light, like a child praying, "You're doing great, sister." She let go of Virginia's head and tried to stand up, all those Scotches belting the hell out of her brain. But Maude found her feet, knowing she was in control the moment she felt her toes in the carpet and stood, using the nightstand that separated the two beds.

She wobbled over to Roscoe, parting the two showgirls and brushing by Al Semnacher with a sloppy wink, and shook her paw up at Roscoe, saying, "What did you do to her, you fat ape?"

"Nothing."

"She's not right. Can't you see? Can't you see?"

"I can see you're a crazy nut who wasn't invited. Either you get her out of my room or I'll throw both of you out the window."

Sherman stood in the doorway. He looked at Virginia and then back at Maude and dismissed it all with the flick of a wrist. "Let's crank up the Victrola."

Virginia started to mumble and then she shot up from the bed, screaming and yelling, eyes wide-open. Roscoe tossed the little hat from his head and threw open the hotel window and leaned outside for a fresh breath of air and then back in. "Would someone shut her up?"

The three girls ringed Virginia, and soon she stopped screaming and began to sob, dropping back prone to the bed and thrashing, tearing at her clothes, ripping away her dress and pleading for God to please help her. The girls held the torn shreds of her clothing, leaving Virginia in a cream-colored slip, and she calmed for a moment before thrashing again and tearing the silk away from her body.

"For Christsake," Roscoe said.

In the other room, Luke started to howl. Roscoe put his hands over his ears.

Maude held Virginia down, pulling the tattered slip from her body and handing it to Alice, who threw it in the trash. Roscoe's face flushed at the sight of the white skin and black patch of hair between her thighs, digging his heel into the carpet and turning away.

"Who invited any of you?" Roscoe asked. "Who invited you?"

Maude pulled the bobbed hair away from Virginia's red mouth. The naked girl, really giving it her all, pretended like she was trying to breathe. But it all only came out in wet gasps, her skin feeling cooked and sticky. Maude could smell the warm, putrid scent of urine mixed with the sweet perfume and gin breath and heard the showgirls starting a bath. And when no one was looking, she pinched Virginia's pink little nipple. "Listen. Listen to me."

But Virginia just lay there. Maude pinched the nipple again.

"Wake up."

Al watched it all and smiled, proud of his little actress, but his goofball haircut and those insanely thick glasses just made him look like a twit. Maude nodded over to the trash can, where Al reached inside for the silky torn slip and bloomers and tucked them into his pocket. He winked back at her.

Alice and Zey came back in the room, all bright smiles, and saying everything was going to be A-OK.

"Is she really in the pictures?" Alice asked.

Zey elbowed her like she was some kind of rube for asking.

"So?" Alice asked.

"Grab her feet," Maude said, stumbling up, feeling sick herself, the world tilting a bit. Freddie Fishback was back in the room, the dark boy with a cigarette dangling from his lips, and he held Virginia's arms while the showgirls held a leg each, Virginia, nude and suspended in space, wriggling like an alligator, as they carried her to the bathtub and plopped her in cold water, where she thrashed and cried and then slowly closed her eyes and nearly sunk beneath the lip of the tub.

She was awake then and moaning and sobbing, blood between her legs swirling in the water like a cloud.

When Maude walked back into the bedroom, Al Semnacher was gone. She ran from the room and down the long hallway to the elevators just in time to see the golden doors about to snap shut, a shit-eating grin on Al's face, Virginia's torn slip and bloomers in the breast pocket of his coat.

"Goddamnit," Maude said.

"So THEN WHAT HAPPENED?" Lowell Sherman asked.

"You were there. Or were you too drunk to recall?"

"Too drunk to call," Lowell said. "That was yesterday."

"Just why are you my friend again?"

"Because I bring a certain sophistication to the party."

"That's rich," Roscoe said. "Thanks for reminding me."

They watched the sun set over the hills of San Francisco, as the ferry made its way from the pier with a steady, slow wake, hugging the peninsula to the Pacific and then back south. Roscoe rolled a cigarette and leaned onto the ferry railing in the soft, perfect golden light. He removed the pair of leather gloves he'd donned while driving the Pierce-Arrow up the ramp and into storage below.

"I recall you and Freddie hoisting that poor girl up like a side of meat and taking her down the hall to another room."

"I wanted her gone," Roscoe said. "I was sick of all the foolishness, so I paid for another room."

"She was pretty foolish," Lowell said. "And silly, too. All that thrashing and moaning. No wonder she never had a part of distinction. Who brought her to Sennett's?"

"Pathé."

"Lehrman? What a gas."

"Do you remember anything else?"

"I remember her lying on that bed completely nude and writhing around while those two drunk girls took turns trying to revive her. They were a hoot."

"What else?"

"I remember the ice."

Roscoe looked away and at the narrow little pass from the bay to the Pacific. "You know they're planning to build a bridge right over the Golden Gate," Roscoe said.

"I'll believe it when I see it," Lowell said. "You don't want me to talk about the ice?"

"I was trying to snap her out of it."

"With the ice?"

"Sure," Roscoe said. "A physician told me that once."

"Hell of a place to put a piece of ice."

"What does it matter? It didn't work anyway."

The ferry chugged out past Alcatraz and down around the Presidio, heading toward the Gate and the fading western light. The men smoked some more and tossed their cigarette butts into the churning wake behind them. The sun looked like a golden skillet.

"I didn't do a thing to that girl," Roscoe said. "I swear to it."

"You don't need to."

"Where is she?"

"Some hospital. What does it matter? It's over now. And there's always the Fairmont."

"She called me a beast."

"Who's that?"

Roscoe flicked his last cigarette over the railing as the *Harvard* found the narrow pass, feeling safe and warm and moist, but cold as they hit the ocean.

"The Delmont woman. You know her?"

"She took advantage of me in the bathroom before all hell broke loose."

Roscoe laughed, the ferry humming along under him, taking in a big breath of sea air and watching as a seagull kept up with them above. He squinted up at the bird looping and flying above the ferry and smiled. "If he makes it to L.A., I'll take him home with me. Buy him a big fish dinner."

"I think I'm going to be sick."

"Go down and rest."

"I don't like boats."

"You'd rather we drive back?"

"All that booze. I'll never touch the stuff again."

"You betcha," Roscoe said, winking at him. "Me neither."

Roscoe crooked his head, popping the collar on his Norfolk jacket, just like those the pilots wore in the war only double-sized. He scanned the horizon for the seagull, catching sight of him by the bow before he tilted off, slowing his wings and riding the wind back to the city.

"Do you think I'm better than Chaplin?"

"Of course, old boy," Lowell said. "That prissy little Englishman stole half of what he knows from you."

"You see the papers? They tore the clothes off him in London. Women faint when he passes by. I remember when he had to borrow my wardrobe at Sennett's and I'd have to coach him through every gesture. The big shoes, the bowler? He borrowed those."

"You're better."

"You seen *Gasoline Gus*?"

"No."

"Don't bother."

"Don't fret about the girl, sport. It's all over."

The gull overhead had gone, breaking away in the fading soft light for the coast, the wake of the *Harvard* churning south.

SAM STAYED IN BED all week, but he suddenly woke up long before daybreak Saturday and turned to his pregnant wife, saying he was feeling much better now.

"And your skull?" Jose asked.

"Still soft."

Jose pulled the covers up to her chin and turned on a bare shoulder, light spilling in from the streetlamps off Eddy. "Back to normal."

Sam found his feet and the bathroom, his clothes and then his cap and laced boots, and he was walking toward Union Square, feeling good walking again, with his hands in his pockets, in and out of the foggy mist, and toward Powell at two a.m., loving the feeling of being in a city and the action and movement even in the middle of the night. Back in Maryland, people ate dinner, said their prayers, and went to bed at eight o'clock.

There was an all-night drugstore called the Owl on the ground floor of the Flood Building right below the Pinkerton offices on Market Street. At the counter, he ordered a cup of coffee and dry toast and smoked four Fatima cigarettes, feeling like a solid citizen again.

"You still working on that book?" Sam asked the girl refilling his cup of coffee. He couldn't remember her name for the life of him. But he knew it was a double name, like a farmer would give a daughter.

"You know it," she said. "And every college professor in America is going to read it."

"That a fact?"

"You betcha," she said. "Do you know how many times I've sat here at this counter and asked myself the question, Are human beings human?"

"Well, are they?"

"They's gonna be a chapter on Fresh Guys, too. Being a Fresh Guy is sort of a habit, wouldn't you agree? I guess I don't know whether it's got a cure or not, but I sure know how to diagnose one. Then they's gonna be a chapter about Finicky Birds. They was born suspicious of food. They stand around weighing the merits of the crab salad against Irish stew until you want to call the Disarmament Conference in to decide the question. They usually finishes by ordering a glass of milk and a yeast cake."

Sam listened and drank his coffee. He liked people—common people— the way they talked and reasoned with things. He smiled at the girl. Not because she was pretty, because she surely wasn't, with big lips and eyes and teeth like a rake.

"You sure you don't want no eggs?"

He shook his head.

"You should eat some eggs or hash or something. You're the thinnest man I've ever seen."

Sam's stomach grumbled, one of his last quarters by the saltshaker.

"You been around, hadn't you?" she asked.

"Some."

"Some? Some, I bet. You look like you been around plenty. You're not from around here. I can tell. You got the look like you're passing through. Where'd you come from?"

"Tacoma."

"Before that?"

"Seattle."

"Before that?"

"Oh, I don't know. Baltimore. Spent some time in Montana."

"Yeah, what'd you do in Tacoma?"

"Lay around a Vet hospital."

"You in the war?"

"I was gonna drive an ambulance but came down with the Spanish."

"What you do now?"

"I'm a fortune-teller."

"Get outta town."

Sam nodded. The waitress with the double name smiled with her eyes and tucked a pencil behind her ear. She pressed her butt against the counter and crossed her arms over her little chest.

"Hey, I ain't even told you about my chapter on Economical Janes yet, but it's going to be a rich one. You want to hear about it?"

Sam looked around. There was an old guy in a corner booth watching a conductor turn the cable car around on Powell. It took three men to turn a cable car on its big swivel, but the mass of it all finally made it and locked, and then the men wiped their hands on their pants from grime and work. The diner was bare except for the short-order cook, who'd fallen asleep on a barstool, a cigarette burning between his fingers.

The wall clock read two o'clock.

"Hey, you make much money telling fortunes?"

"Depends on the fortune. If I tell a fat woman she's about to meet a prince, I get a nice chunk of change. If I see that a rich fella is about to be down on his luck, I might get a nickel."

"So why don't you just lie?"

"Professionalism."

"Get outta town."

Sam shrugged.

A newsboy came in off the street, not more than twelve, in knickers and vest and small newsboy cap and all smiles and young muscle, hefting a thick stack of the *Examiner* tied tight with string. He wiped his brow with his forearm and called the waitress over with a "Hey, sister" and sat there at the counter and drank coffee with his two little hands around the mug, warming himself before cutting his eyes over at Sam.

"What's the news?" Sam asked.

"Give me a nickel and I'll tell you."

Sam reached into his vest pocket and popped a nickel off his thumb. The boy caught it in midair and tucked it into his apron. "Ole Fatty Arbuckle has gotten himself in a pinch."

"The actor?"

"The fat bastard who falls down and gets shot in the ass. He was giving some broad the high hard one at the St. Francis and the damn girl got crushed from the weight. Doesn't that beat all? The cops arrested him at midnight and have him behind bars at the Hall of Justice."

The boy cut open the stack of papers and proudly popped open a fresh edition announcing s.f. booze party kills young actress.

The boy walked over and laid down the paper, and Sam read through the first few paragraphs, getting the gist, as the boy slurped down his coffee and adjusted the cap on his head. He winked at the waitress, pushing out of the door with the papers. The bell overhead jingled as he left.

"Yes, sir. It's going to be a banner day."

THE WORD OF THE ARBUCKLE ARREST was passed from cop reporter to editor to managing editor until the news reached The Chief himself in a whisper from his personal valet, George. George leaned into the ear of William Randolph Hearst just as the wine had been poured at the center of a big round soundstage at Paramount. Mr. Hearst had asked for the set to be cleared for the night and now he was finally alone at the table, a big, solid affair, the kind of table that would befit King Henry VIII himself, with his big turkey legs and goblets and wine and lusty wenches by his side.

The picture was to be called *When Knighthood Was in Flower.*

Mr. Hearst liked big, sprawling historical numbers. On the set, he was sure that every penny had gone into making sure that the era was re-created just so. Even the food on the table was real, but he'd yet to eat, still waiting for the picture's star, Miss Davies, to join him. But the news had stopped the service of the meal, Miss Davies still getting out of her makeup, and he told George to please wait for him outside.

"I have something to cable San Francisco."

Mr. Hearst pushed the big wooden chair back and stood, wiping the wine from his mouth, and walked from one end of the table to the other, and then over to the second set, the bedroom, where that fat actor, Lyn Harding, would play out his scenes with Miss Davies as Mary Tudor.

This was the third adaptation of the book. The first two pictures never got the feel of the story. The bigness of it all. The other productions looked like a school play, not life.

"W.R.?"

He turned to see Marion Davies, in a silk robe and no shoes, shuffle out onto the soundstage, bare of makeup, with a big, broad smile on her face. She turned to the spread on the table. "C-can we really eat there? Real f-food and all?"

She was playing a Brit, but her accent was all Brooklyn between the stutters. Good thing you couldn't hear people talk in pictures.

"We can do whatever we want. Isn't it marvelous? Look at this place. It's another world."

Miss Davies screwed up her face and looked at Mr. Hearst as if he'd gone nuts.

"The set, I mean. It's another world. Can't you just feel the castle and the giant hall. I mean, we're really here."

"We're in Hollywood, W.R."

"Close your eyes," he said.

She stood in that little silk robe that barely covered her knees and closed her eyes just as Mr. Hearst had said.

"And concentrate on the olden times."

"When knighthood was a f-flower."

"When knighthood was *in* flower."

"Of c-course."

"We must go to Europe," Mr. Hearst said. "You can put your hands on the old stones and feel the music resonate."

"W.R.?"

"Yes, dear."

"I s-sure am hungry. C-can we eat?"

"Sure thing."

Miss Davies sat alone at the end of that big table and pulled off the leg of the turkey and wrapped her other hand around a jeweled goblet of wine.

Mr. Hearst paced.

His feet made cavernous clicking noises, and he moved back and forth and back and forth, and then forward, toward the big set for tomorrow's scene at the Tower of London. He leaned into the fake brick wall—just plaster—and felt for the shackles that hung there, thinking of what George had told him, and he whistled for George, and George, knowing what a whistle meant, came running with a writing tablet in hand, ready to cable the *Examiner* offices. The story would be fed to the Hearst wires, cabling from coast to coast and around the globe.

"A virgin. A star of tomorrow. A waif."

George wrote down the words.

"And Arbuckle. A bloated beast. Three hundred and fifty pounds and lecherous and thirsty. An absolute animal."

"The girl?"

"A simple insect drawn into the spider's web."

"Do you want a drawing of that, sir?"

"George, you are a smart one," Mr. Hearst said. "You should be the one running the newspapers."

"I do my best."

"Make sure the spider has the bloated face of the man and that they have plenty of booze bottles in the web."

"Yes, sir."

The air was thin and cold, and the only sound came from electric fans blowing away the heat from the stage lights. But there was a feel to the set, the props became real in shadow, and, in the camera's eye, everything came into focus.

The newspapermen were at the Hall of Justice when Roscoe pulled up in a cab with his manager, Lou Anger, and his attorney, Frank Dominguez. Anger wandered off to talk to the desk sergeant about bail while two cops in stiff blue walked Roscoe and Dominguez up to the second floor and through a big, silent desk pool of plainclothes cops and into a back room where a door of frosted glass clicked shut. Roscoe heard a couple of the cops snicker about him wanting to join the force, and it was all a bunch of laughs because of all those Keystone shorts that made him famous. But the cops sitting across the big schoolhouse table didn't look anything like Al St. John or any of the other Keystone boys. They didn't look like they'd jump at the sound of a gunshot or slip on a banana peel or allow some felon to steal the keys on their hip. These were big, beefy Irishmen. One of them, a cop called Tom Reagan, had a head like a bullet and a thick chest and muscles. He had blond hair and a boyish face, and stood and shook Frank Dominguez's hand but opted not to address Roscoe except to nod over to another big Irishman named Griff Kennedy, with pomaded red hair and pale blue eyes, who just nodded to Roscoe and blew smoke from his nose.

"And this is Assistant District Attorney U'Ren," Reagan said. "Judge Brady is out of town, but he'll be back tomorrow. Mr. U'Ren will be handling the case."

"Not much to handle," Dominguez said. "Is there?"

Dominguez was as big as any of the men in the room. Not as muscled as the cops but not as fat as Roscoe. Just a well-fed Spaniard on retainer for Paramount who wore a two-hundred-dollar suit with a silk neckerchief and a solid gold wristwatch that looked sharp against his dark skin.

"A young woman swore out a complaint on ole Fatty here," Griff Kennedy said, poking his thumb sideways. "She sez she was at the party and Miss Rappe told her she'd been assaulted."

"Roscoe," Roscoe said from the seat, looking down at his hands and then glancing up at the beefy detectives. "My name is Roscoe."

Kennedy looked to Reagan and Reagan looked to U'Ren. U'Ren, the only small guy in the room, glanced down at the files in front of him and then peered up through his pince-nez glasses slid high on a weasely nose and said, "You've been charged with murder. These men will take you into custody as soon as we finish up."

Dominguez stood. "Could someone get me some coffee? This is going to be a long night."

U'Ren stood, too, and began to pace, with hands behind his back, head tilted up in thought, and it was all very theatrical. He stopped after a while, placing little knuckles on the table and leaning into where Roscoe sat across from Frank Dominguez and said, "Let's be practical, Señor Dominguez."

Roscoe narrowed his eyes at Dominguez. Dominguez leaned back in his chair.

"Judge Brady offers a reasonable sentence."

"Any type of sentence isn't reasonable to me."

"Mr. Arbuckle pleads guilty," U'Ren said. "And we can perhaps spare the hangman's noose."

"You don't have a scrap of evidence against my client. And please let me remind you that Mr. Arbuckle here is beloved the world over."

Milton U'Ren grinned, his teeth crooked and sharp in the long, lean face.

"I know of Mr. Arbuckle's reputation in those silly films," U'Ren said. "And I also know he came to our city for his alcohol-fueled jazz orgy at our best hotel. This is gutter-trash morals that we will not tolerate. If you think that's acceptable, perhaps you should have both remained in Los Angeles."

"We're through," Dominguez said. "Either charge us or let us go."

U'Ren raised off his knuckles and wiped his brow with a handkerchief from his tight-fitting coat. He cleaned his glasses and plunked them back on his weasely face. "As you wish. Detectives?"

Griff Kennedy and Tom Reagan took a big arm each and moved Roscoe from his chair and out of the back office and into a hallway, where they prodded him up a large spiral staircase to the highest floor of the Hall of Justice. There they strung a board around his neck with the porcelain number 32052 and told him to turn to the left.

Roscoe looked over at Dominguez and Dominguez shook his head with disgust. Roscoe smiled weakly at him and gave him a little wink.

In a loud, booming voice, Roscoe told the camera man—loud enough for the reporters to overhear—"You don't need to tell me what to do in front of the camera. How's that profile looking?"

The newsboys laughed and wrote it all down.

SAM WENT INTO THE OFFICE on that Monday to pick up his weekly check of twenty-one bucks and to see if anything had come across the wire from the Baltimore office. Usually they'd get some tips on some fugitives from the east or a wandering daughter from New York headed their way. Wandering-daughter jobs were constant. Nine times out of ten, the poor girl split because she was engaged to some lunkhead banker's son and the thought of going through with the act made her physically ill.

The Pinkerton San Francisco branch office was in room 314 of the Flood Building. It was a small office, without the need for an anteroom or a secretary, and Sam rapped on the door before finding old Phil Geauque with his feet up on his desk, dressed in high trousers and suspenders over a crisp white shirt and short red tie. He was smoking a cigar and was in midconversation with a fat Latin man, who stood and was pacing and cursing and didn't stop as Sam closed the door behind him.

Geauque remained seated but introduced the Spaniard as Frank Dominguez, a defense attorney from down south.

"I'll be down at Clinton's for coffee."

"Stay, Sam," the old man said. "We may have something for you."

Sam stood but Dominguez sat. He was a neat dresser, even wearing a red silk scarf tied at the throat. And it was odd for a man to wear a scarf, but somehow on Dominguez it looked regal.

"Mr. Dominguez represents Mr. Arbuckle. I imagine you know all about that mess."

"I've heard a thing or two."

Geauque lowered his big feet to the ground and leaned in to tap a three-inch ash off his cigar. He plunked the cigar back in his mouth and asked Dominguez, "What about witnesses?"

"Roscoe drove up with a couple of his buddies, Lowell Sherman and Freddie Fishback."

"Fishback?" Sam asked. "Hell of a name."

"Who else?" Geauque asked.

"His chauffeur and his dog, Luke."

"I once saw him in a picture where that dog could climb a ladder," Sam said. "I didn't believe it."

"You a fan of Mr. Arbuckle?"

"I've always been partial to Wallace Reid. My grandmother said I favored him."

"No need to worry about Sherman and Fishback," Dominguez said. "They can testify to Mr. Arbuckle's behavior and to the fact that he was alone with Miss Rappe for only ten minutes. At no time did they ever hear screaming or violent sounds coming from the room."

"Who else was there?" Geauque asked.

"Mainly a bunch of floozies and showgirls and the like. A nightgown salesman named Fortlouis. Some fella named Kingstone we can't find."

"Doc Kingstone?" Sam asked. "He's a boxing promoter. Met him down at the Wonderland on fight night. You have the names of the girls?"

"Well, there's Maude Delmont. Mr. Geauque has a copy of the complaint signed. She said the Rappe woman told her that Mr. Arbuckle had forced himself on her and, in doing so, crushed her."

"What do we know about Delmont?" Geauque asked.

"Not a thing."

"The Rappe girl?"

"Typical Hollywood chippie. The papers have been calling her a starlet, but I can't find a soul in Los Angeles who can name a picture she's been in."

"She and Arbuckle friendly?" Sam asked.

"Mr. Arbuckle said he didn't even discover Miss Rappe was in his room until he'd finished taking a shower. She'd passed out by the toilet."

"How'd she get to the bed?"

"Mr. Arbuckle said he carried her."

"Other witnesses?" Geauque asked.

"Cops are looking for a couple of showgirls who were in the room when Miss Rappe made the statement to Maude Delmont. About Roscoe hurting her."

"Names?" Sam asked. He opened his tweed coat for a little notepad and pencil.

"Alice Blake. Zey Prevon or Prevost—something like that. Roscoe said one of the girls, Miss Blake, worked at a joint called Tait's. You know it?"

"Sure," Sam said.

"This Prevon or Prevost woman worked as a cigarette girl somewhere."

"I'm on it," Sam said. And the men turned away from each other, but Sam stayed by the door until Geauque turned back and caught Sam's eyes.

Geauque showed him the palm of his right hand and nodded. "Of course." He reached into his desk drawer and pulled out a check ledger, writing one out to Sam for a week's advance.

"How's Jose?" he asked.

"Big as a house."

MAUDE DELMONT HADN'T LEFT the St. Francis except to visit Virginia once at Wakefield Sanitorium before the poor girl died. She'd told the day manager she just didn't have the energy to change hotels and he instantly started an account to pay for all her room service and phone charges, as she called down to Los Angeles every other hour looking for that rat bastard Al Semnacher. She ordered room service a lot, had her two outfits laundered daily, and read stories in *The Call*, the *Examiner*, and the *Chronicle* about a producer she knew named Henry Lehrman calling Arbuckle a beast for what he'd done to Henry's poor sweetheart. He said if he came face-to-face with Fatty, he'd kill him.

That was a riot. Last she'd known, Lehrman wouldn't answer a single cable Virginia sent to New York.

That afternoon Maude lay on the thick feathered mattress in a black housecoat—thinking black was a nice touch when she had the doorman go out and fetch some items for her—with one arm draped across her eyes, the Victrola from the party now in her room but this time playing a slow funeral dirge and some other kinds of depressing music, mainly opera. She really liked the stuff from *Tosca*, and the bellman told her they were going to do a performance of the opera in a couple weeks, it being opera season and all.

Maude thought San Francisco was some kind of town to actually have a goddamn season for opera.

An hour later, two cops stood at the foot of her bed. Another one stood by the hotel door. A big woman in a big blue wool sweater and big skirt down past her ankles. She wore a woman's version of a police hat pinned to her head and kept a little brown purse clutched to her side, where she probably kept her gun.

The cops, Griff Kennedy and Tom Reagan, introduced her as Katherine Eisenhart.

"Now, these two girls, were they friends of yours?" Kennedy asked.

"No."

"Had you met them before Mr. Arbuckle's party?"

"No."

"Were they with Miss Rappe before she went to room 1219?" Tom Reagan asked.

"Yes," Maude said, dropping the arm from her eyes. "Yes. They were admiring her dress and hair. I remember that."

"What about after?"

"When I beat down the door?"

"When you said you knocked on the door," Reagan said.

"Hammered with all my might against that beastly lock?"

Kennedy looked to Reagan and Reagan back to Kennedy and, for the life of her, Maude could barely tell the two thick Irishmen apart except that Kennedy—or Griff, as he said—had red hair and Reagan's hair was blond, and Reagan's head looked like some kind of melon.

"Do you know where we can find these young ladies?" Kate Eisenhart asked, stepping away from the door and out of the shadows. A window was open in the hotel room and they could hear the high tinny squawk of horns and the clanging of the cable cars out on Powell. The curtains blew slightly in the breeze.

"No."

"What about Mr. Semnacher?" Eisenhart asked.

"I don't know what's become of Mr. Semnacher. He left shortly after Miss Rappe became ill."

"Did he speak to Miss Rappe after she became sick?" Reagan asked.

"Did he know Miss Rappe well?" Kennedy asked.

"Did he see the girl sick in 1219?" Kate Eisenhart asked.

Maude Delmont tossed her head from side to side on the pillow and groaned. "My head feels like it's going to explode. All these questions and I've yet to put my best friend in the world in the ground. Can't I mourn for her?"

Kennedy looked over to Reagan. Reagan walked to the open window looking out over Union Square and the Spanish-American War Monument.

Kate Eisenhart sat on the bed and there was a noticeable shift in the mattress as she felt Maude's forehead and traced the line of her jaw with the tips of her stubby man fingers. Maude smiled up at the big woman and the woman's cheeks flushed.

"Did anyone else hear Miss Rappe say that Roscoe Arbuckle had hurt her?"

"Just the girls."

"Alice and Zey?" Reagan said.

"Yes."

"But you don't know them?" Reagan asked.

"No."

"And you don't know where to find them?" Kennedy said from the window.

"One of them sang at a speakeasy. I don't know what the Zey girl did. To be honest, she was the less attractive of the two, although I think she fancied herself as an actress."

Maude watched the two men grow restless and play with their felt hats in their hands, kneading the wool and exchanging glances, and all Maude wanted was for room service to arrive with her lamb chops with mashed potatoes and a cherry tart on the side.

Maude closed her eyes and opened them again, and Kate Eisenhart was smiling at her, and, from the big weight on the bed, Maude could feel the policewoman's breathing grow heavy and labored whenever she met her eye. The thick roll of fat under Kate's jaw trembled a bit.

"Now, now. I know what it's like to lose a friend. I bet you can't even eat."

"No, ma'am."

"Tom, Griff—you two skedaddle. I'll stay with this poor creature."

"We have a few—" Tom started.

"Thank you," Maude said. "My nerves are raw as a side of beef."

The big fat policewoman tucked the covers up to Maude's chin and turned off the bedside lamp. She stood and pushed Kennedy and Reagan toward the door.

"I dreamed of her last night," Kate said.

"Ma'am?"

"Virginia. She wanted people to know what that Fatty had done to her. He's a monster. A vile, disgusting creature. If I had my way, they'd chop his man bits clean off."

The boys looked at each other again.

"You fools," Kate Eisenhart said. "You poor fools."

"The CHRONICLE'S BEEN RUNNING this serial 'bout this detective named Craig Kennedy," Phil Haultain said. "You got to see this thing. This guy ain't like us. He's a real gentleman. A Nob Hill type, only he lives in New York, and has a manservant and four speedy cars."

"Four of 'em?"

"Four of 'em."

Haultain and Sam walked out back of the Flood Building, heading toward Powell.

"See, this guy's some big brain who can smell a brand of cigarette on a woman and uses a microscope to match hairs found at a murder. He also wears expensive clothes and knows how to talk to women."

"Nothing like us. We can't talk to women."

"See, Craig Kennedy is some man about town but he wants to right the wrongs of society," Haultain said. "The paper's running part four next week, but I think you can catch up. Last time we left Craig he'd been drugged but came out of it to make this big-time raid. But before he could make a raid, the whole goddamn house blew up. Kennedy escaped without a hair out of place, located some underground tunnel, and followed the bad guys just as the chapter ended. I can't wait to find out what happens next."

"You mind if we drop by Marquard's? I'm out of smokes."

"Thought you rolled your own."

"Too much work."

"How's the lungs?"

"Working."

"It's worse in the fog, ain't it?"

Sam nodded.

Sam bought his cigarettes and they cut back across Powell, waiting for a horse-drawn wagon, bumping along, loaded down with fish and crabs on ice blocks. As they followed O'Farrell, the electric streetlights tripped on one after another like dominoes.

"So what's the plan?"

"Wait a couple minutes and follow me inside. When you come in, you don't know me."

"Sam, what do you think happened to that girl?"

"Ain't my problem."

"You just want the truth?"

"I just write reports."

Inside Tait's, a man with a face like a skillet cleaned out sundae glasses and dirty spoons in a sudsy bucket of water. Sam leaned into the counter and asked for a drink and the man said, "It's Prohibition, ain't you heard?," and Sam said he thought this place was a speak.

The ice-cream man snorted and pumped out some chocolate in a glass.

"So what are you, a dry agent?"

Sam reached for the leather wallet in his tweeds and opened it to the Pinkerton badge.

"Just looking for a couple girls. One of 'em's named Alice Blake. The other's name is Prevon or Prevost. No trouble. Just want to ask them a couple questions."

"I know Alice."

"She here?"

The man looked back at the octagon clock on the wall and then at Sam and said, "What'd she do? Break an old man's heart?"

"Exactly."

The door opened, a bell jingled overhead, and three girls flitted past the counter and toward a back door. The ice-cream man's sharp little eyes clicked to the girls, as they disappeared through an unmarked door, and then back to Sam.

The bell jingled again, and Phil stepped up to the bar and asked for a chocolate malt.

"Can you leave her a message?" Sam asked.

The soda jerk shrugged and said something about this being America, and then Sam wrote out a phone number on the back of a business card.

"What's in this for me?" the soda jerk asked.

"Helping out your fellow man."

"That's some racket."

5

o you were there?"

"Sure," Alice Blake said.

Two minutes after Sam left, Phil had sipped his malt and heard the soda jerk ring up the Woodrow Hotel and ask for a Miss Blake. He didn't say much, only relayed that some dick was looking for her and that if she had any goddamn sense she wouldn't come to work tonight. He said the cops had been by, too. Fifteen minutes later, Sam asked a hotel clerk what room his sister Alice Blake was staying in and to please not ring the poor girl because it was a surprise for Ma and all.

"So you dance?" Sam asked, sitting across from the girl in her hotel efficiency, Phil in the lobby, scouting out the stairs and elevators in case she bolted.

"I'm a dancer," Alice Blake said.

"What's the show?"

"Tonight we're doing the powder-puff number, where all the girls come out in their drawers and sing a little song about our sweet little powder puffs, and then we take these big powder puffs, really too big to be real because I guess that's funny and all, and we whack you goofy bastards in the kisser with some face powder. Only I don't think it's face powder, because that would be a damn waste. I think it's just flour, because later on my hands smell like a cake."

"I like cake."

"You gonna see the show?"

Alice Blake was a girl of average height and average build, with a brown bob and big baby-doll eyes. She giggled a lot when she talked, and after she invited Sam into her room her hands shook a bit as she struck a match and lit a little cigarette. A half-packed suitcase sat on a chair below a window looking out onto O'Farrell.

"You want to tell me what happened last Monday?"

"I seen the girl sick." Alice had finished up the smoke and now worked a thick coat of dark paint to her eyelid with her twitching hands, using a mirror above the bureau. She switched to another brush and arched her eyebrows.

"Did Mr. Arbuckle hurt her?"

"I told you. When that Delmont woman started screaming and carrying on and beating on the door with her shoe and all, that's what made me come running."

"Where were you?"

"In the bathroom."

"Which bathroom?"

"I don't know. The big room where they had the Victrola."

"1220?"

"I guess."

"How long were you in the bathroom?"

"Twenty minutes?"

"You sick or something?"

"I was with a fella. That actor buddy of Roscoe's with the funny voice."

"Lowell Sherman?"

"That's the one. So anyway, I finished up having a real nice conversation with Lowell."

"In the bathroom?"

"You can talk in the bathroom same as anywhere else," Alice Blake said. "And so Mrs. Delmont come running into the room, and the way that broad was yelling you'd think the whole St. Francis was on fire or there was an earthquake or some crazy thing. Only she was moaning about Virginia being with Roscoe, and so I sez to Zey—that's my girlfriend—I say to Zey, What gives if old Fatty gets him some tail? I mean, we all need it. I said, Good on him."

"And then what?"

"And then the hotel dick comes and ruins the party, and then Virginia is moaning and thrashing and all that on the bed and that ruined the party, too. God rest her soul." Alice crossed her heart the way Sam's mother had at mass. "And then Maude Delmont and Zey and me tried to help the poor girl out by putting her in a cold bath. Fatty and that good-looking foreign fella Fishback helped, too. We thought she was just drunk is all."

"Did the girl say anything?"

Alice was finished with the paint job and turned her head from side to side inspecting what she'd done with her eyes and apple cheeks. Satisfied with it, she gave her bob a nice little comb through and then felt the weight of her breasts in the lace camisole and smiled.

"You think I have nice tits?"

"Spectacular."

"What did you say your name was?"

"Sam."

She smiled. Then she frowned.

"Kind of a boring name—Sam. That sounds like a schoolboy."

"How 'bout Craig Kennedy?"

"Who's that?"

"A master detective with four speedy cars."

"I love speedy cars."

"Zoom."

"So I was telling you about what I didn't see. I'm telling you like I told the policeman who called me, I didn't see nothing and I didn't hear nothing. They've been hunting me down like a rabbit and my nerves are just about shot. You wouldn't have a little drink with you?"

Sam shook his head and asked, "Who was the policeman?"

"Said his name was Reagan. Didn't say his first name."

Sam smiled. "Did Miss Rappe say anything else?"

"I only know what Maude Delmont said. She said that ole Fatty had crushed that poor girl with all that weight."

"You believe it?"

"She was groaning and moaning and all that. Zey heard her say something."

"What'd she hear?"

"She said Virginia said that she was dying. He said he'd hurt her."

Sam nodded and jotted down a few notes. "'He' being Arbuckle?"

"He being *he*. I don't know who the screwy girl was talking about. We was just there having a good time, and then we tried our best to help her. It's a real shame. It really is. Gosh, I feel bad about what I said about poor Virginia ruining the party. She seemed like a nice lamb. Screwy. But a real lamb. Did you know she was the model for the sheet music to 'Let Me Call You Sweetheart'?"

"Nope."

"She sure was. I like it when you meet somebody who's somebody."

"Everybody is somebody."

"Who are you kidding?" Alice Blake smiled. She had a dynamite smile. "You're only somebody if you get your picture made and people pay a nickel to take a look. The rest of us are just deadbeats."

"Where can I find Zey?"

Alice shrugged and smiled over at Sam.

He mouthed the word *spectacular*.

"Keep talkin', Craig Kennedy."

THE COPS LOCKED ROSCOE in a cell by himself, checking on him twice in the first four hours, and he'd made jokes with them, trying to make them feel at ease, but they'd only answer with curt replies about supper, toilet paper, or a tin cup for water and walk back down the hall. He'd laid back into his narrow bunk, the newsboys already noting his bunk was made for a man half his size, and he'd wriggle his toes in his silk socks and look at the ceiling. Roscoe knew what disappointed reporters most was the fact that he'd weighed in at only two hundred sixty on the Bertillon charts, not the three-fifty he'd told the press men in Hollywood. He loved making up stories for the publicity folks at Paramount about how he ate a pound of bacon and a dozen eggs every morning with a pot of coffee.

The cell was six by six. One of the walls decorated with some nice prison art, stick figures of Gloom and Joy shaking hands, Mary's Little Lamb, and the simple inscription HELL above his head.

But it wasn't so bad. Roscoe had fashioned a coat hanger from a strand of wire from the springs of his bunk. He'd hung the Norfolk jacket he'd had fitted at Hart Schaffner Marx neatly from a single hook and knocked off his shoes by the bed.

He had paper and a pouch of tobacco Dominguez had brought him along with a safety razor and some soap.

When he was a boy, this little place would've seemed like a palace. Sometimes he'd awake from a drunk or a dream and think he was still living in that sod house in Smith Center, Kansas, with dust storms and tornadoes and gully washers that would turn half the kitchen into a pile of mud. Other times he'd be in that dead, dazed time in Santa Clara after his mother had died and he was sent north to live with a father he hadn't seen in years only to find his father had split town and started over again. He remembered the shame of sitting in the train station overnight and waiting for ole Will Arbuckle to show up and finally finding pity from the man who'd bought his family's hotel and offered him a job.

When the old man finally came to claim him, those wild, drunken beatings had returned like some half-remembered dream, and so did the comments about his fattened face and blubbery belly, and, once in a bathhouse, his father lay drunk in a tub and pointed out his son's genitalia with the tip of a burning cigar, calling it a tiny worm. Sometimes Roscoe liked the beatings better than the insults. When the old man took to drink and held the power of the whip in his hand, at least the bastard would shut up.

You fashioned your own way, carried your own water.

Roscoe had always been good at that. When people stare and point and smile, you just do a little dance and make them smile more. It was a hell of a trick he learned.

He heard the guard walking the length of the hall and the splatter of a man pissing in the cell next to him, calling out to Fatty to do some tricks for him. Roscoe turned over and felt for the shaving mirror Dominguez had brought.

He stared at himself for a long time, looking at his pale blue eyes and the odd way God had left his face to resemble an infant's. He smiled at himself and then stopped, and then just looked into his eyes.

He just wished he could remember.

HEARST HEARD THE HORSE HOOVES from a mile up the great hill, as he sat on a boulder he'd known since he was a boy staring out at midnight over the Pacific Ocean. The old campsite at San Simeon was dotted with crisp white canvas tents lit from the inside like paper lanterns, while men worked to unload wagons and trucks, not stopping for the last three months, only working in shifts, to bring in his collection from back east. Little mementos from Bavarian strongholds and Italian palaces that would become the foundation, the cornerstones of his American castle. The foundation had been poured, and already he could imagine the way the stone turrets would rise from the ragged hillside in a way that no man said could be done. So he'd used a woman architect from San Francisco who dreamed without limits.

By the time the horses rounded that final bend on the great hill, he could barely make out the man's face sitting next to the coachman. The white hair, the big nose, and little eyes of Al Zukor, who stared straight ahead under a bowler hat with great annoyance that brought a smile to Hearst's face. He walked toward the wagon as it slowed and Zukor hopped to the ground, dusting off his three-piece suit with the flat of his hands and readjusting the bowler on his head. He still looked like a guy peddling furs on the streets of New York, not the head of Paramount Pictures.

He stood a good two feet below Hearst, who was a tall man. The wide-brimmed hat and big boots on Hearst made him seem even larger, as he gripped the short man's little hand.

"I've cabled you sixteen times."

"I've received them all."

"And you did not cable back," Zukor said.

"No," Hearst said. "No, I did not."

"What's all this?"

"Just a little cottage or two."

"Five miles up in the goddamn air?"

Hearst shrugged, wrapped his arm around Zukor, steered him back to the old childhood rock, and swept his free hand across the expanse that hung in the air like a dream above the clouds. And Zukor closed his eyes and then opened them wide, taking in the way the moonlight caught on the great mossy boulders down along the craggy shore and all the inlets and coves and hardscrabble pines clinging to the hills and wide pastureland with little dots of cattle below. A single stray cloud moved under them and the sight of it made Zukor step back from the edge to find his feet and turn back to the familiar movement of the Chinese workers tearing into great wooden crates and pulling out statues of winged women and horses and thick, beaten columns that Zukor had probably only seen in papier-mâché.

"How much is this goddamn thing gonna cost?"

"Do you Jews only think about money?"

"Yes," Zukor said.

"Let me show you something," Hearst said, steering into a brightly lit tent, larger than the others, pulling the canvas door aside. He took Zukor to a table littered with drawings of great fountains with spitting lions and a mammoth swimming pool copied from a Roman bath, of fireplaces large enough to burn a forest, and of a cleared strip to land his airplane atop the mountain instead of having to be jostled all the way up the hill like poor Zukor.

"How's that Arabian picture coming along?" Hearst asked.

"It's in the can."

"That's the one with the Italian fella."

"Valentino."

"And he's playing a sheik."

"Like a girl from Brooklyn playing a queen. We all like to pretend, Willie."

Hearst grinned at him with his big teeth and breathed, and then smiled a bit more.

"I came for Roscoe."

"I didn't crush that poor girl."

"You're not just crucifying this fat boy in your goddamn papers, you're making the whole goddamn picture industry look like devils. That's bad business. Very bad business."

"I don't tell my men what to write."

"And you don't start wars with Spain either. You must lay off Arbuckle, see? What's with your paper showing him as a drunken spider? The *Examiner* printed that crazy letter from Henry Lehrman. Have you gone nutso?"

Hearst narrowed his eyes and crossed his arms.

"Let's have a drink."

"Don't screw me, Willie, okay? We got a nice thing going with Cosmopolitan and we have a nice run ahead of us with those pictures with Miss Davies, okay? I just can't figure out why you're doing this. Those stories get read in small papers everywhere. In two days you've turned my biggest star into a three-hundred-pound gorilla with bloodlust for snatchola."

"Come now."

"Don't fuck me, Willie. We have such a nice thing going."

"You don't understand journalism."

"I understand when a fella is being fucked in his *tokhes*."

The Chinese had busted apart more wooden crates and they'd started a big fire near the edge of the cliff, the smell of burning pine and salt in the air. Hearst dug his hands into the pockets of his ranch coat and kicked at a stray stone with his big boots. He stole a look from the corner of his eye at dusty Al Zukor, traveling all damn day just to have a second of his time, dusty and hungry and refusing a drink, on this magnificent hill.

"Let's watch the sunrise," Hearst said. "We'll eat our breakfast from an iron skillet like cowboys."

"I know why you're doing this. But I don't know how you did it."

Hearst smiled a bit and took in the expanse of statues brought out from crate and shadow and storage to catch the moonlight on the hill. He recalled being here as a boy with his dad—old rough-talking George Hearst—and the way the chewing tobacco would stain that gray beard and the stories he would tell about Missouri and how he was born to talk to the earth. Hearst would stay awake all night, after the old man collapsed from exhaustion and whiskey, and he'd cling to the rock until morning light and imagine himself a king.

"Who do you think you are?" Zukor asked.

"Would you like a drink, Mr. Zukor?"

"No, I would not."

"Then I have work to do," Hearst said, giving him a hard pat on the back and using the little man's shoulder for purchase as he pushed and moved off to view a new statue he'd purchased of Zeus' three daughters locked in an erotic embrace.

It had always taken his breath away.

Two hours earlier, Sam sat with his wife on the roof of their apartment in the Tenderloin District and smoked a cigarette atop a little stack of brick by the narrow chimneys. Jose sat in a ship's deck chair and finished up a piece of cold chicken Sam had brought from town. She wore a big, loose-fitting dress and smiled back at him when she noticed him watching her. He wore an old Army sweater and a little cap, striking a match on the sole of his boot.

He'd showered and was clean-shaven and wanted a drink very badly, something Jose would not agree to since it wasn't part of the cure.

"Did you take your balsamea?"

"Yes, ma'am."

"And your breathing exercises?"

"Done."

"No more than ten cigarettes."

"Done."

"And no drinking."

"Not a drop."

"You want to feel it?"

Sam stood and walked to her, reaching down to feel the hard wedge on his wife's stomach.

"That's a foot."

"Already kicking Ma around."

"I'm worried we're not going to make it," she said. "I still have an offer from my aunt. I can go back to Montana until the baby comes. We could take care of the rest later."

"This is working."

"For now," she said. "Sam, you still haven't unpacked your steamer trunk."

"I don't own much."

"You did what I asked," Jose said. "For the child. But you don't have to take care of us later. You're not the kind to settle."

"Says who?"

"The nurse who you dallied."

Sam reached into his tweed trousers and pulled out a wad of cash in his money clip. "The old man gave me an advance."

"New case?"

"Big case."

"You want to talk about it?"

"Sure. They got me working on Fatty Arbuckle's train wreck."

"That is big. What do they have you doing?"

"Running down a couple girls who were at the party."

"Did he really do it?"

"I don't know and I don't really care. Have you ever seen one of his films?"

"I used to see him when I was still in Montana. He made a lot of films with Mabel Normand. I remember one where they went to the World's Fair.

They had these little motorized cars you could rent and go from exhibit to exhibit, and it always seemed like so much fun to me."

"I liked his dog."

"Luke?"

"Yep."

"How do they say he killed her?"

"He's being accused of smothering her during rape."

"But she didn't die till four days later. Did he break some ribs?"

"I don't know."

Sam smoked down some more of his cigarette and stood up, stretching up his stick-thin frame and peering down onto Eddy Street and a Model T parking down across from the Elk Hotel, a man strolling across the street to the corner market.

He looked back to Jose.

"You still hungry? I can run to the market."

She shook her head. "How'd he crush her? Did she suffocate?"

"He is a big fella."

"The paper says he weighs two-sixty. Was her vagina badly torn?"

"I love when you talk dirty."

"I'm talking like a nurse."

"I don't know."

"I thought you were a detective."

"I'm paid to interview a couple showgirls, not solve the case."

"And that got your attention. The showgirls."

"I like showgirls."

"Help me up," Jose said.

Sam reached down his hand and pulled her to her feet. Jose waddled to the edge of the apartment building roof and borrowed his cigarette for a puff and then handed it back.

"I've treated girls who've been beaten and raped. That happens a lot in soldier towns."

Sam nodded.

"Can you bring me the autopsy file?"

"What ever happened to flowers?"

The stairwell door opened and an old crinkly woman in a flowered dress walked out. She lived right below their apartment and made moonshine with her old crinkly husband in their bathtub. Sam had tasted better gasoline.

"You got a call," the old woman said.

Bootleggers always had phones.

"Okay."

"Said it's important."

"Okay."

Sam took the call. It was Phil Haultain.

"I got a bead on the Zey Prevon girl. She's working at the Old Poodle Dog."

"I'll meet you there."

The fog rolled in before midnight, flooding in from the bay and along the docks and Embarcadero, sinking the lower maze of San Francisco in a fine mist. Hammett had his tweed jacket on, collar popped up around his ears, and his sporting cap down far on his head. He walked Leavenworth through the curving fog up to Bush, coughing a spot of blood into a crisp handkerchief, and then up Bush and over Nob Hill, passing the Hell's Gate of Chinatown and smelling the garlic and cooked chickens and fresh-cut flowers, and then down a ways, his breath strangled again as he descended back into the static of fog, and toward Bergez-Franks's OLD POODLE DOG sign, lit up with spotlights, and a line of cars that stretched from the front portico down Kearny to Market. Most of the men had on expensive suits with high collars and bow ties, and the women wore tight long dresses and furs and large hats that trailed large, expensive feathers.

Sam tucked his cap into the side pocket of his coat and ran his hand over his white hair to smooth it down a bit. He just hoped no one noticed his laced boots, which could use a good shine.

He walked ahead of the line of sedans and touring cars and little black Fords and into the restaurant. He soon found Phil Haultain back by the kitchen, most of the diners sitting behind curtains in honeycombed rooms where waiters responded to a buzzer to keep a bottle or a mistress private. Downstairs you'd find roulette wheels and blackjack tables and games of faro, and a long hand-polished mahogany bar that stopped serving whiskey only during the Quake.

Sam winked at Phil and followed the big man down a curving wood staircase and past a big door with a sliding view and into a wide-open basement nightclub, where a gathering of negroes played trumpets and trombones, banjos and guitar, in the New Orleans style. The negroes all wore tuxedos and tails and played the wild music with such dignity that Sam thought the whites in the room seemed slovenly by comparison.

Sam leaned against an ornate column, and Phil stepped up next to him as he took in the scene. A bar stretched from one end of the room to the other, with several oblong mirrors and an endless brass rail. Linen-covered tables filled the room. The dance floor a chessboard.

"She sells cigarettes and is wearing a dress above her knees."

"How's she look?"

"Face like a horse. A body that would do Mr. Ziegfeld proud."

"You talk to her?"

"Just found her, like you said."

"Good man."

Phil looked away for a moment, dead-eyed, and then turned back. "Now, there's someone you'd write home to Mom about."

At the long wooden bar stood a tall blond woman, hair almost white, with bright-red-painted lips. She held her booted foot up off the floor on the brass rail in the manner of a man, her hair shorn above her shoulders and covering the right side of her face when she turned. She held a long fox coat across her arm.

The woman looked over the room and then matched stares with Haultain and Sam and smiled a bit, and cocked a dark eyebrow, taking away the curtain of hair over her eye and turning back to face the bar mirror and wall of booze. The shape of her wasn't unknown, as she turned back to the bar, the coat before her now, in her long black skirt that hugged her well-proportioned fanny and legs.

"Sam?"

"I'm here."

"Thought I lost you."

Sam noted a man in black tails and bow tie, thick black mustache and hair split and plastered to the skull and hard-parted with grease. When he laughed, you could see at least an inch gap between his big teeth.

"H. F. LaPeer," Phil said.

"You know him?"

"Biggest bootlegger in the city. How long you been in Frisco, Sam?"

"Since July."

"That's right, you came for that head-busting job on the docks."

"What's the story with LaPeer?"

"Most of the booze in town flows from him. Runs the good stuff from Canada and brings it ashore at Half Moon Bay. Cops here are well paid, and no one seems to want to stop his party."

"He looks like he combs his hair with olive oil."

"Doesn't seem to bother the girl."

The blond girl stood against the long bar now, in the middle of an endless row of men in black suits getting drinks for their women. She smoked down a cigarette and made it look elegant the way she balanced the cigarette while holding the fox coat.

Her eyes looked as soft as her lips.

"That's her."

"You bet it is."

"Sam? Over there."

Phil pointed out a girl wearing a white bodice covered in glinting toy gems flitting her way around the table with a cigarette box hung around her neck. The first image Sam had of Zey Prevon wasn't of a horse but of a Boston terrier. The girl had a sharp nose and soft chin and large bulging eyes, the kind that seemed to be in fashion these days among the movie-picture types. But she was long-legged, with biscuit-colored skin and large round breasts that hung handsomely in the jeweled top when she would lean over the table and the laps of men to light their cigars and cigarettes. The men would guffaw and laugh, and then motion the little twirling girl onto the next gentlemen. Please repeat it, nice and slow, sister.

"Why'd you say she looked like a horse?"

"Horses are ugly."

"Horses are beautiful," Sam said. "Don't you go to the track?"

"What kind of animal has big tits?" Phil asked.

Sam waited for the girl to finish up, and he was going to meet her before she hit the next big table. For just two seconds the negro band stopped on a pin and then launched into "Fidgety Feet," and the girl moved on, counting out cash into her hand and then tucking a few bills into her brassiere.

Two steps forward, Sam moved on her.

But then two large men in flowing overcoats stepped between Sam and Zey Prevon, and he could see only the men's broad backs and then the girl pleading and smiling in profile and then turning down her mouth and sauntering away, one of the beefy men grabbing her arm. The other showed his silver badge. Tom Reagan.

H. F. LaPeer was there now, talking to the policemen and falsely smiling. He pulled out a silver cigar case, offering the men a smoke, but the men obviously declined and instead told LaPeer a few things. LaPeer dismissed them with a wave of his hand, in the thick cigar smoke, the band launching into the first few bars of the "St. Louis Blues," the men and women drunk and going wild with it. A little girl in a flowered dress bumped into Tom Reagan's partner and he tried to strong-arm the girl before she leapt up a good two feet, wrapped her arms around his ox neck, and planted a kiss on his sizable forehead.

"Having fun?" Sam asked.

Tom turned and nodded. "Hammett."

"When you're through, we'd like to talk to Miss Zey here, too. Is it Prevon or Prevost?"

"The papers call me both," the big-eyed cigarette girl said. "I guess you can put one of those things between the two."

"A hyphen?" Sam asked.

"That's it."

"Who's this?" Griff Kennedy, the other cop, asked, finally pushing off the little girl and wiping lipstick from his forehead.

"Pinkerton," Tom said. "Helped me out on that Southern Pacific job last month."

Griff Kennedy nodded. His hair looked to be the color and fiber of copper wire.

"Beat it, Pink," Kennedy said. "We got business with this little lady."

"You gonna arrest her?"

"Does this have a damn thing to do with you?"

Kennedy struck his two fattened fingers in Sam's sternum, moving him a foot back. Sam just smiled at him but didn't turn, only held the gaze, till about the time LaPeer joined the little group again and told them if they had business with Miss Prevon that was their business but they were making his customers nervous.

"You want us to bust open this whole place?" Tom Reagan said.

"Chief O'Brien sends me Christmas cards."

"Har," Griff Kennedy said.

Zey seemed to shrink a little bit as she unstrapped herself from the cigarette box and sat down in a nearby booth, lighting a cigarette she'd taken from the case, and she smoked it, exhausted and bored, her great bulging eyes flashing back and forth between LaPeer and the two detectives.

Sam sat down across from her.

"How'd you like to come with me?"

"I don't think you're any better than those two."

"I'd disagree."

"You're a cop, aren't you?"

"I'm a Pinkerton. I work for the attorneys representing Mr. Arbuckle. You'd like to help out Mr. Arbuckle, wouldn't you?"

She shrugged and laughed, the cops and LaPeer starting to yell and point now but being drowned out by the trumpet player barking out the lyrics to "Bow Wow Blues" and the smart set at the tables and on the dance floor screaming.

Sam turned back to the bar and noticed it was all men now, all dressed in that identical black, the blond woman with the nice shape and the fox gone.

"I don't know a thing," Zey said.

Sam spotted the woman by a door near the stage, pushing away that piece of hair from her eye and readjusting the fox as if it carried a great weight. She had the most wonderful shoulders.

"Alice said you heard Virginia say she'd been hurt?"

"How many times have I got to be asked this? I wish I'd never even gone to that stupid party, but Alice dragged me there because she wanted to meet Lowell Sherman ever since she saw him in that picture where he played a king. You know he's not even English?"

From across the bar, the tall girl with the legs and the snow blond hair scanned the room and nodded. Sam looked over the dance floor that resembled a chessboard and saw a man in a long raincoat and flop hat nod back to the woman and then nod again to another fella dressed just like him by another door. Sam put his hand across the table and held Zey's long fingers.

"What's the idea?"

"We need to go."

"Why?"

"Now."

Just then, the fox coat dropped to the floor at the feet of the long-legged woman and a 12-gauge shotgun appeared in her delicate hands, which slammed out two cartridges into the plaster ceiling, killing the music and cuing the screams.

The girl brushed back the hair from her face again. The face was lovely, heart-shaped, with full red lips and silver eyes that jumped out at you from all that white skin and hair.

Sam found himself smiling with admiration at the girl with the gun.

"Nobody better shimmy a goddamn inch," yelled the girl. "I'm a federal agent and this is a raid."

"DID SHE REALLY shoot into the ceiling?" Frank Dominguez asked.

"She did," Sam said.

"And was she a real beaut?"

"She had a hell of a shape. I don't know if I'd call her a beauty. When the houselights turned on, you could see maybe her nose had been busted at one time. But she had a quality about her. Sleepy bedroom eyes. You know the type."

"And they just let you go?"

Sam nodded and stifled a cough with a handkerchief and his fist.

"And the girl?"

"She went with Reagan and Kennedy."

"You know 'em?"

"I know Reagan. I know Kennedy by reputation."

"And you don't like him?"

"I heard stories."

The two men sat in the center of the Palace Hotel's Garden Court. It was early and a negro woman worked an electric vacuum machine on the carpet. The first light showed through the glass-paneled ceiling that domed the Garden Court, filled with potted palms and fresh-cut flowers, chandeliers that winked with prisms of color. A bird was caught in the ceiling and flew from side to side, slamming and fluttering against the glass.

"You're not going to eat?"

"I'm fine."

"It's on me," Dominguez said.

"Nice place."

"The man who built it killed himself. Jumped into the bay right before his bank went bust."

Sam ordered ham and eggs with hash, but the waiter said they didn't serve hash at the Palace and so Sam ordered toast. It wasn't quite six a.m.

"Coffee?" the waiter asked.

"Sure."

Sam lit a cigarette and settled in. "I talked to the Blake girl. She said she didn't hear anything but Virginia Rappe saying she was going to die. Before she got pinched, Zey Prevon told me she'd heard Virginia saying the same thing."

"And we have Maude Delmont saying Virginia accused Mr. Arbuckle before she died."

"Can you use that?"

"Conversations with someone killed in a crime are completely admissible."

"Did the cops turn over the autopsy records to you?"

"Why do you ask?"

"I'm just wondering how she died. I know the papers say she was crushed. But how? Were her bones broken?"

"Ruptured bladder."

Sam nodded.

"During the rape?"

"There was no rape."

Sam nodded.

"It's a medical impossibility."

"She was hurt in another way?"

"This is a very delicate matter, Mr. Hammett."

"Yes, sir," Sam said. "But I do work for you."

Dominguez nodded and crossed his legs, showing off a pair of bedroom slippers that didn't quite match his pin-striped suit. He tried lighting a cigarette with a lighter out of juice. Sam passed him a pack of matches.

"This goes no further."

"Of course."

Dominguez let out smoke from the side of his mouth and shrugged, leaning into the table. "Mr. Arbuckle's pencil isn't as sharp as it used to be."

Sam sat still.

"In fact, it hasn't written for some time."

"I'd like to see the coroner's report."

"I'd like that, too," Dominguez said. "This whole thing stinks. I just learned last night that the autopsy was conducted immediately after the girl died on Friday at the hospital."

"What's wrong with that?"

"The county coroner wasn't present and wasn't notified. Somebody called the coroner's office Saturday about the dead girl and rang off. After that the coroner called the police and it was the police who talked to Maude Delmont. The autopsy was completely illegal."

"YOU GODDAMN SON OF A BITCH," Maude Delmont said. "Where'd you go?"

"If I got pinched, all our work woulda been out the window."

On the staticky telephone line down to Los Angeles, Al Semnacher's voice sounded as squeaky and annoying as ever.

"Do you know the flaming pile of shit you left me with?" Maude said.

"How was I supposed to know he was gonna kill her? That wasn't exactly the plan."

"But you sure as hell waltzed off with her slip and bloomers. What were you going to do with those, Al?"

"That's why I'm calling."

"Well, fuck you. You can take your apology and shove it up your ass."

"They have them."

"Who?"

"The cops. They came down to L.A. yesterday and they knew all about the slip and the bloomers and they took them from me."

"How'd they know?"

"Those two girls Lowell Sherman brought. They told the cops they'd seen me take the torn clothes."

"Are you in jail?"

"No."

"Are you trying to frame me? Because if you are, I'll tell them about every goddamn con we worked together. I'll sing Hallelujah, you fucking rat bastard, as the stern slips beneath the waves."

"Poetic."

"They know."

"I told the cops I'd taken Virginia's clothes because they looked like nice rags to wash my machine."

"And they bought that crock?"

"Come again? Bad connection."

"They bought it?"

"I think so," Al said. "But I have to come to Frisco and testify to the grand jury."

"Me, too."

"We should talk. You know, before."

"What the hell are we doing now?"

"I'll call when my train arrives."

"Al?"

"Yeah?"

"If you fuck me, I won't think twice about bringing us both down."

"Don't worry, sweetie. If I fuck you, I'll kiss you first."

"You call me sweetie again and I'll bust your head wide-open."

Maude rang off and put the earpiece back on the hook. She walked to the basin and placed a washcloth in some cool water, running the cloth over the back of her neck and her brow and looking at herself in a little mirror. She smiled, admiring her full fanny. She snatched a wide-brimmed black hat off the bed and adjusted it on her head to convey the proper tilt for mourning and took the washcloth to wipe off the paint from her eyes and mouth and bare breasts. A black dress that ran straight to her ankles hung on a hook on the door.

She practiced a few mournful looks until she heard a knock at the door. Staring out the peephole, she saw that gigantic policewoman, Katherine Eisenhart, standing in the hall with a bouquet of flowers.

"Thought you could use a pick-me-up."

Maude nodded and opened the door, taking the dress from the hook, only wearing her bloomers and stockings. "You're too kind," she said so softly.

"Have you even eaten?"

"I've tried, but no."

Katherine walked to the windows, cracking open the frame to let in some cool air. "We have an hour till you're to appear. My God, it's so warm in here."

"I'm so nervous."

"Don't be nervous."

"I've never spoken before such a group."

"Just tell the truth, Mrs. Delmont."

Maude watched big Kate fanning her face with her hand, a healthy flush in the big woman's cheeks. Maude cocked her head and loosely fingered herself across her chest and belly, taking off the hat and pulling the sweaty black hair off the nape of her neck. She used her hands to brace herself against the window frame, letting the cool air come off the bay, nipples growing erect.

"You are such a great friend, Miss Eisenhart."

"You can call me Kate, ma'am. Most everyone does."

"Just how does someone so sweet become a policewoman?"

"Mrs. Delmont, the assistant manager, Mr. Boyle, has been asking me questions about your bill here. He said that you've said the San Francisco Police Department has put you up. I told him that he was surely mistaken, but he said that you had hung up in his face. I know he must be exaggerating his point, but I must let you know."

Kate let her question hang there, making the rest of it seem indelicate. Maude loved women who still thought about indelicate subjects.

Maude sat on the bed, crossed her stockinged legs, leaned back on her elbows, and stared down at her perked nipples as if just noticing them and laughing as if a secret shared between two sisters. Kate looked as if she'd swallowed an entire egg.

"IF MY PARTNER KNEW I was meeting you here, he'd eat my liver out with a side of onions," Tom Reagan said.

"I wouldn't eat your liver, Tom. I guess it's pretty used up."

"Funny, Sam," Reagan said. "What do you want?"

"I came to watch the sea lions wrestle. You know, they look just like dogs to me. Look at that tough old bastard up on that rock. He looks like someone has taken a few good ole chomps out of his hide."

"I can't talk about Arbuckle."

"And I don't want you to talk about Arbuckle."

Sam leaned into the railing of Pier 56, mashing the last of his cigarette against the wood and losing it in the waves beating the crusty pilings. He lit another and stared thoughtfully at the pilings, waiting a few beats before he was going to get to the point, but instead of great timing he found himself in the middle of a coughing fit that nearly brought him to his knees. He covered his mouth, splattering the cotton with phlegm and blood, and hearing bigheaded Tom Reagan say, "Jesus Christ. Jesus Christ."

"No need to say his name twice," Sam said, recovering. "God hears you the first time."

"You never told me you were a lunger."

"You never asked."

"Worse in the cold."

"Doesn't help."

Tom was dressed in his city detective tweeds and no cap. His boots were shined and his milky Irish skin was so clean-shaven the blood vessels across his cheeks and nose glowed blue.

"Why would someone conduct an autopsy without permission?"

"Jesus, Mary, and Joseph."

"You got to bring the man's family into it? I'm just being hypothetical, Tom."

"No, you're calling in your marker for saving my ass in the train yards."

"I didn't say that."

"You didn't need to."

"Why?"

Tom peered down at the waves beating the pilings and out at two sea lions barking at each other and play-biting mouths before one did a somersault back into the bay.

He shrugged. "We don't know."

"But you wouldn't have known about the girl dying or thought of it as a murder without that anonymous tip. Could it have been Delmont?"

"The call came from the hospital. It was a nurse."

"Can I get a copy of the report?"

"It will all be handed over after the grand jury sees it today."

"Did you at least ask for a second opinion? Did the coroner look at the body?"

"He did."

"Tom?"

Tom looked skyward and readjusted his coat, making himself stand taller, as if standing at attention. He leaned into Sam's ear. "It's tough to make a good inspection when some of the parts are missing from the machine."

He walked back on the dock toward the Embarcadero.

"Tom?"

The police detective waved back over his shoulder but never turned around.

Sam handed the man his card.

"I've already spoken to the police, Mr. Hammett."

"You been the hotel dick here long?"

"About a year."

"Rotten work."

"You ain't kidding."

"You got to play babysitter to the lot of 'em."

"Sounds like you know."

"Lots of my jobs have been about the same," Sam said. "My boss, Phil Geauque, said you were a good egg. Said we always trade out for some fair business."

The hotel dick, Glennon, pocketed the Pinkerton card in the lobby of the St. Francis and screwed up his face.

"I don't want to make trouble for you," Sam said.

"Don't look too quick over my shoulder, but you see that fat-cheeked fella in the glasses?"

"The one with the scowl?"

"You got it," Glennon said. "That's Mr. Boyle. You see, earlier today Mr. Boyle brought in the staff and said he'd fire us if we were even to say the word Arbuckle and to forget that Labor Day even came already."

"Mr. Boyle doesn't look like much fun."

"How's Mr. Geauque?"

"Soft as a bed of nails."

Glennon leaned up on the toes of his dress shoes and sucked on a tooth. Loud enough for the lobby to hear, he said, "Mister, I'm gonna have to ask you to leave," and in a lower voice, "John's Grill, thirty minutes."

The restaurant was a couple doors down from the back of the Flood Building on Ellis Street. They served a solid sandwich, and a mean plate of chops with a baked potato and sliced tomatoes when a man could afford it, and if you were lucky enough to catch a good waiter they'd dish out something a bit warmer in your coffee cup. The floor was honeycombed black and white tile and set with small tables and café chairs. Ceiling fans scattered the cigarette smoke.

The dinner rush hadn't started yet, and Sam found a place by the open windows. He said hello to the owner, a tough old Greek he knew, and they talked about ball teams and fighters and some of the tong action that had been popping up in Chinatown. They lamented Prohibition and President Harding, and discussed Sam's becoming a father.

Glennon arrived and the old Greek went back to the kitchen.

Sam offered him a cigarette from his pack of Fatimas.

"I wasn't trying to muscle you."

"Don't worry about it," Glennon said. "The only thing Mr. Boyle knows about detective work is what he reads in the funny papers."

Sam pulled out his wallet and Glennon shook his head. He tugged it back into his jacket.

"We got a call that afternoon about some girl who'd drunk herself stupid at the Arbuckle party."

"Everyone knew about the party?"

"Who'd you think arranged to bring in the booze? They had cases of the stuff that Arbuckle had driven up in that rolling steamer of his. Have you seen it? A custom Pierce-Arrow, with a bar and a toilet. Can you imagine driving down the highway and waving to a fella who's on the crapper? I mean, what does he do? Wave back?"

"Did you see the girl?"

"Sure."

"And what did you think?"

"I thought she'd gotten stupid and drunk."

"And everyone else?"

"They was stupid and drunk, too. Arbuckle, his two buddies. Some fella who sold women's drawers, and then the Delmont woman."

"Tell me about her."

"Wow," he said, "how much time you got?"

Glennon leaned in and turned to look in Sam's coffee cup. Sam looked back to the Greek and signaled for another round of special coffee.

"Listen to this, I ended up screwin' that broad that night. I know that's not professional, but what would you do? She's crying and putting her tits in my face, and we ended up sitting there in the very room where we moved the girl, 1227. That girl was out stone-cold, and Mrs. Delmont had heisted two bottles of the sweetest Kentucky bourbon from old Fatty. We got drunk in the a.m. and told stories, and she's telling me how her old man is a creep and all that. And I'm saying how sorry I am, only I'm not that sorry, only looking at her tits. And finally she grabs me by my ears and plants one on me, and we ended up fucking against the wall. You can say what you want about Mrs. Maude Delmont, but I'll tell you she ain't no frail."

"She say how she knew the girl?"

Glennon stopped as the Greek laid down the coffee cup and he thanked him. "I think they knew each other in L.A. through some guy named Al. I think I saw that Al guy at the party, but I couldn't pick him out of a lineup. He was one of those movie types, too. I got the feeling that Delmont had come with him and he'd split and she was drinking and screwing me out of revenge."

"You look like a wounded bird."

"I couldn't walk straight the next day."

"How long did the girl stay?"

"They moved her out Wednesday."

"And took her to Wakefield?"

Glennon nodded.

"And Maude Delmont is still a guest of the hotel."

"A guest? More like a parasite. She's bought all kinds of stuff, hats and dresses and crap, and charged it to the hotel. She's hung up on Mr. Boyle at least six times. He had to sic the police on her. They're getting ready to throw her ass on the street."

"You two still friendly?"

"She's ice, brother."

"My condolences."

"I wasn't looking to make pen pals."

"So what happened in that room?"

"That's the question. You got two people go into 1219 and one of 'em ends up dying four days later."

"You trust what Delmont says?"

"I wouldn't trust that bitch if she said the earth was round and the sky was blue."

"What did she tell you?"

"I only know what I read in the papers about the dead girl's confession. She never said a word of that to me."

Glennon slugged back some whiskey, lit another cigarette, and stretched his legs out on the black-and-white honeycombed floor. The afternoon light had faded. Some more folks strolled into John's.

"What happened to the bedclothes?"

"Cops took 'em."

"You see them?"

He nodded.

"Blood?"

"Nope," he said. "But someone sure had pissed them good. Both in 1219 and 1227. You know they brought the whole grand jury by the hotel rooms today? Boyle's ticked 'cause those are his primo suites and he's told he can't rent them out."

"Did you hear anything from any maids, workers, Arbuckle's crowd?"

He shook his head. "The cops asked me this already."

"What didn't they ask you?"

Glennon blew his smoke straight up from the side of his mouth, the smoke hitting the fan and scattering across the tin ceiling.

"They didn't ask me about the doctors."

"More than one?"

"Three."

"Who were they?"

"House doctor was out Labor Day, so we had a fill-in. Then the house doctor was back on Tuesday, but Mrs. Delmont didn't want any of that. She brought in her own doctor."

"She know him?"

"Called him Rummy."

"Name?"

"Rumwell," he said. "This guy was a true nut, all nervous and stuttering. Wore his coat buttoned to the top button even when it's so hot you can't breathe. He has a funny-looking eye that goes back and forth and sometimes crosses with the good one. Short little mustache. He's the one that finally took the girl to Wakefield."

"Where she died."

"Where she died."

"You think Arbuckle did this?"

"I'm saying that Mrs. Maude Delmont ain't playing a straight game, and I'm not so sure whose interest she's serving. You ever checked out the connection between Fatty and her?"

"They're burning my films," Roscoe said.

"That was just one case," Dominguez said.

"It says it right here a bunch of cowboys rode into a movie house in Wyoming, shooting up the place, and dragged out the projector and the canister for *Gasoline Gus* and burned it in the street."

"What do those people know? They probably have sex with cattle."

"You want to talk about all the cities banning my films? I've been called indecent, immoral, and a bloated beast. How do you like that alliteration?"

"Only that idiot director Lehrman called you a beast."

"And they put the bastard on the front page. He said he couldn't come to San Francisco to claim the body because he was worried what he might do to me. Pathé? Now, that's a laugh. The *Examiner* had a picture of him showing off a pair of cuff links that he sez Virginia bought for him. Hell, he probably had them engraved himself. 'With Love Always, Virginia,'" Roscoe said, tossing the paper near his hat on the jailhouse floor. "That girl was nothing but a receptacle for him."

"The grand jury is meeting right now, Roscoe."

Roscoe began to shuffle a deck of cards in his hands, bare feet on concrete. Dominguez leaned against the bars, his neckerchief loosened in the heat.

Roscoe began to absently toss cards into his driving cap.

"What haven't you told me about the party, Roscoe?"

"I told you everything, Frank. Ten times I told you."

"You never told me about the Coke bottle."

Roscoe tossed a joker onto the brim of the hat.

"It works better with a bowler."

"We need to talk about everything."

Roscoe felt his face flush and he hated the feeling of it. He stood and straightened his Norfolk jacket on the wire hanger and smoothed down the lapels. He adjusted his shoes by the commode.

"It was just a test. I'd always heard that when a person was knocked out that ice would bring 'em to. If a person was just faking it, you could tell."

"You thought she was faking it?"

"One minute the girl is on my lap calling me snuggle pup and the next she's screaming bloody murder."

"Did you touch her with the bottle?"

"It wasn't a goddamn bottle, Frank. It was an ice cube."

"I got a copy of an interview with this fella Al Semnacher. He says he saw you put something on her lady parts. Who the hell is this guy?"

"I just met him. He said he was an agent."

"He work for Miss Rappe?"

"I never saw him when she was with Sennett," Roscoe said. "Listen, I just put the ice on her to wake her up."

"Did it work?"

"Not really."

"Where did you put it?"

Roscoe sat down on the creaking bed, shuffling out more cards, from one hand to the other, and then eyeing the hat from across the room.

"I put an ice cube from my Scotch on her."

"Where?"

"On her snatch," Roscoe said. "Okay. I put some ice on her snatch. Don't tell me that killed her."

"Did you ever place a bottle into her?"

"Is that what Semnacher said?"

"I don't know. We've heard things. I don't know if the D.A. is going to present this or not."

"A Coke bottle. Jesus."

"Other things may come out, too. I want you to know that. They may say the bottle was a substitution for masculinity."

Roscoe flipped a steady stream of a dozen cards and then moved his eyes up to Frank. He could not stop shaking his head, feeling the shame being directed on him. The worst part about feeling the shame was that it felt like an old friend that he had abandoned long ago.

THE PREVON GIRL LEFT the grand jury room at eleven-seventeen, red-faced and tear-streaked and on the arm of Griff Kennedy, who held up the girl with one hand while slipping into his slicker and hat and pushing past the newspapermen and the camera flashes. Sam stood from the bench where he'd been parked since five and slid around back to the car pool and waited for Griff and Zey, holding up his hand to stop them.

The girl wiped her eyes with a starched white handkerchief and snorted into it when they stopped and looked up at the big red-haired detective for her next order. But Griff didn't say a word to her or Sam, only pushed Sam away with the heel of his hand and pushed the girl into the back of his black machine.

"She's a witness," Sam said. "Not your property."

Griff Kennedy hoisted up the waistband of his pants and spit on the ground before starting his automobile and pulling back around to Portsmouth Square. The girl watched Sam as the machine glided in a wide circle, her big, sad eyes searching out the fogged glass before turning a corner and disappearing.

Back inside, Sam found his bench had been taken up by two fat women knitting. They wore all black and large hats. A few more of the hat crew stood along a circular staircase where another big lady had opened up a picnic basket and distributed coffee poured out into china mugs. By the bathrooms were four more. Three more walked in from the front doors.

"What's this?" Sam asked.

"Vigilant Committee," said a newspaperman.

"What?"

"We call them the Vigilantes," the man said with a smirk. "You can bet these sob sisters are going to be all over this case like stink on shit. Don't you read the papers?"

"Sure."

"You didn't see the part about Mrs. Hamilton and Mrs. Bertola saying they were going to monitor the trial to honor that dead woman."

"Why?"

"'Cause they hate men. They all want to crush our balls in silver-plated nutcrackers they all keep locked up in their purses."

Sam nodded, tucking a cigarette into the corner of his mouth and striking a match. "Jesus, we gonna sleep in there?"

"Already missed deadline."

"The nerve."

"You telling me."

Sam took a seat on the last step of the staircase and stole a glance at a little man with slick black hair, tiny mustache, and one wandering eye. A little past midnight, a bailiff emerged from the great twin doors and called out for a Dr. M. E. Rumwell.

The man jumped to attention and followed the bailiff.

Forty-six minutes later, Dr. Rumwell returned, shaking off a half dozen reporters and exiting out a side door.

Sam followed.

S am had learned to shadow from his old boss in Baltimore, Jimmy Wright. Jimmy had worked for the Pinks most his life, and when he wasn't sending out Sam for sandwiches or cigarettes or running messages to the office boys he'd teach him how to follow a person. Wright wasn't a thing like the detectives in the dime-store novels Sam had read growing up. He didn't have a handlebar mustache or wear tweeds and a bowler. Jimmy Wright was a thick, squat fella, a fireplug, who wore raincoats even when it was warm and had a taste for Fatima cigarettes. He had scar tissue around his eyes and his knuckles, and told young Sam that detective work was a nasty, brutal profession and not a place for a boy who had other options. He told Sam to be a lousy lawyer or a stockbroker or, hell, even a goddamn grocery clerk. But Sam would run those roast beef sandwiches and packs of Fatimas to street corners and back alleys and safe houses where Wright would wait out some con man and bank robber just for a simple word from a man who, although short, towered over his father.

Rumwell headed down California from Portsmouth Square in a lope, probably heading to the Embarcadero to catch a streetcar. But at the Ferry Building, the doctor turned south, not north, and continued walking past an empty streetcar, the off-duty driver reading a newspaper, feet up on the controls. Sam followed him past pier after pier, and endless warehouses that smelled of fish oil and machine parts, and men playing dice next to barrel fires and prostitutes who'd gone long past their day dishing out fifty-cent blow jobs and hand jobs for a quarter.

Sam walked past them all, careful to keep that sacred space, the good doctor never looking over his shoulder as he followed the Embarcadero deeper inside the Barbary, a collection of shanties and clapboard bars that had been open to sailors ever since San Francisco had been a city. It had burned down during the Quake and had been shut down by moral crusaders more than anyone cared to remember. But there was always the sailor's trade for booze and women, and, for the most part, the Barbary became a no-man's-land.

Rumwell turned east up a narrow little alley paved with smooth cobblestones and ballast from cutter ships. Barkers in top hats spit out carnival spiels about harems and belly dancers and shows with Shetland ponies. There were gas lamps and red lamps in bay windows where sad-eyed girls in saggy slips and torn stockings would press their bodies against the warped glass or crook a finger at you. The doctor ducked into another alley and curved again, but Sam did not rush, as he looked both ways, and heard the tinny piano music of a little bar called Purcell's that advertised itself with a wooden sign that swung and creaked in the breeze off the Pacific. A fat man in a little hat banged out the keys to a song about a girl from Kansas City who wore gumdrops on her titties.

Sam wandered in and found the bar mostly empty except for the piano player and another negro, a gigantic man with a shining bald head. The man switched a toothpick from the other side of his cheek as Sam entered and sat down.

"Rye."

The gigantic negro said nothing but uncorked an unlabeled bottle and poured out a generous measure of thin-looking stuff. Despite the taste of gasoline and leather tannins, the burning sensation was quite pleasant on Sam's stomach and deep into his lungs, spreading out a burning warmth and giving him a bit of relief. The bartender's skin shone the color of the deepest black, the whites of his eyes the color of an egg. His hulking form cast a shadow against the brick, with twin notches above his smooth head.

The negro was about to cork the bottle but saw the glass was empty and motioned to Sam, who nodded. He did this several times until the feeling held right and Sam waved him off.

Soon a whore came to Sam, and he smelled her before he saw her, a scent of dried flowers and spawning fish. She wrapped an arm around Sam's neck and whispered in his ear a price. She wore a terrible wig, almost looking as if it were made of straw, and had painted a beauty mark or what most people called a mole at the bottom of her chin. Another look at her told him she couldn't have been more than thirteen.

"I'll suck it for two bits," she said. The bar was dark and filled with red light and the smell of gasoline and urine.

Sam shook her away. In the long mirror, he watched as Phil Haultain walked into the room and took off his hat, as if this was the kind of place that demanded hat removal. Another girl approached Phil, and Sam smiled as he watched Phil's eyes grow big at the offer. Sam was pretty sure he read the boy's mouth saying, "Ma'am?"

The boy took a seat at a table near the piano player. The girl stayed and took purchase on his knee.

Sam rested his head into his hands. It was past one o'clock in the morning and for a moment he lost his place in time. Sometimes his mind played tricks like that when he drank. He could be in Baltimore or Philly or a mining camp in Montana or on the wharves in Seattle or on his grandfather's farm, knee-deep in tobacco, walking endless rows as a summer sun stood red and strong to the west.

He asked for another drink, and in his mind he stood on a dock holding a shotgun in his arms as raggedy men tried to reach for him through fence posts, spitting at him and threatening to rip out his throat. The men wore torn rags, their bodies like skeletons. And then he broke away, hearing calliope music at the edge of a county fair, crushing a cigarette with the edge of his boot and staring up at the brightly lit Ferris wheel that had been boosted from back east.

And then he was back looking at the circle of the glass in his hand.

Sam knew he couldn't return home by morning or else he'd risk Jose knowing he had it on him and what he was doing to his lungs and going against the cure he'd learned from her at Cushman.

The giant black man poured another shot of rye and Sam dished out another quarter, and he sat and he waited and exchanged a quick glance with Haultain, who now had another girl on his knee, and he watched as the girls worked him and bargained. Haultain was young but good at playing the rube.

They played around like that until two, when Rumwell came out from a back room. Even slightly drunk, Sam noticed the man was still put together just so in that boiled shirt and suit and bowler hat. He walked to the bar and moved against Sam, never glancing across at him, and Sam kept his head down and his eyes down as the gigantic negro reached down into his breast and pulled out a thick wad of cash and laid it down on the bar across from Rumwell, and Rumwell, not so much as looking at the black man, counted out the money in his hand and then tucked it into a fat wallet in his breast pocket, and, carrying his brown medical bag, walked briskly out of the bar and onto the cobblestones. Sam turned but found Phil already gone. Following, he clicked open his pocket watch, knowing he had hours to kill before daylight and getting home to Jose and acting like he gave a damn if he lived or didn't.

But he knew he probably wouldn't reach another six months, and the filthy trade he'd been taught by Jimmy Wright might just let him give a few bucks to Jose and the child and, by the grace of God, in a few years they'd forget him like smoke in the wind. Sam had thoughts like these as he wandered in and out of the bars of the Barbary, his lungs feeling squeezed and wrung out, before collapsing into a coughing fit in the great arms of a heiferlike woman with big painted blue eyes who thought he was the most humorous man she'd ever met.

Her breasts felt like great pillows.

"So THE GIRL CHANGED HER STORY?" Mr. Hearst asked the next morning.

"She said that was never her story."

"But the assistant D.A.—what's his name, Pisser?"

"U'ren, sir."

"So ole U-rine is saying the girl was bribed."

"I don't know what Mr. U'ren is saying, but it looks like the girl was coerced into giving the statement. Miss Prevon-Prevost was arrested the other night at that dry raid at the Old Poodle Dog."

"I read the story."

"Yes, sir."

The reporter, whatever his name was, seemed to be having a hard time standing there with his tablet in his hand and ink on his fingers, waiting for Mr. Hearst to spell out the story for him. Or maybe it was because Hearst was wearing war paint and an actual Indian headdress that had belonged to Sitting Bull.

Hearst took off the headdress, much to the disappointment of his six-year-old twin boys, who shot another arrow from the top floor of the Hearst Building out onto Market Street.

Hearst leaned into his desk and jotted out some notes. "Randolph, Elbert: Settle."

The boys, dressed in identical blue Eton suits with knickers, looked at each other and sat down on a short couch, arms crossed over their chests and not saying a word.

"Can we get to the girl?"

"No one can find her. U'ren and Judge Brady put her somewhere. That other showgirl, Miss Blake, has disappeared all together."

"What about this Delmont woman?"

"She's sticking with the story that Virginia Rappe told her that Arbuckle had crushed her."

"Wasn't enough to get murder with the grand jury. What's Judge Brady saying about manslaughter?"

"He says he's looking for a second opinion in police court."

"Will that work?"

The reporter shrugged. "If the police judge agrees, he can still try Fatty for murder."

"What about this other woman?"

"She's waiting outside, sir. That's who I wanted you to meet."

"Would you like a turkey leg?" Hearst said, pulling a big drumstick off a china plate and holding it out to the skinny young man. The young reporter shook his head and walked from the room, returning seconds later with the homeliest woman Hearst had ever seen. She looked like Buster Brown as an old unkempt man.

"This is Nurse Cumberland."

"Good God," Hearst said, and looked to his sons with wide eyes. Randolph whispered to Elbert, and the boys giggled from the little couch.

Hearst said, "Settle."

"Miss Cumberland attended Miss Rappe at the St. Francis."

"And at Wakefield, too," the woman said.

Hearst nodded and tried not to laugh at the woman's haircut, recalling the lawsuit he had with the cartoonist who'd created Buster Brown and now wishing he could ring up the man. The boys continued to whisper and giggle, and Hearst lumbered out of his chair and plucked the bow and a few arrows from their hands. "Boys."

"Miss Cumberland, tell us your story," he said, walking to the window and taking in Market Street and the final rolling slope down to the bay.

The woman looked to the young reporter and the young reporter looked to Hearst.

"Oh, of course," Hearst said. "How much?"

"I don't want to tell nothin' but the truth, mind you."

"And I assure you I'll tell you my price when I know what your truth is worth."

"Miss . . . Nurse Cumberland says that before Virginia Rappe died at Wakefield, she told her that she'd been dragged by Arbuckle, by the arm, into the back bedroom."

"Is that true?"

"God's truth, sir."

"Have you been summoned by District Attorney Brady?"

"Yes, sir."

"Have you given your story yet?"

"No, sir."

Hearst set an arrow into the tiny wooden bow, war paint still on his face, and sighted a big boat pulling away from the Ferry Building, switching his sights to the tiny shape of a man hanging from the Ferry Building's clock. A cleaner of some sort.

He let the arrow go and watched it sail until out of sight.

"Tear up the front page."

"A TALLYWHACKER," Maude Delmont said. "A man's manhood."

The women whispered to each other, dropping their spoons on the china plates and stopping that chattering altogether.

"And that is where the parrot landed?" asked Mrs. W. B. Hamilton, vice president of San Francisco's Vigilant Committee.

"Yes, ma'am," Maude Delmont said, ever so delicately stirring her tea in the great room of the Fairmont Hotel on the Wednesday after the girl had died. She took a little sip and a small bit of sugar cookie.

The two hundred or so women remained silent.

"Were these orgies common?" Mrs. Hamilton used a big voice, loud enough for all the women to hear. There was a stray cough, the light tinkling of a spoon, the shift of the chair, but in it all Maude Delmont had her audience.

"Yes," she said. "A decent moral woman has no place in the film colony. I worked to sell magazine subscriptions to *Ladies' Home Journal*. By the way, I will have subscription cards after I speak. But these parties were no places for a lady."

"And they were nude at these orgies?"

"Completely," Maude Delmont said. "At the party in question, that beast Arbuckle had taken offense with the parrot. The bird called him 'Fatty,' and nothing makes Arbuckle madder than to hear that. He sat there, mind you, in a very drunken state, arguing with the bird and calling it all kinds of foul names, words that would only be uttered in pool halls and houses of ill repute."

My God. How awful.

"It was after he'd disrobed and slathered his whalelike hide with buckets of hot oil, to better lubricate himself and such orifices, when the bird took its revenge and swooped through the party, through the maze of nudity and sea of alcohol, to affix its talons on his man snake."

Oh, my.

Two women fainted. Another woman choked on a delicate slice of coconut cake. A gigantic fat woman screamed.

"I don't quite know how to say this . . ."

The Vigilant Committee members, the dozens of them all dressed in black with great round hats banded with trailing feathers, leaned in, making their folding chairs creak and groan. The room at the Fairmont was all brass and gold and crystal and china.

". . . Arbuckle was making his man snake perform a rare Arabian dance as a man played a flute, as if charming the throb of his anatomy."

More shrieks.

Police Chief Daniel O'Brien, the group's special guest at the Fairmont, finally stood and asked Maude Delmont to take her seat, and said he had heard many stories about the film people down south. But he also said that he'd been assured by many high-ranking, moral, upstanding people that the Arbuckle types accounted for only a sliver of the artists who lived there.

"And in that spirit, I would like to introduce a man who has made grown-ups and children smile the world over," Police Chief O'Brien said, sweeping his hand to a short man with a blunt cut of brown hair who wore a western shirt, leather chaps, and boots, "Broncho Billy."

Maude Delmont rolled her eyes and asked the waiter for more cake. Big Kate Eisenhart leaned in close to her ear and whispered, "The nerve."

Maude wiped her lips of icing.

Broncho Billy hitched a thumb in his chaps and hand-tooled belt and removed the big buckaroo hat from his head and held it to his heart. "May I lead you all in prayer?"

These women were the worst, a black-clad army of grim-faced suffragists, the kind Maude remembered in Kansas who'd march the town streets on a Saturday banging the old drum and causing the whole goddamn country to go dry. The leader of the group was a stout lady physician named Marina Bertola, who stood first and last after Broncho Billy finished up his prayer and promised the group to amass a posse if Arbuckle wasn't brought to justice. As she spoke, the chandelier light refracted in her lenses, making her eyes disappear behind the glass, her eyes twin pools of ice.

"*We have let our ardor cool down,*" Dr. Bertola said. "And for that reason we are all responsible in some measure for the conditions that bring about such outrageous affairs as the Arbuckle party. Our purpose is to secure enforcement of the law. We must be faithful to that purpose, not only in regard to the Arbuckle case but for the sake of the future."

THE OLD MAN listened with great interest to Sam's story about shadowing Dr. Rumwell into the Barbary the night before. He left out the part about getting blind drunk, stopping short of the payoff with the big negro and Haultain tailing Rumwell out of the bar.

"He got on a streetcar and headed back to his place on Lombard," Haultain said.

"How long did you sit on the house?"

"Till this morning," Haultain said. "He left the house for Wakefield. That's where the boy came for me and I broke off the tail."

"Get some sleep," the Old Man said. "Roll back on the job tonight."

"I'll take him," Sam said.

"You find that Blake girl."

"Checked out of the Woodrow on Tuesday."

"Just find her."

"What do you make of this Rumwell making house calls to whores?"

"I'd say he's a true philanthropist."

Sam smiled. "He performed an illegal autopsy on the Rappe girl and may have disposed of some of her organs."

The Old Man took off his gold spectacles, folded them, and tucked them into the pocket of his dress shirt. He wore a pin high and tight at his collar, and leaned onto the desk with his forearms. "That may be. But one problem at a time. Alice Blake is scared. The other little tart is under lock and key by the state. Alice is the only one who can set the story straight about that party. Did you see the afternoon papers? The Delmont woman is on a goddamn speaking tour."

"Does Los Angeles have anything on her?"

"Nope. Someone's on that."

"The Blake girl," Sam said.

"The Blake girl."

"I'll check back with the hotel and run down some people at Tait's."

"You feeling all right?" the Old Man asked.

"Peaches and cream."

"You look like shit warmed over."

"Thanks."

"You need a break?"

"No."

The Old Man looked at Sam a long while and then put his glasses back on and nodded. He didn't add a good-bye or give a speech, only went back to his paperwork, sleeves rolled well above the ink, and expected Sam and Phil to find their way out.

S am found Alice Blake two days later, on a Friday, living in a Sunset District row house with her mother. He'd spent a five spot on a phone number from a dancer at Tait's and used a city directory at the office to find the address, borrowed a machine from a nearby garage, and had been sitting on the house since yesterday. There was a corner grocery up on Irving where he'd buy cigarettes and a sandwich with coffee and use the toilet and pay phone. Most of the houses on the street were brand-new, narrow, two-story jobs with stucco and tile roofs. He'd spotted a nice empty one, directly across from the mother's house, where he slipped through a window and could make himself comfortable on an apple crate with field glasses. It was late afternoon when he saw a yellow cab pull up to the address and saw Alice Blake skip out to the street and get in back.

Five minutes later, Sam was behind the cab in his machine and trailing across the southern part of Golden Gate Park and then dipping down into the Castro, thinking she was headed back downtown but instead watching the cab slow in front of a theater. She got out, paid the cabbie, bought a ticket at the window, and slipped inside. Sam parked and followed.

The picture had already started and Sam had to adjust his eyes in the darkness. The theater was a fantasy palace filled with gilded Oriental and Moroccan designs, the latter being appropriate since the moving images were of sheiks and the desert and far-off places with camels. The ceiling was a night sky, complete with moving clouds and winking stars. The screen was fifty feet high, bordered by balconies and plush red curtains. The effect made you feel as if you were at an outdoor play.

Sam took a seat in a side row where he had a good view of Alice Blake's profile while she ate popcorn and stared, openmouthed, at the moving images. A man sat in front of a great organ, as if he were playing liturgy instead of accompanying a woman outside a sheik's tent, nervous but accepting the invitation to come inside. The flap to the tent was held open and Alice stopped eating. Her big brown eyes remained wide at the sight of the woman removing her pith helmet and belt and the sheik's servants doing the same for him. Caston, the French valet in service of the sheik since his school days, closing the curtain.

Why have you brought me here?

The sheik, with a great smile, saying, Are you not woman enough to know?

Sam turned to the others staring at the huge screen, watching the man Valentino strut in his tent, standing twenty feet tall in the darkness, hands on his hips, robes flowing behind him. Sam leaned back into his seat. The women in the seats around him breathing so loud that it sounded like one great gasp of a chorus. The sheik pointed to his big bed and the woman tried to run. He caught her in his arms and made his eyes real big. The bigger he made his eyes, the more the women in the crowd gasped.

Sam lit a cigarette and settled in.

Alice Blake resumed with her popcorn.

I am not accustomed to having my order disobeyed.

And I'm not accustomed to obeying orders.

You will learn! said the sheik, banishing her from his tent.

It was almost as if you could put your hands up in front of you and touch them or perhaps walk into the screen and be a part of it all. The light of the screen brought a white sheen to the faces of the women, some holding a single red rose.

After a while, Sam fell asleep. When he came to, the picture still rolling and organ pumping, he looked over to Alice Blake and she was gone.

He left the darkness and pushed open into the light, the new world seeming almost unreal against the desert, and looked for the girl, twice checking her seat and the washroom, then walked out into the Castro. A half hour later, he returned to his machine to ride back to the Sunset District and sit on the house. He bought a loaf of bread and more cigarettes and a *Photoplay* magazine to read up on this woman he'd seen in *The Sheik* because somehow the woman seemed like someone he now knew.

When he moved up the landing to the vacant house, he heard a shift and found someone already sitting on the apple crate. The Prohibition agent from the Old Poodle Dog looked over at him, dropping his field glasses by her side, and pulled on a cigarette. She looked at Sam but didn't smile. The streetlight shone off the white blond hair peeking out from under a silk turban.

She turned, cocking a dark brow at him. "Sit down. I won't bite."

MAUDE DIDN'T SEE Al Semnacher, didn't know he was following her, until he plopped down next to her on the cable car just before it started its jerky ride up Powell Street, past the St. Francis and Union Square and slowly up Nob Hill. Maude had to do a double take to make sure it was Al because the dumb son of a bitch didn't say anything, just stared at the people climbing the hill as they glided by in the car, and even casually waved to an old Chinese woman selling persimmons from a corner. Maude shook her head and checked her watch, already ten minutes late.

In the narrow slit in the street, Maude could see the tension of the cable hoisting them all up the hill, the straining of tons of metal and flesh being brought to the top.

"I'm ready to negotiate," he said.

"I don't know what you're talking about."

"I saw your picture in the paper. Cute, really. You with the Vigilant Committee and Harry Carey."

"It was Broncho Billy."

The cable car stopped and three different newsboys from the *Examiner*, *The Call*, and *Chronicle* climbed on like little monkeys scrambling down the row and hawking the latest news of Fatty. The boy from the *Examiner* shouted an exclusive: "Nurse Says Fatty Dragged Girl into Hotel Room."

Maude paid the boy a nickel and looked at the ugly face of that woman who had attended to Virginia at Wakefield. She read the first few lines and shook her head.

"I told the police about the ice and about Fatty threatening to throw Virginia out the window," Al whispered.

"He wanted to throw me out the window."

Two old women down the long wooden bench were craning forward to look at Maude Delmont. She pulled her black hat down deeper into her eyes and gave Al Semnacher a sharp one in the ribs.

"I want a piece," he said.

"A piece of what? I just slipped out of the St. Francis with my bags."

"You mean your purse."

"My things."

"I got you the girl just like you asked for."

"And you stole her underwear and bolted. Why on earth would I trust you?"

"I didn't sign on for this," Al said, whispering. The cable car jerked and strained to the top of Nob Hill, cresting for a moment, the old women getting off at the Fairmont, and then the brake was slowly let go by the conductor onto a turn heading west, and then the car cut hard, flowing down the hill and catching a straightaway on Hyde.

"Then get off."

"You signed a deal in blood," Al said.

"I never signed a deal."

"I want half of what you're getting or next week I'll walk right into that police court and tell them everything I know."

"That you were Virginia's pimp?"

"She was an angel."

"Are you getting a conscience on me?"

"I loved her."

"You didn't even know her, you dumb yegg."

"I'll find you tomorrow."

"It's your stop, Al."

Al leaned in, his musky, sweaty scent of talcum powder and cologne making Maude sick. "You tell your people I'm a part of this."

"Good-bye, Al."

Al stood, pulled the cable car's cord, and stepped down, tipping his hat at a little girl in a sailor suit who took his spot beside Maude.

"Good day," Al said, grinning with his sharp little teeth, "Mrs. Delmont."

"WHY DOES A DRY AGENT care about the Arbuckle party?" Sam asked.

"Besides making us look good in the papers?"

"Besides that."

"Arbuckle broke the Volstead," the girl said.

"A few bottles of gin seems beneath you people."

"We're more interested in where he got it."

Sam nodded and smoked a bit as he stood in the window turret. The girl agent sat on the apple crate, legs crossed, turban perfectly cocked on her head. Light from the blinds fingered out on the wooden floor.

She lit a cigarette, too, and stood and walked to the window, using his field glasses to look down at Alice Blake's place. "How was the movie?"

"Slept through most of it."

"What was it about?"

"This sheik kidnaps this English socialite. He wants her, but she doesn't want him. Then she runs away. Some bandits steal her and the sheik comes to the rescue."

"That's it?"

"There's some kissing, too. The kissing takes a lot of time."

The girl fingered open the window blinds, the arc lamps brightening the streets, the window looking like a framed, slatted picture. Sam could see the Blake house and a Ford parked outside and a man and a woman pushing a stroller across the road.

The girl let the field glasses dangle from the leather strap against her leg and set her head back, smoking.

"Since I saw you at the Old Poodle Dog, I've wanted to ask you something."

"Does it start with 'How does a nice girl . . .'?"

"Something like that."

"I was in a secretary pool when Prohibition broke," she said. "They needed someone to slip into speakeasies unnoticed."

"I wouldn't say you go unnoticed."

She looked at him and brought her lips together, looking down at her velvet shoes with bows, blew smoke up into the ceiling and then crushed the cigarette underfoot.

Sam shrugged and switched to the apple crate. "You after LaPeer?"

"What do you think?"

"I read he was out of jail so fast the ink wasn't dry on his thumbs. You don't have a clue where he gets the stuff."

"We know he has this Australian fella who works for him and we know that same fella was at the St. Francis bringing in cases through the back door."

"But you don't know his name."

"And here we are looking for Miss Blake."

"Seems like a lot of work just for a dumb skirt."

"Maybe she knew the bootlegger."

"Or maybe you think some knucklehead Pinkerton will point you in the right direction?"

The woman walked over to Sam and placed a velvet shoe on top of the crate, hitching up her black skirt just a bit, showing off a nice long stretch of stocking and garter before plucking out a silver flask and handing it to Sam.

"Will you arrest me?" Sam asked.

"Only if you do something bad."

"You have a name?"

"I do."

"Wanna tell me?"

"Let's drink first," the girl said. "Wait till I know you better."

MAUDE MADE THE CALL at nightfall from the back of a mom-and-pop place on Columbus, the kind with red-and-white tablecloths, salami hanging from the ceiling, and dago red sold out of the basement. She had a couple glasses of the red before lifting the handset, giving the operator the number, and hearing the man's voice. Thirty minutes later, she was out on Columbus walking toward Washington Square when a long green touring car pulled up to the curb and a man hung out the driver's side and said, "Sister, you look like you could use a ride."

She got in the passenger side and closed the door and he sped off, rounding the square by the big church, and headed up and over a hill down by the wharf.

It was him.

He didn't say much for most of the ride, one of those tight-lipped fellas that made you all spill it out to them because they know you're feeling uncomfortable as hell in the silences. And usually that was Maude's trick, but not today. Today, maybe because she had two nickels to her name and had been booted out of the St. Francis with nowhere to go, she laid it all out there. She talked about the two beefy Irish cops and the dyke woman Eisenhart, the crazy old Vigilant broads and Al Semnacher following her on the cable car and wanting some more dough.

"Can you believe the nerve of the son of a bitch?"

The man driving said nothing, turning down by the wharf, hugging the last of the Embarcadero, and scattering a gathering of seagulls pecking at a dead fish in the middle of the road.

"He skipped town with the girl's bloomers and now he's coming back for more."

The man was silent, passing the cannery and heading up the hills and south toward Lombard and then taking a turn west up into Pacific Heights, where Maude had once bamboozled a ninety-year-old man out of his dead wife's jewelry. Maude had been running the good ole sweetheart swindle ten years back when there wasn't a man with a pulse who could turn her down. But, God, letting that old man's old wrinkled head between her tits almost wasn't worth it.

They hit a bump. The driver was talking to her. "I said, what do you want?"

"I need a place to stay and the money I was promised."

The man turned to look at her as he drove, leaning over the wheel at an intersection and then cutting up to Union Street. He spit out an open window and looked back at Maude and nodded.

Ever since she'd met him in Los Angeles, the guy had given her the creeps. He wasn't a bad-looking fella, maybe fifty or so, with iron-colored hair and kind of a dark complexion. He wore a black suit with a black tie and a fedora-type hat made of velour. A real dandy.

He kept on driving and nodding to himself before making a big, sloppy U-turn on Union and then meeting Van Ness and heading south again.

"Where we headed?" she asked.

"You tell me. I'm just driving."

"We have a deal?"

"You'll get half tomorrow."

"What about Semnacher?"

"Set a meetin'."

Maude smiled and fixed her hands on the empty purse in her lap, feeling the rumble of the six cylinders under the big, long hood with all that space in back. She adjusted in the seat and stared straight ahead, smiling, and asked him to drop her at the Palace Hotel. As they drove, the streetlights clicked on along Market, shining down into the cabin and showing a good chunk of the man's right ear missing, as if someone forgot to complete the picture.

Sam set the typewriter on the kitchen table and started hitting the keys while Jose reheated some Irish stew from the night before. The windows were open, letting out the hot air from the stove and the hot air in from Eddy Street, while Sam worked in his undershirt and smoked and hammered out a response to his latest reply from the United States Veterans' Bureau. A Mr. Carter had curtly replied that Sam's lung condition rated less than ten percent of a disability, to which Sam replied—in a very official tone—that that was absolutely incorrect, and he requested another evaluation, this time with a lung specialist.

"Mr. Carter again?" she asked.

"I'd like to meet this Mr. Carter," Sam said. "Rotten bastard probably keeps a stack of denials on his desk with a big fat quill pen. Look at the flourish, the way he writes 'Carter.'"

Sam ripped the paper from the black L. C. Smith, held it up to the bulb hanging in the kitchen, cigarette bobbing in his mouth, and read back through what he'd written. "Do you know how many veterans are illiterate or just yes-men and take the government's word as the word of Christ? I read a story in the paper today about this man called Zero in New York who sells off jobless veterans at an auction."

"Do you want bread?"

"Yes, please."

"I mended your socks," Jose said. "They're hanging on the fire escape."

Sam folded the letter and stuck it in an envelope.

He took a seat across from Jose at the little table, the typewriter he'd borrowed from the office pushed between them. She poured him some coffee, and they ate for a while, and it seemed to him that the stew she'd made from the butcher's special was the sweetest meat he'd ever tasted.

"Do you ever wish you'd met an officer?" Sam said.

"I was gunning for a private," Jose said. She smiled with her eyes, which were soft and blue, curly brown hair pulled from her strong, contented face with pins. She wore a housecoat with a soiled apron and no makeup.

"I'd love to take you out on the town."

"Like this?"

"After the baby comes," Sam said. "We'll have dinner at the Cliff House and go dancing on the beach. Later on, we'll find a speakeasy and dance till dawn."

"A speakeasy?"

"Since when did you become a nun?"

"From a reformed Catholic, I'll take that as a compliment."

"Thanks for the stew."

"I think it's better on the second day."

"Has the old woman asked for the rent?"

"Yes."

"And did you stall her?"

"I said she'd have it Monday."

Sam didn't say anything, only fished with the spoon in the bowl.

They had four dishes, some borrowed silverware, the table, and a Murphy bed that folded down at night. A table fan swept the room from its spot in the corner.

"What's new on the Rappe girl?"

Sam finished the bowl and set it aside. He lit another Fatima and leaned back in the chair, mismatched from the other three.

"Just like the papers said, a ruptured bladder."

"Caused by external force."

"That's what they said in the grand jury and what they're taking to police court."

"Still doesn't make sense," Jose said. "No other injuries?"

"She had bruises on her arms," Sam said. "But Dominguez can argue that she got those when they were moving her around."

"Nothing about her vagina being torn or bruised?"

"Not that we know about."

"And no broken bones."

"No broken bones."

"Do you realize the kind of weight that it would take to burst a woman's bladder?"

"They do call him 'Fatty.'"

Jose shook her head and reached for his pack of cigarettes. She smoked and stared out onto Eddy Street, looking through the bars of the fire escape lined with clothes she'd scrubbed in a galvanized pot.

"Unless the bladder was diseased."

Sam looked up at her and mashed out his cigarette. He reached for more coffee.

"The attending doctor ordered an autopsy immediately after the girl died."

"And?" Jose said.

"After," Sam said, "he had several of her organs destroyed. Including the bladder."

"What do you know about this girl's past?"

"What you read," Sam said. "She was an angel plucked from heaven to remain a virgin until Arbuckle met her."

"You know many thirty-year-old virgins?" she asked.

"Plenty."

"I bet."

"Jose, what are you thinking?"

"I'm thinking that a bladder can rupture from all types of things. I've seen some horrible bladder conditions brought on by venereal ailments."

"Ailments?"

"Ailments."

"When do you want to go dancing?" Sam said.

"After we pay the rent," she said. "And when you finally unpack that damn trunk. You make me feel like this is a hotel."

"Fair enough," Sam said, standing and pulling himself into his tweed jacket and pulling his cap on his head. He tucked a little .32 in his side pocket and his Pinkerton's badge at the breast.

"Where you headed?"

"Lucky me," Sam said. "I get to play chauffeur to Mrs. Arbuckle."

"You don't mean . . . ?"

"I do."

HEARST MET MARION DAVIES when she was sixteen and performing in the chorus line in *Stop! Look! Listen!* on Broadway. He'd made the show every night it had run, paying a boy to wait at the stage door with flowers and jewelry and a diamond-encrusted watch that Marion had promptly lost on their third date. But he'd agreed to more watches—that she never wound or checked—and there were secret dinners at Delmonico's and drinks at the Plaza and lovemaking that made Hearst feel half of his fifty-eight years. Hearst's wife, Millicent, had been a chorus girl, too, but back in the nineteenth century, and after five boys she'd lost a bit of her charm and zest for life. With Marion, he'd finally found a solid girl with enough energy to keep up with him and realize that life was just one big rolling party where the world provided constant entertainment. And it was best in San Francisco. There they could escape the prying eyes of the scandal sheets and be out on the town as producer and ingénue, getting ready for the town's world premiere of *Enchantment* in November.

By the time they left the Opera House, they were already feeling a bit of the champagne they'd had at the intermission of *Tosca*, and it had all been a bunch of laughs during the opera, because Marion had dressed as a little Chinese man in a blunt-cut wig and silk pajamas. She'd even made up her eyes to look like an Oriental, while Hearst had dressed as a grand emperor with a flowing red robe decorated with dragons and flowers and a Fu Manchu mustache pasted to his face.

A driver in a Cadillac touring car motored them up Nob Hill from the Civic Center, looping to the portico of the Fairmont, and the grand Chinese Ball that had brought out all the little yellow people from the Chinese colony to serve food, dance, and mix with the elite dressed gaily in their own pajamas and silks.

The lobby air had been perfumed with incense and jasmine, and there was much handshaking and silly bowing by the city elite, and the Oriental people scrambled around with big smiles, offering up pork with bamboo shoots and chrysanthemum salad and little cups of ny ka pa. Dozens of men donned a dragon costume that snaked through the party, and women dressed as men or as Oriental princesses squealed and yelped in the great candlelit room decked out in silk tapestries and gold.

Hearst clapped and pronounced the affair wholly magnificent when approached by District Attorney Matthew Brady and Chief O'Brien. Both men smiled and shook Hearst's hand warmly. Marion did a little bow and stayed in character, rattling off some gibberish that no one in their right mind would think was Chinese. Somewhere was the sound of a xylophone. Cymbals crashed. The giant, bigheaded dragon wove in and out of screaming, laughing women.

"Judge Brady, Chief," Hearst said, "Miss Marion Davies."

Brady said hello. Chief O'Brien kissed her hand.

The men introduced their wives, in jade and ostrich feathers and floor-length Oriental robes. More fireworks crackled in the ballroom. The two women looked uncomfortable meeting Miss Davies, and Hearst put his arm around the smaller woman's waist for reassurance.

The lobby, lit with green and red lanterns, cast the faces in a weird light. Judge Brady was a bit younger than Hearst and had been serious-minded enough to keep on his black tie and tails from *Tosca*. He had a hangdog face and droopy eyes, with gray hair parted to the side, but was sharp and smart and wanted more than anything to be California's next governor.

"No costume?"

"I'm not much for theatrics," Judge Brady said.

"Confucius see," Hearst said. He smiled a big-toothed smile and rubbed the phony mustache. He then smiled normally, dropping the act. "A hold-over from my school days back east."

The men exchanged glances with their spouses. Hearst looked to Marion. The women left.

"Where can a man get an honest drink in this town?" Judge Brady asked.

A little Oriental walked past with small blue china cups on a silver tray. Chief O'Brien stopped the man and gathered three. The pointy straw hat on O'Brien's head seemed out of place with his walrus mustache, giant gold-rimmed glasses, and bright blue eyes. The seams on his black pajamas were about to burst.

"Manslaughter?" Hearst asked.

Brady looked to Chief O'Brien. Chief O'Brien cleared his throat and said, "Our detectives have some new information."

Hearst squinted his eyes, slid his hands into the opposite sleeves of his silken robe, and bowed. "I see . . . I see."

Hearst toasted the men and took his drink.

Judge Brady finished the drink, pronouncing it god-awful, and placed his hand in the pant pocket of his tuxedo. He glanced around the room, his eyes staying away from Hearst's stare, which was making him nervous. Hearst could always do that with the stare, could watch a man incessantly without prejudice or malice, his eyes merely lingering on the man's face, making strong men grow shy. It was almost as if some felt Hearst's gaze to be too private, too intimate, the way his eyes could rove over you and take in all of you and seem to know what you were thinking even as he was trying to figure it all out.

Miss Davies bounced up and bumped her behind to his and handed him another cup of the ny ka pa and said, "What's the h-haps, Daddy?"

And Hearst smiled at that. The chief and the D.A. looked uncomfortable with the informality of the exchange. Hearst bowed, formally and very Orientally, and took Miss Davies's arm and led her into the deeper red-and-green light and the smell of sweet jasmine. He slid his large hand onto her lower back, the spread of his fingers encompassing the base of her spine, and whispered into her ear, "I wish I could take you here in front of everyone."

She squealed and said, "W.R.!"

The feeling of her so close, even in the silliness of a costume ball where they could be anyone and no one, made his heart race. He remembered only days ago standing with her alone at the beaches of San Simeon and taking pictures with his big box camera as she would emerge from the sea, a Venus with golden locks, covered in sand. Her beautiful, healthy body glowing from sun and sand and vitality and life.

He made love to her there in a cove along the shores and in the gentle sound of the surf, the cool night creeping in from the Pacific, and he could feel the rage drumming in his blood and in his ears until he thought his entire body would ignite in flame.

"Are you okay?" she asked. Her breath a sweetness, a cooling mint in his face.

"Just fine," Hearst smiled. "Let's dance."

THE TRAIN WAS LATE.

Eight hours late from the east, coming in on the Overland Limited, some trouble with another train's wreck in Iowa, and now the big Southern Pacific clock on the wall of the station terminal read two in the morning. Sam went back to the paper, sitting on the large bench drinking a cup of coffee he'd bought from a blind man at the newsstand. He massaged his temples, reading up on five men busted in Bakersfield for trying to organize oil workers on strike in Kern County. The *Examiner* called them "card-carrying reds" and agitators with the International Workers of the World. The sheriff rounded them up, drove them out of the city, and turned them loose to walk south toward Los Angeles. The paper said if the owners of the oil rigs couldn't handle their men, they'd take over the job.

Sam folded the paper and leaned back into his seat, his cap sliding down in his eyes, as a conductor walked into the giant cathedral in Oakland and announced that the Overland Limited would arrive in ten minutes.

Sam checked his watch and made his way to the platform, watching that giant eye of the locomotive grow closer in the dark, chugging and steaming. He yawned and rested a hand against a metal support beam and then noticed all the men crowding behind him carrying writing tablets and pencils and box cameras and flashes. The Old Man had told him there was to be some sort of announcement at the station and that one of Dominguez's men, a fella named Brennan, would handle it. But after Arbuckle's wife said a few words, to take her and her mother back to the city by ferry, making sure they weren't hassled by any newsmen.

The giant engine shook the platform and steamed and hissed as it slowed to a stop, metal on metal, brakes screaming, wheels slowly circling to a stop. As cabled, Minta Durfee, vaudeville songstress, film comedienne, and the estranged wife of Roscoe Arbuckle, waited for a little negro porter to mount the steps before her and she walked down, hungry newspapermen shouting and taking photos, and she smiled glibly—as one would expect the wife of the accused to act—showing more attention to helping a little gray-headed woman with a sunken-in toothless smile and round black hat onto the platform.

Sam introduced himself to a man in a suit who carried two hatboxes. The man, Brennan, introduced Sam to Minta and "Ma."

Minta told them the terminal would be quite fine for a short meeting with the newsboys. But Sam could tell she was quite tired, as she stood under the big clock, now at two thirty-two, and read off neatly folded sheets of paper.

"Upon my arrival here I have only one request to make of all the fair-minded people of this city. I simply ask them to be fair to Mr. A. I ask them to give him only that to which he is entitled in all fairness, and for which San Francisco is noted around the world—a square deal. I know and his friends all know that he is innocent. He is entitled to a trial by a jury made up of men and women whose minds will be receptive alone to the truth. Only one side of this story has been told, and I know that the people of this good city will wait until the other side comes out in the proper, orderly fashion of the court. I believe everyone will agree with me that first impressions gained from rumor and report are most times found, on closer investigation, to be false, and that when the truth is heard in this matter—when the entire story has been unfolded—that my husband will be completely exonerated, and his good name will be thoroughly cleared, and that he again will take his place in the hearts of the American . . ."

But as she continued to speak, the newspapermen and photographers broke away, filing back out to the platform, leaving Minta alone to look at Ma and Ma just to shrug her bony shoulders. Brennan had already made arrangements with the porter to bring their trunks to the waiting car, and from there they would take the ferry back to the city.

Sam left the attorney and filed back out to the platform, watching the newspaper men standing in a great huddle, not at the Overland Limited coming in but at the Owl making ready to head south to Los Angeles.

The strobes of the big flashes looked like pockets of lightning in the early dark as Sam walked toward the openmouthed crowd and watched as four negro porters carried a white coffin onto the last car and two negro boys hoisted armloads of pink lilies onto the train.

Sam could smell the fresh-cut flowers from where he stood.

"Read us the note," a newsman called out.

The porter shook his head and pulled the sliding door shut with a giant clank.

An hour later, a faint gray dawn broke over the city, as the ferry made its way over the bay to San Francisco. Sam sat with Minta and Ma in their stateroom and waited for more knocks and to make more threats, sending the newsboys away. The ferry rolled and bobbed, and Ma's head was slumped with a snore, her hat fallen onto the seat beside her.

Sam caught Minta's eye and smiled.

They were alone.

"You see the coffin?"

"Yes, ma'am."

"He's innocent."

"Yes, ma'am."

"I spent two days in Chicago looking for people who knew that little tramp."

Sam leaned forward. "It was awfully nice of you to come."

"Of course." Minta looked at Sam, confused. "I love Roscoe with all my heart."

AL SEMNACHER never cared to be on stage. He was just fine being a bit player in Hollywood, standing in the shadows helping along a career or two, having lunch at Musso & Frank's, putting together a deal, maybe working a con or two on the side. The conning didn't start until he met up with Maude, and she'd kept him busy as a jackrabbit in the spring. Back then it was just plain old Maude Parker from Wichita and she'd needed some cash, so he'd introduced her around, and Hollywood had been a real gas. Soon she'd set her sights on a couple of actors and they'd pull a rape, or set them up with a man—one director was particularly into that type of thing—and they'd get a statement or take a photo and the money would soon be turned over to Maude. They'd live in high style for a few months till the tank was empty.

But now here was Al sitting in the lobby of the Palace Hotel, ten o'clock or so at night, waiting for Maude to show up and make good on their deal. He paced the lobby until he drew stares from the doorman and hotel manager and he told them he was a good friend of Mrs. Delmont's. But by midnight, he knew she was there but wasn't going to take his calls or come down to the lobby till hell froze over, and so he said to hell with it, retiring to the hotel's Rose Room, a little back-corner restaurant where they'd moved the hotel bar since the dry laws were on.

He ordered a Scotch and sat at a corner table. The rest of the Rose Room empty.

The walls were stained paneled wood, with a lot of low light and brass, and a large mural against the far wall that the waiter had said once hung over the bar before they broke it up.

The painting was of a strange-looking old man dressed in a harlequin checkerboard getup leading children away from a village by playing a flute. The little children raced with determination to catch up while others walked along bored or sat under great twisted trees the way you find trees in California, corrupted by the salt air from the Pacific.

Al had another Scotch and stared so long at the mural that it became real to him. The rough boulders, the failing light of day, and a giant stone castle on the hill. One boy in particular seemed so strange and foreign but known to him. He seemed the most important of the bunch, racing in jutting determination with the Pied Piper, mirroring the older man, trailing in the failing yellow California light and going somewhere over the rough little hills and boulders whittled away with time. The boy and the Piper the same, walking with the same stride, the same face, only the man much, much larger, towering over them all, but walking with a youthful stride, seeming to know exactly where he was headed.

Al finished his drink, knowing he couldn't pay for it.

He decided to put it on Maude's tab and had a laugh at that.

About that time, he watched a fat man enter the bar in a silk bathrobe and slippers and recognized him instantly as Frank Dominguez. He'd never met Dominguez officially but had seen him plenty on the Paramount lot and knew he was a regular at Jesse Lasky's poker games.

Dominguez took a seat under the mural.

Al smiled at his luck.

With a self-confidence that only a strong drink can give, he pulled up a chair and sat down.

"Can't sleep."

Dominguez shook his head.

"Lots to worry about with the police court and all."

"We're not talking to the press."

"I'm not the press."

"Then who the hell are you?" Dominguez said, putting fist to mouth in a giant yawn.

"Your new best friend."

Dominguez signaled the waiter, slumped against a back wall, for another round.

11

When Minta arrived at the Hall of Justice it was early morning and Roscoe had been asleep on his bunk, dreaming of the dusty town where he'd lived as a boy in a little hotel closet alone, scrubbing floors and cleaning spittoons and falling in love with this nineteen-year-old singer who smelled of lilac and taught him to harmonize and dance. The meeting of their voices on a tinny old piano had made him smile and feel warm as he slept until he heard the clank and turn of the key and he imagined he was driving a wagonload of meat, reins in one hand, some little girl's knee in the other, and the wagon suddenly buckled and tilted on a wide dusty road and the whole thing tipped and fell and he awoke on a stone pillow looking up into the face of Minta.

"Hello there, honey dear," she said.

He smiled.

"How's my boy?" Ma Durfee said.

The door jangled closed and the lock clicked.

Roscoe found his feet and fisted the sleep from his eyes. He stood and hugged Ma first and then Minta, still feeling inside a dream. He held Minta close and saw her angelic face, the soft reddish brown hair peeking out from a silken turban, beads of gold dangling from one side of her face like a veil.

Ma smiled a toothless smile and pinched his cheek.

"How 'bout a family shot for the boys?" asked a man with a camera.

Roscoe picked up the bunk rail with one hand and twisted it to run lengthways with the wired wall of the cell. He gathered Minta to sit on his right and Ma on the left, their backs turned to the dozens of newspapermen who the jailer had let in. The newsboys called to them and muttered but never moved, standing close to the wire wall, listening and scribbling down every breath and gesture.

Roscoe placed a meaty paw around Minta and Ma and whispered, "My best friends in all the world. How was the trip?"

"There was a train wreck in Iowa," Ma said. "They served minestrone soup and cheese biscuits. Twice."

"We stayed an extra day in Chicago," Minta said in a whisper. "I met people who knew the Rappe girl."

"Later," Roscoe said. "Have you a hotel?"

"Mr. Dominguez got us a room at the Palace."

"You'll love the Palace. Say, Ma, they have this wide-open space in the middle of the hotel called the Garden Court. The ceiling is made of glass, and it's so big that sometimes birds live their whole lives inside, hopping back and forth on the fig trees."

"Do you like minestrone?" Ma asked.

"Better than this jail grub."

"I spoke to Mr. Dominguez's partner, Mr. Brennan," Minta said, pulling off her gloves and placing them in her neat little jeweled purse. "He met us in Sacramento and rode with us to Oakland. He's going to cable men in Chicago. This girl had a very low start, Roscoe. She was an orphan who turned to men for money. She has a child and was known to be quite loose."

Roscoe walked to his homemade coat hanger and slipped into a fresh dress shirt, pulling suspenders over his large shoulders. He washed his face in a small bowl and stared at his ruddy cheeks in a rust-flecked mirror.

"I have to be in court today," Roscoe said, toweling off. "I wish I could show you the city, Ma. I'd take you down to the wharf and we'd eat steamed crabs and motor down to this wonderful garden in the park. You'd just love it. You could get lost there for days."

Roscoe felt Minta's eyes on them.

"Come now, Minty," he said, "Mr. Dominguez will straighten all this out. You know I didn't touch that girl."

"Roscoe!" Minta said.

"I'm sorry," Roscoe said, looking down at the beaten-wood floor and the silk socks on his feet.

"Why would you say such a thing to me?" Minta asked.

"You look thin," Ma said. "I'm sending out for food. How 'bout a big plate of spaghetti?"

Roscoe hugged them, pulling them both in close, their backs silhouettes and questions to the newsmen. He heard the men grumble and groan, big flashes exploding and popping in the long hall. One reporter complained to the jailor that the big gorilla wouldn't even turn around and that he wanted his dollar back. And finally Roscoe had enough, releasing his weight from the bunk and stepping toward the mesh-screen wall, an open frame looking back through the little wire squares at the newspapermen, and he asked who'd called him a gorilla.

The men scribbled and grinned, one more than the others, and he smiled even more as he mashed a cigarette under his heel. Roscoe put his hand to the mesh, running his hand over the wire, and looked at the man, saying, "How 'bout five minutes alone in here, bub? Anytime you like."

The flashes snapped so quickly they blinded Roscoe and he hit his hand hard against the cell frame, rattling the cage, not eliciting fear but excitement, the questions coming at a furious pace.

Why'd you do it?

Did she scream when you squished her, Fatty?

How's the dryin' out taking you?

He bashed the wall with the flat of his hand until Minta grabbed his wrist and led him back to the bunk, where he rested the weight of his head in his large hands. Ma stood and walked over to Roscoe's suit of clothes and shifted them on the hanger, straightening out the wrinkles, and pulling a scarf from her purse to buff out his shoes.

The newsboys were still calling out questions as the jailor ushered them out.

"How long has it been?" Roscoe asked, kissing the side of Minta's face. She smelled of French perfume and the cleanness of powder.

"Five years."

"How's the money?"

"Check comes every month as promised."

"This business won't affect any of that," he said, running his hands over his profile and through his hair. "Jeez, I'm sorry about all that. I feel like an animal in here."

"You remember what I told you when we first met?"

"You said, 'I don't like fat men and I don't like blondes.'"

"After that."

"In Long Beach? At the Byde-A-While?"

"Backstage at the theater."

Roscoe shook his head, feeling something wet running down his cheek.

"I told you to quit apologizing. I know who you are."

In many ways, the girls from the Arbuckle party had been getting more ink than Roscoe himself. Alice Blake's pretty mug was on the front page of the three papers almost every day, with police looking for their LOST WITNESS, while little personal tidbits about her affairs and those of Zey Prevon got to be regular fixtures in the news. The world learned that Zey was from Alabama and that Alice had grown up in the city. Alice's repertoire of songs and dance numbers were cataloged, as were her dreams of making it to the screen. Some even wondered if Zey Prevon was using the name Prevost because maybe she was related to the Prevost sisters, who'd made it big down in Hollywood.

Sam rolled a cigarette and sat back down on the apple crate.

Since dropping off Minta and Ma, he'd been watching the house owned by Alice Blake's mother and logging entries in a little notebook. Back at the Flood Building, he'd type it all up in a neat report for the Old Man, who'd then make his own report and cable it on to the home office in Baltimore.

It was six a.m. Sam picked up the *Examiner.*

He read yet another story about a girl he hadn't even known had been at the St. Francis. Her name was Betty Campbell, and it turned out that Betty was the true virgin at the party. Or so she said. Despite the big front-page spread, with a photo of Betty and Lowell Sherman wrapped in a heart, she admitted she barely met Arbuckle, let alone Virginia Rappe, who'd already taken sick and been moved to a room down the hall. But the boys sure got this Miss Campbell to call what she witnessed a "gay alcohol orgy" and to share how Lowell Sherman had tried to trick her into going to a back bedroom with him.

Sam wondered if Lowell Sherman ever got tired, because this would've been after his in-depth conversation with Alice in the bathroom.

He finished the cigarette and put down the paper, wiping the fresh ink on his pants.

It was early morning on the street, and men in suits and ties were starting their machines and driving into the city. Negro women with large baskets of cleaning supplies knocked on doors to start their days. Wives emerged from doorways with baby carriages or children in hand, heading to the market.

A little after nine, Sam thought about walking over to Sunset and Irving and trying out a little diner he'd seen that advertised a plate of eggs and bacon with coffee for fifteen cents. He checked his watch again and noted the time.

Slipping out the back door, he rounded his way to the front lawn and sidewalk just about the time three police cars slowed to a stop and a half dozen men in uniform climbed out. A plainclothes man that Sam didn't know walked up to the house and knocked on the door.

Sam stood from across the street and watched.

A half minute or so passed and the fella in plainclothes stepped back and nodded to a couple red-cheeked Irishmen in blue. One of the cops held an ax.

They knocked again, and then, seconds later, the big cop tore into the front door of the narrow home, breaking apart the wood and lock. He kicked inside, followed by his uniformed brothers.

Sam lit a cigarette.

The men soon pushed Alice Blake, screaming, hands behind her back, wearing nothing but a nightie and one stocking, out onto the street. She craned her neck and caught Sam's eye, giving him a hateful glance and spitting in his direction. She screamed and yelled that the men hadn't got any right, but all that stopped when they pushed her in the back of a car.

Sam noted the time.

He wrote it into the book.

MINTA PICKED OUT a blue suit for Roscoe, a new one Dominguez had brought from Los Angeles, and a crisp white shirt with a red-and-blue-striped tie. He was clean-shaven, his shoes spotless thanks to Ma, and he smelled of Bay Rum and powder, walking between two guards down the jailhouse steps and around a cove toward the Hall of Justice police court. He had a smile on his face, chewing gum, waiting for this big mess to blow over. But when he entered the second-floor hallway, the guards had to stop and cut a path through a room choked with women. They sat on stairways, on benches, leaned against walls, and blocked doors. Hundreds of them. Some were young with skirts almost to their knees, but most were gray-headed, with thick brooches, fur hats, and long black dresses. The room smelled of perfumed sweat and stale breath, the big courthouse windows not helping with the September heat wave.

According to the papers, the temperature was a record setter.

All heads turned to Roscoe and he didn't meet an eye, following the guards, Minta and Ma already waiting for him inside, as the tall doors parted. Roscoe walked an endless path lined with more women dressed in black, the sweetness covering up a mass body odor so strong he placed a silk handkerchief over his mouth, everyone silent, wooden benches creaking as the women strained to get a good look at Roscoe C. Arbuckle.

He felt a trickle of wetness on his neck and at first thought he was sweating, but then he felt more pock on his cheek and suit coat, like the first drops from a rainstorm, and he craned his neck away from the path and looked up into the sea of faces up in the court balcony and the old women with eyeglasses and fur hats and prune faces who looked sour and distant. A few more bits on his face. The old women spat on him and whispered, murmured, sounding like the summer buzzing of insects high in the trees.

The policemen called out for them to stop.

The judge, Sylvain Lazarus, entered the room in his long black robe and quickly took control, and hit the gavel over and over until the women stopped the noise and took their seats, and he launched into a big speech about how the women were in a court of law, not a Broadway spectacle, and if they came for entertainment or to make comment they might quickly find themselves tossed out on their ear.

"Are we understood?" asked the judge.

Roscoe took a seat beside Frank Dominguez and his young attorneys, Brennan and Cohen. Minta and Ma at the table. Minty sat beside Roscoe and reached under the heavy wooden table and squeezed his fingers.

Roscoe took a breath. It felt like the first breath in a while, as he used the silk hankie to remove sweat from his brow and spit from his cheeks and lapel. Judge Lazarus said something about the court not trying the film star but in a larger sense the community was trying itself.

Roscoe wanted a drink.

His heart would not stop jackhammering in his chest and he was afraid to turn around and look back at all the hate-filled faces staring at him. He felt the stares, their eyes on his back, the heat of it all burning so badly that he shifted in the chair. Minty's hand squeezed his even tighter.

The court called Al Semnacher.

The big doors parted and the man passed Roscoe, taking the stand beside the bench. He was sworn in and faced Milton U'Ren from the district attorney's office, and Roscoe tried to remember where he'd met Semnacher before the party but failed.

Roscoe wanted a smoke.

He looked down at the nicotine-stained fingers of his free hand.

Semnacher was a small-eyed man, even in those big horn-rimmed glasses, with a thick head of graying black hair and thick, furry eyebrows.

Roscoe looked to Dominguez and Dominguez gave a polite nod, a confident smile, and soon got to his feet, replacing U'Ren before the bench.

"Did you see Mr. Arbuckle under the influence of liquor there at any time?" Dominguez asked.

"No, not under the influence of liquor."

"His conduct was perfectly proper the whole time?"

"Yes, sir."

"And that of a gentleman?"

"Absolutely."

"Did he show any marked difference in his treatment of any one of the ladies there at all?"

"No, sir. He was the entertainer of the party."

"In other words, he treated all the ladies who were present the same way he did Miss Rappe, isn't that true?"

"Yes, sir."

U'Ren was on his feet spitting out objections, his weaseled face red and pinched and sweating. Words were exchanged, and he returned to his chair, only to return minutes later before Semnacher. Roscoe watched but didn't whisper over to Dominguez or shake his head or show any bit of emotion. He'd just let it all play out, let the fellas tussle on their own.

"Did Mr. Arbuckle say he had mistreated Miss Rappe?" U'Ren asked.

"No, sir."

U'Ren gave a little laugh. A crooked little smile.

"He didn't make the remark that he'd placed a piece of ice in Miss Rappe's person?"

Roscoe held his breath, watching the smile on the lips of that bastard, knowing where it was all headed. He clenched his jaw, his right hand trembling.

"I don't recall."

"You don't recall if he made the statement or where he placed the ice?" U'Ren asked.

"I never said 'in.'"

"What did you tell the detectives, sir? I remind you that you are under oath."

"*On.*"

"Where was the ice placed?"

Semnacher looked right at Dominguez, only catching Roscoe's eye, and then back at U'Ren, shifting in his seat, uncrossing his right leg and then crossing it again. *Come on, you bastard.*

"On her vagina."

Roscoe let out all his breath.

"Would you please repeat the exact word told to you by Mr. Arbuckle? Or would you prefer me reading your statement to Detective Reagan?"

"It's not proper."

"Sir?"

"I said it's not proper."

"It's completely proper in the context of the proceedings."

Semnacher glanced over at Judge Lazarus, who nodded with his chin.

"He said he placed it on her *snatch.*"

Women gasped. One squealed with horror. Roscoe turned in his chair to see the words repeated into an old woman's tin horn. The old woman's eyes grew large and she began to choke.

"But you don't consider the placement of a piece of ice on a nude young woman improper?" U'Ren asked.

Dominguez stood and objected. Roscoe dropped his face into his waiting fingers and rubbed his eyes and forehead.

"He was trying to revive her," Semnacher said.

"Would the court please instruct Mr. Semnacher to only answer the question?" U'Ren said. "He is not here to speak on Mr. Arbuckle's intentions."

Through his loose fingers, Roscoe watched U'Ren turn to the courtroom. He leaned a skinny arm against the witness stand, looking as loose and disjointed as a scarecrow. He peered up into the ladies hanging over the balcony railing and for a second gave a little grin. A confident batter at the plate.

"At what time did you hear Mrs. Delmont screaming for Mr. Arbuckle to open the door to room 1219?"

"I didn't hear her scream."

"Mr. Semnacher?"

"I don't recall her screaming."

"Surely you heard her banging on the door with the heel of her shoe?"

"That's not what I recall."

"Are you having memory problems, sir?"

"The mind is a funny thing."

"Some minds are funnier than others."

U'Ren paced back and forth in front of Judge Lazarus. Judge Lazarus followed the little lawyer with his eyes, never moving his big jaw from his hand. U'Ren walked back to the prosecutor's table and exchanged whispers with the district attorney, Judge Brady. Judge Brady stood and walked to the railing, leaned over, and whispered something to the Delmont woman.

Maude Delmont, dressed all in black, nodded her head and wiped her nose with a handkerchief. Roscoe looked to Dominguez and Dominguez raised his eyebrows, hands resting on his large stomach waiting to see what was about to be sprung.

"Is it not true that you left the party with Miss Rappe's undergarments? Her brassiere, bloomers, and garters?"

"I fished a waistcoat from the trash bin."

"For what purpose?"

"I planned on joshing her later about her condition."

"Did you not tell Mrs. Delmont, the very person who accompanied you to the Arbuckle suite, that you needed the clothing to wash your machine? Which was it?"

Women laughed. Lazarus stopped the court and spoke for a while, and U'Ren asked the question again. Al Semnacher leaned forward from the witness stand and cleared his throat, speaking loud enough for the ladies in the balcony.

"Maude Delmont is a known liar," he said.

———————

MAUDE DELMONT GASPED, closed her eyes, and pretended to faint. Kate Eisenhart caught her and hoisted her into her big lap, tapping Maude's hand over and over and calling her name. Women craned their necks and whispered, and policewoman Kate Eisenhart told the lot of them to get back as she picked up Maude Delmont, threw her over a shoulder, and walked her from the courtroom like a big-game prize. As she walked, Maude opened one eye and looked back at Semnacher on the stand.

That bastard. That lousy prick.

Big Kate took her down the steps and out the front door of the Hall of Justice and told them newspapermen if they took one snap, she'd kick 'em all in the balls. She yelled for a glass of water, fanning Maude Delmont's face and unpinning the wide-brimmed black hat. Maude fluttered her eyes open and then closed them again.

"Maude?"

She opened her eyes and righted herself on the granite steps, looking out on Portsmouth Square.

"That horrible man," Kate said.

"The heat is awful," Maude said. "All this black."

Kate had a copy of the *Examiner* she'd plucked from the hands of a curious newsboy and waved it high up and down, breezing Maude's face. A cup of water was placed in Maude's hand and she stood.

"He can't make up those things," Kate said. "Not in this town, he can't."

"Movie people are all alike," Maude said. "I'm never returning south. It's a place without shame or a conscience."

Kate shared a smile with her. The midday sun was a burning white.

"Could you please call me a cab?" Maude asked.

Kate disappeared. Maude waited at the foot of the steps of the Hall of Justice for several minutes until Al Semnacher skipped down them, a mongrel group of newsmen at his heels. He tipped his bowler hat at Maude and there were pictures taken.

"I see you've made arrangements," she said.

"How are things at the Palace? Heard the St. Francis kicked you out."

Maude turned her head away. "I had my luggage moved to the Palace. The accommodations are much more to my liking."

Al laughed. "Luggage? The only luggage you ever carry is a fresh set of bloomers in your pocketbook."

Maude leapt at his throat, black hat rolling from her head, dropping her pocketbook and reaching her fingers around Al Semnacher's skinny neck, trying to wring it like a chicken. His glasses were knocked off and Al fell to his back, swearing and cussing and calling her a nasty whore, and she kneed him in the balls and slapped him across the face until she felt a big arm reach around her waist and pull her back, the sweet voice of Big Kate telling her that her cab had come.

"Mrs. Delmont, are you okay?"

Maude put her hand to her chest and just breathed. "I have no idea what came over me."

12

Sam walked with Dominguez up Kearny Street away from the Palace Hotel and toward the Hall of Justice. It was the second Monday since the Arbuckle party and the third day with Judge Lazarus and police court, and Frank Dominguez said he wouldn't bet heads or tails which way the judge was leaning. The fog had burned off in the early-morning heat and Sam got a nice breath going, trying to pace out his answers so as not to sound winded to the fat attorney. He wore tweed pants and a tweed vest with a white shirt Jose had boiled for him, a cap and laced boots.

"How solid is your information?" Dominguez asked.

"Solid."

"You want to tell me where you got it?"

"I'd rather not," Sam said. "If it's all the same with you."

"U'Ren and Brady are putting up three docs today," Dominguez said, not winded a bit, taking the hill, the talk, and a big cigar in easy stride. "All three will testify that the girl's bladder burst from external force."

"Rumwell?"

"Not Rumwell," Dominguez said. "One doc who performed the autopsy with Rumwell at Wakefield, one fella, a Dr. Strange, who performed the second autopsy for the county, and a doctor who treated her at the St. Francis."

"What does the county man say?"

"I haven't seen his official report yet," Dominguez said. "I was told it was still being typed up and I'd have ample time to question the man in court."

"For some reason, I don't think Brady is going to bring up the missing parts."

"And I don't want to look like a fool for asking unless we're sure."

"We're sure," Sam said.

Bankers, lawyers, and businessmen of all types flowed down the hill, walking past Dominguez and Sam in their buttoned-up coats and waxed mustaches, heavy leather satchels in hand. Two streetcars passed each other on Kearny, electricity sparking off the wires.

"Think this could be enough to throw out the case?" Sam asked.

Dominguez puffed on his cigar, lengthening his strides, cresting the hill at Portsmouth Square. A crowd had gathered on the front steps of the Halls of Justice. Dominguez clicked open a gold timepiece that hung on his waist.

"I don't believe we'll get a murder indictment," Dominguez said. "I think that Lazarus will rubber-stamp the grand jury decision for manslaughter. Probably tomorrow."

"And we prepare for real court."

Dominguez puffed more on the cigar and squinted his eyes in the smoke.

"I'll need you to go to Los Angeles," Dominguez said. "Miss Durfee spoke to you about what she learned in Chicago about the girl?"

"Some," Sam said. "But I can't leave the city. My wife's about to burst in a week or two. Really, anytime."

"I can make sure you're compensated, Sam. A new family needs money."

"We have operatives in Los Angeles."

"And they haven't found a scrap on that girl."

Sam put his hands in his pockets.

Dominguez crushed the last bit of his cigar under his shoe. He watched the dark mass of Vigilant women growing in a great black curtain on the steps.

"You understand what we'd need?"

"I do," Sam said.

"Sam, you're not looking at me."

"It's not my favorite type of work."

"We wouldn't have long," Dominguez said. "Weeks at most. I don't want any more time for Roscoe to get crucified in the papers."

Sam watched a woman unload sandwiches and a teakettle from a large wicker basket. Another woman brought her own chair, placing it at the foot of the great steps and knitting away with giant, sharp silver needles.

"When's the Delmont broad up?"

"She was supposed to go first," Dominguez said.

"Make any sense that U'Ren would keep the woman who swore out the complaint, their main witness, off the stand?"

"No," Dominguez said. "No, it does not."

Dominguez walked toward court, turning back a few steps later, and yelled, "Talk to your wife, Sam."

MAUDE DELMONT let reporters into her room on the fifth floor of the Palace Hotel earlier that morning and held court all the way through breakfast. She sat on the bed, fully clothed, but rested her head back like an invalid and stared at a ceiling fan while she spun wild stories about Virginia Rappe and their enduring friendship, a friendship Maude said lasted even into death. When the questions became too personal, too detailed, Maude would only have to stretch her forearm across her head and say she'd grown tired and the newspapermen would ease off, taking a few of the scraps she'd fed them.

"We met at the Million Dollar Theater," Maude said.

They'd met in Al Semnacher's living room, parceling out a bottle of laudanum and taking disgusting turns with Al.

"I had never seen her touch alcohol until the Arbuckle party."

In the three weeks Maude had known her, the girl always had a stomach full of gin and an arm full of heroin. She liked cocaine. Sex was as easy as wiping her nose.

"We often went to church," Maude said. "She was little but had the most lovely, strong voice."

The girl was ripe, full of curves and solid meat, and couldn't have found a church in Los Angeles with a road map.

"Will you make her funeral?" a newsman asked.

Maude sadly shook her head, standing from the bed, grabbing the now-trademark black hat and veil, readying for court.

"I can't," Maude said. "Her former fiancé, Mr. Lehrman, is taking care of the arrangements. I'm needed here to set the truth straight."

"Did he kill her?"

"I only know what the poor girl told me only moments after her encounter," she said. "I can only imagine the horror of what that blubber must have been like. Please, I must be alone. I can't breathe."

Maude had scurried the boys out, picking up a pint of whiskey one had left her for her nerves and taking a swig before closing the door. But a big old foot clogged the way. She asked, What gives?, and the door was pushed forward by the bigheaded cop, Reagan, with his partner with the red curly hair behind him, Kennedy.

"Hey, boys."

"Mrs. Delmont," Reagan said.

"Take your hats?" she asked. "I'll be ready in a jiff."

The boys looked to each other, like a couple steers eyeing the same heifer.

She watched herself in the beveled mirror as she pulled on the hat and slanted it just so. She could see the men standing side by side behind her, in their dark blue suits and serious faces.

"You two have something to say?"

"Captain Matheson would like to talk to you."

"But I'm due in court," she said. "Did you talk to Judge Brady about this?"

"He knows," Griff Kennedy said.

"Does this have something to do with what that fool Al Semnacher said about me?"

"No, ma'am," Tom said. "We'll ride down with you. We have a man holding the elevator."

Maude stood a good two feet below both of the detectives and looked back and forth to each one's face before launching into a smile. She let her eyes linger on them.

Nothing.

"Oh, well," she said. "Let's go."

A little bald man wearing a red coat across his sagging shoulders held the elevator door and rolled the caged door in front of them. He turned the key and the elevator rumbled to life, floating and bumping, floating and bumping, down the shaft.

"We're going to be late," Maude Delmont said. "I hope you two fools know that."

She watched the floors slide by the door, keeping her eyes on the needle pointing down toward the lobby.

"Mrs. Delmont, have you spent much time in Madera County?" Detective Reagan asked behind her.

Maude Delmont kept her eyes forward, letting the elevator slow to a stop and the gated door open. Without a word, she walked ahead of them.

"SO ARBUCKLE IS A FREE MAN?" Mr. Hearst asked.

"Yes, sir," said the young reporter.

"You saw him walk out of jail?"

"Yes, sir. Bail was five thousand."

"Did he smile?"

"He grinned."

"That's a smile."

The big black locomotive steamed south from San Francisco to Los Angeles, the young reporter still looking uneasy from when Hearst asked him on the journey, still worried about making the morning edition. The young man sat across from Hearst, afraid to touch the plate of food that George had carried from the kitchen, the roast beef and potatoes growing cold on the gilded china.

"Do you think he deserved to be tried with more than manslaughter?"

"I don't know, sir."

Hearst sliced into the roast beef, adding a touch of mashed potatoes on the fork. The gravy was creamy and bloody, fresh green beans on the side. He asked George to pour more wine and looked out at the flat, barren northern California countryside as they sped along, the occasional whistle blowing from the engineer.

"When should we expect a trial?"

"In a month or so."

"What else do we have for the afternoon?"

"The disarmament conference begins in a few weeks. The Tong War continues in Chinatown. Mollie Merrick has a piece on the high rate of college coeds never marrying."

"I mean on Arbuckle."

"They bury the girl tomorrow in Hollywood. I've brought you the story of her viewing from the wire."

Hearst set it by his elbow and scanned the story, George refilling his wineglass. The young reporter nervously checked his wristwatch, wanting more than anything to be away from the man the newsboys called The Chief and off his goddamn train.

8,000 AT L.A. VIEW BODY OF VIRGINIA RAPPE. *Eight thousand persons—gray-headed matrons with their daughters, men in overalls who stood hat in hand, and schoolgirls with braided hair down their backs—all inspired by love, friendship, or morbid curiosity, viewed the body of Virginia Rappe, beautiful motion picture actress, as it lay in state between the hours of 10 a.m. and 4 p.m. at the undertaking establishment of Strother and Drayton in Hollywood today.*

Draped in a white satin shroud, with flowers in her hands, the body of the girl, central figure of the tragedy which startled the country last week, looked extremely lifelike and natural. The casket was banked high with flowers, including the 1,000 tiger lilies ordered by Miss Rappe's fiancé, Henry Lehrman, from New York, and across it was a white satin ribbon and in gold letters this: To my grave sweetheart. —From Henry.

Hearst closed the folder over the story and looked across the table at the young reporter fidgeting.

"Aren't you going to eat?"

"Sorry. I'm a little nervous."

"Of what?"

"I'm sorry, sir."

"At least drink your wine," Hearst said, downing the rest of his. "I never trust a newspaperman who doesn't drink. Shows me he doesn't have ink in his blood."

He smiled, watching the reporter down the glass.

"I want Arbuckle smiling up high. I want you to show his cockiness and aloofness from the judge's decision. What was the first thing he did when released?"

"Got a shave, sir."

"A shave. From whom?"

"A neighborhood barber offered him one for free."

"Set it up with the smile, walking out a free man for now, and then the smugness of getting a shave and a big meal at the Palace Hotel. He did have a big meal, I assume."

"I can find out."

"He's not concerned about the girl at all. She's dead, lying cold in a mortuary with her adoring fans swarming over her, and Arbuckle just wants to stuff himself to satisfy his mammoth appetites."

The engineer blew the locomotive's whistle again, and soon hovels slapped together from scrap wood and tin showed in the long coach windows. A fat Mexican woman cooked meat on an open stove, dirty children playing by her feet, a skinny baby on her bosom. Coolies hefted boxes from the backs of wagons and trucks to the train platform, and soon the locomotive slowed and drew to a long, steady stop.

The only sound in the cabin came from the hissing of the engine as the train took on more water and wood.

"You can go," Hearst said. "Take the story on the girl."

"Here?"

"Another train will come through," Hearst said. "If not, just write your story and have it cabled to the office."

The reporter stood and grabbed his coat and hat and nervously shook The Chief's hand and walked back through the coach, George already holding the door open and then shutting it with a tight pop.

"Odd little fellow," George said.

"They all are."

"Are you okay, Mr. Hearst?"

"I'm fine. I'm fine."

Hearst stood and watched as George cleared the china plates from the table. The coolies and Mexes looked up from their work at the strange black train pulling only two coaches. Hearst waved at them, and made his way back to the bath, shutting the door and locking it behind him, splashing water on his face and trying to steady himself from the nausea.

There had been a picture attached to the wire story on the girl's burial. He had decided it was too much, the Rappe girl, with her insides cleaned out and sewn back whole, photographed in her Sunday best and covered with that goddamn white veil, a sweet smile upon her dead lips. Hearst ran cold water and wiped his giant eyes with a moist towel.

But his legs gave out and soon the big man was on his knees, hands wrapped around the brass commode and vomiting out the roast beef and potatoes, George knocking on the door.

Hearst yelled back that he was fine and to fetch some ice water.

Hearst, still on his knees, steadied himself. The image of the girl would not shake free of his mind. When he saw the girl's face, it wasn't the Rappe girl but Marion, pennies covering her eyes.

He felt feverish as he stood and tried to calm himself.

THE CAPTAIN OF DETECTIVES, Duncan Matheson, was an odd-looking duck, thought Maude Delmont. Odd because he looked so much like a policemen that she figured him to be a stock player in Hollywood. He wore one of those thick, waxed mustaches and smoked a pipe while he interviewed her in his little partitioned office made of pebbled glass and oak. His eyes were as black as coal, and he would ask questions as if they were statements and Maude didn't know whether to answer, nod her head, or call him a liar.

"You've been married for a year or so."

She decided to nod.

"To a Mr. Woods of Madera."

She nodded again.

"Are you aware that Mr. Woods has been searching for you for months now and only knew you were in the city when he picked up a newspaper?"

She shook her head. It called for a shake.

"Are you in the process of divorce?"

"No, sir."

"Mr. Woods has complained you left him without explanation."

Maude's throat felt dry and cracked. She had started to sweat. She never sweated. She almost closed her eyes, waiting for Captain Matheson to ask her all about the bonds and cash she stole from Cassius Clay Woods's safe.

She held her breath and dropped her head into her waiting fingertips.

"I can explain," she said. "Please. This has all been so traumatic."

Captain Matheson stood. He was a great deal shorter than he looked sitting behind the desk and appeared downright minuscule as he passed Detectives Kennedy and Reagan, who stood against a brick wall lined with photos and fancy inked documents.

"I don't want to meddle in your affairs," Matheson said. "I was just asked to pass on this news and ask you to call your husband. I think he'll understand the trauma you have been through. And no matter what else, a woman needs a husband to make sense of things."

Maude nodded and said, "Of course."

She stood. But Captain Matheson held up his hand, asking her to sit back down. He refilled his pipe and sat on the edge of his desk. He got the pipe going with a set of matches and stared at her, evaluating her for several moments before blowing out a big mouthful of cherry-scented smoke and nodding to himself as if arriving at a decision.

"You drove up here with Mr. Semnacher."

"Yes."

"Are you and Semnacher intimate?"

Maude put her hand to her mouth.

Matheson waved away the worry on her face. "Do I look like a goddamn minister? I just said you need your husband now because I think that Semnacher fellow is a menace."

"He is."

"You don't care for him anymore."

"We were friends. Not now."

Matheson looked back to Reagan and Kennedy and then back at Maude. "We understand that you and Mr. Semnacher had adjoining rooms at the Palace Hotel before this Arbuckle fiasco."

"I stayed in the room with Miss Rappe."

"You never opened the door that separated you."

Maude took a breath, took off her hat, and floated it onto a free chair. She stood up and pressed out the wrinkles in her dress, feeling the cool air coming off the desk fan. She smiled and looked at the little man. "Put it this way, Semnacher stuck me with the bill."

Maude made a big show of plunging her thumb back to her breastbone.

"So you wouldn't try and hide his whereabouts."

"He took off?"

"He was due back in court yesterday. That's why police court broke up early."

Maude laughed, a little giggle at first but spilling over into a gut buster, then she sat back down and asked Griff—really calling Detective Kennedy "Griff"—for a cup of joe and a cigarette.

"I wouldn't hide that sorry ape if he was my own brother."

"He hadn't checked out of the hotel."

"Come again?"

"He left his possessions," Matheson said, drawing on the pipe and then speaking with smoke coming out from his mouth. "The front desk said he checked messages two days ago, tipped a doorman, and walked away. His Stutz is still parked at the tunnel garage."

am hired a taxi at the Los Angeles station early the next morning after taking the Owl south late the night before. Arbuckle was free for now, and Sam had his instructions from Frank Dominguez and the Old Man. He read off the only address they had for Virginia Rappe to the cabbie, taking him through the downtown lined with wrought-iron streetlamps and palm trees, and then out onto Wilshire and up on Western, through orange groves and large mansions being built on loose, dusty soil. The machine hit potholes and jostled him up and down as they made their way north to Hollywood around where the cabbie said the circus had just started.

"You think it was bad yesterday," said the cabbie. "Today they bury the poor girl. There ain't no telling how many people want to see that."

"Why would they care?"

"People feel bad for her. Say, what kind of work do you do?"

"I work for the Fuller Brush Company."

"I'm bald, so no need to work your spiel on me."

"We also sell many items for the ladies."

"I read this morning that Arbuckle was smiling when they let him out of jail. That made me sick to my stomach. They say he walked right out of jail not feeling bad for nothing he did, only going down to see some barber and getting a free shave. You think the bastard would at least pay for it, him driving a thirty-thousand-dollar machine."

"Why should he feel bad if he didn't do it?"

"Come on. Where you been? The guy's an animal."

The little taxi painted canary yellow turned onto Melrose, two cars honking at the driver from the crossroad and him waving them off with disgust, turning so hard to the left that Sam thought the machine would lift up on two wheels. But all was steady as the driver headed east, passing the big barn buildings marked with signs for different studios, all of them surrounded by high fences and shut with gates.

"I pick up girls like that at the station all the time," the cabbie said. "They come in with their little suitcases, all big-eyed and bragging about winning Miss Corn Queen or the like, everything they own brought in from Bumfuck, Iowa, and wanting to be the next Mary Pickford."

"I think we might give a fella a break till his day in court."

The cabbie turned around in his seat, the cab rolling into oncoming traffic, and said, "Didn't you hear the bastard stuck a Coca-Cola bottle in her pussy? Where I'm from, you find a rope and the tallest tree."

Sam didn't say anything as they passed a long fence and a corner grocery and finally turned into a little neighborhood of bungalows. Most of them freshly built, the kind they advertise in the papers for veterans to start families. These were California specials, with stucco and red tile roofs and a dwarf orange tree in every front yard.

"Hey, you got a friend with you?"

"Come again?"

"That little Hupmobile has been following us since the station."

Sam turned and noted the shadows of two figures in the coupe. He reached down to his ankle and slipped the .32 in his hand. His arm rested on the backseat, the gun in his lap, and he told the driver to keep circling.

"That's the house right there."

"Keep going," Sam said. "Don't circle back till I say."

ROSCOE WAS bowling to opera.

Minta and Ma watched, eating ice cream from the little parlor he'd had built in the basement of his mansion on West Adams. It felt so damn good to be back home that the last weeks felt like a feverish nightmare, something from one of his pictures where he'd been locked up and whistled for Luke the pooch to come running with keys.

Luke, who was really Minta's dog, sat at her feet under the wire parlor chair and waited for her to finish her sundae to lick up all the ice cream and pineapple sauce.

Roscoe let out all his breath and closed his eyes, taking a few steps down the lane and watching the ball glide and float to the pins, taking out all but two. A little negro at the end of the lane cleared off the downed pins as Roscoe hunted for another ball out of the dozens shining and gleaming on a brass rack.

"Ma, how 'bout another sundae?"

She shook her head, the spoon still in her mouth.

He smiled over at the pair, finally ditching the depressing black they'd worn in the police court and now dressed like normal folks. Minta in a green-and-white print dress and Ma still in her housecoat she'd worn since running the servants from the kitchen and cooking a skilletful of bacon and eggs.

Roscoe chose a red ball, eyeing the two pins, and stood at the line. Holding the ball up, he took a single step before hearing the warning bark from Luke, and he stopped to see Frank Dominguez coming down the curved wrought-iron staircase into the basement.

He was alone, still dressed in his black suit and red scarf, a fat leather satchel at his side.

Luke continued to bark and jut in and out at Dominguez's feet without ever really taking a bite. Dominguez coolly smiled and threw down a biscuit the butler had given him, and Luke wandered off to a corner.

Dominguez said hello to Minta and Ma and then took a seat at the parlor bar.

Roscoe put down the ball and walked behind the bar and started to make Dominguez a sundae without him asking. He made a hell of a one with three different scoops of ice cream and three different sauces with chopped nuts and fresh whipping cream. A few cherries to boot.

"When did you put this in?"

"Last year," Roscoe said. "You want to bowl a game?"

He slid the sundae before Dominguez at the bar. Dominguez rested his satchel on the barstool next to him. He smiled to Roscoe, a really tired, worn-out-looking smile, as Roscoe cleaned out a couple dirty glasses in some sudsy water, his shirtsleeves rolled up to his elbows.

"Any word from Fishback or Sherman?"

Roscoe shook his head.

"You've called them?"

"A million times," Roscoe said. "Lowell's still in New York. God knows what happened to Freddie. I even wrote the son of a bitch a letter when I was in jail."

"The Pinkertons can't find him either. They believe he skipped Los Angeles right after you were arrested."

"Some friends."

"We need 'em."

"They'll come around," Roscoe said. "Hey, how's that sundae?"

It remained untouched.

"Freddie Fishback was in that room right after the girl took ill. He could testify that the girl was too far gone to be making any dying accusation. He also moved her into the bath and could account for those bruises on her arms and legs."

"People think I got the leprosy."

"You'll be back on the lot before the year's out."

"All my pictures have been yanked, Zukor has stopped paying me till further notice, and when I got back from Frisco I found most of my furniture had been repossessed. Did you see upstairs? We don't have a place to sit. Lucky the bastards didn't come down here or they woulda taken every last pin."

"Let me handle Zukor," Dominguez said. "We have a contract."

"A million a year only if I work. How am I supposed to work if they won't let me on the lot? They pulled *Gasoline Gus* and it had only been out five days. No wonder the picture didn't show a profit. Those goddamn bastards."

Dominguez looked down at his sundae and then up at Roscoe.

"You got anything stronger?"

"What's eating you?"

Roscoe dipped his hand into the cooler and came out with a bottle of jackass brandy. He poured a generous amount into a coffee mug.

"They want to replace me."

Roscoe laughed. "Who?"

"Zukor. Lasky. Paramount wants you to go with a bigger name. I think they've been going behind my back with that big swinging dick in Frisco. He's the one who took on the Jack Dempsey mess."

"'Cause of that shimmy girl, Bee Whosis, who shacked up with him?"

"Yeah."

"That was just a dumb case," Roscoe said. "The girl's beau sued Dempsey for theft of love."

"But the newsboys like him and he's local. Might make a difference with the jury."

"You still sore at how that son of a bitch U'Ren kept calling you Señor Dominguez?"

"I'm just saying this fella, McNab, is local. You should do some thinking on this, Roscoe. Don't get all loyal and stupid on me."

Dominguez finished the brandy, picked up his satchel, and told Minta and Ma good day.

Roscoe followed Dominguez with his eyes as he twirled around the iron staircase and disappeared up into the mansion. Roscoe set Dominguez's untouched sundae on the floor and whistled for Luke.

"Roscoe, you're going to make him fatter than he already is," Minta said.

Roscoe took a seat on the steps down to the bowling lane, eyeing those last two pins, and rolled a cigarette. He massaged Luke's nub ears as the dog licked the glass clean and asked him, "What about you, boy? Can you see the future?"

THE ADDRESS WAS A BUST.

Sam read out another.

The cabbie U-turned and headed west on Sunset, away from the city, along the long, barren road, and then cut up toward the cool, dark hills and zigzagged up a rough-cut path.

The house was in the old Mission style, a big, fat adobe number built up a steep drive and surrounded by high shrubs and palms. The early-afternoon shadows showed a set of twin hills, and the air smelled of citrus.

The cab parked at the curb. Sam walked to the gate and stared up at the mansion. The day was cool, sky blue, and down below a bunch of men in overalls were digging a trough through an orange grove. Up a long, curving driveway, a butler washed a long Packard touring car.

Sam whistled to him from the gate.

The man didn't hear him. Or pretended he didn't.

Sam whistled again and the man stuck the brush back in a suds bucket and wandered down to the gate.

"Like to see Mr. Lehrman."

"He ain't here."

"Tell him I'm a detective from San Francisco."

"I don't care if you're the Emperor of Japan, he still ain't here."

"When will he be back?"

"Next week," the man said. "Leave a card."

Sam left a card and walked back down to the cab and told the cabbie to wait. On foot, he followed the wall of shrubs until there was a break and he found a wrought-iron gate.

The gate was unlocked.

Sam let himself inside and walked down a winding path through some exotic trees and bushes. There was hibiscus and lime. Lemon trees and palm. Flowers planted along a spindled alabaster wall and up a little staircase to behind the mansion.

Sam found three people sitting by a little round pool with a fountain in the center. Two men and a woman.

All were very naked.

Sam smiled and took off his hat.

"I guess I'm a bit overdressed."

A man with tight slicked hair and a tiny mustache got to his feet. He was tall and bony and hairless and made no attempt to cover himself. He just wanted to know how the hell Sam had gotten into the garden.

"Let myself in," Sam said. "Nice to meet you, Mr. Lehrman."

"Please leave."

"I came all the way from San Francisco."

"Are you with the police?"

"I'm a detective," Sam said.

"Please sit," Henry Lehrman said, sweeping his hand to a small lacquered table bordered by four silk pillows. "Would you like some tea?"

"Sure."

"I hope our nudity does not shock you," Lehrman said. "We find it to be quite natural and nothing to be ashamed of. This is my home and we have our own customs."

"I heard I was born that way."

The woman remained seated by the pool, eating an apple. She was young, maybe not twenty, redheaded and freckled, her skin flushed with sun. Sam made a note of her form as she was introduced as Miss Leigh. She smiled at Sam and Sam smiled back, liking the smile and shape.

Henry introduced the man as his spiritual adviser, Dr. Bagwa. The man wore a jeweled headdress and it jingled as he bowed. Sam couldn't hide his smile, which wasn't lost on "Dr. Bagwa," who returned back to his spot by the pool with Miss Leigh.

"Dr. Bagwa is an expert in soul painting," Lehrman said. "Have you heard of it?"

"Can't say I have."

"He can see the colors of man's soul without the flesh and bone."

"That a fact."

"He's quite wise, you know."

Lehrman rang a little bell and a maid appeared and he asked for two cups of flower tea.

"I'm sorry about Miss Rappe," Sam said.

"She was my fiancée."

"What about Miss Leigh?"

"She's my secretary."

"I see."

Lehrman looked off for a long moment, seeming to study the hills, and turned back to Sam. "She was my muse. *My love. My friend.* I don't know if I can work without her. She was to be the star of my next film."

Sam set fire to a Fatima and laid the pack and matches on the table. "What was it going to be about?"

"The film? Does it matter now? It's all lost."

"How long did you know her?"

"I've already answered these questions for Judge Brady."

"Just a few more, if you don't mind."

The tea came. The maid thankfully brought a robe, an Oriental affair, that Lehrman slipped into and belted at the waist. He sat cross-legged on the pillow and lit a jade opium pipe.

"She was just an extra," he said. "But she had a quality. You know they say she was born from royalty?"

"I read that. Is it true?"

"Virginia never knew her father," he said. "I suppose it could be true."

Lehrman pulled on the pipe and closed his eyes. He looked quite content on the little pillow.

"She lived with you?"

"She lived in the wing of the house with my aunt."

"All very proper."

"Well, of course."

"And you loved her."

"I did."

"And how did she know Mr. Semnacher and Mrs. Delmont?"

"I don't know."

"But she was with them?"

"I've met Mr. Semnacher and find him to be quite distasteful. I know nothing of this Delmont woman."

"You didn't care that she'd gone to San Francisco?"

"We were free to live our own lives."

"But she was your fiancée?"

Lehrman set down the pipe. He made a show of smoothing down the little black mustache. The wind blew off the shadowed hills, smelling of orange blossoms and tropical flowers. He made a sad face, looking more comical than sad. Sam watched him and fished for another Fatima.

He stole a side glance of Miss Leigh, laughing and talking with Dr. Bagwa.

"When did you meet Miss Rappe?"

"Two years ago."

"She was in one of your pictures?"

"Yes."

"And you fell in love?"

"Madly."

"And she moved in here?"

"Yes. What does it matter?"

"Did you know any of her people in Chicago?"

"We decided not to speak of her past or who we were before we met."

"I see."

"Did she have many friends?"

"Of course."

"Who were they?"

"I'm finding this tiresome, Mr. . . . ?" Lehrman raised an eyebrow.

Sam introduced himself and laid out his hand. Lehrman looked to his hand and stood, holding on to the jade pipe and excusing himself. "This all has been quite a troubling ordeal. If it wasn't for the good doctor, I don't know what I would have done."

Lehrman took a crooked path back to the house. The glass doors rattled with a sharp slam.

Sam sniffed the tea and then took a small sip. It tasted like chopped flowers and sugar. He stood and stretched his legs, smiling over at Miss Leigh. She smiled back and crossed her shapely long legs. She wore her hair loose and it fell softly against the fine shoulders and the tips of her full breasts with small pink nipples.

Her eyes were wide set and an innocent green without a trace of paint.

Somewhere a farmer was missing his daughter.

So intent on the girl, Sam missed the good Dr. Bagwa as he took a seat at the table, pulling loose a Fatima.

"Whatta you say, Pete?" Sam said, turning his eyes back to the girl.

"Thanks for not blowing it, Sam."

"Man's got to make an honest living."

"You ain't kidding, brother."

"How long you been with this four-flusher?"

"A month."

"Dr. Bagwa," Sam said, laughing. "That tops your minister act in Portland. Or the English duke in Cleveland."

"I try."

"You know where I can get a decent plate of ham and eggs?"

Pete the Fink told him. Sam said he'd meet him there in an hour.

"And Pete?"

"Yeah?"

"Make sure you wear some goddamn pants."

14

They met at a little place called Philippe, a short walk from the train yards near the Mex district on Aliso Street. Sam finished up three cigarettes and two cups of coffee before Pete showed up in a dark suit with a red tie. He'd switched out the turban for a beaver hat he laid on a hook by the front door and slid into a booth across from Sam, folding his hands together like he was about to pray, with a devilish smile on his lips.

"Thanks for losing the getup."

"You should see this robe I got," Pete said. "It's made of Chinese silk and little emeralds. They look like stars."

"Nice."

Pete was medium height, medium weight, with brown hair and brown eyes. He could be a million men, if judged by Bertillon. No scars, no marks. Even if you'd never seen him, you'd think he was someone who used to date your sister.

"You'll like this place," Pete said. "They make roast beef sandwiches on thick rolls like they do back east."

"I just ordered some hash and eggs."

"You're a hash-and-egg kind of guy, Sam."

"So tell me about Lehrman."

"Hey, aren't you gonna give me the stroke? Ask me about the boys in San Quentin or whores we've known. Butter me up a bit before you stick it to me like that."

"You want coffee?"

"Sure."

"So tell me about Lehrman."

"I mean, he is what he is. He's a guy who needs a guy like Dr. Bagwa. I came up with the idea when I was on the train from Chicago, I read up on this guy in New York, some Oriental, who did these soul paintings. I didn't make it a night before I had these movie people lined up around the block for me to smear some colors on the canvas. That's the beauty, Sam. I can't even draw a fucking cat."

Sam scratched his face. He needed to find a cheap hotel and a shave. He hadn't slept the whole way on the train, thinking about Arbuckle and the Vigilant women, and Jose about to burst and what he was going to do with a kid without two nickels to rub together.

"Breakfast on you?"

"I'll expense it."

"How much for the goods on Lehrman?"

Sam smiled and scratched his face again. He drank some coffee. He looked at the time on a big clock over the lunch counter where workers in overalls had come in from the train yards. They carried lunch pails and punched time clocks and worked with their hands in the same place every day, getting a regular check from the bossman.

"Go ahead and tell Lehrman about me," Pete said. "The son of a bitch is broke."

"Living in that ole shack?"

"Place belongs to some fella in Boston who backs his pictures. It's his family's place and he lets Lehrman stay there. The guy is a big fucking phony."

"Coming from Pete the Fink."

"I know who I am, Sam. I don't confuse myself. Lehrman believes he's some kind of artist 'cause he makes moving pictures. He calls himself an artist with a capital *A* at least a hundred times a day. Oh, and he's a fucking psychic, too. The other day he tried for half an hour to move a saltshaker across the table. Finally when he'd closed his eyes, I moved the fucking thing and then clapped for him. I thought he was going to cry while I started telling him again about the eight principles of peace. That's what 'Bagwa means'—I read up on it at the library. You can find out all kinds of things at a library. Books make you smarter. It's true."

Pete the Fink fished into his coat pocket for a matchbook. When he opened the cover, it read BETTER YOURSELF IN TEN MINUTES A DAY.

"It's no joke," he said.

The waitress brought the hash and eggs. Pete ordered something called a French sandwich and a seltzer.

"He mention Virginia Rappe?"

"Are you putting me on? That's all he's been talking about since the girl went and got herself squished in Frisco. He's called every newspaper in the country, reversing the charges, making me send telegrams to William Randolph Hearst himself."

"About what?"

"About the dead girl. It's all bullshit about these cuff links saying 'To My Love, Henry' and all that. He doesn't even have cuff links. The bastard doesn't wear clothes except when he leaves the house. He's a nut. I mean, you get used to it, wandering around with your schlong waving around. I think he likes the breezes down there or something because I never seen him with a boner even when his girlfriend, Miss Leigh, is naked. I got to sit down and kind of cross my legs, think about things that aren't sexy like baseball, or this one time I walked into the crapper and saw my grandma in the tub. God, she had tits like flapjacks."

Pete winced with the memory.

"He knows Hearst?"

"He's fishing for money. I took the telegram to Western Union for him and thought, *Good luck*. But it wasn't two hours later that he got a goddamn telegram back from Hearst himself. Can you believe that? William Randolph *Fucking* Hearst. He answered back with two hundred dollars."

"I had a run-in with some of Hearst's people once."

"What were you doing?"

"Strike busting."

"And they call me the fink."

"So Lehrman lied about knowing the girl?"

"He talks about her too plain to make it all up in his head. Because he ain't that kind of crazy to make up things that never happened and repeat them back like they really did. I think, at the heart of it, he knows he's a phony bird. That's halfway between crazy and a con man, and that's the middle of the road, brother."

"Tell me about the girl."

"She lived with him at the mansion for maybe a year or more. He was punching her ticket but wasn't trying to make her a star. Lehrman's a doper and so I guess she probably was a doper, too. I heard from the help that she'd become a real mess and finally he threw her out. She kept on coming back, yelling at him from over the fence like some kind of cat in heat about how much she loved him. But he was done with her, moved on to Miss Leigh, and that was that."

"She ever in his pictures?"

"How should I know?" Pete asked. "I don't go see pictures. It's a fad. People will come to their senses and realize they're just looking at a big flip-book. Remember when the Jew street peddlers used to hustle those in New York? I had one with a silhouette ice-skating. The world has gone nuts. Women wanting to marry that Valentino fella after seeing his picture. Folks chasing down Charlie Chaplin in London, ripping off pieces of his clothes and trying to sell them. I mean, these people are just making pictures of what I've been doing all my life, and that makes their shit not stink. They ain't princesses or sheiks or little tramps or any of that. I remember when they used to bring actors to town in stages, like circus animals."

"What happened to the girl? After Lehrman?"

Pete looked down the counter at a waitress carrying his French sandwich. He tucked a napkin into his shirt collar over the red tie and thanked the woman, calling her sweetheart.

"I don't know."

"Can you find out for me?"

"For a price."

"I'm buying that goddamn sandwich."

"You're a smooth talker, Sam."

"Hey, Pete, I went and got myself married."

"Come on."

"It's true."

"Well, congratulations."

"A baby on the way."

"Well, there's hope for all of us."

"Amen," Sam said.

"Amen," Pete said.

"I THOUGHT I told you never to come here."

"You told me not to come to your house," the Dark Man said. "This isn't your house."

They were on the beach, and the Dark Man and Hearst followed the shoreline, salt water retreating and then breaking over Hearst's bare feet. His trousers were rolled to his knees and he carried his shoes and socks in his hands, a little dachshund trying its best to keep up with its little legs.

"What if someone saw you?" Hearst asked.

"No one saw me besides your driver."

"That's George. He's not my driver."

"Quite a spread."

"It belongs to a quite talented and beautiful lady."

"Your mistress."

Hearst stopped walking. The surf came up high above his ankles as he stared at the man. "I was told you're good at your job."

"That's true."

"Then please do not speak unless spoken to. Do not arrive anywhere unannounced. Am I understood?"

"Yes, sir, Mr. Hearst."

"I note a tone of sarcasm."

"No, sir."

"I suppose here is as good as anywhere."

"You wanna know if Fatty killed her?"

"Well, did he?"

The Dark Man shrugged. He still had on his dress shoes but had removed his hat and his black hair whipped down across the ragged half ear. His wool suit and jacket were too warm for the climate, but the man didn't seem to notice or to perspire.

"That's a question I can't answer," the Dark Man said. "It seems Miss Rappe and Mr. Arbuckle are the only two who know. The door was closed."

"What about your man?" Hearst said. "The one who arranged the party?"

"What about him?"

"Does he know?"

"No."

"This whole affair has been quite troubling," Hearst said, picking up the little brown dachshund and rubbing the dog's ears. He smelled the dog's fur and the scent reminded him of Bavaria and the wonderful food and people. How he loved Germany.

"I didn't come for money," the Dark Man said.

"I would hope not."

"The police know about Mrs. Delmont," he said. "They know about the cons. They probably know about her string of husbands, too. I don't expect the district attorney in San Francisco to keep the same level of interest."

Hearst nodded and looked down at the much shorter man. He kissed the little brown dog on her head and smelled the sweet scent. He just simply smiled at the dark, very troubling man. The man was compact and muscular, giving the impression of a loaded spring about to snap.

"The case may fall apart," said the Dark Man, adding, "Mr. Hearst."

"That's where you're wrong."

"How's that?"

"Mr. Arbuckle's trial is already over."

Hearst whistled for the dog and walked briskly away from the man, leaving him to chew on the idea.

"How 'bout a ride?"

"No thanks," Sam said.

"It's me, Daisy. Remember the Old Poodle Dog? I was the girl with the shotgun."

"I remember."

The Hupmobile trailed Sam along Aliso Street, the engine clicking and whirring, some faceless dry agent at the wheel. The girl rested her head across her forearm on the open window, trying to play it blue and lonesome. Sam kept walking and checking his watch.

"Where you headed?" she asked.

"I'm gonna hop a streetcar over to Echo Park."

"What's in Echo Park?"

"Mabel Normand."

"Mabel and Fatty," she said. "What a team."

"You've been following me since I stepped off the Owl."

"You bet."

"Why?"

"Looking for a bootlegger."

"I'm not."

"Does the name Hibbard mean anything to you?" she asked.

The Hupmobile drifted on at about five miles per hour. A machine behind them honked its horn twice before speeding by.

"What about Jack Lawrence?"

"Nope."

"You without a machine and us without a lead," she said.

"What's in it for me?"

"A rest for your feet."

"I like your hat," Sam said.

Still resting her head across her forearm, she rolled her eyes upward at the little velvet hat cocked just so.

"Nice angle."

"Yeah? I thought so, too."

Sam stopped walking. He checked the time. He steadied his breath.

"Get in," said Daisy Simpkins, famous female dry agent.

THEY DROVE BACK into the downtown, to a building called the Bradbury, a big, old hulking brick structure built before the turn of the century. The roof was made of glass and the inside had been designed like the exposed guts of a machine. Scrolled iron balconies boxed the open atrium, with two caged elevators zipping up and down, large iron wheels turning whirring cables. The light inside seemed almost to be magnified, more real than it was on the street, and Sam followed the girl and the other agent across the big, wide lobby and to a staircase they mounted and followed, and Sam looked at the elevators zipping up and down and stopped to rest on the second floor, his hand on an iron banister as he caught his breath.

"You okay?" Daisy asked.

"Dandy."

They followed the balcony ledge on the third floor to an office advertising U.S. GOVERNMENT on the frosted glass. Inside, it bustled with the activity of a dozen or so men working in their shirtsleeves and ties, talking into telephones and typing out reports. One woman waited at a front desk and led them to a back office, where Sam was introduced to a delicate young man named Earl Lynn and a toadlike older man who didn't get out of his chair to shake hands.

He grunted at Daisy.

He was Lynn's father.

Earl Lynn was in his early twenties and handsome in a girlish way, with perfect slick hair, a flawless shave, and long thick eyelashes that seemed to flutter nervously. He took a seat by an open window and crossed his legs at the knee. He wore silk socks with small gold designs and a vest that matched his pin-striped suit. He had a rose on his lapel and smelled of flowers.

The flower smell was soon covered by the scent of Old Dad's wet stogie that he relit with fat-thumbed flourish. His son tried to get a cigarette in an ivory holder going but failed at least three times.

"Mr. Lynn is an actor," Daisy said. "He contacted us yesterday about the Arbuckle party."

"You were there?"

"My God, no," Earl Lynn said. He pulled the cigarette from the holder and broke it in two as if somehow it was the cigarette's fault for failing to catch fire.

"Mr. Lynn had a run-in with one of the party guests," Daisy said. She found a spot on the end of the desk, sat down, and crossed her thin arms across her bosom. They were nice bosoms, high and tight, and Sam had to redirect his attention back to the young man.

"Maude Delmont claimed she got the high hard one from my son and carried his seed," said the father.

"Father," Earl Lynn said.

"Six months ago, I paid that woman five thousand dollars to peddle that story somewhere else."

"You and Maude?" Sam asked.

Earl Lynn tucked his tongue into a cheek and rolled his eyes. "No. Absolutely not."

"But you did know her?" Sam asked.

"We went to the same parties. Knew the same people."

"What people?"

Lynn named some and they meant nothing to Sam, Hollywood people, but he wrote them down anyway.

"But you two weren't . . . ?"

"My Lord, she's an older woman!"

"So you got roped."

He nodded.

"Why'd your old man pay if the baby wasn't yours?"

"There was no baby," Lynn said. "But I have an image, characters known to women in the world, and to think that I had impregnated a married woman . . . Well, it's that simple."

Sam took a seat beside Daisy. Even from the back office, you could hear the giant iron wheels turning and moving and groaning and stopping the elevators. An elevator stopped near the floor and he could hear the gate slide open and then slam shut, the wheels turning again. Sam felt like he was on the inside of a clock.

"What do you do, Mr. Lynn?"

"Me?" the old man grunted. His head looked to be the size of a melon, with a nice slab of fat hanging from his insignificant chin. He resembled a contented hog.

"Oil."

Sam nodded.

"Why'd you call the dry agents?"

Earl Lynn tried with a second cigarette in the ivory holder and finally got the smoke going and watched it trail up to the ceiling and then stared back at Daisy and Sam. "I thought the government should know what kind of people were at this party. Mrs. Delmont surely had something to do with that liquor. She's a lush. A hophead, too."

"You think she conned Mr. Arbuckle?"

Earl Lynn sucked on the ivory and held the holder loose in his long fingers. "I would not be surprised by the depths of her evil. She once got me drunk and tried to unbuckle my trousers."

"The horror," Sam said.

"Can we go?" the old man barked. "This man is a tiresome smart aleck."

"Did you recognize the others?" Daisy asked. "At the party?"

"I know Lowell Sherman, of course. We play tennis. But he'd never be mixed up with a woman like Mrs. Delmont. That was my own error in judgment."

"The other women?" Sam asked.

"I met Virginia Rappe once. She didn't impress me. A little tart. A leech."

"Fishback? Semnacher?"

"Al Semnacher is the one who introduced me to Mrs. Delmont," Earl

Lynn said. The tip of his cigarette had grown long and fell off with a plop in his lap. He brushed off the ash with lots of busied annoyance.

"How did you know him?" Sam asked.

"He's in the business. Haven't you read the papers? He books acts for Mr. Grauman at the Million Dollar."

Sam smiled at Earl Lynn and then back at the fat father, who'd rested his thick hands across the top of his stomach. The old fat man looked like he might doze off in the thick leather chair, the cigar smoldering in the corner of his mouth.

Sam tucked a Pinkerton's card in the man's stubby fingers. He jostled awake with a snort.

"We'd like to see you at the trial," Sam said.

Earl Lynn said it would be his pleasure.

"Does the name Jack Lawrence mean anything to you?" Daisy asked.

"Should it?" Lynn asked.

"He supplied the liquor, and maybe the girls, too," Daisy said. "Mr. Lawrence may be the source of the biggest bootlegging ring in California."

Lynn repeated again that he didn't know the fella. His father seemed to grow awake very quickly, fast enough to stand and relight the cigar before walking out. "Okay? All right? Are we done here?"

Sam took the fat man's seat. He could still smell Earl Lynn's perfume.

"He's a pretty one," Daisy said as the door closed.

She sat behind the desk that displayed a brass marker reading DIRECTOR and lit a cigarette. She placed her feet up on the desk, and finally said, "Why won't Arbuckle name the man who brought the liquor?"

A small fan on the table whirred and spun.

"Besides the confession leading to a federal indictment?"

"Besides that."

"Maybe he's a standup guy," Sam said. "That's what I'd call a fella who doesn't rat on his friends."

"You know what I'd call a fella who buttons up with his ass in a sling?"

"Please tell me."

"A fool."

15

The Arbuckle mansion door was wide-open and Sam followed the hall to a great room with wide, buffed plank floors, a big bank of windows, and not a stick of furniture. Roscoe sat on the floor in a square of sunlight shining in from high windows and watched as his dog Luke walked from bush to bush, marking his territory. He sat like a sullen child on his butt, with his legs spread, holding a cigarette in his fingers and barely noting the two entering the room. He wore fine tweed trousers and shoes with silk socks.

His red suspenders hung over his bare, meaty torso.

"Mr. Arbuckle?"

He turned.

"I work for Mr. Dominguez."

"I guess you haven't heard."

"Heard what?"

"You'll hear it."

"I'd like a second."

"Who's the skirt?"

"This is Miss Simpkins. She's a dry agent."

"And you brought her here?"

"She's not interested in you," Sam said.

"That's a switch," Roscoe said.

"She's looking for a man named Jack Lawrence who delivered liquor to the party."

"Don't know him."

Sam raised his eyebrows and Daisy opened a pair of French doors out onto a large patio. She tugged away a baseball from Luke and pitched it far off into a blanket of freshly cut green grass.

"She's okay," Sam said.

"I'll say."

"I'm having a tough time running down folks who knew the Rappe girl," Sam said. "I understand you knew her when she worked at Sennett's. But the only person I can find who knew her is Henry Lehrman. I guess you worked with him?"

"He used to direct some of my pictures," Roscoe said, still sitting in the same childlike pose. "We used to call him Pathé. Like the French picture company. The rumor was that he'd told DeMille that he'd worked for them in Paris. It was all a bunch of hooey, but the name stuck. He's an arrogant bastard. Have you read the letter he wrote about me? He called me a goddamn beast and said he wanted to kill me. He knew I didn't do a thing to Virginia. He knows I'm not that kind of fella."

"Tell me about the girl."

"Listen," Roscoe said, pointing the end of a half-smoked cigarette for emphasis, "I've been over this ten thousand times with Frank. I met her a few times, knew her when she was with Lehrman. She was cute. A lot of fun. When she showed up at the St. Francis, I hadn't seen her for years. I barely remembered her name. I was in the shower, and when I came out—"

Sam held up his hand and shook his head. "I don't need that part. Just who would know the girl?"

Roscoe smoked some more and thought. He wobbled as he tried to get to his feet and then wandered out of the room, and Sam heard water running and then a commode flush and for a second thought about showing himself out. But soon Roscoe was back and asked if Sam would like some coffee because the coffeepot was about the only thing he had left.

"That and a skillet."

"What about friends outside Lehrman?"

"Hold on," Roscoe said and walked to the foot of an endless oak banister to the second floor and yelled up for Minty. Minta Durfee appeared at the top of the landing and asked what he wanted, and he told her about Sam, and she said she'd be down in a minute.

"Can you believe she came all the way from New York for me? Have you met her ma? She's a peach."

Sam sat at a small, wobbly table that was dwarfed by the size of the kitchen. The four chairs that surrounded it were crude and mismatched and looked as if they'd been picked up at a rummage sale.

Minta came into the kitchen wearing a flowing red robe and a kerchief on her head. She smiled at Sam and said it was nice to see a familiar face and then poured him a cup of coffee to go with his cigarette. All of them sat at the little table.

Outside the window, they could see Daisy playing with Luke.

"Who's the skirt?" Minta asked.

Roscoe laughed. They drank their coffee and made idle talk for a while, and then the subject rolled back to Virginia Rappe.

"I was gone by then," Minta said. "Have you talked to Mabel?"

"Minta and Mabel," Roscoe said. "My girls."

"I was headed there this afternoon," Sam said. "Are you sure she'll talk to me?"

"Sure thing," Minta said. "She'll like you. You're a handsome fella, Sam."

Sam smiled at her.

Roscoe smoked and made a puzzled smile. He snapped his fingers and leaned into the table. "Say, I know you from somewhere. You ever spent time in Bisbee?"

"Nope."

"But I know you. I'm not crazy. Sometimes it comes to me, people I've met. I may not have even spoken to them, but I remember a face."

"The Palace Hotel," Sam said. "Last week."

Roscoe looked at him.

"You should really put on a shirt, Roscoe," Minta said.

"Did Frank introduce us?"

"I was sitting in the lobby in a chair reading a paper. You stepped off the elevators and spotted me right off."

"Did I say something?"

"No, but you gave me a look that coulda melted paint."

"I suppose I took you for a newsboy. You look like a writer."

"No such luck," Sam said. "I only made it to eighth grade."

"Self-made man," Roscoe said. "How 'bout a drink?"

"Are you kidding?" Sam asked. "That's the toughest, meanest dry agent in the state of California out there playing with your dog."

"She's got a hell of a figure," Minta said. "She with you?"

Sam felt his face heat but he managed a smile. "I suppose one drink. You wouldn't happen to have Scotch?"

ROSCOE WAS DRUNK and two hours late for his meeting with Al Zukor. But he was clean-shaven and showered and smelling sweet as he stepped into the dimly lit room at Musso & Frank's and straightened his tie. The bourbon had given him kind of a loose, resolved dignity, as it seemed to him—maybe he only imagined—that all voices fell silent, forks stopped scraping on plates, and the clink of glasses had all but ceased. In his standard corner was little Mr. Zukor in a high red leather booth, and the little white-headed man stood and smiled and waved Roscoe over. Roscoe knew that being seen in public with an outcast truly pained Al, but it was all show business, and being given a good handshake by Al Zukor in Musso & Frank's was rock-solid.

He made his way through the maze of tables following the same little maître d' that was always there but whose name Roscoe could never remember. And he'd about made it to that back booth when he spotted Broncho Billy at a side table over candlelight, guffawing it up with a couple tarts in sequins and hats that looked as if they were made with dead squirrels, and so Roscoe waved over to Mr. Zukor and stumbled up to Broncho Billy and asked him with great sincerity, as he—Roscoe—straightened his diamond cuff links, where the two broads killed that squirrel.

Broncho Billy stopped the guffawing and stood, slipped his pearl Stetson back on his head, and shifted his gunless belt on his waist. He stood toe to toe with Roscoe, and Roscoe looked at the little man with the big nose and bigger ears. Billy sucked a tooth, trying to figure out what to say.

"You have a good time in Frisco?" Roscoe asked.

"Someone has to make the picture business clean."

"If you keep hanging out with broads like that, your pecker is gonna turn green."

Little Mr. Zukor inserted himself between Billy and Roscoe and smiled, sweet and calming, but tough, too. Because even though Mr. Zukor was a pint-sized little bastard who used to sell furs on street corners, he was a hard-edged son of a bitch that no one in their right mind wanted to cross if they ever wanted to step foot on a picture lot again.

"Our table."

Roscoe followed and squeezed into the booth. Every bastard and bitch in the restaurant craned their necks to get a good look at the zoo animal. Roscoe rubbed his face and straightened the cuffs of his shirt under his pressed suit jacket. He took a deep breath as a waiter laid a napkin in his lap and handed him the menu.

"How 'bout a fucking drink?" Roscoe said.

Mr. Zukor made a face, as if Roscoe had just dropped a turd on the table, and sent away the waiter with a flick of the hand.

"Aren't you hungry?"

"I'd like a drink."

"Not here," Mr. Zukor said. "Not like this."

Roscoe shrugged. "I'm plastered anyway. So what's the difference?"

"That's a spiffy suit you got there, Roscoe."

"Bought it in Frisco," Roscoe said. "Labor Day. You might've heard about a little party I threw. I crushed some woman while I was giving her a solid lay."

"Please keep your voice down."

"These people are cannibals," Roscoe said. "They'll eat your flesh from your bone."

"It's a tough business."

Roscoe leaned back into the comfort of the leather booth and lit a cigarette with a gold tip. He removed a spot of tobacco from his tongue and met the stare of a beautiful woman across the way. When she matched eyes with him, she turned her head.

"Let's talk about Frank Dominguez," Zukor said.

"What's to talk about? You fired him."

"I didn't fire him. I discussed your trial with him. We'll need the best."

"Frank *is* the best."

"Frank is your drinking buddy, the guy you play poker with when you're feeling lonesome. Not the best, Roscoe. Maybe down here, but not up there."

"So you want this McNab fella? Who's he?"

"The best defense attorney we can buy."

"I didn't do this, Al. I did not touch that girl and they got no one to say I did."

"Sometimes men become a target for hate. When I was a kid, people used to say they were cursed. You're a cursed fella right now. But a fella I got a lot of dough wrapped up in."

"The checks have stopped."

"They'll resume after the trial. I have investors worried."

"What if I'm guilty?"

"I don't think it will come to that."

"How many cities have banned my pictures? How many?"

"Let's eat, Roscoe. Just like we used to. Let's laugh and remember old songs. Okay, friend?"

"I'd like to walk right over to that Broncho Billy and piss in his drink."

"I don't think that would be such a good idea."

"I don't want you to fire Frank," Roscoe said. The words sounded slurred, but he goddamn well meant them. "Okay?"

"He's not fired," Al said, spreading his hands wide, pleading. "He served you well during all that preliminary mumbo jumbo."

"I need him."

"You'll be fine," Al said. "McNab is just a little, um, insurance."

Roscoe looked across the room at all the laughing and talking starting up again. The people had stopped staring. In fact they weren't looking at Roscoe at all. Even when his eyes would meet another's, it was as if he was invisible, or, worse, just another Joe.

Roscoe pinched the bridge of his nose, trying to breathe. His face felt hot and moist, and he just stared at the blue of the linen-covered table. Tears dropped one after another and he wiped them away before looking up again.

He felt Al's small hand rubbing circles on his back and again sending away the waiter, telling him to just give them a minute.

"Mein Kind," Mr. Zukor said.

"Why does everyone leave me?" Roscoe said, saying it as a question for himself. "Why do they do that?"

It was midnight, and Sam rode with Daisy way the hell out of town on Wilshire to the Ambassador Hotel and the Cocoanut Grove nightclub. Long after she'd killed the machine's engine, they sat there in the front seat of the open cab and watched a long line of Kissels and Kings and Nashes and Hayneses wheeling up to those carved wooden doors where the crowd walked up the red carpet and was swallowed into the great mouth of the pulsing shell, jazz floating out on the warm wind.

"So how do we know who's Lawrence?" Sam asked.

"I know a fella who knows a fella."

"And that fella's gonna give you the nod."

"Right."

"Shouldn't we go inside?"

"You're a puzzle, Pinkerton."

"How so?"

"You're a lunger, aren't you?"

"I am."

"Still running down dank alleys and climbing fire escapes and beating the truth out of stoolies."

"I don't run so much."

"And you wear a ring."

"I do."

"And you have a wife."

"She goes with the ring."

"Children?"

"One on the way."

Daisy nodded, both hands placed on the wooden steering wheel, watching the line of cars move in a slow, delicate dance like the mechanical turn of a carousel. There was the opening of the car door, a hand for the lady, and the slick greasing of the palm. Sam rubbed his jaw, finding himself thirsty, and balanced his hat on his knee. He looked over at Daisy, in her silk dress and soft turban, clenching that tight little jaw. She'd changed into a dress with a fur collar and the warm wind made the fur ruffle as if it were alive.

"How 'bout you?" Sam asked.

Daisy kept watching the door and the carousel movement, and Sam noted that she saw it all in the exact same way. "How 'bout let's have a drink?"

"Don't you find that hypocritical?" he asked.

"I call it an agent's job to not make themselves known. Hell, it's in the manual."

"Dry agents come with a manual?"

"On some things."

"And the rest?"

"The rest is all intuition, Pinkerton. Don't you ever find yourself in a situation that ain't according to Hoyle and you have to just use the noodle?"

The Cocoanut Grove was a big bubble of jazz and smoke and cocktails and laughter. Stars twinkled in a plaster-domed sky. There were twenty-foot palm trees that looked so real, Sam had to reach out and touch them to check his eyes—a woman at the bar said they'd been brought straight from the set of *The Sheik*. Fat paper lanterns hung from the drooping fronds and brightly colored tents had been set up all over the nightclub, where people smoked and laughed, walking in and out of silky floating curtains like a hazy, smoky dream. Women lounged on large pillows and danced on tables, a paper moon going down over a painted lake far on the wall, a horizon that made you feel unsteady, almost as if you could drown yourself in it if you stared long enough. And there was Daisy at a bar with a bartender dressed as a sultan, and Sam watched the drape of her hair down the reach of her long neck and the elegant placement of her thin arms across the bar, and she turned to Sam and smiled with that red mouth.

And Sam smiled back.

A mass of people separated them, but Sam could see through them to Daisy, the way your eyes can make out shapes and patterns of trees and roads through the fog. There was laughter and dancing and jazz and the sound of a trumpet.

He walked toward her.

Daisy put her finger to her nose and sloughed it off, turning to a skinny fella in a black suit bopping his way though the party. Sam could not see the man's face but noted the way his shoulder blades cut up into the material of his jacket and the long droop of the neck. He walked with speed—deliberate yet loose and disjointed.

Sam followed him out onto the hill and then lost him in the mass of a hundred machines, finding him again as he piled into a Studebaker Big Six, Sam knowing it was a Studebaker by the insignia as it shot past close enough to feel the engine's heat on his face.

When he turned, there was the Hupmobile idling next to him.

"Do I need to spell it out for you?" Daisy asked.

16

The Studebaker drove east, back through downtown, with its flashing signs and jostling streetcars, and joined up with Valley Boulevard until there was nothing but pasture and produce trucks and lonesome gas stations and the odd farmhouse or seed store. Daisy hung back a quarter mile, watching the Big Six's courtesy lamp on the driver's side like a beacon. Sam commented on the lamp being a great thing and Daisy shot back that it didn't really matter because there was nothing else out here besides farmers and cows and orange trees. The hills were silver and rolling in the moonlight, the wind coming through the Hupmobile's cab warm on Sam's face, the dashboard glowing under the instrument panel and showing off Daisy's lean legs as she mashed the accelerator when the Studebaker would disappear around another lone turn.

VISIT GAY'S LION FARM read the billboard. At El Monte on Valley Boulevard.

"You don't think?" Sam asked.

"I don't like animals."

The Studebaker rolled off a little access road and Daisy slowed to a near stop. There was a dusty lot and a broad stucco entrance bragging about the place being *Internationally Famous,* and from his vantage point Sam could see the figure of the lean man walk through the gates and disappear. Daisy followed, parked, and killed the engine. The only other machine in the lot besides the Hupmobile and the Big Six was a long flatbed truck with slatted sides.

Flies buzzed in the back of the truck, and in the moonlight Sam could see rancid meat and blood.

The entrance gate was open, and they followed the man down a winding path of crushed pebbles. Signs to the lion cages were fashioned from bamboo and oak trees canopied the path, past small red barns and little kiosks that sold postcards and stuffed lions and gum and cigarettes. They were well down the path when they heard the first scream.

"What's that?"

"The King of the Beasts," Sam said.

"They keep 'em locked up, don't they?"

"One would hope."

There were more screams and roars—definitely roars—and Daisy stepped back from the lead to take a stride beside Sam, too worried to lead but too proud to follow. The trees looked old, spared from the bulldozer and plow, and it all seemed natural and prehistoric in the moonlight.

They stopped and listened for steps but only heard the screams until the screams seemed to be coming from all around them. It was a great ring, a chain-link circle as wide around as a baseball field, at least thirty feet high, with bleachers and long nets strung from what looked like telephone poles.

"Where are they?" she whispered.

"I don't see 'em."

"You see him?"

"I don't," Sam said.

"This was a goddamn fool thing to do."

They kept on the path, over a little bamboo bridge and toward a long red barn lit up with tiny white bulbs. Sam nearly ran into Daisy when she stopped and pulled him behind the large trunk of an oak. From the barn, an engine started, and soon another flatbed truck, identical to the one parked in front, came rambling down the path, breezing past their hiding place and slowing to an idle by the giant cage. The headlights lit up the center of the ring, and the long, lean man, Jack Lawrence, unlocked a gate and walked inside. Sam and Daisy stood watching at the narrow spot in the path well back from the idling truck.

They watched Lawrence squat on his haunches and walk backward with the edge of a tarp, the dust and gravel falling away and choking the night air. The beams of the headlights caught the dust as Lawrence emerged into the light and removed one large wooden beam and then another before disappearing for several moments down below and returning with a large crate. They could hear the bottles jostle and rattle against one another as he slid the crate into the truck and went back for more. On his third trip down into the hidden hole, Daisy walked down the path and into the headlight beams and locked the cage door.

Sam followed.

Soon Lawrence emerged with another flat of hooch and walked to the closed doors and looked puzzled, before he saw Daisy and asked, "What gives?"

Daisy twisted her knee inward and removed the pearl-handled .22 and aimed it through a diamond in the chain-link. "Got to hand it you."

"Who are you?"

"Daisy Simpkins, federal dry agent."

"This isn't what you think."

"What is it?"

"It's mineral oil," Lawrence said with a noticeable Australian accent. "For the animals."

"Sam, hold 'im."

Sam walked up to the man, who was still hoisting the crate in his arm, and he pulled a gun and showed it. He winked at Lawrence.

"I didn't do nothing."

Sam smiled back.

"Hey," Lawrence said. "What's she doing? Hey!"

Sam heard the rusted bars and the metal gates swing open one after another. The cries of the lions had stopped, and as the animals filled the ring through their now-open chutes there was soft, contented purring. Lawrence dropped the hooch. The bottles cracked and broke, and Sam shook his head at the damn shame of it all.

"Keep the gun on him," Daisy called out.

"Them animals will kill me," Lawrence said.

He rattled the door and Sam squeezed the padlock with a tight click.

The purring became more insistent, and in the headlights Sam noted one male, with a large, regal mane, and three females. The male hung back, his noticeable set of balls moving to and fro, while the females circled the bootlegger.

A long, trailing spot of wetness showed on Lawrence's trousers.

"Tell us about Frisco," Daisy said.

"It's a nice town," Lawrence said.

Daisy fired off the .22 at his feet. The cats growled.

"I'll shoot you in the leg, sure as shit," Daisy said. "You brought the booze to Arbuckle."

The man held up his hands in the light. The truck continued to idle.

"We met at this garage," Lawrence said. "This man opened his trunk and we loaded him down. I was paid and the man drove away."

"Who was it?"

"His name was Hibbard."

"First name?"

"I don't know. Jesus, I don't know."

"Hibbard," Daisy repeated. "The stuff you brought matched cases we took out of a joint called the Old Poodle Dog in Frisco. That jackass brandy came in the same bottles. The Scotch was bonded out of Canada."

"So what?"

"You work for H. F. LaPeer."

"Never heard of him," Lawrence said.

"If those big cats smell a little blood, they're gonna want a taste," Daisy said.

"You're crazy."

"When's LaPeer's next shipment?"

One of the female lions sauntered over and ran herself between's Lawrence's legs, purring and growling. The male jumped from five feet away, knocking Lawrence flat on his back, his screams not unlike those of a little girl. The male straddled his chest, balls in Lawrence's face, and yawned. Another female licked at the man's hand while yet another sniffed at his crotch.

"I can find out."

"What's that?"

In a whisper, "I can find out. I can find out. I can find out."

"And what about the Arbuckle party?"

"It's all I know. Jesus, God. Holy hell. Mother Mary."

"What do you think?" Daisy asked.

"I think the man has been properly motivated," Sam said.

Roscoe found Freddie Fishback at the Cocoanut Grove bar at midnight, talking to a barmaid wearing a beaded headdress and veil, a golden bodice, and a long flowing skirt. She was laughing at one of his jokes and Freddie was laughing, too, until he saw the shadow of Roscoe over him and his smile simplified into something more like Freddie, droll and impersonal, and he offered his hand.

Roscoe looked at his hand as if it were a dead mackerel.

Freddie shrugged and puffed on his cigaratte.

The girl in the Arabian getup looked to Roscoe and bit her lip before moving on back down the bar. People were whispering and pointing, and Roscoe didn't give a good goddamn.

"You look very sharp," Freddie said, his Romanian accent more pronounced. He wore a tuxedo. He was very dark, with black hair and eyes. The kind of guy with a heavy brow and thick fur on his hands.

"Your housekeeper said you were in New York."

Freddie took a sip of his cocktail and said, "She was wrong."

"I got ditched when you stepped off the *Harvard*," Roscoe said. "I pulled my Pierce off the ship and waited for you to load your bags."

"I don't like to wait. Do you mind, Roscoe? People are staring."

"You'll get used to it."

Freddie turned back to the bar. Roscoe touched his shoulder.

"Don't be a stupid man," Freddie said and raised his eyebrows. "The papers?"

Freddie ordered another drink, a cocktail served in a champagne glass with a cherry. "The soldiers made this up during the war," Freddie said. "Call it a French 75. Like the big guns. How 'bout a drink? We drink and we forget, okay?"

"How 'bout I shove that champagne glass up your ass?"

"Why not a Coke bottle?"

Roscoe gripped Freddie by the front of his tuxedo shirt and twisted him into his face. He ground his teeth so hard, he could hear them grind and pop deep into his jaw.

"I only wanted to ask you a question," Roscoe said. He could feel a barman or a doorman or someone's hands on his arm. "Just a question."

Freddie looked at him. The champagne cocktail had rolled from his fingers onto the bar, the thin glass breaking into shards. Freddie stared at him and breathed, a little smile on his lips.

"Why'd you bring her there? Why Virginia? You knew, didn't you?"

Freddie's smile widened.

"You goddamn son of a bitch."

SAM AND DAISY stayed up that night, finding an Owl drugstore downtown just like the one at the bottom of the Flood Building. Daisy ordered eggs. Sam ordered toast. They both had coffee and cigarettes, which was a fine thing to Sam at four a.m. when you were too tired to sleep.

"What's it all about, Sam?" she asked.

"A good shot of rye and a warm bed."

"You don't let anyone get in there, do you?"

"In where?"

She moved her knuckles over to his forehead and lightly knocked.

"What about you, sister?"

She sipped her coffee, elbows on the lunch counter, watching the fat man at the grill burning up a steak, bacon, and some home fries. Outside, a streetcar zipped past, littering electric sparks in the leftover night.

"You got a man?"

"Nope."

"Family?"

"Back east."

"Did you see the set of balls on that lion?"

"I did," she said. "That one's got it all figured out."

"So why you working for the G?"

"What if I told you H. F. LaPeer killed the man I loved?"

"I'd tell you to peddle your story to the pictures."

Daisy drank more coffee. The fat cook laid down a plate of ham and eggs and she didn't touch it. Sam placed a pack of Fatimas on the counter.

"That's not true, is it?" Sam asked. "About your man?"

Daisy shrugged. She reached for his cigarettes and lit up. The smoke was in her eyes and she fanned it away.

"Why do you gals paint your lips in the center?"

"The Kewpie doll effect," she said, pursing her lips and closing her eyes. She opened them and parted her lips and smiled at Sam. He turned back to his plate and grabbed a slice of dry toast.

"You don't give a damn about Prohibition, do you?" he asked.

"I didn't make the law."

"But it bothers you that some places are off the books? Like the Cocoanut Grove?"

She shrugged again, looking good every time she shrugged, and took a bite of eggs. Her soft light blond hair tucked behind her ears and a slouch hat tucked over her head. Sam reached out and traced the edge of her jaw with his middle finger and she cut her eyes at him but kept eating, and he kept his eyes on her until she met his gaze.

Her eyes flicked back to the window and Sam glanced over his shoulder, watching a very dark, very compact man in a black suit staring in the window. He turned back to her and removed his fingers and hand and caught his smoldering cigarette in the ashtray. He looked back to the window and saw the dark man again.

Sam left his toast and laid down some coin and walked out the door. Daisy followed, and soon they were on the street, catching the back of the man and his dark hat and long coat, a coat too warm for Los Angeles. Sam was not shadowing him but calling out to the man's back, which slumped as his legs pumped fast around the corner. He heard the start of a machine and Sam called out to Daisy to retrieve the Hupmobile.

He saw the car turn and pass him with a lot of speed, and he caught the dark man's profile again, all so familiar from somewhere, some town, some old report.

"You could've said something back there," Daisy said.

"I know him."

"Who is he?"

"I'm not sure."

"So why do we care?"

"It wasn't his face," Sam said. "It's because he ran."

The road led a quarter mile up the mountain into more cleared roads, more gravel and half-finished houses and open lots. Sam jumped out of the machine and searched the landscape, with his .32 in hand, for shadows and movement, finding only the gentle flickering of eucalyptus leaves and the burning smell of a big ancient oak on a smoldering pile. He rounded a large stack of brick and timber and made his way into a house without a roof, the ceiling big and black and pockmarked with bright stars, seeming not as real as those at the Cocoanut Grove.

He listened for feet and heard none.

A flash of headlights crossed over the open mountain ground and Daisy skidded to a stop and hopped out of the little automobile. She followed Sam on foot up a hill and into the elbow of an embankment. There were poured foundations and clearing machines. Fat, gnarled trees had been left naked in the cleared land and they looked prehistoric and skeletal in the moonlight.

They heard an engine crank and saw headlight beams flash from the back of a hill, and then the car was up and over the hill and coming straight for them. Sam pulled Daisy into him and around the back of a brick pile, and the car left dust and smoke and taillights as it disappeared over the lip of the mountain and down into the curving roads leading back to the city.

Daisy ran to the Hupmobile and circled back for Sam, soon catching the glow of taillights appearing and disappearing around curves and more straightaways, and then she headed west down a fire road, the bounce of the car nearly throwing Sam from his seat. Daisy smiled, grinning with her big white teeth, and leaned forward into the wheel, mashing the accelerator for all it was worth, skidding and spinning down through the dust and gravel, the beams catching the fender of the machine they followed. She drove through a tunnel of tree branches and across more cleared land, up the mountain and down again, and looping back on another fire road, coming out this time into a narrow entrance where the road just stopped.

There were giant earthmoving machines with large bucket scoops and heavy tracks as wide as a car. The car they followed had stopped cold at the mountain wall but then doubled back and idled.

The earth around them carved out like a huge bowl.

Sam told Daisy to switch off the lights and the two piled out of the car, moving for the rear and glancing around corners, waiting for the dark man to make his next move.

A few seconds later, the man fired. It was a big goddamn gun, something like a .44 that a man could feel hard into his elbow and shoulder and which could deafen an ear a bit, too.

Sam responded with a couple shots from the .32 that sounded tinny and small but clacked and echoed in the big earthen bowl. They squatted down behind a rear tire, and the man fired again, Sam and Daisy both covering their heads, the solid *blam, blam, blam* from the .44 like a drum all around them.

The bowl felt damn-near Roman to Sam, as he waited for the dark man to either speed forward his machine or keep trading bullets with them.

"I can't see the bastard."

"I hope he can't see us."

Sam squeezed off another few rounds from the edge of the Hupmobile. *Blam, blam, blam.*

The radiator cap blew off Daisy's machine and steam shot out.

"Goddamnit," she said.

Another big shot from the .44 and a tire was out.

Sam reached into his coat pocket and reloaded some more bullets. The .44 answered before he could even aim.

"I think you pissed him off," Sam said.

"Me?"

The big black car of unknown make or model, just a big goddamn closed-cab machine, built up speed, heading straight for Daisy's little two-seater, as Sam squeezed off all six, aiming straight between the headlights and up for the driver. But it just kept coming, sounding like a choir out of hell.

Y ou're lucky you weren't killed," Minta Durfee said.

It was early afternoon the next day and Minta and Sam walked the ringed path of Echo Lake, not far from the Mack Sennett Stage. Men rowed boats with their honeys relaxing, the men trying to not break a sweat with their suits busting at the seams. There were flower gardens and park benches, tall palm trees and drooping, tired willows dangling their branches into the water. Swans shuffled their way through the tall grass and into the lake, making it seem so damn easy, all the action going on below the surface.

"You drew your weapon on him," Minta said. "You stood strong while his machine raced toward you."

"I squeezed off a few rounds so he'd know I was armed," Sam said. "He could've killed us if he'd wanted."

"But you protected that dry agent. That's what matters."

Sam scratched his cheek and they kept going around the lake, this the second pass on the loop.

"She tackled me out of the way," Sam said. "The son of a bitch in the car kept going and sideswiped her Hupmobile. Nearly knocked the damn thing over."

"And then you shot the man."

"He got away."

"And how did you get back?"

"We walked."

"And Miss Simpkins?"

"She's fine," Sam said. "She headed back to deal with the busted machine. She waited till it was daylight 'cause she didn't care for all the coyotes."

"Did you see many?"

Sam smiled. "I told her I saw hundreds. All of 'em with mean red eyes."

"Did she really lock that bootlegger in a cage with lions?"

"She enjoyed it."

"You're quite the storyteller, Sam."

Minta and Sam left the loop and walked across an arced bridge to a small island in the center of the lake. Minta wore a wide-brimmed straw hat with a big-flowered dress that hugged her full frame. Sam offered her a cigarette but she declined, landing on the island and pointing out a small bench.

"So, tell me more about your sleuthing in Chicago."

"I found the woman who'd raised the girl, a Mrs. J. Hardebach. By the way, the girl's name is just plain ole Rapp. She added the *e* and accenting after she'd returned from a trip to Paris."

"What else?"

"I told Mr. Dominguez most of this."

Sam smoked and thought, a brief pause. "Let me hear it again, if you don't mind."

Minta took a deep breath.

"The girl was born in 1894 to woman named Mabel Rapp who worked as a chorus girl and perhaps a prostitute. The father was either a big Chicago banker or British nobility. No one seems to buy that one. Mabel died when Virginia was eleven and Virginia went to live with her grandmother. Before she was sixteen, the girl was pulling up her skirt for the asking. She had a total of five abortions and gave birth to one child. A daughter."

"You're good," Sam said. "So, where's the daughter?"

"Given to an orphanage."

"Is there record of that?"

"I don't know."

"Go on."

"Virginia's grandmother died ten years ago and that's when she went to live with Mrs. Hardebach. This was after she'd had the child. Apparently Mrs. Hardebach provided more structure for the girl. She said she was the one who taught Virginia to be a lady and pull up her bloomers for a while. She also gained her employment as a model and as a salesgirl at Marshall Field's. Virginia became a style expert of sorts and a shopper for society ladies. This led to a trip to Paris where Virginia caused a big scandal by dancing in her nightie with another woman. Apparently she kissed the woman full on the mouth."

"How'd she come west?"

"She came to San Francisco for the Exhibition."

"In '15."

"And from there, she moved to Los Angeles."

"Where she met Henry Lehrman, who got her into pictures."

"Mabel will know more about that than me," Minta said. "I'd already left for New York by that time."

"You'd make quite a sleuth, Minta."

"I just want to help Roscoe."

"So when do I meet Miss Normand?"

CAPTAIN OF DETECTIVES Duncan Matheson checked the time on the wall clock and then flicked open his gold timepiece. Satisfied they matched and all was right in San Francisco, he clicked it closed and hung it back in his vest pocket. He took a seat across from Maude Delmont and smiled at her. He offered her coffee. He offered her a cigarette.

He wanted to know more about Cassius Clay Woods in Madera. She said it had been a misunderstanding. She said he'd beaten her.

And then he asked about Earl Lynn in Los Angeles.

"Come again?"

"Surely you know Mr. Lynn?"

"I may have met someone by that name."

Griff Kennedy coughed behind her and the cough was so sudden and sharp that it made her jump a little. "According to Mr. Lynn, you bragged about carrying his child last year. Musta been a quick meeting."

"That is a personal matter."

Kennedy coughed again. Maude couldn't see him, and his talking and coughing and general harrumphing was starting to piss her off. She turned in her chair to glower at him a bit.

"I have a speaking engagement at two," Maude said.

"It can wait," Kennedy said.

"Where's your partner?" she asked.

"Tom? He's in Los Angeles."

"I see."

"With Mr. Lynn."

"Does the San Francisco Police Department normally poke into the affairs of taxpaying citizens? I find poking into the private life of a woman to be quite unsavory."

"Un-what?" Kennedy asked.

"Unsavory."

Harrumph.

Matheson walked. He twirled the end of his mustaches like a one-reel villain. He looked out from his glass wall into the pool of detectives smoking and talking with stoolies, con men, rapists, and robbers.

Maude straightened her hat and readjusted the black parasol in her hand. All her wardrobe was black now. She's become known for it, her signature. She planned on buying a little black dog perhaps, a little dog that would attend the trials with her, and she thought about naming the little pooch Virginia after her poor, dear dead friend.

"Mr. Lynn claims you wanted five thousand dollars to make the baby go away," Matheson said.

"That's a fool's talk . . ."

"Mr. Lynn has agreed to be a character witness in the trial."

"He's a liar."

"He says he has documentation that you asked for money," Matheson said.

"He told Detective Reagan that he was not or could not be intimate with you," fathead Kennedy said. "That ring any bells?"

Maude remembered an old grifter adage, one she'd learned long before California from an old-timer in Wichita, but the rule was simple and everlasting. When they're on to you, you brass the son of a bitch out.

Maude stood.

"I find this talk to be gutter talk and unfitting to a woman. While you two should be out finding women who have been ill-treated by that beastly Arbuckle, you are here questioning my character with lies and rumors. From what I recall, Mr. Lynn is a mixed-up little man who has no interest in women whatsoever. He is what is called in polite society a 'sissy.' Why would I have anything to do with a soul like that? Now, if you'll excuse me, I have a speaking engagement with the fine women of this city. Apparently Chief O'Brien will be there to discuss the orphans' fund that I'm now heading. You both must know that the chief found his own little lost bundle on his very doorstep last week. The matter of orphans is very dear to him, and I'm sure he'll find it quite interesting to see how I, a respected woman in this city, was treated."

"Take a breath, sister," Kennedy said.

Maude turned to him. He had a cigarette bobbing out the side of his big bullet head.

"Slow down when you talk," Kennedy said. "Makes it easier to breathe."

She snarled at him. She gave a short bow to Matheson. Kennedy opened the door wide. He used the hand gesture of a doorman, a smirk on his face as he pretended to tip his hat.

The bastard didn't even have a hat on his fat Irish head.

"How was I to know?" Mabel Normand asked. "I thought it was some kind of fever. All I knew is that Mack didn't want that girl on the lot. He was afraid it would infect the whole crew."

"You know what it was?"

"Mack would know," Mabel said. "He's had all those social diseases. Isn't it funny that they call them that, 'social diseases'? Makes it almost seem dignified, as if you got 'em from shaking hands or doing the waltz."

Mabel Normand reminded Sam of a child's doll, with her milk-colored skin and saucer black eyes. Her hair in ringlets. She looked even more like a toy as she perched on top of a cracker barrel, her feet drumming on the wood while she talked about the good ole days with Fatty and Minta and the craziness on the lot at Keystone.

"Minta's a good egg," Mabel said. "I don't know if I'd stand by Roscoe in all this."

"She says she loves him."

"That's another kind of sickness. I got the same sickness and it's terminal, brother. Say, do you have a smoke?"

Sam fished out a cigarette and handed it to her.

She remained in her stage costume, that of a turn-of-the-century washerwoman, complete with a frumpy dress and slouch hat. When Minta introduced them on the back lot at Sennett Studios, Mabel showed off the pruning of her hands from all the wash she had to do for the part in *Molly O'*.

"I swore to myself I wouldn't step foot back on this lot without killing Mack, but, here I am, crawling back to the son of a bitch. I shoulda stayed with Goldwyn. He's an all right fella, if he'd just keep his hands off my ass."

"I heard that Roscoe had a thing for Virginia."

"A thing? He had a hard-on like a divining rod for that piece. Every man on the lot did. She showed up here from somewhere back east, with her polite smile and those gorgeous clothes, and every boy knew they had some pie fresh from the oven. Little did they know she gave it away for free."

"Was she ever with Roscoe?"

"She wouldn't," Mabel said. "Said he was too fat. She said she didn't like fat men. But he sent her flowers and candies and took his hat off when she walked by. Even when she was with Lehrman, he tried."

"You know this?"

"I saw this. He acted like a fool."

"You know, I saw you once in a nickelodeon in Baltimore," Sam said.

"I never been to Baltimore."

"I saw you in one of those things you crank and the photos flip."

"Anyone ever tell you that you look like Wallace Reid?" Mabel asked. She smiled at him and Sam decided she had a very nice smile.

"All the time."

"Well, you do. If the detective thing doesn't work out, you could make a fine living as his double."

"I don't think I could live here."

"How come?"

"Too spread out. I like a city where you can walk and get to know the neighborhoods and back alleys. A real city you can know on your feet. I'd get lost here."

"This is no city," Mabel said, looking down the row of wooden barns and façades of a city set. "Sometimes I think I live in purgatory. I had the craziest dream the other night. I dreamed I was bleeding from my mouth and couldn't breathe or see. Say, you wanna get a drink, Sam?"

"I'm catching the three o'clock back to Frisco."

"Too bad," Mabel said, finishing the cigarette and flicking it into the dusty streets of the lot. "Next time you're here, give me a ring."

"Does the name Hibbard mean anything to you?"

Mabel Normand, the old little girl in makeup and ringlets, looked to Sam like he was some kind of rube.

"Don't you read the papers?"

"Mainly the comics," Sam said. "I love *Mutt and Jeff.*"

"That's Roscoe's buddy."

"I don't follow."

"Fred Hibbard. The Romanian. He calls himself Fishback now. He thinks it's pretty goddamn funny because he directs comedies."

"I LOVE YOU."

"I love you, too, W.R."

"Are you ready to open your eyes?"

"Where are we?"

"Quit fiddling with that blindfold," Hearst said. "Two more steps and we're there."

"I been b-blind since you picked me up," Marion Davies said in that cute staccato Brooklyn accent. "You ride me all over the city up and down hills and around c-corners and I don't know which way is up. Do you call that fair?"

"What's that?"

"K-keeping a person blind for the whole goddamn drive? It's c-c-cruelty."

"It's a present."

"Because you love me."

"Yes."

"Can I t-take this off now?"

Hearst was silent. And then he thumbed open the bottle of champagne, making Miss Davies jump back, maybe thinking it was a gunshot, as she fingered open the silk blinds on her eyes and smiled. He could almost hear her smile, the moist parting of her lips, that small cracking noise of lip on teeth, as she spun around in the center of the theater, in the middle of all those slabs of wooden seats. She crooked her head up at the ceiling, still half done—the sloths—but enough done to see those Spanish patterns and curves and buttresses and delicate designs he'd had hand-copied from Madrid.

"Where are we?" Miss Davies asked.

"Miss Davies, we're in your theater."

"Mine? Don't k-k-kid me, W.R."

"Have you ever known me to joke about a gift?"

Davies raised her eyebrows and shrugged a bit, pursing her lips. "No."

"It's called the Granada. Isn't that just a wonderful name? The perfect place to premiere *Enchantment*."

"You b-bought a whole theater for one picture?"

"Why not?"

He walked tall and erect down the aisle toward the stage, not a soul in the place, just as it was supposed to be. The screen wasn't up yet, or the big red curtains he'd handpicked from a hundred samples, but he just couldn't wait another moment. She had to see it.

"The stage will be set on the seventeenth of November. When the clock strikes one, the guarding doors will swing wide for those lucky San Franciscans who will first taste the glories of the new Granada. 'A surprise upon surprise awaits. A foyer smiling beautiful—a palace where quiet luxury warmly glows—and then thousands of comfortable, hospitable seats.'"

"You ham."

"Now for the program," Hearst said, mounting the steps and comfortably finding the stage. "*Enchantment*. Heralded and accepted by New York—of course New York, letting all these San Franciscans know about the true tastemakers—as an exquisite photo comedy—and chosen for the Granada's opening program in competition with the best current, super features, '*Enchantment* will add a captivating climax to an event already big.'"

"You fool."

"Do you love me?" Hearst asked from the stage.

"I love you."

"Even as a ham?"

"Even as a f-fool."

The theater was as large, or larger, than any movie house in New York. The façade was just grand, the opening mouth to a palace, a castle, a cathedral onto Mission Street. He could see all those faces on opening night, their mouths agape, looking at the black-and-white images floating across the screen. Miss Davies's angelic profile, her lithe form, the goddess in ringlets smiling at all of them. He felt his heart shift inside him.

"W.R.? You okay up there?"

"Fine."

"You looked as if you'd pass out."

"I did this all for you, Miss Davies."

"C-come down this instant."

"I like it up here."

He mouthed the words "All for you."

Marion found the staircase and the stage and walked to him, finding a spot under his big arm. He pulled her into his stiff black suit, the kind George said reminded him of an undertaker, her head not even reaching his shoulder.

"I miss the eye contact," she said. "When you're on stage, you c-can see people having a good time. B-b-but in a picture, you're just one of them."

"Isn't that the point?"

She smiled up at him and pinched his cheek. Hearst felt his face turn red as he looked out onto the empty seats, feeling the jitters of opening night coming into play. Everything was set. All there was to do was sit back and watch the thing play out.

"How 'bout dinner?"

"More champagne?" she asked.

"Always."

"In p-pajamas?"

"Of course."

"You screwy boy."

"So HE'S A LIAR?" the Old Man asked.

"He's not so much a liar as he just left some things out," Sam said.

"With his fat ass on the line, you'd think he could stand to be a little more truthful," said Phil Haultain.

"He probably left out that the Fishback fella brought the booze to keep him out of trouble," Sam said.

"What about lying about knowing the girl?" the Old Man asked.

"To keep himself out of trouble," Sam said.

"He should've figured he'd get found out on that one," the Old Man said. "I wonder who Brady has lined up to tell about Arbuckle's passion for Miss Rappe."

"Plenty," Sam said. "I heard Tom Reagan was down, too."

"You run into him?"

"No," Sam said. "But I hear he was talking to the same people."

"You think they know about Maude Delmont running that con on that fairy actor?"

"I'd bet on it," Sam said.

Phil Haultain walked to the windows and looked down on Ellis Street. You could hear the sound of the cable cars zipping up and down Powell and the yelps of the little newsboys hawking the afternoon editions. The big lug was wearing his big brown Stetson and a double-breasted suit and nodded while the Old Man and Sam talked, as if making sure they knew he was all right with what they were saying.

"I wouldn't screw that Delmont broad," Haultain said. "She's old as my mother and twice as ugly."

"You're a romantic, Phil," Sam said.

"I likes what I likes."

"Phil, stick with those two women."

"I got to know Miss Blake and Miss Prevon on an intimate basis," Haultain said.

"Where are they?" the Old Man asked.

"Living on the hospitality of Ma Murphy."

"And who's Ma Murphy?" the Old Man asked.

"Mother of George Murphy, young assistant district attorney in the employ of Brady," Haultain said. "She runs a rooming house and they got guards round-the-clock."

"Sam, go home, see your wife, take a shower, have a hot meal."

"Will do."

"And then I want you to shadow Maude Delmont. I want to know what the coppers know. You understand?"

"Yes, sir."

"There's something at that party we've missed," the Old Man said.

"That's why I followed Jack Lawrence," Sam said. "But the more I know about that party, the less I know."

"You don't trust Arbuckle?" the Old Man asked.

"Not as far as I can throw him."

Sam looked to young Phil Haultain and he smiled back.

"You got this guy running shadows now?" Sam asked.

The Old Man cracked a smile. A rare smile for the Old Man, who didn't seem to know what a smile was all about.

"Stir the pot," the Old Man said. "See what floats to the top."

"Even if we don't like it?" Sam said.

The Old Man placed his feet on his desk. He lit a cigar. The sounds of people and machines and cable cars came from outside. He smiled but said nothing.

"It's good to know," Sam said.

"You bet," said the Old Man, the cigar a burning orange plug in the side of his mouth. "Even if we want it buried."

Weeks later, the morning of November 11, Sam awoke to military bands warming up by the Civic Center and City Hall—the first few chords of "How 'Ya Gonna Keep 'Em Down on the Farm?"—and the metallic sounds of the testing of amplified voices from where President Harding would address the crowds later in the day. The apartment windows were open onto Eddy; a soft, cold breeze parted the torn curtains and brought in the early sounds of Armistice Day. But Sam soon closed the windows to shut out the racket and returned to watching his daughter sleep. Her name was Mary Jane, perfect and tiny and pink, with the sad soft eyes of her mother and the long delicate fingers of his mother's family, the Dashiells.

After the baby had been born, Jose didn't miss a beat, changing and washing diapers, soothing the late-night cries, and walking that creaking floor with the child just about the time Sam would come in from a shadow job. He'd sit with the child, after a long day on his feet, and rock her, careful not to breathe close, head turned and sometimes holding his breath, at the doctor's request. Sam made camp on the Murphy bed, an alarm clock and bottle of balsamea kept nearby for company, while Jose and the baby slept in the bedroom.

Sam left the crib and Jose and the bedroom and set a match to the burner on the iron stove, making coffee. He was off today, as was most of San Francisco, but was already showered and dressed, his military papers tucked securely in the vest pocket of his tweeds. The *Examiner* had run a story the day before about veterans being given food and coal, and even toys for their children, and this was the first day since making his way west that he'd been proud he'd signed up for the goddamn circus. He'd been ignored by pencil pushers, told the sickness he'd caught back in camp wasn't worth a damn, and was now forbidden by docs to be close to his daughter. He'd be damned if he wouldn't get every scrap offered by his government.

The coffee boiled and he strained it over a mug. On a hook by the door sat his old Army-issue coat and cap. He heard Jose stir and she came tiptoeing into the room and leaned down to kiss Sam on the cheek.

"You think we'll have room in the icebox?" Sam asked.

"We'll make room."

"The paper said to come to the Civic Center."

"Do you hear all that?"

"It's what woke me."

"You think you'll see the president?"

"I'll give him your best."

"I'd like to get the baby out."

"It's shoulder to shoulder," he said. "Drunks and fat politicians. I won't take long."

Sam stood, finished the coffee, and walked with Jose to the door, sliding into his Army coat and cap.

"I don't think I've seen this," she said.

"From my steamer trunk," Sam said. "The only thing worth a damn I got from the Army."

She buttoned him up into his coat and pulled his hat down into his eyes.

"It's cold."

"Who turned out the lights?"

Eddy Street was choked that morning with flivvers and cabs and crowded buses in from the county. Men in overalls and women in catalog dresses looked lost on city streets. Newsboys shouted out special editions from every corner and every other old woman wore a paper gold star on her breast. There was a legless man in ribbons and medals propped atop a wooden crate and holding a tin cup. A blind man walked in the opposite direction of Sam, being led by a nurse in white wearing a flowing black cape. Sam turned onto Van Ness, passing over Turk, and was almost over Golden Gate when he saw the thick heads of folks clear and heard a police whistle, an arc forming around the open door to a hotel.

The Mariah was parked out front, doors wide-open and waiting for a gaggle of red-faced cops who emerged from a flophouse, pushing out three men—two in their undershorts and shirts and a third with no shirt but pants and shoes—out into the street. One man was yelling at the cops. Another man's face was spiderwebbed with blood from his nose. The yelling man got a beefy fist to his stomach and was told to shut the hell up. Sam stood there in his heavy coat, collar popped high and hands deep in his pockets, and watched the cops toss all three men into the back of the paddy wagon.

Sam asked the driver of the wagon, "What gives?"

"Filthy communist scum," the man said. "Wobblies."

"What did they do?"

"Nest of 'em," the driver said. "In our city organizing, stewing up all that red bullshit for a family parade. I'm proud to give them a ride to San Quentin."

"Not the Hall?"

"San Quentin, brother," the man said. "Filth like that doesn't deserve a trial. It's goddamn Armistice Day."

Sam continued watching another cop walk from the flophouse with a metal printing press hoisted in his thick arms. He threw it in the road, where it cracked and broke like a dismantled engine, and the cop dusted off his hands on his trousers with a big smile. One of the Wobblies broke free from the cop pushing him along and the big man caught him by the arm and began to beat him about the face and neck and back with his nightstick.

Sam yelled for him to stop and the sound coming from him felt odd, like it hadn't been his own.

He ran for the cop and grabbed his arm, but the big cop just jabbed

Sam in the stomach with the nightstick, squeezing every ounce of breath from him, and dragged the man into the Mariah, where the back door closed with a hard click. The wagon started and disappeared, and the circle of people grew smaller and smaller until there was nothing but people walking around Sam as he sat on the ground trying to find some air and his feet.

Sam could hear the crowds and noise and music down the hill at the Center and he staggered toward it.

"THIS IS A NICE CAR, ROSCOE," Gavin McNab said.

"Glad you like it."

"It's like sitting in your own living room."

"Glad you like it."

"You don't like me much, do you?" McNab said.

"I'm tired, my ass hurts from the drive, and I'm not exactly thrilled about visiting San Francisco again."

"Don't worry."

"Don't worry," Roscoe repeated, staring out the wavy glass of his Pierce-Arrow at the endless pastures and hardscrabble little gardens. The engine hummed and purred and vibrated the limousine carriage in a fine, even way.

McNab was a big man, with a balding, closely shorn gray head and a pair of tremendous black eyebrows. His face was craggy and weather-beaten, his eyes a light blue, not as soft as those Roscoe found in the mirror but washed out and penetrating. They'd been out of Los Angeles for four hours and his new lawyer had yet to take off his black suit jacket, buttoned up over a black vest and tie, with his boiled shirt pinned tight to his thick neck. Most of the trip so far had been McNab telling tales of how he'd made it from bellhop to law school, and what it was like being right in the center of the city in '06. He laid it on real thick about all the stone rubble and fires and smell of dead horses cooking. Gavin McNab was a hard guy all the way around.

In the bench seat across from them, the young attorney Brennan made a pillow from his jacket and leaned against the window, slack-jawed and sleeping, as the California nothingness rolled by. The driver, Harry, separated by glass, blissful and unaware, worked the wheel up a straight leg north. Good ole Harry.

"Don't let one bad thing ruin Frisco for you," McNab said. "It's only after those old bitches got the vote has it been like this. Christ, they have a bull's-eye drawn on every set of testicles they see. They won't be happy till they turn us all to geldings."

"Good to hear."

"Hey," McNab said. "I hear you have a shitter in here. Where is it?"

"Under your seat."

McNab got up, bent at the waist, and removed the leather cushion from where he was seated. "So it is. Genius."

"And a bar?"

"It's empty."

"Good. Good."

"I'm on the wagon."

"Good. Good."

McNab rubbed his craggy face and stared for a moment at the sleeping young Brennan. He reached for a lever that brought down a skinny tabletop before him and opened a briefcase made from the skin of a crocodile. There was a silver flask inside and he took it out for a moment before taking a long sip. He offered it to Roscoe and Roscoe shrugged and then grabbed it and took a long pull.

With glasses on the end of his nose, McNab made small checks on lists of names and occupations.

"The jury?"

"Potential names."

"Where'd you get that?"

McNab glanced over at Roscoe, shrugged, and then turned back to the sheets of paper.

"I didn't kill her, you know."

"I don't care if you did."

"But I didn't."

"So much the better," McNab said. "I think you'd like knowing we've located two witnesses in Chicago and three in this state who will testify that Miss Rappe suffered serious ailments before."

"What kind?"

McNab reached into his briefcase and pulled out another file, using the tip of his empty pen to find a few names and check over notes from a neatly typed report. "Apparently the girl had spells like this before. Whenever she drank alcohol, she'd become agitated, frustrated, begin to tear at her clothes. This happened quite often, and she wouldn't find release from the pressure until she was very nude."

Roscoe looked at him and then rested his head on his knuckles. They passed oil wells now, little herds of them in the flat, grassland earth pumping in a mechanized rhythm.

"You're not happy?"

"I'm sure it took a lot."

"One of the women, a Mrs. Minnie Neighbors, attended a hot springs with Miss Rappe and saw her under one of these spells. Another," McNab said, checking his list, "another is a Harry B. Barker. He'd apparently gone with Virginia for five years before she moved to California. He said Miss Rappe suffered from enough venereal ailments to kill a sailor."

"She was lovely," Roscoe said.

"Of course she was, Roscoe."

"She had soft brown eyes."

"And a warm, wet pussy, too, I bet. But let's not get nostalgic. We have hours till San Francisco and there are things you must know."

"Invented things."

"Facts."

"How much?"

"How much?" McNab asked.

"How much will this cost me?"

"It's not your tab."

"Unless you lose."

"I never lose, Roscoe," McNab said. He didn't turn to Roscoe when he said it, just said it like he was talking about a box score or the weather, a certain fact. "We'll make sure of that."

"With facts."

"Call 'em what you like," McNab said.

Roscoe's driver, Harry, hit a pothole, and all their asses jimmied around for a second, slugging Brennan's head against the window frame, startling him, perking him right on up.

He rubbed a hand over his face and opened his eyes wide: "Did I miss something?"

THE ENTIRE BREADTH of City Hall and the Civic Center was crammed with people. People brought their babies to see Harding. Immigrant people—Chinese, Italian, Japanese—came to wave little American flags on sticks. More people, Gold Star mothers, who came in tribute to their dead sons. People who'd fought in the war, even some old ones who'd fought the Spanish or the aged ones who'd fought each other in '65. Box cameras were set atop of cars. Ragtag bands played Sousa. Men sold hot sausages from makeshift grills and sacks of popcorn for pennies. By the time Sam got to the park before City Hall, he saw it, what the *Examiner* called the largest American flag ever on display. The Stars and Stripes hung from high under the rotunda—modeled to a larger scale than the Capitol in D.C.—covering the columns and bleeding down and swaying at the top of the steps.

A large path had been cut between the people and the steps, and in the center police dressed in their most crisp blue stood ready to march. Sam figured almost the entire San Francisco Police Department was there on foot and horse, all the top men up front to lead the parade near the band. He saw Chief O'Brien and the white-haired D.A., Judge Brady, and behind them stood Matheson, talking and smoking with detectives Reagan and Kennedy. The horses nervously skirted the edge of the regiments, waiting for the damn mass of blue to get moving.

Sam shouldered his way to a rope run down to the foot of City Hall. On the side opposite of him, the people parted as a dozen or so policemen cut an opening and held up the rope, letting in a tall man with great bulging eyes. He wore a homburg and tall coat with a fur collar. Smiling and holding leather gloves, he strode across to the mayor and the police chief, Brady and their ilk, and shook a lot of hands.

Sam didn't recognize him. But he heard whispers of "Hearst" all around him.

The band started up.

The police began to march to Market Street.

The D.A., the chief, and mayor, and William Randolph Hearst led the way.

Boots marched from City Hall, along the cleared roadway, and past the big Bull Durham advertisement on the last building standing on the cleared grounds. The trees newly planted and immature, the lampposts all new and polished. The smiles on the leaders' faces. Hearst confident, hands in pockets, sharing a quick joke with Judge Brady. A quick smile from Chief O'Brien.

"Say, how about making way for a kid?"

Sam felt an elbow in the back and looked back to see a man with a ruffian boy on his shoulders trying to catch a glimpse of the big blue walk. The kid smiled with amazement, and his father handed a tiny flag up to him and he waved it and yelled. His father held on to his legs and smiled at the syncopated rhythm of the police boots, the strength of it.

Sam stayed there until the blue parade moved down onto Market, heading toward the Embarcadero. The crowd began to mass up toward the steps of City Hall, where workers put the final touches on a great wooden dais. Soldiers walked the grounds, spending time with country virgins and proud old men. They shook hands and patrolled with rifles strung across their backs. Sam asked one of them about the handouts for the veterans, and the soldier, a pink-faced boy with hair the color of straw, pointed him to a series of trucks parked along Larkin in front of the library.

Sam waited there in line for nearly two hours before being handed a pound of flour and a hand-painted greeting card thanking him for his effort overseas.

He stared back at the old soldier who'd handed this to him, the old man himself leaning on a crutch and missing part of his left leg. The soldier smiled with apology, offering a warm hand, and turned back to the next in line, the line of cripples, lungers, and shell-shocked boys—now men—stretching down around McAllister Street.

Sam kept the flour and tossed the greeting card into the trash by the public library.

He sat on the steps and smoked two cigarettes. CHAUCER. SHAKESPEARE. MILTON. HAWTHORNE. POE. Other names he didn't recognize carved in marble on the library walls.

He walked up the steps and went inside.

19

There's no way this Petrovich fella is smarter than Craig Kennedy," Phil Haultain said.

"He's pretty sharp," Sam said. "He understands people."

"Well, so does Craig Kennedy. Craig Kennedy isn't just a detective, he's a scientist. He uses his knowledge of chemistry and physics to chase down criminals. Does that fella Petrovich ever look through a microscope?"

"He's got a sense for body language."

"Does he have a nice car?"

"The book was published in 1866."

"How 'bout a horse?" Haultain asked.

The men were side by side in long separate tubs filled with hot mud. Sam smoked a cigarette. Phil smoked a cigar.

They'd driven north up through Napa Valley the day before and found rooms in the old wooden hotel downtown. Calistoga was a terrible town for shadow work, only about a half dozen buildings along a single street. The girls were staying at a resort down the road, but Phil said they came in for dinner every night. Phil knew their schedule and movements, the shifts of their guards, and the whole racket. He'd been watching them for nearly a week before picking up Sam. But there wasn't much sense in watching them today, so they'd taken the afternoon off, waiting for the girls to come back to town.

"You're going to ruin your hat."

"Some steam is good," Phil said. "That mud helping you breathe?"

"Like an elephant on my chest."

There was a strange sense about lying neck-deep in the mud—you lost the sense of your body, your outline, and shape. You didn't see yourself anymore, couldn't find yourself. Phil seemed fine with it, though, a big smile on his face and chomping on that wet cigar, refusing to take off his big brown Stetson.

"So she knows who you are?" Sam asked.

"Sure," Phil said. "No sense in hiding it. I think Zey kinda gets a kick out of the danger. She slips out with me at night, kinda like we're a couple kids. She doesn't care for Ma Murphy a bit. The old woman puts them on a schedule of when they eat, when they take their exercise, and probably when they go to the toilet."

"How many guards?"

"Two."

"You know 'em?"

"Couple Frisco cops. Uniform boys outta uniform. Never seen 'em."

"Can we get the girls out?"

"Sure."

"Arbuckle's new attorney, Gavin McNab, wants 'em."

"When?"

"Soon as we can."

"The problem won't be the cops. The problem is the girls."

"How's that?"

"They got the life up here. They get served a big fat breakfast and go for walks and swims. They take mud treatments and mineral baths. I mean these girls don't have to do a thing."

"Maybe they're bored."

"Can we have one more night with 'em?"

"Sure thing."

"I don't know if I could stand much more anyway. I'm up in the hills with my field glasses when they go for their treatments, when they dip 'em in mud and massage 'em and all that. I'm there when they come outside to the hot springs. Do you have any idea what that can do to a man?"

"It's a rough assignment, Phil."

"You bet it is," Phil said. "They come out in robes, their bodies all slathered in dried mud, like they got some kinda tight brown dress on, still showing their curves and humps and all that, and then dip down into the little hot springs. All that steam and heat bubbling up from the earth, the women not even having the decency to stay covered. They get up and play on the rocks and just plain frolic."

"It's the frolicking that bothers you."

"You bet. You ever seen a nude woman frolic? Let alone two? It ain't good for your head."

"I'm real sorry, Phil. Nude showgirls. Tough stuff."

"You'll see."

A very large woman in white walked into the baths and without a word opened a large spigot over Phil's tub, dropping in more mud, and then opening another over Sam. Sam closed his eyes and tried to breathe with the heft on his chest. He thought of being outside himself and liked that idea, hoping he could emerge from the bath with a repaired body but knowing better.

"What's your favorite part?" Sam asked.

"Of what?"

"The girls."

"Zey has a mole on her ass. I don't know why, but it does something for me."

"We should get the car gassed up tonight."

"Will do."

WHEN ROSCOE FIRST SAW Judge Louderback, he thought to himself, *You got to be kidding.* The guy looked like any other Joe walking the street, playing the market and punching the clock at some downtown firm. He was thin and young—too young, in Roscoe's estimation, to be a judge—with neatly combed brown hair and a casual, friendly way of addressing the court. Light smile and eyes, soft voice. Roscoe thought a judge should be an old man with a weathered face and crooked fingers that wrapped around the gavel, not some young businessman type.

McNab sat by Roscoe as they waited for Louderback to finish up his docket before they started the first round of jury selection. A frail Chinese man in silks with a down-turned head and a woman translator stood small and distant before Louderback as Louderback read out a short list of charges, most of them dealing with theft. Apparently the Chinese man, Yuk Lee or something like that, had stolen five bags of rice from a grocer and then gunned down the grocer.

Louderback continued to run down the list of charges, his eyes skimming the papers before him, and then casually and with little anticipation sentenced the Chinaman to be hung. The gavel was swift and hard and final, and the Chinaman was led away, dead-eyed and emotionless, and tossed into the arms of a big fat deputy who yanked him into a back doorway and disappeared.

"For rice?" Roscoe whispered to McNab. Roscoe loosened the tie at his throat.

Louderback called the next order of business, the people of San Francisco versus Roscoe Conkling Arbuckle, charged with the manslaughter of Virginia Rappe. McNab stood and nodded to Roscoe and walked through the short swinging doors and launched his crocodile briefcase on a waiting table as if he were a dog pissing on a rock to mark his territory. Arbuckle and McNab stood before the judge with Brady and weasel-faced U'Ren beside them, shoulder to shoulder. Words were spoken, legal motions made, and with all of 'em standing there Brady said the prosecution objected to several witnesses added to the list.

"Which ones?" said Louderback.

"Where do we start?" Brady asked. "This hotel detective, Glennon. He was recently released from his position due to dereliction of duty. And these so-called character witnesses from the south who serve no other purpose than to blacken the dead girl's character."

Big Gavin McNab stood with his arms folded across his sizable chest. He shuffled his feet and rubbed a hand over his gray bristly head, never looking over at Judge Brady, only seeming to wait for Brady to take a damn breath so he could speak.

"Mr. Glennon has exceptional information on the girl's condition and statements made before she died," McNab said.

"He is a disgruntled ex-employee of the St. Francis," Brady said.

"Since you've chosen not to produce Mrs. Delmont, we have no other course."

"Where did you hear that?" Brady said, turning to the larger man. His face reddened. "Where did you hear that?"

"Well, are you?"

"Of course."

McNab smiled. "We're so pleased."

"I will take this all under advisement, gentlemen," Louderback said, shuffling papers from a large file. "Shall we start? We have a long day ahead of us."

"There is one other matter, Judge," McNab said. His voice, deep and weathered and melodious. "The girls."

"Who?" Louderback asked.

"Miss Prevon-Prevost and Miss Blake," McNab said. "The district attorney's office has spirited the women away, giving us no chance for interviews. I understand these young women are being held against their will in some secret location. Since these girls are some of the few witnesses to the party, we should have every chance to talk to them. Or perhaps Mr. Brady is aware of a separate school of law?"

Brady's face was crimson.

"Mr. McNab will have every opportunity to speak to the young ladies. They are being looked after for their own protection."

"Under armed guard," McNab said.

"That's simply a lie. A rotten lie."

McNab cracked a smile. "Two guards with the San Francisco Police Department."

Brady turned to U'Ren and U'Ren looked away. The exchange wasn't lost on McNab, who couldn't help but smile.

"Their changing statement of what occurred in that hotel is troubling," McNab said. "It's almost as if the girls were being coerced."

"May I remind Mr. McNab I do not bow to his social position in this city and I resent his implications that I diddle with the law," Brady said. "I am the district attorney of this county and will prosecute this case the way I see fit."

Roscoe looked up to the judge on the bench. Judge Louderback looked at his watch and stifled a yawn. "I will take this under advisement. Shall we begin?"

Roscoe just stood there staring at the bored judge, curious and incredulous, but felt McNab's big paw on his arm leading him back to their table. Roscoe opened his mouth, too confused to speak, Louderback tilting his head and knitting his brow.

IT WAS DINNERTIME at the Calistoga Hotel and Phil and Sam sat at a corner table not far from a stone hearth with thick logs blazing, red wine in their glasses and hot rolls between them. Sam helped himself to another glass as an old woman set down a plate of pork chops with mashed potatoes. The hotel, a big, ramshackle wooden number, reminded him of some places he'd been in Montana, places left over from another century, a world away from streetcars and movie houses and airplanes. The wine was good and felt warm in his chest. He wondered if the baths and all that mud didn't have some kind of effect on his condition. He felt better than he had since before the war.

"Don't worry," Phil said. "They'll be here. Would you pass the butter?"

"Maybe Zey met someone else."

"You wanna bet? She's crazy about me. After we take care of matters at hand, I let her wear the hat."

"You're kidding."

"She loves it," Phil said. "Sometimes she wears it while we're taking care of the business, riding me like I'm a horse."

"Yee-haw."

"You think I'm crazy 'cause I said these girls are trouble. You don't know about women trouble. Look at you. You're married and have a kid. It's easier that way. You know what to expect every day. You got a beautiful wife, Sam. That counts for a lot. I'd love to have something like that. A man knows where he stands. When did you know it was good with Jose? You know, for keeps?"

"I had to make a choice."

"How'd you know?"

"It was the right thing."

"Do you ever stop thinking about women? That'd be the hardest part for me."

Sam cut into his pork chops and took a bite. He took a sip of wine and just looked over at Phil. The younger, larger man smiled back, a slight grin on his face. His eyes then cut over to the tall front doors and watched as the two now-famous showgirls entered. They handed their coats to a crinkle-faced old woman who hobbled after them. They passed by the table, Phil smiling up at Zey and Zey smiling back at Phil, and they found a spot by the warm fire. It was all dark and very cozy in the room. Hearth fire, kerosene lamps on the tables.

"You met that Blake girl once, right?"

"I did."

"Kinda screwy."

"Kinda."

Sam finished off half the plate and pushed it away. Phil finished his and asked for some more potatoes. They were already onto a thick slab of apple pie topped with melted cheese with a pot of coffee between them when the girls joined them. Zey was all smiles and giggles and huddled up close to Phil. Alice sat down next to Sam, who drank his coffee and smiled over at her as she said, "Craig Kennedy."

Phil looked to Sam and Sam shrugged.

The old woman was chatting away with the two cops who'd joined her. They were Irish lunkheads, beat cops, who would squint over at the table and then back to Ma Murphy. Probably jealous the girls were talking to some other men. Zey swung her arm over Phil's shoulder.

"How'd you shake loose?" Phil asked.

"We said you were a couple salesmen we met at the springs," Alice said. "They can't say no to us. I said we were getting bored. They don't like it when we're bored."

"Good to see you, Zey," Sam said from across the table.

She acted like she didn't remember him and played with Phil Haultain's ear.

Alice smiled over at Sam and Sam pulled two cigarettes from the Fatima pack and offered one to Alice. Alice said, "Thank God," telling him that Ma Murphy wouldn't let them smoke or drink and the whole thing had been murder on her nerves. She wore a black dress with a fur collar, maybe rabbit but not mink. Her makeup was lighter than he remembered it, and she was prettier without all the red paint on her lips and cheeks.

"You know, my real name isn't Kennedy," Sam said.

"You don't say."

She grabbed the matches and lit her own and then handed the pack to Sam. Sam lit a cigarette and pushed away the pie, keeping the cigarette going on the coffee saucer. Phil whispered something to Zey and she cackled so loud that people across the room turned their heads. She put her hand over her mouth but kept on laughing.

Ma Murphy screwed up her face when she noted the cigarette in Alice's hand. Alice looked over at the prune-faced woman and stuck out her tongue.

"We've been drinking all day," Alice said. "That's all there is to do around here, drink. We go for treatments and a swim. I'm tired of all that goddamn mud. You got to take ten showers to get it out of all your cracks. I want to go back to Frisco."

"That can be arranged."

"How?" she asked. "Those boys sleep outside our door. Did I tell you that Ma Murphy tried to get both of us to start wearing a corset? Can you imagine? This is 1921!"

Alice breathed in a long drag from her cigarette and turned her head to the ceiling, blowing out the smoke. Zey said they needed to get back, meeting the eyes of the nervous cops and Ma Murphy up by the hearth.

Alice leaned in, her eyes brown and sleepy, and felt for Sam's fingers under the table. She moved his hand over to her knee and slid it up her dress, his hand crossing over her stockings and deep up her thigh, and he could feel the warmth of the sun on her skin. The higher she moved his hand, the warmer it got.

Sam just kept smoking and nodding and talking across the table to Zey and Phil. Zey talking about going horseback riding tomorrow. His hand reached the end of her leg, fingers delicately moved across a warm patch of silk between her thighs. Sam took the cigarette from his mouth with his free hand, met Alice's eyes, and shook his head.

She leaned in and with hot breath said, "Come for me tonight."

And with that, she pushed his hand away from under her skirt and back to his own knee and very pleasantly stood and said good-bye to Phil. The girls returned back to Ma Murphy and their guards.

"You were right, Phil."

"About what?"

"It ain't easy," Sam said.

"Told you."

"Fill up the machine?"

"Yep."

"You can get by the guards?"

"Cake."

"We go tonight."

20

The girls stayed in a small white cottage fitted among a half dozen along a dirt road called Palm Row. The little cottages had little front porches with rocking chairs, picket fences, and small chimneys, some blowing smoke up into the cold night. A full moon shone silver on the endless patchwork of brown-and-green hills and across acres of grapes dying on the vine, toppled trellises broken apart by dry agents. Sam took in the scene beside the little flivver they'd taken from the Pinkerton motor pool and in the darkness smoked and checked his watch. They'd made arrangements with the girls to make the move at midnight when the guards would change. But here it was, eleven minutes after, and Phil walked back to the Ford to tell him that the fat Irish kid was still sitting on the girls' cottage porch with a shotgun and reading a goddamn copy of the *Saturday Evening Post*.

"Can we get 'em out back?"

"Back leads to the springs. Sometimes the other fella's out there."

Sam checked his watch. "Aw, hell."

Phil and Sam climbed the wall and circled the hot springs, now throwing off a mess of steam since the temperature dropped. The springs bubbled up in a little grotto surrounded by the chest-high wall of stone, and the men followed the circular path by moonlight, leaving the guns in the car in case they got caught, and trailed a row of shrubs to the back window of the cottage.

They heard giggling and music from a Victrola. Inside the wavy panes of glass, Sam saw Alice jumping up and down on the bed, a big suitcase nearby latched with a thick man's belt. He knocked on the panes softly and then harder, and that got Alice down to the floor, where she removed a needle from the record. The music stopped.

She tilted her head and walked to the glass, a big smile on her lips, and opened up.

"It's just me, honeybee," she said.

"You girls come on," Sam said. "And be quiet about it."

"Zey's not going."

"Come again?" Sam said, whispering.

"She likes it here," Alice said, leaning down, whispering, elbows laid across the threshold. " 'Sides, she ain't got a job since the Old Poodle Dog was busted. She's got no dough and nowhere to stay. Did you have the fried chicken tonight?"

"Pork chops."

"You shoulda had the chicken."

"I'm coming in," Sam said.

Phil laced his hands together and propped up a place for Sam to stand, lifting him through the cottage window. Sam fell with a thud to the floor and waited there for a moment, and, not hearing anything, then whispered to Alice about where he could find Zey.

She whispered back, "I'm telling you, it won't do no good. She likes the treatments, too."

Alice Blake closed the window and curtains behind him and walked to the bed. She lay back into the mattress, propped on her elbows, and crooked her finger at Sam. "We got time."

Sam gritted his teeth and took a breath.

Alice started to unbutton the length of her dress and Sam watched her, unable to speak until the entire front of the dress was open. She wore a brassiere and bloomers, lots of lace and silk, tall laced boots, stockings, and garters. She ran her fingers across her stomach, stroking her white belly, the way a proud owner shows off a fine machine.

"I'm married."

"I won't tell."

"I'll know."

"Poo."

Alice smiled and parted her legs. She crooked her finger again. She reached down and unsnapped a single garter. Sam walked to her and reached for her hand, pulling the short girl to her feet. He put a hand to her shoulder and closed his eyes. Her eyes closed, too, and her mouth parted just as Sam snapped the garter back and began to work on the buttons up the line, stitching them closed.

"I thought you were fun," she said.

"A damn dirty lie."

Sam followed her into a long hallway, noting the front door to the porch was closed, and Alice rapped on a bedroom door twice. Zey appeared in a long Oriental robe, hand on her hip, and said, "About goddamn time. Where's Phil? And where the hell are my goddamn records, Alice? Are you trying to take the Victrola, too?"

"Phil's outside," Sam said. "Waiting."

"Outside? That doesn't do us any good."

"Come on," Sam said. "Get packed."

Zey made a pouty look and shook her head. The inside of her room smelled of lavender and candy-sweet perfume and glowed red from a silk handkerchief she'd placed over a lamp. Undergarments and stockings were strung across the room and over bedposts. An open armoire spilled out unfolded clothes. A bottle of unmarked wine sat on the bed stand with two teacups.

"Where's the Victrola, Alice?" Zey asked.

"Take it."

"And the records?"

"They're yours. But I packed that new one though. 'Dangerous Blues.'"

"I liked that one. You know I liked that one."

"Ladies," Sam said, holding up his hand, Zey still keeping herself wedged in the doorframe, hand on her hip. "All the way to Frisco."

"Well, you tell Phil that if he didn't have the class and decency to come in and say good-bye, then I don't care if I ever see him again," Zey said. "No, tell him I hope he gets hit by a bus. All of you can go straight to hell."

She slammed the bedroom door.

The front porch creaked and the screen door opened. The copper knocked on the front door. "Hello?" the man called out, sounding more like a boy. Sam motioned to Alice with his head and she followed him back to her room.

The knocking grew frantic and the cop called out for them again. Zey poked her head out and held her teeth clenched and said, "Sorry."

Sam ducked back into Alice's room and slid open the back window, tossing the suitcase through the curtains and motioning for Alice to come on. The banging on the front door was tremendous and Phil was muttering, "Come on. Come on."

Alice stood there paralyzed, hands against her mouth, with Zey now in the room saying, "I want that record."

"Zey," Sam said. "Answer the door."

"Please, Zey," Alice said.

"Really?"

"Really. I can't breathe here. Ma Murphy with her corsets and hot-water bottles gives me the creeps. Tell her to take her corset and stick it."

More banging. A click. The door opened. The copper called out.

Zey walked into the hall and told the cop there was no trouble, none at all, but the man wanted to check the rooms, make sure everything was on the square. And Zey said everything was just beautiful, peachy in fact, and asked him if he'd like a drink. The man asked again to see the rooms and Zey said she had something better to show him, saying it real sexy and slow.

Phil helped Alice out the window. Sam slid out himself and down to the ground. Phil stood there in the full moonlight holding the big suitcase and listening. He walked slowly to a side window, peeking in, and Sam touched his shoulder.

"Phil?"

"Do you see what she's doing to him?"

"She's saving us."

"She's naked."

"No, she's not," Sam said, peeking in and then turning back to Phil. "Guess she is."

"She dropped that robe to the floor and started biting his ear. That was supposed to be my ear. She said she only did that for me."

"Come on."

"Goddamn women."

Sam looked back inside and the man's hands were on Zey's naked white backside, squeezing her butt cheeks, while Zey crooked one of her legs around his legs. The cop turned his head to the window and Sam ducked down.

When Sam looked again, the man was headed back to Alice's room.

Phil, Sam, and Alice found the path around the springs and heard someone yelling from the open window, curtains billowing about the cop's head, the cop yelling, telling them to halt, the word *halt* seeming kinda comical coming from a boy. They ducked down behind some hedge as the cop, a young kid with freckles and jug ears, came barreling out yelling, and Zey followed moments later, back in her robe, and catching the young boy at the hot springs. The boy saying "goddamnit" at least fifteen times before she reached her arms around him and planted one right on his mouth.

He still had the 12-gauge out in his hand, over her shoulder, and was waving it around all crazy like he might start shooting at the bushes.

"Alice went for a walk," Zey said.

"With her suitcase?" asked the boy.

"Not much you can do now," Zey said. She grabbed the young boy between the legs and started to rub. The boy was saying, "Hold on, Miss Prevost, hold on," but Zey kept working him like a piston and kissing his neck. Behind the shrubs, Alice had her hand over her mouth, snickering, but Phil turned his head in disgust. The cop was now begging for Zey to stop, please stop, but calling her "Miss Zey." Zey just kept kissing and rubbing, the boy standing taller and more rigid and breathing hard until his body convulsed, the shotgun clattering to the rocks. The boy said, "See what you done? I was savin' it."

He kicked at his gun and walked back to the cottage, his head down.

Alice snickered so hard she about fell over. As the three followed the moon-lit path back to the gassed-up flivver, Phil said, "I thought she loved me."

"Oh, go give yourself a good slap," Alice Blake said as they piled in the car. She checked herself in a compact mirror, rubbed some more paint on her lips, and, satisfied, clicked it closed. Sam smiled and Phil started the machine and pulled off, dust trailing behind them in the red glow of the taillights just as they heard the screaming and yelling and profanities of a woman.

For a moment Sam thought Zey had changed her mind, but behind them he saw an old woman in a housecoat, Ma Murphy, trailing like a stray dog, trying to keep up and shaking her gnarled fist at the moon.

MAUDE DELMONT STARTED THINKING something was truly wrong with this picture when she turned that final corner on the first floor of the Hall and began to follow the policeman down a marble staircase into the basement. She got to the first landing, well in sight of the bottom floor and a long caged storeroom where they held court files and mug shots and bullets and fired pistols and some of the recently dead. She stood there on the landing, halfway upstairs or halfway down, and waited and listened to the masses of men and women being called for jury selection for ole Fatty. She could hear their feet above her that morning shuffling like horse hooves.

Soon another policeman came to the landing and shouted down that Miss Eisenhart had been called as she'd requested. Kate would understand. Big Kate would get to the bottom of all these snobs in Brady's office giving her the high hat.

Maude yelled back up the dimly lit stairs, but the cop was already gone.

When Big Kate finally arrived an hour later, Maude leaned against the wall of the landing and smoked a cigarette, confessing it must be her feminine assertiveness that scared Brady. Eisenhart leaned against the wall, too, dressed in her woolly blue uniform, and scratched her head, listening. The silver badge on her chest seemed tiny and strange, like a toy pinned on her big fat bosom.

"Scared him to death," Maude said, pointing a closed parasol as a cane.

"Men don't know how to take an assertive woman. They find it threatening or, at the least, offensive. He doesn't want me in that courtroom because I'm a woman, a powerful woman with a mind of her own, who will do everything in her being to make sure her dear friend's last words are heard."

She squashed the spent cigarette under her pointed boot.

"Dearest, District Attorney Brady doesn't want the jury to hear about your past," Kate Eisenhart said, her frown turning her fat face into dough. "In the eyes of the law you are a bigamist. You'll ruin his case."

"Good gracious me," Maude said, holding her chest as if expecting a heart attack.

"You must divorce a man before you marry another. Or didn't you learn that in Wichita?"

Maude narrowed her eyes at the fat policewoman.

"This is all a slow boat of slanderous lies because I'm now a known person," she said. "My former husbands who treated me terribly can't stand that I am now a public darling. They seethe on it. Did you know I've had offers to tell my life story on film? On film!"

"Truly?" The look she shot at Maude was that of a schoolmarm questioning a whopper told to her from the back of the room.

"Miss Eisenhart, is there something you wish to say? I've been waiting on this landing for more than an hour. I thought we were sisters."

"And how did you figure that?"

"I know how you feel." Maude adjusted her big black hat and smiled a bit. She touched the edge of Kate's badge, rubbing her fingers across the emblem.

"Who are you?" Eisenhart asked, crooking her head to get a better angle at Maude's face. "Really? Because the trusted friend of Virginia Rappe doesn't work for me anymore. Or the divorced wife of Cassius Clay Woods. I do believe you could be the woman who tried to bamboozle a young actor type in Los Angeles who, as it seems, prefers the company of men. Just why were you and Mr. Semnacher at that party with Mr. Arbuckle? What was your angle? I guess Mr. Semnacher has jackrabbited from here, but you still stick around waiting to be heard. What is in it for an aging grifter like you?"

"Good Lord, you fat old bitch," Maude Delmont said, turning and raising her hand to slap Kate Eisenhart. But Big Kate caught Maude's hand in midstrike and held it there. She looked Maude in the eye for a long time and then muscled her arm down, using her thick man muscles and man ways to control her. There was a slight sheen of perspiration on Eisenhart's upper lip.

Maude adjusted her big hat.

"I think you like it," Kate said. The smile wasn't smug but knowing, which pissed off Maude all the more.

"Like what?"

"The cameras, the newspaper boys, the boys on the corner hawking the afternoon edition with your name on it. You can't let it go, even if it will lead you down the flowered path to prison."

Maude's indignant face and fetid manners dropped, much like the first layer of wax burning off a candle. She breathed it out. "You want me. You want us to make love like man and wife. You wish me to wear a bedpost between my legs?"

"You disgust me."

Maude turned to her in the streaming light and dust, row upon row of boxes holding court cases and reports of criminal acts and faded mug shots. Maude watched her, feeling her breath coming in uneven gasps.

"I find your advances and your false manners repugnant," Eisenhart said. "You find the Vigilant women stupid? You think all it takes is a black dress and a large hat and some kind of silliness and you're one of us? Do you have any idea where I've been all night? This silly group of women are the ones who tune the deaf ear of our chief of police. Three weeks ago, a fourteen-year-old girl, a child in ribbons, was brought to this city by an uncle to work at a hotel. I won't say the name of the hotel because it is of no consequence. But at the height of her employment she was forced into relations with more than forty men in a single afternoon. When the girl complained to us at the Hall, her story was written off by a city detective who believed that only a young girl's foolishness, naiveté, or lust could have produced it. Dr. Marina Bertola attended to this young girl's wounds personally and, mark my words, Mrs. Delmont, they were horrifying and deep."

Maude just stared at her. "What's your point, sister?"

"I expect this conduct from men, but when a woman sells out her own kind it turns my stomach."

Kate Eisenhart ripped the big black hat off Maude Delmont and tossed it down the stairwell, the hat pin wheeling on its brim until hitting a wall. The large policewoman picked up the heavy blue dress from her boots, well above the dirty stairs, and made her way back to the first floor, where Maude could hear a crowd beginning to gather.

THEY COULD HAVE BROUGHT the being to him in a box or cage, Hearst decided. The man was so scrawny and scared that he reminded Hearst of a feral animal presented for inspection before being locked in a zoo. He had the eyes of a monkey, nervous and quick, and Hearst half expected the man to leap onto his giant desk and steal an apple. Two hired men had stayed at the Hollywood cemetery all night to find the odd little fellow clutching the pink tiger lilies and Hearst could not wait to get the first interview with this man everyone wanted to know. He was the key to the mystery, the paradox solved—the man who worshipped at Virginia Rappe's grave daily. He was real but created by Hearst, an international sensation storied in ink and then unmasked for all, and the reason he'd been whisked onto a train north to the city and brought right into the *Examiner* offices as if he were their own property.

"Your name is truly Crystal Rivers?" Hearst asked.

"Yes, sir," the odd little man said. "I am."

The top floor of the *Examiner* office was brisk with publicity men, and four projectionists, nine florists, and at least one organ player. There had been four, but he'd fired the others for not getting the feel of *Enchantment* right. Tonight was the premiere.

"And you were acquainted with Miss Rappe?"

"Oh, yes, sir."

"How so?"

"She loves me."

"You?" Hearst said, laughing. He nudged the ribs of the young reporter who was taking dictation, standing by his side at the great desk. The young reporter smiled back but continued to write. A florist held up a handful of roses and Hearst nodded. A publicity man placed a still shot of Marion Davies in his hand and Hearst shook him off. "She loved you? You have proof of this?"

The skinny little man with enormous ears and hands peered down at his long skinny fingers with those great bulging eyes and shook his head. "She smiled at me once."

"And where was this?" Hearst asked. He opened a top-floor window to let in some air and it smelled of the sea and salt and of ragged adventure stories. He thought about what he would serve to Miss Davies after the premiere. He needed someone to call the Fairmont. Or had that been arranged? There was also the question of getting a massive chandelier to the Grenada Theatre before the doors opened. It had to be moved from the docks and inside with great care.

"In a movie house," Crystal Rivers said.

"Did you speak to her?"

The silly little man shook his head. "How could I? She was up there." He pointed to the open windows behind Hearst.

Hearst looked at him, puzzled, and walked behind his great desk, hands behind his back, looking down at the wharves, the ferry buildings, the ferries with the big, frothing wakes heading to and from Oakland. "I'm sorry?" Hearst asked, as if suddenly being reminded of the answer.

"And here," the man said. He fumbled for a broken, sad little suitcase and got to the floor of Mr. Hearst's office at the feet of the dozens waiting to be heard and opened it with great pride, pulling out clippings from newspapers and magazines and sheet music. "She's here. All of her. She was mine."

Hearst looked to the young reporter and the young reporter to him. Hearst paced the office. "The world wants to know why you did it."

"I only wished to lay flowers on her grave."

"You laid wreaths and baskets of pink tiger lilies for days," Hearst said and chuckled. "When my newspapermen would come to you, you would run from them like some kind of criminal. You became somewhat of a figure, I guess. You know my papers have been writing about you for weeks now? The American people want to know who you are."

Crystal Rivers, bony and thin in ill-fitting rags and a poor hat he wrung in his hands, turned his bulging eyes back to Hearst. "Am I going to jail?"

"I'm not the police, you silly little man."

"They told me I had to come to the city."

"They gave you money, too."

Crystal Rivers started to gather his clippings together, working on his hands and knees, and placed them all back in neat piles of liturgy and closed the case with a tight click. Hearst spotted something on the floor, the young reporter noticing Hearst's gaze and reached for a publicity photograph, handing it to his boss. A yellowed, frayed clipping of a girl that could be Virginia Rappe, perhaps not—too portly, too full in the mouth.

"I did nothing wrong," Crystal Rivers said, wiping his face. "May I please go?"

Hearst nodded, silent and agreeing, meeting the man's eyes. The man stared. Hearst blinked.

"Why won't you all just leave her alone?" Crystal Rivers said, starting to sob. "Haven't you all done enough? Leave Virginia alone!"

Hearst set the photo upon his desk, littered with maybe three hundred or so photographs of Miss Marion Davies.

"I only wanted to touch her," Rivers said. "But when I touched the light, the light from the projector, I felt nothing at all, not even warmth. Why is that?"

Hearst looked back to the young reporter, a sly smile on the newsman's face, a slack, humiliating smile for the poor little fellow. Hearst shot the reporter a hateful look and bounded from the room, slamming the door behind him so hard he wondered why the glass didn't shatter.

21

The Old Man poured Sam a drink, glasses were raised, and a toast was proposed for bringing Alice Blake back to the city. The drink was bad stuff, poor imitation Scotch, but, despite the taste, the stuff did its business and Sam gladly accepted a refill. Phil Haultain sat on his desk, a goofy drunk grin on his face, the kid just learning to hold his liquor while he told stories to the office boys about the sounds old Zey Prevon-Prevost could make. The office boys, just kids like when Sam started out in Baltimore, laughed and egged him on for more, and he was setting into a story about the mole on her ass. There was something about that mole, Phil said.

"McNab wired a bonus," the Old Man said. "The girl says she was forced to change her statement. Mr. Pinkerton called personally."

"Will it matter?"

"Brady won't put up the Delmont woman, too risky. These goddamn showgirls were all he had."

"So what will Alice say?"

"She sez Virginia Rappe said, 'He hurt me,' without identifying the *he*. Brady tried to force the girl into saying, 'Arbuckle hurt me.'"

"The *he* could have been Fishback when he threw her into the bath."

"Exactly what McNab will argue."

"They got nothin'."

"But they got this far."

Sam raised his drink and finished the glass of bad Scotch, a cigarette burning between his fingers. The Teletype was clicking in the adjoining room, while some other ops were pounding on typewriter keys with their fists. Or elbows. There were con men to nab, jewels stolen from hotels, runaway daughters joining cults. Nobody slept.

"Fishback or Hibbard or whatever the bastard's name is is back in the city for the trial," Sam said. "The Palace."

"You need help?"

"I wouldn't slough off, Phil."

Phil walked back to the Old Man's desk on cue and told Sam there was a call for him. Sam took the call, thinking it was Jose, but was greeted with the excited voice of Pete the Fink.

"Thought you'd lost me."

"I'd never lose you, Fink."

"I got it. I got it, brother."

"How 'bout a hint?"

"I got something that will blow the lid right off ole Fatty's case."

"I'm dying with anticipation."

"How'd you Pinks like to have the broad who was Virginia Rappe's personal nursemaid for two years?"

"How would I?"

"She'd be happy to talk about some sort of spells where the woman cried out in pain and ripped her clothes off. What you call that?"

"A con."

"Straight up."

"Don't screw me, Pete."

"The word of a grifter."

"What's it to you?"

"It'll cost. But it's on the level. Gold."

"How much?"

"Five hundred."

"You're kidding."

"A free man."

"Who is she? Your sister?"

"Name's Irene Morgan. Swedish. Blue eyes. Blond hair. Big tits."

"I like her already."

"We need you to wire the money."

"Come off it."

"For the Owl. Two seats."

"Why do we need you?"

"I'm her agent."

"Jesus Christ."

"You pay when you meet her."

"You're that sure?"

"Does Dr. Bagwa lie?"

"Frequently."

Sam rang off and replaced the earpiece on the telephone cradle. He propped his feet up, smoking and looking out the window to Market Street, seeing nothing but night. It was getting late and Fred Fishback awaited. Walking to the rack, he grabbed Phil Haultain's Stetson and tossed it to the big man still telling his stories and said, "Ready?"

WHILE McNAB AND MILTON U'REN interviewed potential jurors, Roscoe played with his hat. He used his fingers to lightly knock off the dust, twirled the band on his fingers, and when he got really bored he reached for an elastic band on top of McNab's papers. He stretched the band between his fingers, made it fit over his thumb and forefinger like a gun, and even sighted down U'Ren as he paced and asked a prospective juror if he had the goddamn sense—not saying "goddamn" but implying it—to tell the difference between Roscoe Arbuckle the man and Fatty Arbuckle the sweet, stupid face on the movie screen. Roscoe was about to let the elastic fly on that last remark but Brennan closed his hand around Roscoe's fingers and silently shook his head.

"What do you mean?" asked the potential juror, a white man in a blue suit.

"Have you seen Mr. Arbuckle's films?"

"Yes."

"Did you enjoy them?"

"I guess," said the man.

Roscoe rolled his eyes.

"Can you tell the difference between the man who sits at that table and the character you saw on screen?"

"I should say so."

"Do you believe Roscoe Arbuckle is just a funny, sloppy buffoon wandering his way into trouble but meaning no harm?"

"I only seen one picture, it was him at Coney Island, and he got hit in the head with a mallet."

"Did you think it was funny?"

McNab walked toward the judge and held up his hand in a wait-a-minute motion. And Judge Louderback said, soft and bored, "Get on with it please, Mr. U'Ren."

"I guess so," the man said. "But I don't think he's anywhere as good as Charlie Chaplin."

All the newspaper boys and Vigilant women had a real laugh at that, and even McNab had to smile. Roscoe reached for his hat and began to twirl. He raised his eyes up to watch McNab, who took over and walked that lawyerly walk, back and forth, pacing and thinking. Roscoe knocked out some indentions in his hat.

"I don't know why we're wasting your time, sir," McNab said to the possible juror. "We have a self-constituted judge and jury already."

Louderback looked down at McNab who looked out in the courtroom filled with newsboys and Vigilants. McNab looked back to the judge with an expression of *Do I lie?* He continued to walk and think, a man thrown from the proceedings trying to find which way was up. But it was all theatrical and done for show, and the gray ole dog had something to spring. Roscoe quit twirling the hat, his eyes now on McNab.

"Who is that man over there?" McNab said, pointing to Roscoe.

"Fatty Arbuckle."

"Is he real?"

"Sir?"

"Is he real or a projection?'

"I don't understand."

"Answer the question," McNab said. "Is he flesh and blood?"

"Yes, sir."

"That will be all," McNab said. He stood there before the judge, crossed his arms over his black suit. His craggy face and gray bristled head looking as if they were chiseled from granite. When two doors shut behind the juror, McNab turned to Judge Louderback and said in an easygoing tone, "Judge, I'd like to stop this foolishness and go ahead and make a motion to dismiss."

"Motion denied." Louderback didn't even look up from his paperwork.

"Judge, it seems that the prosecution has so graciously consented to eliminate both the Golden Rule and Pontius Pilate from the proceedings."

The newsboys snickered. The Vigilant women gasped and muttered.

U'Ren was a jackrabbit on his feet, pointing his long, crooked finger at McNab and saying, "If you think you can spit polish this once-successful motion picture star—"

"This whole thing is a frame-up, boy," McNab said. "You put those showgirls in cold storage until they read a script you wrote."

"He is a liar," U'Ren said. "Judge, this is all a lot of poisonous gas for the benefit of the press."

"Go ahead and proceed," McNab said, standing firm. "And I'll prove this city's prosecutor intimidated witnesses."

"And if you do," U'Ren said, "I'll resign."

"Stop this," Louderback said. "Bring in the next one."

A deputy walked in a scrawny young man who held a cheap hat in his hand. His face was reddened and chapped from a poor shave. He nodded and smiled a lot, agreeable and friendly and, in some crazy way, wanting to be part of the circus. Roscoe watched him and liked him. He smiled over at the man. The man smiled back. The bastard U'Ren was still fuming over the exchange with McNab and didn't even see it.

"Have you read much about this case?" U'Ren asked.

"Not much."

"Has it been on your mind at all?"

"Not really. I work too much."

"Has it been on your wife's mind?"

"Sir, I don't know my wife's mind."

And this brought another chorus of laughter from black-hatted Vigilants and newsboys alike. Roscoe clenched his jaw and looked over at Brennan, shaking his head. He was so glad he could still provide laughter for the goddamn masses.

THEY PICKED UP FREDDIE FISHBACK as soon as the gold elevator doors parted at the Palace Hotel and he wandered over to the tobacco stand to pick up a pack of Tuxedos. He was tall and well dressed, with the posture of an athlete but the rough, loping walk of a teenager, and for a moment Sam thought the man was surely drunk. Phil fell in stride beside Sam as Fishback followed Market Street, turning off immediately on Kearny and heading north. The men didn't talk and there were enough people, even after nine, coming and going from the hotel and restaurant trade, that Fishback wouldn't notice. Sam didn't think the man would notice if they'd been hiking through the Salt Flats. The worst was when you had some fella window-shopping and taking in the sites, keen to new things, new people, maybe catching a glance of you in a store window.

He was taking long strides, lean and determined, and headed somewhere specific, maybe even a little late. Fishback checked his watch at least four times since leaving the Palace.

The fog was something terrible, wet clouds that hit Sam like a fist, and as he walked he cloaked his mouth with a bleached handkerchief. Fishback sped up, Sam slowed down. He felt like someone was squeezing him dry. Breaths came in sharp little spurts, ragged and small. A breath caught in his throat and wouldn't spread. He felt light-headed, knees weak. It was a cold night, but Sam's shirt had grown damp.

"You take him."

"You okay?"

"I'll try and catch up."

Sam caught the firm edge of a brick town house. He tried to fill his bum lungs with cigarette smoke, the way pearl divers do with air before disappearing down into the depths. The smoke made him feel better, eased the breathing. He could hear the lungs, scarred and cracked, a wheezing in his throat. As he steadied himself, he could see inside the town house, where a man and a woman sat at a silver-set, linen-covered table. A negress appeared in the room, setting a large bowl of soup before a child, and the young boy clapped and clapped, his parents laughing, as the negress tucked a comically large napkin around his skinny neck and a silver spoon in his hand. The heat from the soup floated over the boy's face like a phantom.

Sam found his feet and kept walking uphill, catching the top of Haultain's hat as it crossed California, the men separated for seconds by a cable car. But then the cable car was gone, ringing off back down Nob Hill, and there was that big Stetson turning up on Grant and into Chinatown. Phil never looked back, kept an easy tail, and it was several blocks up Grant, all the way into the colony, that he found his partner under an Oriental lamp, a gold dragon wrapping the post, hat down in his eyes and a sly nod down the street. Sam overtook Phil now and they passed grocers with dead chickens hung by their feet and huge sacks of rice and long strands of dried peppers. Street hawkers yelled to the white men with silks; tiny yellow women called to Sam from the second and third floors of flophouses where laundry ran in tattered lines across black-holed alleys.

One woman called to Sam and threw down a key.

He kept walking, Phil keeping the pace on the opposite side of Grant, a little too close. Fishback was there, stiff-shouldered and athletic, perfectly oiled hair, tailored tweeds, and then he was gone. Sam kept on, picked it up a little. He could hear the paper lanterns strung over Grant beating in the wind. But the closer he walked, he heard music. *Jazz.* Fishback had dipped into a back-alley speak. Sam pointed to Phil, and Phil heard the music and smiled.

The door to the joint was a garish red with a long vertical sign overhead saying THE MANCHU. The door was opened, music and laughter grew louder, and Phil disappeared. Ten minutes later, Sam followed.

22

oom, chisel, chisel!" sang the Oriental gal on stage, dressed in a long silk getup, with an embroidered gold dragon crawling from ankle to bosom. She wore long gold gloves, her raven black hair twisted atop her head with chopsticks. "Boom, chisel, chisel!" the girl sang again, and the jazz band stopped and then started again, and a fat Oriental man with the pleasing round face of a Buddha asked Sam where he'd like to sit and, not seeing too many tables or Haultain or Fishback, Sam just shrugged. The fat man brought him to a far corner, and it was a good spot to watch the little tables scattered across the floor, but the light would be tough, nothing but red lanterns spread across the ceiling, drapes covering second-floor windows, with a single spotlight on the girl and her all-Oriental band. The fat man was behind him again, neat and spiffy in a freshly laundered dinner jacket, and asking Sam would he "like setup?"

"Sure. Rye."

"Ice. Ginga-rale?"

"Sure thing."

The man snapped his fingers and more Orientals appeared and laid down a bowl of cracked ice and a single glass with a pint of brown alcohol. The man proudly displayed the cap sealed with wax.

"Five dollar."

"What?"

"Five dollar."

"You got to be kidding?"

"The 'Dragon Show.' The 'Dragon Show,'" he said, pointing to the stage as if any of that made a lick of sense. The fat man looked confused.

Sam poured the whiskey but didn't add ice. He drank and pointed to the girl on stage. The man smiled a big row of crooked teeth and said, "No, no, no," before walking away. Sam shrugged, feeling good to sit down, and poured another. Phil Haultain, hat in hand, walked by, leaned in and whispered, "At the bar," and moved across from Sam. Sam pointed to one of the boys for another round and another glass. He poured one for Phil and left him at the table with all that beautiful booze, cracked ice, and ginger ale.

The bar was a long black-lacquered affair, with two skinny Orientals in white coats pouring. Fishback was turned toward Sam and talking to the woman who'd been on stage, and she seemed friendly and at ease with him as he touched the chopsticks in her hair and did a twirling motion with his fingers to make her turn around. The girl gave an easy laugh. Sam still couldn't see Fishback's face, only the long red nails of the woman clutching the Hollywood director's shoulder and laughing. She held a cigarette in a long holder and spilled smoke from the corner of her mouth as if she were uptown. Fishback's hand twisted around the girl and placed it flat on her fanny and the girl leaned in and whispered.

Fishback kissed the girl on the cheek.

He left the bar.

Phil picked him up by the door.

Sam waited a beat, pushed his way through a long, confusing red curtain and walked out onto a short balcony, into the night, looking down on Grant. He spotted Phil, who'd stalled under the awning of a grocer and then turned to the alley running alongside the Manchu. Rows and rows of laundry hung over the narrow shot, obscuring his view, and Sam saw Fishback only in breaks until he stopped and spoke to someone. Fishback turned and looked up at the Manchu, seeming to look right at Sam, but turned back and started talking to a man Sam couldn't see.

Sam saw hands shake. There was a fat envelope. The director accepted it and walked away.

Fishback headed back out the alley. Phil followed.

Sam bounded down the steps to the first floor, made it to the corner, and then saw a man emerge from the mouth of the alley and turn the opposite way onto Grant. He was short and in a gray suit, gray hat. His hair silver and clipped close on a swarthy neck.

Sam made his way to the opposite side of the street, the man passing over Washington, Jackson, but turning west at Pacific and then looping south again on Stockton. Sam stopped and smoked a cigarette and looked into the window of an import/exporter, surely made. He started to cough again, the sweats on him rough. He felt feverish and sick, knowing the body had turned again and knowing the work was too much. He coughed more into the rag and there was blood.

The man in gray did not look back but continued to walk through Chinatown, back to Clay. Sam took a ragged breath, looked behind him, and nearly vomited.

He saw darkness and lights and then rows and rows of headlights coming from a concrete mouth. Sam reached into the pocket of his tweeds, wiped his lips with the back of his fist, and followed the dark man into the darkness and cold wind of the Stockton Tunnel.

THE CHANDELIER COST sixty thousand and weighed nearly a ton, and one hour before *Enchantment* was set to roll at the Granada the workers couldn't hoist it. Hearst was furious beyond words, watching a dozen men with ropes and pullies working like mules up the gentle slope of the theater, muddying the red carpet and trying to get the damn thing up into the gilded ceiling. The architect was making apologies for the foreman, the foreman was blaming his workers, and the workers didn't speak English. As ten employees surrounded Hearst, in tails and holding his top hat, he simply held up his hand and walked away, trailing up the stage and behind the screen and nodding past two guards as he entered Miss Davies's dressing room.

Marion sat in a chair, looking like a discarded doll. She wore the same chiffon frock and beaver hat from when he'd seen her that morning. The gown he'd ordered from Paris hung from a hook. The jewels still in their velvet cases.

"What's the matter?"

Marion just looked up at him with those enormous sad eyes and bowed little mouth. The mouth quivered a bit.

"I f-f-feel like I'm gonna be sick."

"Don't you worry."

"What if they don't like it?"

"They'll love it. Besides, you know what I say."

"Only r-read the good reviews."

"Right."

"But it seems the only good r-reviews come from Hearst papers."

"Now, that's a lie, Marion. Everyone is in love with you."

"I don't need this, W.R. We c-can live without all this."

"You are the most naturally talented little woman I ever met."

"Little woman?" she smiled, her little bowed mouth pursed like a flower.

He leaned down from his heights and kissed her on the forehead. "Now, get on with it. Smiles. All big smiles."

Hearst returned out onto the stage and watched the men, now double in strength, pulling and straining with the chandelier. The wooden roof creaked, but the joists were built of redwood beams, large enough for a clipper ship. He stared out at all those empty red velvet seats and into the balconies where they would watch the premiere. Thousands of roses would be brought in just moments before the film started, letting those in the theater live the experience, that soft sweet smell blending in their mind with the picture on the screen. Marion, soft-focused, so lovely, forty feet tall, and so modern.

Enchantment, the perfect vehicle for Marion, Hearst so proud to have directed the writer. The story centers on a girl, Ethel Hoyt, a modern girl in every way, spirited, beautiful, and lively, with numerous suitors. The girl spends her time dining and dancing, going to parties with different men, with her father back home worrying about her and knowing the only thing he can do is find a proper suitor for her, and it's on the night of her birthday—how very proper—that he takes her to a performance of *Taming of the Shrew*. There he finds the man who can tame Ethel, a man named Edison—Hearst's idea because of the connotations of inventiveness—and from there Edison suggests Ethel for the lead in his next play, *Sleeping Beauty*—again, Hearst's suggestion to the writer—and as Edison falls for Ethel, so will the audience, to see Marion as Sleeping Beauty—in ringlets, with her moist lips parted—as one of the most fantastic, erotic images ever put on film.

"Mr. Hearst?"

"Hmm?"

A little newsboy held up a copy of the afternoon edition of the *Examiner* and Hearst reached down from the stage to grab the copy. The boy tipped his cap at Mr. Hearst and Mr. Hearst reached into his pocket and flipped him a silver dollar off his thumb. The boy caught it in midair with such a natural gusto that it brought a smile to Hearst's face, and he unfurled the paper and saw the banner headline: ENCHANTED SAN FRANCISCO. He flipped below the fold to see a photo of the fat man at the defense table, his new attorney, McNab, held in conference, the fat man looking confused and worried, starting straight into the camera as if a startled animal.

He'd brought it all on himself.

Hearst looked up from the pages to watch the chandelier finally rise off the ground, tinkling, crystal winking in the light, the men grunting and straining and marching down the aisles up to the waiting doors through which fans of Miss Davies would soon pour. He looked back at the photo and stared at the face of the fat man, so dumb and confused, a sick animal, with animal virtues and animal desires. How drunk would a woman have to be to see something in that soft, doughy face and stupid eyes? How drunk and confused would a woman have to be to let herself be bedded by a millionaire brought into this world in a Kansas mud shack who lived his days cleaning out saloon spittoons before becoming a buffoon to millions?

Hearst had sat in darkness for days when the detective had come to him about the party. He had told him about the actors and Hollywood types who had filled the beach house with their gay laughter and alcohol and jazz music from a Victrola brought out onto the sand. They had danced away the last night of 1919 with cases of the last legal alcohol in this country and the fat man had been the king there, twirling around small, fresh Miss Davies, plying her with drink until even his doughy face could be attractive. All his tailored suits and manicured nails and twenty-dollar haircuts couldn't hide what he'd been. And the thought of him sleeping under the roof that Hearst had built for Miss Davies made him want to vomit, but how could he be angry at Marion? How could he ever fault Marion for the appetites of a fat man? A buffoon.

The fat man had simply walked away that first day of 1920 without a moral headache of consequence—maybe the bright sunlight had brought him some discomfort or perhaps he could not gorge himself on cakes or pies that day. But he had escaped without a bit of gentleman's remorse, the tainted, now-illegal liquor in his blood, driving in his ridiculous automobile like a circus oddity. Hearst rubbed his head and his eyes. He must gather himself. Someone called to him, but he waved him away. Someone called to him again.

He had not a bit of remorse for what he had done. He had only wanted Fatty caught, pants around his ankles, his appetites and vileness and poor breeding known to those who sat in the darkness and giggled at his antics. And now that that had happened, he was finished with the man. He had nothing to do with the death of that girl, absolutely not a thing. That girl was an extra, a supporting player, in a perfectly designed drama written and produced by Hearst with direction from that odd Hungarian fellow, Fishback, although Fishback hadn't the slightest idea who'd given him the script. The Dark Man handled it all for Hearst, finished it off for Hearst, and now the justice for the fat man was in the blind woman's hands.

Hearst heard yelling and grunting and opened his eyes, suddenly aware of all those watching him up on stage and in the light. The beams in the ceiling groaned and strained, the chandelier halfway up through the mammoth space, rising to the very top, the topping to the wedding cake, and Hearst saw the faces marvel at the theater, the perfection, every attention to the slightest detail. Hearst stepped back, hands in the pockets of his tuxedo, and placed the top hat back on his head.

"Yes?" he asked, turning to those who called him.

And then there were yells from the men, the whoosh of the hemp rope from calloused hands, the release of tension of the creaking beams above, and finally a giant, spectacular crash of the chandelier breaking and scattering across the Granada, the thousands of hand-fitted crystal pieces raining around him on stage and into the seats like sleet. Hearst turned his head, a piece of glass ricocheting off the floor and tearing across his cheek.

"Mr. Hearst! Mr. Hearst!"

He turned, the broken crystal all at his feet.

"Mr. Hearst, are you okay?"

Hearst nodded and stepped forward in a crunch.

"You're bleeding."

Hearst reached for the silk handkerchief in his pocket and touched his cheek, dabbing off a bit of blood. He said to no one in particular, "So I am."

SAM SAW THE MAN twice in the glow of scattering headlights. The long brick cavern grew black again and soon there was only the sound of feet clacking in the tunnel and a constant drip of water from the roads above. He walked straight into the darkness at a decent clip, the man a good distance ahead of him. Another car passed and Sam caught sight of the fella looking back over a shoulder; another car passed and the man was gone, maybe running now, Sam knowing he was in no shape to follow. He kept walking, darkness and light, two machines at a time and then three, the constant rhythm of his leather soles thwacking hard and ugly under him. He could just make out some streetlamps from where the tunnel ended under Bush Street. Sam stopped and listened, the tunnel dripped, no cars, little light. He stood still and lit a cigarette.

In the strike of a match, he saw a man's face.

Sam fumbled for the match and it dropped to the wet ground with a hiss.

He felt the point of a gun in his ribs, smelled sulfur, and heard a voice say, "Keep walkin'."

Sam kept moving down the slope toward the mouth of the tunnel, a hand rough inside Sam's jacket pulling the .32, where streetlamps bled light into the cavern. A little Essex Coach roared past them, honking its horn twice. The man kept close, Sam smelling his ash breath on his neck. When the machine had disappeared, Sam closed his eyes, waiting for a bullet to tear through his spine.

But they kept on, the tunnel growing into a wide open mouth. He could see people coming out of an apartment building and a billboard advertising cigars. THE SIZE PLEASES YOU. THE QUALITY PLEASES YOU. THE PRICE PLEASES YOU. DON'T ARGUE. DON'T INFER. A NICKEL WILL PROVE THE ASTONISHING GOODNESS OF THE NEW CURRENCY CIGAR!

Fog seeped outside on Stockton, headlights cut through banks, while more machines roared into the tunnel. Sam's shirt was completely soaked now, and he moved dead-leggedly, feeling feverish and sick. When the light met them gray and weak, the gunman faced him. Sam's breathing stopped for a moment, but he stared back at him, dead-eyed, with a steel bluff. The man recognized it and smiled back, calling it.

He handed Sam back his gun. "Beat it."

Sam pointed his gun into the man's ribs.

"Why don't you reach for my wallet?" the man asked.

"I'm not a thief."

"Reach for it."

Sam reached inside the man's jacket and pulled out a fat, battered leather wallet.

"Come on," the man said. "Open it."

Inside, Sam found a small silver badge like the one he carried. PINKERTON NATIONAL DETECTIVE AGENCY.

"You get it now, Sam?" he said, smiling and snatching the wallet and placing it back inside his coat. As he turned, Sam noted half the man's ear was gone and he felt a stab of recognition.

Anaconda mines. Montana. Four years back.

Sam wavered and for a moment lost sight, hearing the feet steadily fade. Sam held on to the tunnel wall, tried to follow, but knew the man was gone. All he could think about was watching Frank Little swing from under the railroad trestle like a pendulum.

You scared me plenty, Sam," Phil Haultain said. He laid an old horse blanket across Sam's shoulders and handed him a hot cup of coffee. "Wandering around like that, muttering to yourself about some man named Little. What was that all about?"

"The TB can sometimes make you screwy."

"You're talking straight now," Phil said. "Glad of it. Now, what's this about Fishback meeting with another op?"

They sat in the middle of Phil's little apartment, Sam in the only chair in the room and Phil on his Murphy bed drinking straight whiskey. An illuminated clock on his nightstand read four in the morning. Sam massaged his aching head and coughed in a spasm longer than was comfortable. Phil handed him a handkerchief and sat back on the bed, leaning forward to listen.

"He had a badge," Sam said.

"Coulda been phony."

"Sure."

"But you don't believe it?"

"I don't know what to believe."

"Drink that coffee up. You still got the chills."

Sam had never been to Phil's apartment before, a basic city special, a studio with a bathroom and a small kitchen with a narrow gas stove topped with a speckled coffeepot. On the wall hung a small painting of an Indian on a horse holding a spear up in the air, ready for battle. Haultain's big hat hung on a hook by the front door over a rain slicker.

Sam finished the coffee and stared at the painting of the Indian. "I can't do this anymore."

"So you had a bad night."

"That guy coulda knocked me out with his breath."

"You're the best shadow man I've ever seen, Sam."

"My body's giving out."

"You gonna die?" Phil said, looking genuinely sad.

Sam shrugged and smiled. "Would you come to the funeral?"

"You betcha."

"You're a good egg, Phil."

Phil stood up and walked back to his small kitchen and brought the coffeepot. He poured out some more into Sam's mug and laid the pot back on the stove.

"You know, I got an escape plan," he said.

"Go figure," Sam said, warming his hands on the coffee mug.

"No foolin'."

Sam watched him head for a small closet and pull out a few boxes.

"I wanna show you something." He pulled out a small wooden box and sat it on the edge of his bed. With great care, he opened the top and a few old rags and then held two halves of a black sphere, about the size of a cantaloupe. He broke the halves apart and held one aloft, the light from the single bulb that hung from his ceiling catching winking jewels and carved designs.

"That's a hell of a soup bowl," Sam said.

"It's the skull of a very holy man," Phil said. "A lot of museums would like me to give it to them. But unless they have the funds to buy it, I'll keep it as a family heirloom."

"Who was the holy man?"

"A guy who had a good skull."

"What's that spoon and stuff for?"

"I understand it was used to sip blood from human sacrifices."

"Come off it."

"An uncle of mine who lived in Calcutta sent it to me. It was taken as loot by a member of the British Younghusband Expedition to Lhasa, Tibet. I always figured the original owner mighta put a curse on it."

The cold wind whistled around Phil's boardinghouse and the single orange bulb in the room dimmed and buzzed back to life in time with the shaking power cables outside. Sam drank more coffee and reached into his coat, grabbed a pack of cigarettes, and lit one. Phil handed him the halves of the skull and he studied the way the jewels had been laid along the separate pieces.

"Heck of a story."

"I hide it pretty good," Phil said. "You're the first I showed it to. Well, that's not true. I showed it to some gal a few months ago. You know, to impress her that I wasn't just a deadbeat and had some cash if I wanted it. But you know, it gave her the creeps."

"Go figure."

"I didn't. I thought she'd like the jewels."

"Can you imagine what some crazy collectors would do for that thing?"

"They'd probably try to bump me off."

"I'd guess so."

"Sam?"

"Yep."

"You gonna talk to the Old Man about what you saw?"

"I am."

"What if he sez to lay off?"

"I don't know."

"I'd lay off, Sam," Phil said. "Just like you say, bang out that report, sign your number, and go home with a clear head."

"That's not so easy anymore," Sam said.

"You're not well, Sam."

"No," Sam said. "I guess I'm not."

AT NOON, SAM WALKED BESIDE JOSE, pushing Mary Jane through the Civic Center Plaza in a carriage she'd borrowed from the bootleggers downstairs. It was Sunday and Sam still had not slept, the sun bright and shining and harsh in his eyes as he kept up with his family, other families lounging on the green grounds with picnic baskets set up in front of City Hall. He felt wrung-out, dry, but too tired to sleep. He'd lain down for two minutes on the Murphy bed when he'd first come in, Jose on her way out, but he wanted to walk with them, leave the apartment, clean his head out and forget about the Arbuckle case.

"I read your notes," Jose said.

"Which ones?"

"From Virginia's autopsy," she said. "Interesting stuff."

"Let's talk about something else."

"Like what?"

"Mary Jane."

"She's asleep."

"So she is."

"Didn't you say Arbuckle's lawyers have found people to testify that the girl suffered from spells brought on by drinking?"

"They did. I have to meet one of 'em in about an hour."

"Who's that?"

"A buxom Swede."

"You're a great kidder, Sam."

"You know me."

"I particularly like the part about 'a young woman who lost her life so that San Francisco shall not be made the rendezvous of debauchee and gangster.'"

"Debauchee," Sam said. "Good word. I like the way it sounds."

"The autopsy troubles me."

"It troubles me, too."

"The city coroner said when he checked the pelvic cavity, he found it packed with cotton."

"Pandora's box."

"Sam."

Sam lit a cigarette and walked. "We know all this."

"And the bladder, uterus, and rectum were absent."

"They were removed and studied," Sam said. "Destroyed soon after."

"You got to ask yourself, why would a doctor do that? What's he protecting?"

Sam shrugged, changing places with Jose, now pushing the carriage. Jose followed beside him. Sam tipped his hat at another couple walking in the opposite direction with their carriage and baby. The sunny kind of day brought on that kind of thing.

"And this lawyer, McNab, will argue the bladder was already diseased."

"Yep."

"Why would those first doctors cover that up?"

"I assumed they wanted a stellar virgin presented to the altar."

"So the police pushed a cover-up?"

"I think so."

"But this was done before the police were involved."

Sam nodded. He pushed the carriage with one hand, smoked with another. "You know, we could carry a bar in this little buggy. It's perfect. All that jostling around would mix a cocktail or two."

"You are hopeless, Sam."

"Too true."

"You look terrible."

"It's the lighting."

"You need to see a doctor."

Sam looked at his watch. "I need to go."

"Please come home. Lay down."

"Just this one thing," Sam said, winking at her. "I have to meet with an old friend."

PETE THE FINK SPOTTED SAM just as soon as he stepped into the Ferry Building terminal, waving with a free hand and dragging a big leather suitcase with the other. A woman a good head taller walked beside him, carrying a small pink hatbox and wearing a hat and snug black dress trimmed around the neck and sleeves with white fur. She was a true blonde, with blue eyes and red lips and a beauty mark just beside her mouth. She looked nervous as she waddled behind the Fink and didn't stop glancing all around the big Ferry Building even as she was introduced to Sam, Sam noting they stood at the same height as she said "How do you do" with a noticeable accent. She smelled like powder and perfume, and although a large woman, she wasn't fat, just big and healthy.

Sam grabbed her hatbox, letting Pete continue to drag the big suitcase, and they walked through the main terminal, as large as a couple of football fields, a glass ceiling letting in the bright afternoon light. Pete nudged Sam in the ribs as they watched the big Swedish girl move ahead of them, her muscular and healthy buttocks swaying from side to side. The girl attracted attention from every man she passed, all of them craning their necks, just about tripping over their feet, mouths wide-open, watching the girl show a nice set of calves below the hem.

"Where you fellas puttin' us up?" Pete asked.

"Are we supposed to put you up?"

"Sam, if you screw me, me and Miss Morgan here will get right back on that ferry to Oakland and be back in Los Angeles by midnight."

"We got a place. The Golden West."

"Sounds like a flophouse."

"It's where I had my honeymoon."

"Don't I feel much better," Pete said. "Say, can I have some help with this? Irene, honey, what'd you pack, some rocks?"

Sam walked beside Irene and she was aware of him but kept glancing around the terminal at the shoeshine men and porters and bustling masses visiting the city for the weekend. Many men smiled at her. She smiled back. They tipped their hats. She smiled. Chinese men bowed. It was all so universal, Sam thought.

"First time in the city?"

"Yes."

"So, you're from Sweden."

"Gutenberg."

"Like the Bible."

"Sweden isn't in the Bible."

"I see."

They kept walking, Sam's detective eye noting her breasts of the appropriate and recommended size for a nice Swedish girl.

"Pete tells me you knew Miss Rappe."

"I work for her for two years."

"As a nurse?"

"I go with her to gymnasiums to keep with exercises. I make sure she take steam. I give her massage two times a day. All like Mr. Lehrman say."

"And you saw her get sick?"

"Many times," Irene Morgan said. She stopped and grasped the dress at her large bosoms and started to pull the material down. "Like this. When she drink alcohol, her clothes are gone. Woosh."

She pulled down so that Sam could see her brassiere. He put a hand on her hand to stop her from going further and said, "Does Mr. Lehrman know you're here?"

"He fired me."

"When?"

"When Miss Rappe leaved."

"When was that?"

"Oh, long time," she said. "Months."

"Why'd she tear at her clothes?"

"She would get sick when she drank."

"Did Pete tell you to say that?"

"No. No, I tell him," she said. "I don't want to get in trouble, okay? I don't want people to think I'm bad of character."

"Why would they do that?"

"A policeman come to see me and said if I say these things about Miss Rappe that it would ruin me. He said the government could even send me back to Sweden. I told Pete these things and he said you were a good policemen. Is that right?"

"Absolutely," Sam said. "I'm a great policeman."

"That man told me I could be hurt."

"No chance," Sam said. "We'll look out for you. We got our best man on it."

"Who?"

Sam smiled. "Me."

Pete walked beside them now, a black porter pulling the big suitcase, and Pete, hearing that last comment, winked over at Sam. "Don't be modest, Sam. Tell her the way it is."

The three moved outside the Ferry Building, waiting for a yellow taxi to take them back toward Union Square. Sam readjusted the cap on his head and offered a cigarette to Irene. Pete the Fink sat on the big piece of luggage, legs on each side, like he was riding a horse.

"It's scary," she said.

"What's that?"

"The city."

"It's not so bad."

"It killed Miss Virginia."

"I don't know what happened to Virginia," Sam said. "But it wasn't the city."

"That poor girl," Irene said, shaking her head. "And with child, too."

Sam turned his head, cigarette hanging loose from his lower lip. "Come again?"

"Of course you know she was pregnant with Mr. Lehrman's baby?"

24

The rains came that Monday, and Roscoe felt strangely comfortable inside the Hall of Justice, listening to the tapping on glass, water running down the high windows, and mainly just falling into the routine of sitting behind the desk, a water pitcher in front of McNab, Minta and Ma sitting behind them. They'd eat lunch together at good restaurants during the breaks, and sometimes Minta would fall asleep during the medical testimony because pretty much all of it was the same only repeated by different doctors who saw Virginia before she died. But not a bit of it made Roscoe tired—they were off, the trial had started, and the twelve folks, five women and seven men, sitting up there in the box, spectators taking notes on the little details that Roscoe was beginning to know by heart. He just sat there and listened, McNab having told him earlier to stop playing with those goddamn elastics and his hat. He said juries didn't like men on trial who didn't pay attention, it showed they didn't give a shit.

The room changed a great deal after lunch, Roscoe knowing the feel and energy of a room better than anyone. This room was electric. The word was that the showgirls were going to take the stand, and you could hear the whispers about Alice and Zey throughout the hall and along the corridors and down the steps and even out onto Portsmouth Square.

Zey was first, the girl all smiles as she was led into the courtroom, dressed in blue broadcloth with a fur hat, black stockings, and silk ballerina shoes. She smiled at the judge. She smiled at the jury. She smiled at U'Ren and

Brady but didn't look once at Roscoe. U'ren led her through it, just as he had at the coroner's inquest and police court, and she sat there with an idiot grin on that doughy face, nodding and repeating things, finely trained and parroted, and looking to Roscoe like a thousand girls who'd read lines. Roscoe closed his eyes and leaned into the desk, rubbing his forehead.

"And what did Miss Rappe say?" U'Ren asked.

"She said, 'He hurt me. He hurt me. I'm dying.'"

Roscoe opened his eyes. He turned to McNab. McNab looked back to the girl, thumping a pencil on the desk, thinking, changing strategy, restless energy ready to pounce on her. The girl continued on about how Virginia had entered room 1219 first and then moments later Roscoe walked in behind her, and she wasn't sure of the time but at some point later Mrs. Delmont—that goddamn woman—started banging on the door with her fist and the heel of a shoe. That's when they found the girl writhing in pain and tearing her clothes off.

U'Ren cleaned his glasses, placed them back on his feral little face, mouth puckered like he'd sucked a lemon, and looked as if he was inspecting his creation for anything he might have missed. But he was finished with her and McNab was on his feet, brushing by U'Ren, nudging the man's shoulder ever so lightly, but seeming to do it all in a rush by accident. He began to speak almost immediately, the words in his throat for the last twenty minutes. "The girl said, 'He hurt me. He hurt me'?"

"That's right," Zey said, kind of rolling her eyes like McNab had wax in his ears or was too old to remember.

"She said it twice?"

"Yeah."

"And then said, 'I'm dying'?"

"That's what I said," Zey said, looking over at Brady and U'Ren, and McNab caught her eye and moved his bulky bearlike body right in her line of vision. She narrowed her eyes at him like *What's the big idea?*

"Do you recall making the statement earlier that the girl had said, 'He killed me. Arbuckle killed me'?"

"No."

"Are you sure?"

"I know what I heard," she said. She rolled her eyes again, and Roscoe noted she was pretty damn good at it. Maybe even practiced it in the mirror, copying Mabel Normand.

"Your Honor, we'd like to read her earlier testimony into the record," McNab said. He read every word from her sworn statement but didn't stop there. With a hell of a flourish, the gruff old man read her testimony into the record and did his best to sound gay and flighty, with every other sentence he read ending with "I sez I don't remember nothin'. It's all mixed up, I tell you." McNab ended with U'Ren asking the girl where she lived and the girl saying, "I don't want to tell you because I don't want my mother drawn into this."

Zey Prevon-Prevost stifled a giggle. Some on the court laughed. Roscoe noticed no one on the jury even cracked a smile.

"Did you sign your name to this statement?" McNab asked.

"Yes."

"Were you forced?"

The girl tried to look around McNab to the prosecution table, without any luck. McNab let the question hang there, not saying a word, letting the big damn silence of the wood-paneled room suck it from her.

"No."

"Where have you been for the last month?"

"Calistoga."

"By yourself?"

"With Alice."

"Alice Blake?"

"Yes."

"And did you two decide on this trip yourselves?"

"I don't know," Zey said. "I was just sent there."

"By who?"

"Mr. Brady."

"Did you have a nice time?"

"I guess."

"I hear the treatments are quite relaxing," McNab said. "Especially when it's on the taxpayer tab."

U'Ren and Brady stood in unison, Louderback shot down a stare from the bench. McNab just rubbed his craggy face and stretched his neck, and he continued on while Zey looked as if she was sitting on a griddle, turning and readjusting, crossing her leg and showing her black stockings and silk ballerina shoes, her smile plastic.

"Did Mr. U'Ren tell you that you had to sign that statement?"

Zey shook her head.

"Please state your answer."

"No, sir."

"But now you're saying the statement is incorrect."

Zey's mouth opened, her pudgy little face dropped, and she put her hands to her head. "I don't know. I don't know."

"Please answer," Judge Louderback said.

"It's just all mixed up," Zey said. "All of it is all mixed up."

"Then," McNab said, pointing to her and then turning to the jury, Roscoe watching him work like a goddamn acrobat, even turning back to Minta and Ma with a look on his face like *Look at that bastard go*, and Minta winking back at him. "You could have mistaken Miss Rappe's statement that day?"

"I don't know."

"Hadn't Miss Rappe just been immersed into a cold bath by you and Miss Blake and a Mr. Fishback?"

"Yes," Zey said, shaking her head, trying to find his meaning.

"Mr. Fishback had hold of her arms?"

"Yes."

"And even the contact of her clothes hurt her, isn't that true?"

"Yes."

"So when Miss Rappe said 'he,' she could've meant that it was Mr. Fishback and not Mr. Arbuckle that hurt her?"

"I don't know."

"You don't know if she meant Mr. Fishback, do you?"

"I don't know."

"Then you don't know if she meant Mr. Arbuckle, do you?"

"I don't know."

"Your Honor, I would ask you to direct the witness to answer my question and remind her that she is under oath and failing to do so amounts to perjury. Punishable by imprisonment."

Zey smiled and shrugged.

"Objection," U'Ren said, shouting and jumping up.

"Objection to the crime of perjury?" McNab asked, smiling a bit.

"Sit down, Mr. U'Ren," Louderback said, before leaning toward Zey. "Please answer the question yes or no, Miss Prevon."

"You don't know if he meant Mr. Arbuckle was the one who hurt her, do you, Miss Prevon?" McNab asked.

Zey glanced at U'Ren, before she said in a small, soft voice, "No."

"Because it's quite possible she could have been referring to Mr. Fishback when she said 'he,' since you and Mr. Fishback had just roughly handled her and tossed her into a bath of very cold water to cure what you thought was a bad drunk?"

"I don't know."

"Your Honor?"

Judge Louderback leaned toward her. "Yes or no."

"Yes."

"*Yes*, she could have meant Mr. Fishback hurt her and not Mr. Arbuckle?" McNab asked, voice booming.

"Yes."

"No further questions," McNab said.

McNab sat back down next to Roscoe and Roscoe smiled at him, giving his lawyer a soft shot on the arm, but the old crotchety bastard just looked at him like he'd just pissed on his shoe and returned to the papers spread out before him.

———————

HEARST DIRECTED GEORGE to drive him to the Embarcadero, having him slow behind a streetcar and wait until it rambled off into the rainy night. The Dark Man was at the curb and spotted the Chandler limousine, hat tilted over his eyes, black umbrella in hand, looking to Hearst like a funeral director. Two more streetcars passed, each going the opposite way, the inside of each great rattling box filled with artificial light as it rambled past the piers and endless fishing boats. Old men sat under lean-tos fixing fishing nets by the light of kerosene lanterns. The Dark Man closed the umbrella and crawled inside with Hearst.

The limousine pulled out onto the roadways hugging the bay and headed up past Market Street and the Ferry Building, more piers flashing by the windows, George now overtaking the streetcars. The big black car seeming to glide on rails. Hearst held his head in his hand as they rolled along and stared out the glass, feeling the Dark Man staring at him but saying nothing. They soon wound around the Cliff House and the Sutro Baths and the terrain grew rocky and ragged, the road narrowing, the headlights cutting a wide path into the rain.

"I read *Enchantment* was the best picture ever made."

Hearst stared at the man and took in his black suit, smug grin.

The man flipped open a writing tablet and read. "Her name is Irene Morgan."

"Is she genuine?"

"I think so."

"I will not have Miss Rappe's name besmirched.'"

"You want some advice, Mr. Hearst?"

"Did I ask you for any?"

"Sometimes people just die," the Dark Man said. He removed the hat from his gray head and shook loose some rainwater. The outline of the rocky coast looked like jagged silhouettes. "That wasn't the plan."

"They want her to be called a whore."

"You ever play cards, Mr. Hearst?" The Dark Man's face was half lit in the lights from the baths, the other split in shadow.

Hearst just looked at him.

"You get out when the gettin' is good," the Dark Man said. "And that was some time back."

Hearst continued to stare. The man stared back. Hearst called for George to circle back downtown. The big, lumbering car found a spot along the cliffs and made a wide, squeaking turn. Rain began to fall harder now and the windows were completely obscured with grays and blacks, the rocky outline and silhouettes gone. The man across from Hearst smelled of heavy cologne and Hearst took him as someone who needed to cover up a strong offensive odor.

"But you're not done poking at this?" the Dark Man said. He smiled, understanding.

Hearst turned and watched the rain fall across the window, the light coming into the limousine's carriage again across his face and eyes, and he said nothing.

JUST OUTSIDE the Flood Building, Sam heard someone call out to him from across Ellis Street. He turned and stared into the long, driving sheets of rain and just made out the face of a man and an umbrella. The man was smiling and offered a hand and Sam stepped back, watching for any quick moves.

"George Glennon," the man said, "the St. Francis?"

Sam shook Glennon's hand and told him he was sorry. "A little nervy, I guess."

"Let's get out of the rain," the hotel dick said.

They walked a couple doors down to John's Grill, where Sam sat next to the pudgy fella up at the bar. They ordered a couple coffees and were disappointed when the cups came back as plain joe. Sam asked the Greek what gives and the Greek pointed to a couple cops eating a steak dinner by the front door.

"As if they care," Sam said.

The Greek shrugged and walked.

Sam drank the coffee and had a smoke. Glennon did the same.

"You ever get a bead on that Dr. Rumwell?"

"I did," Sam said. "Thanks for the tip."

"What'd you think?"

"Strange little man, nervous, jumpy. I tailed him one night out into the Barbary and watched him attend to a mess of whores at a place called Purcell's."

"That's mighty white of him."

"He got a big wad of cash for the effort," Sam said. "Dr. Rumwell works the unwashed trade, no telling what the sailors bring to port."

"How's he know Mrs. Delmont?"

"Don't know," Sam said. "I got pulled off to work some business down south."

Glennon smoothed down his mustache, scratched his neck, and drank more coffee. He thought about it, added some more sugar to his coffee, stirred it a bit, and then said, "That bastard manager at the St. Francis let me go."

Sam listened.

"I gave a deposition to Gavin McNab last week saying that Virginia Rappe told me personal she didn't know what was wrong with her. Suddenly there are two pigheaded Irish cops in my lobby, showing their muscles and badges and swinging their dicks around wanting to charge me with dereliction of duty."

"And they fired you?"

"Yep," Glennon said. "The cops say they'll charge me if I see McNab again."

"Ain't the legal system a beaut?"

Glennon shook his head and drank his coffee. Sam let the cigarette burn in his fingers and watched the rain outside on Ellis Street. The arc lamps were on, shining gold patterns of water running naked down the road.

"I'm sorry," Sam said.

"It's not your fault."

Sam shook his head.

"I didn't come to tell you a sob story," Glennon said. "Before I left I watched a team of policemen go upstairs to the Arbuckle suite. They removed three big doors. Two from 1219 and one from 1220. It took four men to carry each of 'em out."

"Fingerprints?"

"Some guy named Heinrich and a broad named Salome Doyle," he said. "Get this. When they entered the lobby, this Heinrich guys sez to the cops, 'Make way for Sherlock Holmes and Dr. Watson.' He's a complete screwball."

"Did they dust the room before that?"

"Not that I saw."

"And they just did this when?"

"Friday," Glennon said. "I wanted to keep you wise."

He handed Sam his old business card from the St. Francis. GEORGE GLENNON. HOUSE DETECTIVE. An address. An extension number. Sam flipped the card and on the back was written, "Kate Brennan."

"Fine Celtic girl."

"Who's she?"

"A hell of good maid," Glennon said. "Fired her, too. You folks may want to ask Mrs. Brennan if she wiped down the doors after Arbuckle checked out."

"They fixed it."

"Is that possible?"

"I know a guy who can add any set of prints you want for fifty bucks."

Sam offered his hand. Glennon took it with a wink and disappeared back onto Ellis. Sam finished the coffee, too poor to pay for a meal, and smoked a cigarette on his way back to the Flood Building.

It was late when he reached the third-floor office. The Old Man had gone home. Haultain was out on assignment. Sam recognized a couple other ops at their desks and one young boy who worked the Teletype and telephone in case something big happened. Sam found a desk, not his desk but a desk they all used, and called his landlady, the bootlegger, and asked her to send word to Jose that he'd be home in an hour or so.

In a half hour, the room thinned out. The ops gone. Just Sam and the office boy.

Sam asked the office boy to place a call for him to the Baltimore branch. He wanted to run down the name of a possible op: medium build, with iron-gray hair, brown eyes, and half an ear missing.

25

D oes this goddamn rain ever stop?" Roscoe asked. "How do you people live here?"

"You lived here," McNab said. "You tell me."

They sat in a private booth, along with Minta and Ma, at the Tadich Grill off Washington. The Tadich was all dark paneled wood and soft yellow lights. The floors were honeycombed black and white and the waiters wore stiff bleached linen. Roscoe felt human in a good restaurant again, straightening his tie and relaxing into the booth. The waiters called him "sir" and brushed away bread crumbs.

"Before the Quake," Roscoe said, "Sid Grauman hired me to work for seventeen bucks a week. I sang to illustrated slides, songs like 'Tell Mother You Saw Me,' crapola like that. Remember that stuff, Minta? Just like Long Beach. Good money back then. But then there was the goddamn Quake and I was out in the street, hauling rocks into oxcarts. Ma, you shoulda seen the city back then, everything was on fire, any able man was given a shovel or faced the point of a gun. I never seen anything like it, and hope I never do again."

"Roscoe?" McNab said.

"Yeah?"

"I was here, too. The Quake was tough on all of us, but we dusted ourselves off, buried the dead, and built a brand-spanking-new city. Let's skip over memory lane and to the shitstorm at hand. 'Scuse me, ladies."

Roscoe adjusted his silver cuff links, put his hand on Minta's knee, and winked across the table at Ma. Ma winked back. He loved Ma.

"We're not so different, me and you," Roscoe said, pointing the nubbed end of his cigarette at McNab. "We're both performers with our own set of talents. We both know how to work a room, feel a crowd."

McNab looked uneasy and shook his head.

"You know the secret of working a room?"

"Tell me."

"You have to be quick on your feet. If a joke bores 'em, head off into a dance. If they don't like dancing, try a little physical stuff on stage. A crowd isn't just a bunch of people, it's a single thing, and that single thing reacts as one person. You just have to find that vein and tap into it."

"Why risk it?" McNab said. "You talk too much and people think you're a liar. You talk too little and they think you have something to hide. Hell, Roscoe, you're a fat man. You sweat. The jury will think you're nervous."

"That's not what I was saying."

"Sure it was."

"That's Zukor talking."

"Did I say a goddamn thing about Al Zukor?"

"You don't have to," Roscoe said, plugging a fresh cigarette into his mouth and striking a match. "Zukor doesn't think I'm able to take the stand. He thinks I'm a kid no matter how much money I've made that bastard."

"Roscoe," Minta said.

Ma broke off a piece of bread and chewed with her toothless mouth.

"Zukor is a Jew bastard," Roscoe said, breaking a match and starting a new one. "I said it. Have I heard from him once since I left Los Angeles? He's waiting to see how this plays out. I think he wants me locked in San Quentin. That way he can wiggle out of that contract."

A waiter opened the curtain to the back booth and brought the table a bottle of white wine and three bowls of soup, a loaf of sourdough. Roscoe poured wine for Minta and McNab. Ma didn't drink. The soup was hot and steaming and perfect on a cold, foggy day. He could stay here all afternoon, enjoy lunch, enjoy dessert and coffee, smoke a bit, tell a few jokes, sing a few songs. Every time he walked into the hall, he felt like a goddamn circus elephant paraded down Main Street.

"Who do you work for?" Roscoe said, pointing the end of his spoon at McNab.

McNab leaned back in the booth and took in Roscoe, as if seeing him for the first time. His craggy old face split into a smile, "I work for myself."

"You work for Paramount."

"I do what's best for the client," McNab said. The waiter came over and tucked a towel around McNab's neck, setting a big bowl of steaming mussels and sea creatures in front of him. The crusty old lawyer ate with beautiful manners, dipping the spoon away from him, very little splattered on the linen.

"Well?" Roscoe said.

"A jury isn't vaudeville, Roscoe," he said. "It can be a mob."

"I can make 'em love me," Roscoe said. "They haven't taken that away from me, have they?"

McNab looked up from the soup and over at Minta and then over to toothless Ma and there was a steady silence in the booth, the sounds of the restaurant carrying on, until they'd finished eating and made their way back to court. Roscoe wasn't two steps outside when someone tapped him on the shoulder and called his name. At first he didn't place the rail-thin man, maybe the thinnest man he'd ever seen, but then he knew it was the Pinkerton he'd met down south.

McNab stood beside Roscoe and stared at the young detective.

"He's all right," Minta said, waiting for her mother to get in the limousine and then following her. "He's with the Pinkertons."

McNab looked at his gold timepiece and crawled into the limousine and slammed the door. "Hurry up with it."

Roscoe buttoned his jacket and pulled his hands into some leather gloves. "What a shit day."

"What's your connection to William Randolph Hearst?" the Pinkerton asked.

Roscoe shook his head.

"You know him?"

"I met the man once," Roscoe said. "He's been giving me a hell of a trashing in the papers, but that's no secret."

"He have a reason?"

"He's an asshole. You need much else?"

"He works with Paramount?"

"He gets Paramount distribution."

"And they get Hearst press?"

"Something like that."

"Then why's he laying into you, Roscoe?"

Roscoe shook his head again but felt himself sweat underneath the coat. He tried to keep a light smile and shook the detective's hand warmly. "I got to go, Pinkerton. Judge Louderback doesn't like to be kept waiting."

The detective just stood there, watching him, waiting for an answer.

But instead, Roscoe gave him an old pat on the back and climbed in the limousine, the door barely closing before the big machine rolled up the hill and toward Portsmouth Square. Roscoe took a deep breath, feeling more trapped than ever, thinking of what it must be like to be swimming under a sheet of ice.

WHEN DR. RUMWELL saw Maude sitting in his parlor having tea with his wife, he looked as if he'd just shit his drawers. His little mustache, the one that looked like he dyed it with boot polish, twitched under his nose and his eyelids fluttered as he removed his hat and black overcoat, leaving his well-worn medical bag by the door.

"Mrs. Delmont is such good company," his wife said, laughing. "So charming."

Rumwell just stood in the doorframe staring down at Maude, who crossed her legs and took another cookie his wife had offered. She sipped some tea and smiled up at Rumwell from the lip of the cup.

"Won't you sit down?" Maude asked him.

He shook his head. He'd begun to perspire at the brow.

"Darling," his wife said, "Mrs. Delmont has been waiting on you for more than an hour."

"She may see me during office hours."

"But I tried to call the clinic," Maude said. "They told me you wouldn't see me."

"Quite right."

Rummy's wife looked shocked and put down her tea. She was the kind of frail woman who wore going-out clothes around the house, got the vapors, and would invite some complete stranger into her little velvet parlor and serve cookies and tea. Her husband's manners were making her physically ill.

"But, Doctor," Maude said, "you remember that itch I have? You've treated it before."

She smiled at him and took another bite of cookie. The frail wife left the room, the kitchen door swinging back and forth behind her, the woman muttering something about dinner burning on the stove. Rumwell looked as if he'd swallowed a turd.

"You must be going," Rumwell said.

Maude stood and walked to him. He held out a hand as if she was some kind of leper and all that unease was making Maude pretty damn happy. She smiled at him, walking slow and swatting her giant hat from side to side and against her buttocks. "Come on, Rummy."

"Not here."

"I don't believe you'd see me anywhere."

"I will if you'd please leave."

Maude turned from him to a little wooden cabinet and opened a glass door. She pulled out a little porcelain curio of a kitten and held it in the palm of her hand, staring at it, appraising it. "Darling."

"I will ring you at the Palace."

"I'm not at the Palace."

"I thought you were getting the royal treatment." He said it snotty. "It was in all the newspapers."

"Yeah, I was getting the treatment all right, out on my ass."

"What do you want?"

"Two hundred dollars."

"You must be joking."

Maude shook her head and said, "Nope." She reached back into the glass cabinet and found another little figure, this one of a little girl holding a basket of flowers. She twirled it up in the failing light coming from the front door and smiled. "Doesn't this look like Virginia?"

Rumwell grabbed her arm and his fingers were tight and strong, but he couldn't budge her. She smiled at him. "Do you remember Mrs. Spreckles's party? You took me from behind in the garden. Like some kind of animal. We've had so many adventures. I've brought you so much business."

"I won't pay you."

"I have nowhere to go."

"That's not of issue."

"Rummy," she said. "Be a gentleman."

The wife returned, now composed but flushed, and worked her best smile. She asked her husband if Mrs. Delmont would like to join them for dinner. She was baking a chicken and . . . But Rumwell stopped her, saying that Mrs. Delmont had to be returning south, kind of giving the wife the old brush-off, the frail getting his meaning and disappearing back to the kitchen.

Maude held the figurine up to Rumwell's face and twisted it there. "Does it hurt when you fill them with air?"

"This instant," he said, raising his voice, spit flying a bit.

"You hear it doesn't hurt," she said, "but I would feel like a balloon inside while you worked. And hands—you must have very steady hands."

"I will call the police."

"And I will tell them about your delicate work," Maude said. "Your specialties."

"So be it," he said, disappearing into the kitchen.

Maude returned the figurine to the cabinet and took a seat back on the little settee. She sipped from the delicate china and watched the pendulum swing on a large grandfather clock. A large gray cat stumbled into the room and found a spot in Maude's lap, settling in, and she stroked the animal and played with its tiny paws.

Rumwell came back, minutes later.

"It's done."

"Don't be foolish."

"They're coming for you now," he said.

"Who?"

"The police," he said. "They have warrants for your arrest."

"On what?"

"Bigamy," he said. "They called me this morning at the hospital and I was given instructions to ring them if I saw you."

"You must think I'm a fool," Maude said, smiling. "This is a wonderful little home, Rummy. The rugs alone must've cost you a fortune. That big clock, all this mahogany. Very strong and solid. Do you have children? I can't believe I never asked."

"You may wait here if you wish," Rumwell said. His wife, high-collared and sweating, returned, locking her arm with her husband's. She swallowed but would not make eye contact with Maude.

Maude could hear the pendulum of the great clock, the gears whirling inside making the hands move. She finished her tea, stood, and walked toward the receiving area of the home. She brushed straight past the two of them, placed her hat on her head, and adjusted it in the mirror of a hall tree.

"Two hundred woulda saved you some heartache, kids," Maude said.

"I can't be bribed or bought," he said.

"Good man," Maude said. "And you'd be a hell of a doctor if your hands didn't shake."

"You wanted to see me, sir?" Sam asked.

"Close the door," the Old Man said.

Sam closed the door. He took a seat in a hard wooden chair and waited.

"I hear you've been making inquiries about an op from back east."

"Yes, sir."

"Why didn't you ask me?"

"I figured this fella was off the books."

"Did you find anything?"

Sam nodded. He pulled out his cigarettes and struck a match, settling into the chair. The Old Man had a cigar that had expired in a full ashtray on his desk. His shirtsleeves were rolled above the elbows and he stood and stretched and opened up a shade on the window.

"You got a name?"

"Yes, sir."

"And what else?"

"The fella is on retainer to Hearst Corporation. He's been assigned to them for years."

"What's he have to do with all this?"

"I saw him making a payment to Arbuckle's buddy, Fred Fishback."

The Old Man looked back at Sam from the window. "I'll make sure McNab knows. He called over here earlier today mad at hell. Said you gave the bum's rush to Arbuckle outside the Tadich Grill."

"No, sir," Sam said. "I asked Mr. Arbuckle what he had to do with Hearst."

"You know it's just the *Examiner* trying to dig up some dirt, sell some lousy newspapers."

"Maybe."

"They were probably paying off that Fishback fella to tell his story. Inside the St. Francis party and bullshit like that."

"Why hold a meeting at a Chinatown speak?"

"Privacy."

"I've seen this op before," Sam said. "Before the war, I was assigned to bust up some labor in Montana. This fella approached me in a bar, bought me a drink, and offered me a respectable payday if I'd take out the fella making all the trouble. Next day, the guy winds up dead."

The Old Man reached across the desk, grabbed the dead cigar, and tried to light it with three or four matches, finally getting the stinking thing going, a giant plug of orange growing red-hot.

"The mines were owned by Hearst."

The Old Man settled back into his creaking chair, smoking and thinking. He shrugged. "So?"

"So this ain't the kind of fella doing a nosy newsman's work. He's still on the tab for Hearst."

The Old Man nodded and let out some smoke. His shoes, ragged-soled old jobs, twittered on the desk. "Let's let this one lie, Sam."

Sam watched him.

"Those two showgirls are done with their act, and Phil's keeping watch on that big Swedish gal you found down south," the Old Man said. "Really nice job on that one. She may be the real ace in the hole."

Sam watched the Old Man and the Old Man gave him a soft, weathered smile. He had twinkling old eyes that saw everything in the room while keeping good contact, trying to pass along something without saying it.

"I need you on another job," he said. "A ship called the *Sonoma* comes in early tomorrow. We just got cabled that somewhere between Honolulu and Frisco, she got robbed."

"How much?"

"Half a mil in gold," the Old Man said. "We think it may still be on board."

26

They didn't speak to Maude the entire way out of the city, rumbling along in a black Dodge Brothers, the kind with the steel-frame construction and hard top. All business, the only action coming from the fatheaded cop, Kennedy, when he cracked open the windshield as they drove over the county line. They headed out onto a bumpy road, hugging the coastline south, hardscrabble vegetation clinging to the rocky edge, the roadway growing thin and narrow. The cops didn't have to say it, but she figured she was headed back to Madera to face the last one, Cassius Clay Woods, in court and then finally all the way back to Wichita to face Mr. Delmont. Or would they get it all over at once? Maude hoped it was the latter, she thought, as the road wound and curved, snaking more and more the farther south they got, breezing through wide, rolling green pastureland, cows impossibly perched on the vertical hills, grazing, Maude not sure she knew how they found their footing.

She lit a cigarette and offered one to Big Kate, but Big Kate didn't even acknowledge the question as the smoke flitted out the side window, a cool breeze shooting through the open cab and between the two lunkhead detectives dressed identically in black suits. Just as Maude settled in, flicked the cigarette from the window, and laid her head against the window, the car slowed.

Nothing around but the dirt road, a long fence, and those goddamn crazy cows making their way up the steep cliff.

"We outta gas?"

"Out," said Griff, the lunkhead driver.

"I'm not squatting before you men."

"Out," Kate Eisenhart said, nudging her in the ribs with an elbow, pushing her toward the door being opened by Tom Reagan. She stood in the roadway, the sun high and golden. Maude pulled her hat down to shield her eyes.

"You are not to step foot back in San Francisco," said Reagan, his head shaped like a bullet. Big head. Good teeth.

"Am I to walk back to Los Angeles?"

"Up to you," said Griff Kennedy. He lit a smoke and leaned back against the Dodge Brothers business model, arms across his chest.

"What about the charges you mentioned?"

Detective Reagan shrugged. "It's all up to you now, Mrs. Delmont."

"Hopper-Woods," Kate added.

"You're a laugh riot," Maude said.

Kate stood wide-legged in a big black dress, black coat, and matador hat. Her double chin bunched under her disapproving mouth.

"Is that it?" Maude said. "You can spare the lecture."

"I don't think she heard us, boys," Kate said.

"Kate," said Reagan, grabbing her arm, "c'mon, let's go."

"I'm not through with the twist."

"Kate," Reagan said again.

Kate shook his beefy hand off her. She walked toward Maude and Maude looked at her and shook her head with pity, gathering her black dress from her feet and starting for the road. Kate grabbed hold of her dress and spun her around. "You are to never return. Not under any name."

"I heard you."

"Good."

"Please remove your hand," Maude said.

Kate slowly let go, still staring right at Maude, but before Maude turned she gathered a good deal of spit in her mouth and let it fly into Kate's chubby face. Kate hauled back with the palms of her hands and pushed Maude to the ground and, red-faced and angry, marched back to the machine.

Maude found her hands, looking for her feet.

"You people," Maude said. "You don't want to know what happened."

"What happened?" Tom Reagan said, offering her hand.

She stood on her own and dusted herself off. "You'll never know. You idiots."

Big Kate returned from the Dodge, coat flying behind her, matador hat hanging crazy on her head, clutching a baseball bat. Her face heated, breathing excited, she looked as if her body would swell and explode like a balloon. Tom blocked her path.

"Outta my way, Detective Reagan. This saucy bitch needs a talkin' to."

"Not like that," Reagan said.

Griff Kennedy remained leaned back on the machine, flicking the butt of his cigarette and coolly lighting a new one, watching the action play out through the smoke.

Kate hoisted the baseball bat in her hands. Tom stood in her way.

"Don't you care?" Maude said, screaming. "Don't you care? Rumwell is a liar."

"Dr. Rumwell is respected," Kate said, getting a better grip. "You are gutter trash."

"Dr. Rumwell is an abortionist. A killer of children."

"Liar," Kate said, howling. "Black liar."

Tom made a move for the bat, but Kate eluded him, circling Maude Delmont in all that open, hilly green space. The wind cold and salty off the Pacific. Overhead, a hawk circled.

"He killed her," Maude said. "There you have it."

"Black liar."

"He removed the child from her the day before the party," she said. "She was ill. I don't care if you crucify the fat bastard, but there you have it. Take it."

Griff Kennedy perked up at her words and moved in beside Tom, Tom slacking his shoulders as if the other Irishman could talk down the dyke. Instead, he handed Tom a cigarette, the bullet-headed man looking over at his partner, the partner slipping his arms around his big shoulders and leading him away.

Kennedy looked back at Maude. "I didn't hear what you just said, and I hope for your sake you never repeat it."

"You don't want it," Maude said, laughing. "I serve the truth to you on a silver platter, but you're so far gone with it you don't want it. How wonderful. How pious."

Kate choked up on the bat, the cop Reagan trying to get away from Kennedy when the fat policewoman took the first swing into Maude's stomach, knocking out all the air, the second blow knocking out her legs, and then two hard blows against the back, pushing her in the dirt. The beating was savage and quick and dull and hard, until the screaming and profanities from Kate become gibberish, her fat ass pulled from Maude's back. The big Dodge started and pulled off, moving away from the sun and into the shadow, and above and over a hill, until they were gone.

Maude spit out sand and blood. Her dress torn, ribs cracked, body battered. She wavered to her feet and tried to find the road south.

SAM WAS ON THE DECK of the *Sonoma* all of ten minutes before he was introduced by the captain, a man named Trask, to Daisy Simpkins. Daisy smiled at Sam and shook his hand as the captain explained she was a federal dry agent snooping for any alcohol that may have made it to Pier 35 unchecked. He kind of smiled about it, like it was such a big joke, as the morning sun shone over Oakland, the wind harsh in his ears. Behind Daisy, the light made her hair seem more gold than white, a lock covering up one of her silver eyes, red mouth pursed into a wry smile.

Sam walked beside her on the long, endless deck of the ocean liner, other Pinkertons interviewing hundreds of passengers and checking their trunks and suitcases before they could head down the gangplank. City cops prowled the guts of the big ship, Sam spotting Chief of Detectives Matheson and Tom Reagan; Reagan caught Sam's eye but turned back to interviewing the purser.

"I heard it's not a half mil," Daisy said. "They carried a half mil, but the robbers only got a hundred and a quarter."

"Still, a nice haul."

"Would set me up for a while."

"You check every boat that comes in?"

"We had a tip about LaPeer," Daisy said, walking beside Sam, strolling the top deck like an average couple taking in the sights, through the backed-up passengers and out onto the aft deck loaded down with bunches of green bananas. Daisy wore a cape with a blue jumper dress, and the wind blew the cape up off her shoulders while they walked. "But I figure they already dumped the hooch at the three-mile limit."

"You miss me?"

"I ached," she said. "In the gut."

"Funny girl."

"How 'bout you? How's that baby?"

"A girl. Very pretty."

"What's her name?"

"Mary Jane."

"Wife okay?"

"Dandy."

"I like the tie."

Sam looked down to see which one he put on with the tweeds that morning. Red with blue dots. He readjusted the cap on his head to block out the morning sun, finding the end of the boat and then turning around the bow and heading back around.

"So what happened, after you were south?"

"You shoulda seen Jack Lawrence after the bit with the lion. He was scared to death of me, practically begged to work for us. I think it was the lion balls in his face that did it, emasculated him. So, I set up a little meeting in Frisco with my boss, F. Forrest Mitchell, and he thought Lawrence was on the square, too. And we turned the son of a bitch loose."

"And he ran."

"No, not then," Daisy said. "He was a good boy for a while. He went back to the same ring that supplied the booze for Fatty and ended up getting sent to Plumas County to help run a moonshine still with this fella named Clio. This old-timer Clio. You shoulda seen this guy, looked like a real miner forty-niner type with the whiskers and flop hat and all. He ran a fifty-gallon still in this abandoned lumber camp that was only eight miles from the Blairsden railroad station, where they'd move a lot of the stuff. We knew every move LaPeer was going to make but played it patient waiting for the good stuff to make its way from the Philippines or up in Canada. But all of our plans got shot to shit."

A little girl in a straw hat with a pink ribbon turned to stare at Daisy with an open mouth and then leaned back over the ship's railing and tossed bread crumbs to a dozen seagulls. The seagulls just hung in the wind, barely moving their wings, catching and fighting over the crumbs, another dozen joining the others squawking and fighting.

"LaPeer sniff him out?"

"Mr. Mitchell and I figure we got a rat on the inside," Daisy said. She stopped walking and found a spot to lean over the rail and look out at the fishing boats heading out through the Golden Gate. "A few weeks back, LaPeer sends Jack Lawrence back to the old lumber camp with a letter, telling him to hand it off to Clio. And of course what does Lawrence do but open the son of a bitch. It read something like, 'I don't know whether to trust this Australian bastard or not, keep one eye open.' That being kind of a joke between LaPeer and Clio, I guess, because Clio only had one eye."

"Then he ran?"

"Scared shitless."

Sam offered her a smoke.

"Don't you have a coat?" she asked.

"I hocked it."

"For what?"

"A nice cut of meat."

"Hard times."

"Not too bad," Sam said. "I got some bum lungs and a lousy job. You read about all these vets who come home shell-shocked out of their mind and end up checking out early with a .45."

"That's a solid way to look at things, Sam."

"It's the truth," he said, leaning over the railing with her, about the same spot over the edge and meeting her eye. She smiled at him and he smiled back.

"Don't you need to work?"

"Guess so," Sam said. "Waiting for the cops to finish up with the purser and then I'm headed down below."

"What's below?"

"Where they kept the money," he said. "Stronghold. So they say it's an inside job?"

"That's what I heard."

Sam nodded, still staring back at Daisy. He wanted to touch her face. She had a lovely cleft in her chin.

"They pulled me off the Arbuckle case."

"This is a big job."

"Wasn't the job."

"What was it?"

"Greed."

"From who?"

"You ever feel like you're no better than a prostitute?"

"Every day," she said. "You got an alternative?"

THE THREE HUGE WOODEN DOORS were brought in during lunch and placed within the witness-box. Roscoe knew about them and the finger-prints, expected them, but didn't think they were going to get into the whole mess today. When the jury was brought in, the men and women stared at the doors, as if they'd propped up a corpse for the viewing, some-thing tangible, the first physical piece of the St. Francis they'd laid eyes on. Roscoe poured some water from the pitcher and leaned back into his seat. He took a swallow, and as U'Ren began Roscoe started to examine his cuti-cles, glancing up to the man sworn in by the judge.

E. O. Heinrich. A tall, gangly man in a rumpled black suit. He wore glasses but still needed to stare up at the judge and out at U'Ren. He was nervous and bookish and that all suited U'Ren well as the bastard continued to call the witness "Professor" on every occasion.

McNab waited a minute for the accolades and then pushed back his chair, standing and cutting off U'Ren's reading of Heinrich's résumé credentials.

"Your Honor, we challenge this witness as an expert."

"On what grounds?" Louderback asked.

"We have no issue with Mr. McNab asking the witness a few questions before we proceed," U'Ren said, a cracked smile showing. "In fact, we insist."

McNab pursed his lips, nodding, moving toward the witness, wasting no time. "What cases have you testified for in this state?"

"In this state?" Heinrich asked.

"Yes."

"None in this state."

"So you have never testified in the state of California on fingerprints for any district attorney."

"No, sir."

"Where else have you testified in the Superior Court or a court of criminal jurisdiction?"

"In the state of Arizona and the state of Washington."

"How often have you testified on fingerprints in the state of Washington?"

"Once."

"How often in the state of Arizona?"

"Once."

Brady and U'Ren stood in unison, Brady putting his mitt to U'Ren's shoulder and seating the boy. He said, "Perhaps it would please Mr. McNab to have Professor Heinrich take the fingerprints of every jury member, have them secretly numbered, and then test his abilities."

McNab stuck a thumb in his vest pocket and looked over the jury box and shook his head. "No," he said. "No. That won't be necessary."

Louderback yawned and told U'Ren to please resume questioning the witness. And there were degrees and citations and awards and scientific papers, and as they continued McNab started to fidget and tighten his jaw, his rough, old-man breathing growing louder until he pushed back the heavy chair and stood. "I think we're quite aware of Mr. Heinrich's gold stars. May we continue?"

Louderback rolled his fingers for U'Ren to move on and U'Ren smiled with his ragged little teeth and asked for the assistance of Miss Salome Doyle, who worked in Heinrich's lab.

She was a skinny redheaded woman, flat ass, no tits, and a nervous little grin, aware of everyone watching her and loving it, as she set up an artist's easel. Roscoe half expected her to curtsy. On the easel was an enlarged photograph with what looked like fingerprints made of silver. Roscoe leaned in, nicked a rough cuticle off with his mouth, looked down at his hands and then back at the easel.

This skinny fella Heinrich was led by the nose through the setup: Three doors from the St. Francis. Two handprints on a panel. One belonged to Virginia, with an overlay of prints belonging to Roscoe.

Roscoe looked over to McNab, but McNab showed nothing. His hands crossed over his big chest, breathing, resting like an old fighter in the corner. Roscoe thought McNab might doze off in the heated courtroom.

"And what does this pattern say? How does it speak to you, Professor?"

"It says that at some point Mr. Arbuckle had his hands over Miss Rappe's by the door."

"In what manner?"

"It's of a scientific opinion that there was a struggle," Heinrich said.

"Objection," McNab said, on his feet. "The witness is an expert in identifying fingerprints. No body of work exists that allows Professor Heinrich or Salome Doyle to read them like tea leaves."

"What did scientific methods show?" U'Ren said, glad of the correction, smiling and pacing. Mouth closed, waiting for Heinrich to spill what he'd been coached to say.

"My methods conclude me to believe that Mr. Arbuckle was trying to prevent Miss Rappe from leaving the room. You can plainly see the patterns formed in the aluminum dust."

"Objection," McNab said.

"Sustained," Judge Louderback said. "The jury will disregard the witness's testimony as to the events precipitating the fingerprints."

Several jurists scribbled into notebooks. Roscoe looked at them and then back at his hands. Big paddle fans wheeled above them all. Stray coughs and seat shuffles while U'Ren drove home his points.

When he finished, McNab took his place, pulling his watch out on its gold chain to check the time and buttoning back his black coat.

"Is it possible to have these doors reexamined?" McNab asked.

"No."

"Because too many hands have touched them."

"In the courtroom."

"Perhaps even wiped down with a cloth."

"Perhaps."

"Calling up your methods and as an expert in such matters, could these surfaces show sufficient prints after being wiped down and scrubbed with a cloth?"

"I would say not."

"Prints would be obliterated."

"Yes."

McNab nodded, thoroughly interested, digesting what Heinrich had to say, slowly looking over to skinny Salome Doyle and nodding at her.

"On what days were these doors removed from the St. Francis and taken to your laboratory in Berkeley?" he asked.

"I don't recall."

"Did you not make notes?"

"I most certainly did," Heinrich said, opening a thick but small ledger. "September sixteenth. It was Friday."

McNab smiled.

"Eleven days after Miss Rappe took ill?"

"The room had been sealed."

Brady was on his feet and the judge motioned him over and there was much squabbling, words that Roscoe couldn't hear. And then Brady walked back to the prosecutor's table and sat back down.

"Was the room encased in glass?"

"The doors were locked."

"And not a single person touched these doors since Miss Rappe was moved into 1227."

"Yes."

"A record of the events frozen in time."

"Most surely."

"And you're sure even the most gentle wiping of a dustcloth would remove such evidence?"

"The tests could only be conducted in my laboratory with Miss Doyle's help."

"Not to be repeated now."

"Yes."

"Because the doors are tainted."

Brady stood and frowned. "Judge?"

Judge Louderback looked down at McNab. "Cover new ground."

"Your Honor," McNab said, "to ease the confusion of the court and the jury, I wish to call a rebuttal witness at this time."

Louderback waited.

"A Miss Katherine Brennan."

Louderback looked annoyed and bored. Roscoe poured some more water.

"And who is that?" the judge asked.

"The good woman who cleaned that room the day after the Arbuckle party. Since we're calling her work into question, it's only right that she has the opportunity to respond."

THE STRONG ROOM on the *Sonoma* was a solid steel box, sealed with a solid steel door that took three keys to open. The keys belonged to the first officer, the purser, and the captain. According to the rules, all three had to be present when the door was opened and when it was closed and locked. The captain told Sam he'd made regular trips, night and day, to test the door's integrity. But he did not open the door nor could he see inside. The strong room had no windows, no barred peepholes, and, as far as the captain knew, the loot had been stolen shortly after he'd seen the safes loaded inside at Honolulu. Fifteen chests, each one containing ten thousand gold sovereigns.

"Mr. Houdini couldn't find his way out."

"How much do they weigh?" Sam asked, examining the three locks. "The chests?"

"Eighty pounds."

"And five are missing?"

The first officer nodded. The purser joined them and then Captain Trask.

Each man showed Sam the lock procedure. Repeating it twice more.

"Fifty thousand gold sovereigns. Four hundred pounds," Sam said. "Could they have been off-loaded with the booze?"

"What booze?" Captain Trask asked, mustache twitching.

"The booze crates you dropped at the three-mile limit."

The captain's eyes were very clear and very blue, and he soon blinked and simply said, "No. I watch that shipment myself."

Trask pushed open the steel door and it groaned and clanged against the inside wall. The men waited for him outside as if their presence would taint his work. The strong room was oval and painted with a pink primer to stop the rust. Sheets of metal formed the curved corners, rivets driven in flush with each piece. Sam felt over the smoothness of the room, the gentle curves, and below him he could hear the humming and pulsing of the engine room, a *woosh, woosh* sound that was comforting.

The ten remaining chests lay in an orderly row, side by side. Everything else had been removed from the hold. Sam dropped to his knees and touched the blackened scars on the pink primer where chests had been dragged from the room. The black marks went straight for the steel door, and there were no signs that any other point of entry was possible, no ventilation ducts, no signs of drilling. Sam felt the tracks, gouging deep into the paint, where the gold was ripped from the room. He moved his hands along the path, feeling something wet and, smelling his fingers, knowing it was some really good Scotch.

The Scotch formed a very small puddle in a low spot in the steel sheeting. At some point, maybe this voyage or maybe one from years ago, a single rivet had been yanked away in the path. Most of the Scotch had drained out through the tiny hole and Sam wondered if there wasn't a lucky crewman below who thought his prayers had been answered.

He stood in the room for a long time, hearing that gentle *woosh*, and cursing himself for not seeing the obvious.

"Sir?" asked the first officer.

Sam turned.

"We need to lock back up," he said.

Sam nodded and stepped through the bulkhead. The door sealed and locked by all three men.

"Any clues?" Captain Trask asked.

"Your lock is brass, not steel like the others," Sam said. "The thief or thieves changed out the captain's lock before the trip and made impressions of the other two keys."

The purser and first officer exchanged looks.

"It's an inside job by someone who could get close enough to you two," Sam said. "Now, let's start with a list of the crew."

The captain said he'd get a list, and they walked back through the mail room and out to a stairwell, and Sam told the men he'd like to snoop around a bit. He wound his way around the guts of the ship, through hallways of staterooms and offices. There was a barbershop and a shoeshine stand. An empty restaurant with tables changed out with fresh linen and crystal and silverware laid out for the cruise back to the Pacific. Daisy Simpkins was back by the kitchen with another dry agent. When she saw Sam, she said something to the agent and he bounded around Sam and headed up the stairs to the top deck.

"Your booze is gone," Sam said.

"Half Moon Bay?"

Sam shrugged and Daisy followed him out to the dining room. "You know which way is up?"

She smiled. "You lost?"

He nodded.

They followed a long hall through the guts of the ship and then up a ladder to a level with passenger cabins. Everyone was up on deck, clamoring and pissed off at the search, doors wide-open into the little rooms with unmade beds and piles of linen. You could hear the feet above and the wind around the ship, portholes open, a biting cold coming through the halls in all that desolate space. As they walked, Sam was aware of Daisy grabbing his hand and pulling him into the next empty cabin, closing the door, leaving the light off, and kissing him full on the mouth.

"If they don't find the gold, the office wants me to take this tub back to Australia."

"How long?"

Sam shrugged. She kissed him again.

"What about Arbuckle?"

"Like I said, they pulled me off it. 'Sides, he's too far gone anyway."

"He's gettin' what he deserves."

"It's not that simple."

They kissed for a while in the dark room. She smelled wonderful.

"The girl came up to The City with something," Sam said. "She got hurt when it was taken from her. She was dying before she stepped foot in that party."

"You want to talk straight?"

"I can't, angel," Sam said. "How 'bout you?"

"Shut up," she said. "I hate talk. It's all in what you do."

27

Roscoe stood outside the courtroom in a little corner by the big staircase made of mottled marble. Reporters gathered by the doors as spectators already started to fill the seats. Word had spread about the masseuse from down south who was going to testify about Virginia's condition, about her having fits whenever she took a drink. Roscoe leaned against the wall, the newsboys sensing a black mood, knowing he wasn't going to bullshit with them like most days. Roscoe started a smoke, saying, "The way I figure it, it's damned if we accept those prints as mine. They're trying to say I screwed that poor girl against a door."

"He's a fraud," McNab said. "The professor. That chambermaid woulda been out on the street if she didn't clean that suite properly. That room was cleaned time and again."

All of a sudden the newsboys were on their feet and chattering with each other, a gaggle of them running out of the courthouse, a few running upstairs to the police offices. Roscoe followed McNab to court, getting into the rhythm of the days there, not much different than being on-set, only he wasn't called to do a damn thing but watch.

"Where's the fire?" Roscoe said to a couple fellas from *The Call*.

"You don't know?"

"I give up."

McNab held the great door open for Roscoe, trying to move him along.

"Your witness, the Swedish broad, is in the hospital," the newsboy said. "Someone went and poisoned her."

SAM PATCHED TOGETHER what happened to Irene Morgan from a stack of reports from the op who interviewed her and from reading the tale in the afternoon editions of both *The Call* and the *Examiner*, no one really knowing if the girl would live or not. The whole series of events piecemeal from fact and fiction, headlines from the newsboys and statements from Morgan, rumor and fact. But apparently the girl had grown bored that first night and snuck out of the Golden West Hotel with another Arbuckle witness, a woman named Leushay. The pair made their way to Geary on foot, hopped the streetcar to Pierce, and then walked two blocks up to the Winter Garden Hall, where single girls could always find a dance and men could take their pick from 'em clustered on long rows of church pews. The unattached would sit and wait, hand-painted slides projected against a cracked wall as an all-darkie band played love songs from the South. The last little bit of information came from Phil Haultain, who sat across from Sam at a partners desk, reading the same report, smoking and laughing and peppering the facts with little insightful and sometimes off-color comments.

Irene never had to sit that night. As soon as the big blond Swede—or, as Phil called her, "the woman with incredible tits"—walked through the doors, she was accosted by at least a dozen men and chose two and then chose another two and so on. Her dance card was filled for hours, while the Leushay woman sat on a hard seat and drank bottles of Coca-Cola and chain-smoked cigarettes and gave wan smiles to the blonde as she made her way across the dance floor as large as four basketball courts. By the time Irene was tuckered out, maybe two hours later, she'd convinced some nervous, sputtering gent to give Miss Leushay a solid try while she was cooling her heels. And that was about the time that Miss Leushay's side of the story ended and the op's interview of Irene Morgan took over.

Irene had just come back from the ladies' room and was making her way back to the floor, refreshed and ready for more songs, another twirl, a broad shoulder on which to lay her head, bootleg booze from a flask passed underhand to her. But this odd fellow tapped on her shoulder, much too old for her tastes, maybe about fifty or so. Dark skin and gray hair. She found it odd that the man wore a hat indoors. He asked for a dance and she politely refused, but the man pretended not to understand her accent and grabbed her rough by the elbow and took her for a twirl anyway. She recalled his breath smelling of cigarettes and mint, part of an ear missing, and him not talking much, being a horrible dancer, and finally landing her back where she started, where a much younger man with neatly oiled hair bowed to her and kissed her hand.

Say, didn't that fella who jumped you in the tunnel have part of an ear missing?

Sam nodded and kept reading.

Irene was halfway through another song when she realized she'd seen the older man before at the Hall of Justice. He'd asked her for the time. Irene put off the whole affair, until it was midnight and Miss Leushay was bored again and worried the girls could get into some kind of trouble with Judge Louderback. Irene said her good-byes to the men, getting a purseful of business cards, finding it strange how many American men, especially shorter ones, had no problem dancing close, head upon her bosom like a child.

She's kidding, right? I bet they were like soft pillows.

She was a bit drunk and tired when the older, dark man pulled to the curb in a new machine, a long green touring car, and asked the girls if they'd like a ride back to the hotel. She couldn't even reply before Miss Leushay hopped in the backseat of the car and motioned for Irene to come on, Irene staggering from the curb and crawling inside, the car moving down Geary, heading down to O'Farrell, and dropping Miss Leushay at the Manx. Miss Morgan said she thought she was on the way back to the hotel when the man did something very kind.

"He offered me candy," she said in *The Call*. "He said it was homemade."

Didn't her mother tell her better? Candy? Jesus.

She didn't know she was only a few blocks away from the Golden West. For all she knew, she could've been on the other side of the city. But the man kept them moving around in circles, up a street, down a street, a long ride along the Embarcadero, and then a long march up Market and back again, circling Union Square four times. She told the man she was beginning to feel a bit odd, a little queer, and he recommended she try some orange juice, slowing at the first drugstore, maybe the Owl. Miss Morgan ran inside, had a small glass, and then stumbled back to the car. She had the back of her hand against her forehead, as they drove some more, the very motion of the machine making her ill, and finally pleaded for the man to take her back to the hotel that very instant. He said some more candy would settle the stomach.

"And so I ate several pieces," she said.

At the Golden West, she got out fast, knowing the man would want to walk her to the door. But he stayed in the machine, only letting down the driver's window of the long green automobile and smiling at her. The smile was what struck her as odd and she wandered to him, cocking her head, and waiting for him to say what he had to say.

He smiled more.

"What?"

He looked her dead in the eye and said, "Go to hell."

Irene covered her mouth with her hand, stumbling into the lobby, but never made the elevator. The last thing she recalled was collapsing in a heap and the bellman calling for a doctor.

How is she?

Docs gave her oxygen. Whatever was in that candy didn't sit too well with her. We got an office pool going. You want in?

"THEY'RE CALLING FOR another witness," McNab said, leaning over the table to talk to Roscoe. Roscoe was seated but turned around to tell Minta and Ma. Minta had on a blue dress and fringed hat. He'd never noticed that much about what she wore, but it sure was reported every day in the papers. Everyone wanted to know what the famous Minta Durfee wore to court as she stood beside her man. Roscoe decided he liked the blue, while watching Minta whispering in Ma's ear. She had to whisper twice because Ma was deaf as a post.

"Who's up?" Roscoe said, folding his hands over his stomach.

"Your pal," McNab said, "Fishback or Hibbard, or whatever he calls himself."

"Thought that wasn't till later this week?"

McNab shrugged.

"That sick nurse gonna be okay?" Roscoe asked.

McNab shrugged again. "Do I look like a goddamn doctor?"

McNab approached the bench, and Louderback nodded and answered a few questions. McNab said hello to Brady and Brady just eyed him and turned on his heel. McNab laughed at that, walked back, and took a seat beside Roscoe, the jury trailing in as chipper as a funeral dirge.

"Do they always have to look so solemn?" Roscoe asked in McNab's ear.

"Quiet," McNab said and began a fresh sheet of paper for notes. "I didn't call this son of a bitch."

There were more whispers and loud talking. Jurors sat up straighter and notebooks appeared in their laps. Freddie was brought in from a side door and placed on the stand, where he stood and raised his hand. He was dressed to the nines—blue aviator jacket, crisp pleated trousers, and polished riding boots. His black hair had been oiled just so, and, as he turned, his profile looked like a silhouette from *Photoplay*.

Roscoe stared right at him. Fishback caught the stare and kept his eyes on Brady, who got the jury up to speed on who Fishback was, what he did, that he did indeed drive up to the city with Roscoe in September, all that business.

"And you directed Mr. Arbuckle in several moving pictures?"

"No."

"But he is a friend of yours?"

"Yes."

"And you've known him for how long?"

"Since '16, somewhere around there."

"Where were you born, sir?"

"Romania."

"And you took the name Fishback why?"

"I thought it was funny. It makes you think of the bones of a fish."

The court laughed. Mainly women. Roscoe always kept Freddie around because his dark looks and athletic shoulders could pull some tail. Roscoe wrote on a piece of paper, "Why was he called?" He passed the paper over to McNab, who wrote back, "I am not of the psychic arts."

Roscoe leaned back in his seat.

"Did you see Miss Rappe ill?"

"Yes."

"And what did you think when you saw her?"

"I thought she'd had too much to drink."

"So you tried to help her?"

"Yes."

"What did you do?"

"I placed her in a cold bath."

"Were you rough with her?"

"No. Not at all."

"Did you bruise her?"

"No, sir."

McNab stood. "A person hardly knows when they've inflicted a bruise."

Roscoe leaned into the table. His heart raced a bit. Ole Freddie wouldn't look at him. If he'd just give him a quick glance, Roscoe could tell if he was still with him. But he was sitting there, erect, stiff, answering yes or no, like they'd never met, never shared a drink, a song at a piano.

"But this was not the first time you'd met Miss Rappe?"

"No. I had met her some years ago."

"When you worked at the same studio with Mr. Arbuckle?"

"Mack Sennett's."

"The master of comedy?"

"That's what Mr. Sennett says."

The court erupted in laughter again, the crowd loving handsome Freddie.

Roscoe looked up at the ceiling at the fan breaking and spreading apart the heat and wind in the room. There was a strong odor of bad breath and old stale sweat around him. He folded his arms in front of him and straightened his navy vest.

"Did Mr. Arbuckle know Miss Rappe?"

Roscoe's eyes shot back to the stand and then back to McNab.

Freddie was still, composed, reading off his lines, not moving his eyes except to punctuate his words with the jurors and knowing goddamn well how to perform, direct the play, move the herd.

"He did."

"Were they friendly?"

"They had met," Freddie said. "The film colony is quite small."

"There was a time when Roscoe asked for some help getting to know Miss Rappe?"

"Yes."

Roscoe took the slip of paper and scrawled in all-capital letters, BULLSHIT.

"He said he wanted to play a joke on her?"

McNab got his ass halfway out of his chair, Brady catching the move and saying, "How was the introduction to be made?"

"He wanted a key to her dressing room."

Roscoe underlined BULLSHIT four times. McNab's big hand enveloped Roscoe's and gripped his fingers to the point of pain, no expression on the hard old man's face.

"A joke?"

"He wanted to sneak in her dressing room."

"Did you get him the key?"

"No."

"Was he angered?"

"Very."

"I told him this is where the girls, the Bathing Beauties, shower and such things. It was not proper. But he was insistent."

The son of a bitch shrugged. *Freddie shrugged.* A move of "What can you do?"

And he performed it so well for the jury.

If only he would look at him. But Freddie just trailed away as McNab took a stab at him, asking him questions that Roscoe could not hear with the hot blood wooshing through his ears. The final insult was McNab asking Freddie if he was sure that it was Roscoe Arbuckle who asked him for the key, couldn't he have been mistaken for another person on a very crowded lot, another portly man?

Freddie calmly caught Roscoe's eye then and Roscoe stared back at Freddie, time seeming to stop as Freddie pointed his long index finger—never being asked to—and shot it straight at Roscoe.

Roscoe did not move. He could not breathe.

He felt McNab's disappointment as the old man falsely gathered his papers, making motions, actions while he tried to make sense of what had just happened, like a man in shock after being run over by a bus. Roscoe leaned in and said, "I want to see the Pinkerton."

"There are a dozen Pinkertons on your case, Roscoe."

"I want the tall one. The thin man. The one who came south."

"May I ask why?"

SAM WAS BACK on the deck of the *Sonoma*, working in the heated bowels of the ship, shirtsleeves rolled to the elbow, only taking a break for a quick smoke, checking in with the other ops to see if they'd found anything. There was a commotion down below on the pier where flashlights worked around the dark green water and on the mooring lines. A man in a diving suit had been dropped a half hour ago, an air pump chugging away, the lifeline running down into the black depths. Sam checked his watch. It was past nine.

He hadn't eaten since morning.

They'd found some of the coin, the robbers dropping the strongboxes over the side of the ship suspended from hemp rope. More coin was found in drainage pipes, raining down on the heads of sailors when an old salt unplugged them to lay down a coat of paint on the deck.

There was still twenty-five thousand somewhere, but Sam figured they were all going through the motions now. The money long gone. A seaman by the name of Ducrest having disappeared hours ago.

He returned belowdecks, the ops being paid by Seamen's Bank to go room by room, slowly down each level. And now Sam was back near the engine room, grease on his hands and forearms, still smoking a cigarette, checking out ventilation ducts. He ran a flashlight into them and pinged them with a rusted wrench, duct by duct, room by room. He wanted to get home.

Two hours later, there was a sound. A solid dull thud instead of a ping.

He used the flashlight to look into the shaft. Nothing. He reached deep into the grimy, oily shaft, stretching with his right arm and fingers until he touched the brass top of a fire hose and grabbed hold, pulling it out.

Sam was alone. Two levels down from the main deck.

The hose was heavy and full. He unscrewed the nozzle and found a continuous trail of loosely packed gold coins that jangled with heft in his hand.

When he glanced back up, he could see an image of himself in the glass of a porthole. Grease covered his face like war paint. He used a handkerchief to clean himself off, some of the white cloth spotted in blood. He looked back at himself and then lifted the hose back into the shaft, pushing it far back into the pipe and screwing it tight with a pocketknife.

He was back on deck when he saw a man he recognized as one of Arbuckle's lawyers, the young one, Brennan. Brennan nodded at another nameless op and the op pointed over toward Sam.

Sam met Brennan halfway on the deck, still wiping grease off his hands.

"Mr. Arbuckle would like to speak with you."

"It's a little late."

"It wasn't my idea."

Sam checked the time again. Below, men were helping the fellow in the diving suit out of the water, a great brass helmet on his head that they had to remove with wrenches. The man had been out of air and took in great lungfuls when the helmet was removed.

"Where is he?"

"Waiting in the car."

"What's this about?"

"I haven't a clue."

"I've been reassigned."

"This is important to Mr. Arbuckle," Brennan said. "He's having trouble sleeping."

"Tough day in court?"

"The worst."

"Okay," Sam said. "Lead the way."

28

M inta thinks you're a good egg," Roscoe said.

"Minta is a sensible woman."

"That she is."

There was a long silence between the two men in the rear of the Pierce-Arrow limousine. Roscoe was dressed in pajamas and a robe. He rolled another cigarette, fumbling around with the paper and tobacco until he got the thing made. The leather inside the cab reminded Sam of a fine saddle; it all smelled rich and oiled.

"Now we got that settled," Sam said, "I need to get back to work."

"I read about that gold," Roscoe said. "They said it was a 'Mystery at Sea.'"

"Not much of a mystery," Sam said. "We found most of it."

"You found the robbers?"

Sam shook his head.

"Can I call you Sam?"

"Sure."

"Sam, I was set up."

"I know."

"Fred Fishback directed the whole thing. He arranged the trip, called the girls, and brought the booze. The son of a bitch blindsided me. All that crap he said on the stand about me asking for the key to the ladies' changing room is a bunch of hooey."

"Why?"

Roscoe looked out the window, the machine idling at Pier 35. A group of sailors passed his car, eyes wide with amazement at the fine machine. He smoked and shook his head. "I don't know."

"You remember me asking about you knowing Mr. Hearst?"

Roscoe didn't say anything.

"Why'd you lie?"

"I said I've met the man once."

"He's taken an interest in you."

Roscoe turned from the window, his profile in the glass.

"His bagman paid Fishback," Sam said. "I saw it. That same man poisoned the woman who'd come to the city to testify on your behalf. Between Hearst and Brady, the facts will never be heard. The real truth has already been buried or burned up in an incinerator."

Roscoe looked confused but nodded, and then nodded some more.

Sam leaned into the space between them. He checked his watch and rubbed his head.

"Why do you continue to protect him?"

Roscoe shook his head.

"He's walking all over you," Sam said. "Hearst is making you look like a fool. You keep on keeping whatever you know a secret and you're headed to San Quentin. Why a grown man would want to be anyone's whipping boy is beyond me. My ass would get sore after a while."

Roscoe looked at him and Sam saw more rage than he expected. But the rage soon softened and he started to cry, and he was very open about it. Sam had never seen a grown man so open about weeping before another man. He looked like he was about ten, wiping the mess away with his fists.

"I'm not protecting Hearst," he said. "I'm no one's whipping boy."

Sam leaned into the soft leather seats. He lit a cigarette, reached into the bar and poured himself a drink from a crystal decanter. "Jesus Christ," Sam said, taking a long pull.

Roscoe reached over and poured him another.

"I could get used to this."

"No, you couldn't," Roscoe said, not looking at him anymore but staring out the window and thinking. The hand-rolled cigarette burned between his fingers. His robe was silk and probably cost more than Sam's suit and shirt and shoes put together. "All this makes you soft."

"I left my hat on the boat," Sam said, reaching for the door.

Roscoe held up his hand. "Hold on. Christ, let me think. I just don't know. God damn. I don't understand any of it. It's making my head hurt."

"It's a simple story, Roscoe. You walked into a frame job and the frame job went really wrong. About as wrong as it can get. And that isn't your fault. But to hold out on me with anything isn't just pigheaded, it's damn stupid."

"Do you know that for the weeks I spent in that jail, all I did was try to remember what happened in that room?"

"What happened?"

"I couldn't. I thought maybe I did kill her. I could imagine it. I could imagine me falling asleep on her, touching her too rough."

Sam finished the glass.

"I'm so goddamn clumsy when I drink," Roscoe said. "I wanted to die. If there had been a gun in that cell, I would've stuck it into my mouth. I convinced myself that I'd killed her. I read the stories and those stories rolled in my head. I saw myself crushing her. I didn't really stop blaming myself until today. When Freddie turned on me, I knew it had been a frame job. He worked me goddamn perfectly. He arranged the sets, brought in the actors, and had it play out just like he'd written it."

"Except for one thing."

Roscoe looked up at Sam.

"The girl wasn't supposed to die."

"Sure she was."

Sam shook his head. "She was sick. No one was planning on that. But when it happened, they changed the script and rolled with it, and now you're being railroaded to prison. So why don't we cut out all the bullshit and you tell me why William Randolph Fucking Hearst wants to destroy your life."

It began to rain outside. The rain pinged on the waxed hood of the big machine. Roscoe flipped a switch and told the chauffeur to drive. The wheels rolled.

"I don't want her hurt."

"A woman," Sam said. "Always a woman."

"She's a hell of a woman," Roscoe said, as the chauffeur kicked it in gear and they headed down the never-ending row of piers, arc lights blazing the way, the rain catching in their bright glow. "She saved my life. And, above all, I want her name left out of this. She's sweet and gentle and caring. She saved my life."

"You said that."

"Well, it's true."

"And just how did that work?"

"There was a New Year's party," Roscoe said. "Two years ago. She owns a beautiful beach home that looks like an old-fashioned plantation. We were all very, very drunk."

"What's her name, Roscoe?"

"Marion," he said. "Marion Davies."

"The film actress?"

Roscoe nodded.

Sam nodded. He waited.

Roscoe didn't say anything.

"And who is Mr. Hearst to her?"

"A friend," Roscoe said. "Her benefactor."

"I bet."

"You ever have a woman care for you when you're down-and-out? When you feel like you're at the bottom of a well and can't see for the dark?"

Sam glanced away.

"I had problems," Roscoe said. "With my manhood. I confided very personal issues to her. I was drunk and told Miss Davies. I was quite drunk. Very drunk."

"So you were drunk," Sam said.

"She said I lacked confidence and the whole business was in my head," he said. "We walked on the beach when all hell was breaking loose with fireworks and champagne bottles uncorking and all that, and she led me by the hand behind a sand dune."

"And proved you wrong," Sam said. He ashed his cigarette into his hand. Roscoe noted the gesture and handed him a cut-glass tray.

"This is all in confidence," Roscoe said. "You must assure me."

"I assure you."

"Miss Davies isn't what I call chaste," Roscoe said. "Surely Mr. Hearst understands that. He's quite a bit older, and for him to go to all this trouble . . . She's known to entertain other gentlemen."

"God bless her."

"No one saw us."

"Oh, someone saw you," Sam said. "You just didn't see them."

"The only thing on that beach was shadows and moonlight," Roscoe said. "I never told a soul."

"They'll convict you, Roscoe," Sam said. "If Miss Davies is the friend you think, she'll give us the goods on Hearst."

Roscoe shook his head.

"This man has destroyed your life."

"I don't believe it," Roscoe said. "Why would a man like Mr. Hearst go to all that trouble?"

"Do I need to draw a picture for you?" Sam asked. "You screwed his girl."

"Mr. Hearst doesn't have time to take such an interest—"

"I've seen him take an interest in a lot less."

Roscoe watched Sam. Sam drank some more. There was more rain and headlights cut across the darkness of the cab.

"Miss Davies is—"

"I've done some work I'm not proud of," Sam said. "I know for a fact Mr. Hearst once sent a man, the very same man who paid Fishback, to kill a fella by the name of Little. All Little did was try and help some miners and he ended up with his neck stretched under a train trestle."

"That sounds like a business matter."

"It wasn't just money," Sam said. "Hearst couldn't control him. He spoke out louder and better than any Hearst stooge. He attacked Hearst in his speeches and on street corners. Workers listened to Little, respected him."

"I can't."

"Get a message to Miss Davies," Sam said. "I'll take care of the rest."

Roscoe shook his head, arm casually resting against the door. The cigarette smoldered in his hand, Roscoe seeming to forget about it.

"Hearst may have set the trap, but I was dumb enough to be snared," Roscoe said. "I'll carry my own water, thank you."

"If you don't speak up, they'll win," Sam said. "This isn't just Hearst, it's the lot of lousy bastards."

"Who are we talking about?"

Sam studied the fat actor's profile.

"He's already won," Roscoe said. "And dragging Miss Davies into the mud won't do a goddamn thing."

"Thinking like that is the reason this country is a goddamn mess."

"I don't follow."

Moments passed. The big black Arrow rolled on. Sam ran a handkerchief across his sweating face. He felt his breathing slow as he composed himself and smiled at Roscoe.

"How's your"—Sam pointed to Roscoe's crotch—"now?"

Roscoe crossed his legs. He turned his eyes back to Sam, face breaking into a grin.

"Every time I see those Vigilant women, I feel like a scared turtle."

THANKSGIVING MORNING, Sam awoke to the baby crying. He could smell coffee and bacon in the tiny kitchen and hear Jose rummaging around with the groceries and dry goods he'd brought home. He found his watch and his cigarettes, neatly made the Murphy bed and closed it up into the wall. He was still working on the cigarette when he walked into the kitchen, Jose handing him a warm cup and smiling. He kissed Mary Jane on the head. It was cold in the apartment. He owed the landlady for the heat.

"And a turkey, too?"

"A turkey, too," Sam said, sitting at the rickety table. "Not a bad-looking bird. Bit skinny. Kinda felt sorry for it."

"How much was this?"

"It's Thanksgiving," Sam said. "Rumor has it, we're supposed to stuff ourselves."

Sam rubbed his head and yawned, Jose laying the baby in his arms. She cried and cried and he stood and rocked her, walking around the tiny flat and to the window, fogged in the early morning. All of Eddy Street seeming gray and cold.

"Jose, I may have to leave for a spell."

"Don't worry," she said, "I'll keep dinner warm."

"Longer than that. Not today, maybe next week. I may have to take that ship back to Australia. They haven't located the loot and the Old Man may want me to sail with her."

"I read *The Call* last night," she said, face never changing. "I heard the purser located some of the gold through a dream. I found that odd."

"So did we," Sam said. "But the fella we make for it jumped ship yesterday morning and hasn't been seen since."

"How much is still missing?"

"Twenty thousand," Sam said. "I'll make sure you and the baby have plenty. I can pay up the rent for some time."

"How?"

"It'd be taken care of. You wouldn't have to worry for a thing."

"I never asked for a thing, Sam."

There were just the sounds in the kitchen for a while and the silence just kind of hung there between them for a long moment, Sam searching for something to say but Jose speaking first.

"I read about Mr. Arbuckle, too," she said, cooking eggs now, hard-frying them, and browning the toast alongside in the skillet. "Doesn't look good. His friend Mr. Fishback said that Arbuckle asked him to sneak into the women's changing room to see Virginia."

"Don't believe everything you read."

"You want some of those preserves?'

"You bet."

"Say, you're good with the kid, Sam. She asleep?"

"Like a baby."

"Ha."

"I've been doing some thinking about Mr. Arbuckle."

"You have some theories?"

"I don't think the autopsy was covering up her being pregnant. I think one of the reasons she came to the city was to get rid of the child."

"Why do you say that?"

"There's a doctor," Sam said. "The one called by Mrs. Delmont to the St. Francis. I shadowed him sometime back and, among other things, he treats whores."

"Doesn't mean he's an abortionist."

"Easy enough to find out."

"But you don't believe he was protecting Miss Rappe's virtue when he destroyed her organs."

"Nope."

"You believe he was covering for something he botched."

"Yep."

"You don't say much."

"Nope."

He smiled.

She laid down his plate of eggs. He slowly, very carefully, passed over the sleeping child to her. She took the handoff with a smile, the kid still dozing.

"That would be a hell of a thing to prove."

"It's not my case anymore," Sam said. "Other men are on it."

"But you're still poking around?"

"A fella I think is a good egg asked me to."

"That simple?"

"Yep."

"You're a good egg, Sam."

Sam didn't respond.

IT WAS MIDAFTERNOON when Sam stepped foot back on the *Sonoma*. A couple of seamen in coveralls painted the deck and smoked cigarettes. He recognized one of them from the days before and gave him a short wave and hello, looking for the first officer, McManus or Captain Trask, but was told that both of 'em had gone ashore to meet with their families. Sam was headed back down, stepping onto a staircase leading belowdecks, back to the engine room and the hidden vent shaft, when he heard his name called.

He turned.

Tom Reagan stood there looking down on him. He wore a black slicker and black fedora and motioned for Sam to come on back up. "We need to talk."

Sam followed him.

The wind on deck was a cold bastard. He lit a cigarette for warmth. Tom did the same.

"Hell of a place to be on Thanksgiving."

Sam nodded.

"I think that gold is long gone," Tom said. "How 'bout you?"

Sam nodded.

Tom smiled at him and it was a knowing smile. Sam shuffled on his feet a bit.

"'Course it wouldn't take much to hide a coin here or there. A man could fill up his pockets and walk right out."

Sam studied Tom's face, his granite features pinching, taking a draw on the cigarette. Those small eyes in that bullet head squinted at Sam.

"I guess that's right."

"Something's not sitting well with me, Sam."

Sam watching him. He waited.

"I don't like when someone isn't straight with me. I like 'em to be honest.

I like to lay out the truth, plain and unvarnished, for all the world to see. I don't like cheaters. Even when I wrestled back in school, I knew the rules and played 'em straight."

"Get on with it," Sam said.

"Now, hold on. I need you to listen to me. 'Cause I'm not even sure what to do about this."

Sam's heart started to race. He took in a breath of cold air and dropped his hands into his pockets. He could smell the paint fumes from the deck ahead of them and it was making him nauseated. He grabbed the edge of the railing and felt it was slick with paint, which he wiped off on his clean handkerchief.

"Goddamnit."

"I like you, Sam," Tom said. "I think you're a straight shooter and I respect that. I want to give you a fair chance."

Sam nodded. "How'd you know?"

"Something's been wrong from the start. You can't blame a person for cheating, but this . . . this is something else altogether. Makes me ill."

"Tom—"

"Hold on," Tom said, putting up his meaty paw. "Hold on. Hear me out. I don't want a word of this coming back to me. You hear me?"

Sam nodded.

"Arbuckle is being crucified," Tom said. "Brady knows he's innocent."

"What?"

"There's more," Tom said. "But I need you to figure some stuff out on your own."

Sam took a deep breath, wiping more paint from his fingers. The sun was behind Tom and it was weak and white through the clouds. The men painting the deck whistled while Sam found his footing. He lit another cigarette and began to walk side by side with Tom.

"You're okay, Tom."

"You look sick."

"I'm okay now."

"So what do we do?"

"What can you tell me about Rumwell?"

"You don't fool around, do you? You go straight to it."

Sam shrugged.

"So you know?"

"I guess so."

"I don't know what to believe," Tom said, beside him, making Sam feel small although the men were the same height. "Everyone on this case is a liar. It can make you screwy."

"I say we talk to him about what we know."

"Rumwell?"

"Why not?"

"He won't admit a goddamn thing."

"It's a funny thing the way the conscience works on a guilty man."

"You look like a man with experience, Sam."

THE PINKERTON OFFICE kept a running list of every greased palm in every hotel in The City. You worked the city by who you knew, who you kept up with, who you routinely paid for the privilege. And they had a beaut of a list, starting with the top hotels, with names and numbers of the hotel dicks, on-duty managers, and doormen. After meeting with Rumwell for a solid three hours, Sam went to his apartment and then returned to the office, placed exactly four calls, and soon came up with a time and place, the Fairmont Hotel tearoom atop Nob Hill. He waited in the office for an hour, used the time to type and then retype a short letter, and then hopped a cable car up Powell.

He wore his best suit—his only suit—freshly pressed, with shoes shined.

He was able to make it to the tearoom before being stopped.

From where he stood, talking to the maître d', he could see the big party. The table stretched behind marble columns and iron banisters, taking up nearly half of the restaurant. Men wore their best black and ladies wore their newest hats. There was gay laughter and toasts and mountains of food. Turkeys with dressing, hams, fresh fruit, and pies sitting atop silver stands. Sam smiled as he watched Police Chief O'Brien uncorking a bottle and pouring a bit for District Attorney Brady, Brady proposing a drunken toast, Mr. Hearst himself wiping crumbs away from his mouth and answering the toast back, clinking glasses with Mrs. Hearst and winking over at two boys who looked nearly identical.

The maître d' was arguing with Sam, telling him that he could not enter. He said it was closed, private, and the accent was vaguely German. Sam reached into his coat, offering his apologies, and told the man he had urgent business from Mr. Hearst's office and it was absolutely imperative that this letter reach Mr. Hearst's hands and no one else's.

The man took the envelope with great seriousness, taking pride in the task in the way that only Germans can. He shook Sam's hand warmly and told him to consider it done.

Sam tried to pay the guy a nickel for his trouble, but he looked at the coin in his palm like it was a dog turd.

HEARST RECEIVED THE LETTER not from the maître d' but from his valet, George. And he left the letter next to his half-eaten plate for many minutes, almost an hour. He drank more red wine, just to taste, since he was not a man to indulge in a weakness, ate a turkey leg, and clapped with joy at the sight of the Baked Alaska.

While the men sat back to cigar stewards and glasses of cognac, Hearst shared a story with the table about serving the flaming dessert to Pancho Villa. He said Villa had been a guest at his mother's ranch, and after demonstrating some of the most abhorrent table manners he'd ever witnessed the revolutionary jumped from his seat and cocked a pistol at the flaming Baked Alaska.

"He was convinced I'd brought him a bomb."

There was cordial laughter and much harrumphing from the men, the mayor, the chief, and the D.A., all of San Francisco's elite. Millicent, Hearst's wife, smiled over at him, quite tired from her journey west with the twins, prepared once again to make their way back to New York.

Hearst would miss the boys.

Millicent, as always, had begun to bore him with her incessant talk of the Milk Fund.

While the men grew sleepy from the food and drink, plied with more cognac, cigars burning and satisfied, the women's talk began to dominate the table. Chatter of the latest styles from Paris and of that handsome Italian Valentino. They particularly seemed to like his eyes, finding them oddly hypnotic, and Hearst thought to himself that perhaps he should reexamine the man's films, learn the technique that had transformed a dishwasher into a lustful attraction.

As his plate was cleared, he remembered the letter, and tore at the envelope with his thumbnail. The message was as simple and straightforward a group of sentences as he'd ever read, so Hearst thought that it had to have been written by one of his newspapermen, an insider. But the last line made him know differently, and he looked up from the cleared linen and smiled, just catching the last few words from Millicent about the boys' antics when they visited the British Museum and begged their father to buy them an ape.

"He not only can climb a tree," Hearst said. "But he can serve cocktails."

"He cannot," Millicent said, blushing.

"He's quite talented, you know. Better than a Chinaman."

More laughter from Hearst's side of the table, and Hearst stole a glance at George, who leaned against a marble column. Hearst crooked his finger, and as soon as George was at his side he looked up from the long row of family and friends, smelling of sweets and smoke and hearing laughter and great mirth. "Take care of this, will you?"

He dropped the envelope into his man's waiting hands as if the edges had been set afire.

oscoe picked lint from his hat and wondered what life would be like in prison, judging if he'd grown too soft, those times working laundries and barrooms too far away. But he decided he'd made a good go of it in the city pen, making friends with the jailers and hoods. He should have expected this shitstorm anyway, knowing that's the way life works—that sucker punch coming when you least expected. He picked more lint, remembering what the Pinkerton had said about him being a whipping boy. He didn't like to be anyone's whipping boy, feeling that old shame heat up his face.

Satisfied with the crown, Roscoe went to work on the brim, picking, and slowly bringing his pale blue eyes up to the stand as Dr. Rumwell continued talking about the dead girl.

"The first thing I did was inspect the body," said the little man with the shrill voice. "I decided that she was about twenty-five years of age and about five foot five inches and weighed about a hundred and forty pounds. And then I looked at the external surface of the body. I used a measuring stick for precision."

Rumwell was small and lean. He wore a black suit of no style and a matching tie of no style. The man looked as if he'd shopped from a street vendor. His thin black hair was oiled and creased, and he wore a small black mustache under a reddened, bulbous nose.

Roscoe inverted his hatband and then tucked it back along the rim.

Milton U'Ren paced before the judge and witness. "Go on," he said.

"I examined the body and limbs, both the lower and upper," Rumwell said. "I examined the face and the head by inspection and did not notice any marks on the face or head or on the scalp. But on the arms I noticed a few areas of ecchymosis."

"Please speak to us in plain terms," Judge Louderback said. He yawned, the whole goddamn show boring him to tears.

Rumwell looked up and over at the judge, mouth open, and then turned back to the courtroom. "Well, ecchymosis is a bruise. I think ecchymosis would be the more definite term."

"How many bruises did you see on the right arm?" U'Ren asked.

"May I refer to my notes for the exact number?"

"Yes, sir."

"There was a large area of ecchymosis—bruises—three inches above the external condyle of the right humerus . . ."

Roscoe looked over the McNab and let out a long breath. He readjusted himself in his seat and turned back to Ma and Minta. Minta had on a little fur hat and it was very attractive, and he wondered if the newspapermen would write about it, trying to make some sense of why she wore squirrel now and not monkey or mink. The newsboys always tried to make something out of a little detail. Like that time Roscoe couldn't bring a manicurist to the jail. They wrote it as if he was trying to be uppity when really he just wanted someone to cut his nails. They even wrote about his playing with elastics, and would probably write about him cleaning his hat in the afternoon editions.

He placed the hat down on the table.

"This is the external condyle of the humerus, this bone called the humerus," Rumwell said, pointing. "And this would be the arm and this the forearm. This was three inches above the external condyle of the humerus. And it varied in width from half an inch to an inch and it was exactly four inches long—that is, measuring from the posterior surface of the arm."

McNab stood, tucked his hands in his pocket, waiting for the judge to let him speak. "I wonder, Your Honor, please, if the doctor couldn't describe that a little more technically?"

Much laughter in the court. Even a few of the jury laughed, which was good because Roscoe had rarely seen them laugh at anything. McNab sat back at the desk, straight-faced, like a good sidekick. Roscoe nudged him in the ribs and winked.

McNab didn't even respond.

"Over to the left arm," U'Ren said. "What did you find?"

Roscoe could not take it anymore. It took everything in him not to stand up, walk out into the hallway and out to the park for a smoke. He imagined the whole farce in his head. Not as Roscoe Arbuckle on trial but Fatty. Fatty would be dressed as an infant and they would place him behind the judge's bench, a rattle for a gavel, and the Kops would bring in his father in shackles. Al St. John would play the part as a wandering drunk, maybe even drop in a role for Luke the dog. They'd dress up Luke as the district attorney, and when a motion was overturned he'd lift his leg on the witness's leg and run off, a chase would follow, out of the courtroom and onto dusty Hollywood streets. Al St. John would ride a giant bicycle, shaking his fist in the air. They'd rig Baby Fatty's high chair as a machine and he'd begin pursuit.

Roscoe laughed.

Testimony stopped.

McNab gave him a hard look. Testimony started up again.

"We commonly call that the shinbone?" asked Judge Louderback.

"Yes, sir," Rumwell said. "A bruise over the shinbone and to either side of the shinbone, oval in shape."

"Did you examine the back of the deceased?" U'Ren asked.

"There were no marks on the back."

"No marks on the back at all?"

"No."

"And all the marks, discolorations, or bruises you found were on the front of the body?"

"Front and a little to the side."

"Well, Doctor, from your experience in general practice, and from your knowledge and education and your training as a physician, were you able to determine from those marks what caused those wounds?" U'Ren asked. "Was it force or something else that caused—"

"Your Honor," McNab said, shaking his head. "That calls for an opinion and is not based on anything that he has observed."

"You misunderstand the question," U'Ren said. "I mean as to the general nature of the wound, whether it was inflicted by a blow or a hypodermic syringe, a medieval sword or a red-hot poker—or what?"

Louderback held up his hand to stop the lawyers from arguing. He leaned back in his great high-backed chair and stared at the ceiling. You could hear the wood bend and creak beneath him. He wasn't speaking but contemplating. Roscoe thought it would've been much better if he'd used the fist under his chin; that way, it would translate to the folks in the back row. "I should say this, gentlemen, not qualifying as an expert myself, but what I imagine all the doctor could say, or give, would be a general cause, without any particular specifications."

"My opinion—" Rumwell began.

"Objection," McNab said.

"Overruled," Louderback said. "Please answer."

"Those smaller bruises were fingerprints," Rumwell said. "As far as the others, I could not tell just what agency caused them."

"Shall we move onto the internal organs?" U'Ren said. "Did you examine those, postmortem?"

"I made an incision through the skin in front of the median line extending from the middle of the chest down to the lower end of the abdomen," Rumwell said. "And before I made the incision, I noticed that the abdomen was moderately distended . . ."

Roscoe hoped to God Rumwell wouldn't produce the photos again of Virginia lying there on the marble slab like a piece of butchered meat. Her body cavity folded open, and you could see her rib bones cut away, her heart removed. Close-up shots of her legs and arms, little bruises that looked like spots to him but that would be made out to be prints from big, fat clumsy fingers that held down the girl while he entered her like a wild animal at a zoo.

"The tear in the bladder wall did not seem to be quite fresh," Rumwell said, the bastard's bad eye wandering a bit. "But it was not very old, either, because it was not lined with any visible amount of new tissue. Then we investigated—"

"Doctor, what in your opinion caused the death of the deceased?' U'Ren said, finally getting to the goddamn point, leading them from head to toe, eyes to anus, and finally getting where they wanted to get, Fatty crushing the little waif beneath his whale body.

"My opinion?" Rumwell said. "Rupture of the bladder."

Roscoe looked down, grabbing his hat. There we go. He let out an enormous amount of air and felt the jury's eyes all upon him. He looked at his hands, folded them neatly and respectfully for what was about to come.

"And what would cause such a rupture in a woman who was in the very pink of condition?" U'Ren said, walking and smiling, really good at both, keeping that smooth motion down, waiting for the final exclamation from his witness.

Rumwell swallowed, his Adam's apple enormous.

"Well, sir," Rumwell said, one eye moving back in line and both lining up dead on McNab and then back to U'Ren. "Upon further examination I found the bladder to be quite diseased."

Brady was on his feet, yelling. U'Ren could not speak, Roscoe believing the weasel had choked.

Roscoe dropped his hat and it rolled off the table and onto the floor. Louderback was hammering the desk with his gavel to stop the goddamn buzzing in the bleachers.

"Possibly from a venereal ailment," Rumwell said without being asked. "I believe gonorrhea. Yes, gonorrhea. I have the bladder in a specimen jar if you'd like to see it."

"Dr. Rumwell," U'Ren said, shouting. Rumwell merely blinking back,

seemingly confused by all the action. "You will be charged with perjury. I
have full transcripts of you earlier testimony . . ."

Roscoe rubbed his eyes, half waiting for Luke to run down the center
of the courtroom and bite U'Ren square on the ass. It would be a hell of an
ender, a close shot on Luke's ugly, satisfied mug.

SAM FOUND FISHBACK staying at the new YMCA in downtown Oakland
registered under the name of F. C. Hibbard. He took the ferry across the
bay and a taxi to 1515 Webster and walked up the great stairs and into what
looked like a massive assembly hall. Only instead of chairs and a platform,
he saw vigorous men jumping rope, tossing medicine balls, and stretching their bodies with an odd assortment of pulleys and racks. The whole
thing looked like torture to Sam, but Fishback seemed to enjoy getting a
good sweat while tossing the medicine ball back and forth to a fat man.
Fishback was smoking a cigarette, the front of his white undershirt bathed
in sweat.

Sam introduced himself and handed him a Pinkerton card.

Fishback dropped the card on the ground.

"Hell of a show at the Manchu."

Fishback shrugged. He was a good-looking guy and knew it, with an
aquiline nose and dark brown eyes. His cigarette hung out of his mouth and
he just nodded or shook his head to the questions Sam asked.

"You are not a member here," he said finally.

"But I'm an upstanding young man," Sam said. "And an occasional Chris-
tian."

"You're not the law," Fishback said. "You are not a policeman."

"Why'd you turn on Roscoe?"

The ceiling was very high and very elaborate with moldings and
designs. The windows high and bright, sunlight making long shapes on
the wooden floors. Fishback tossed the ball around some more, lit another
cigarette. "Ty Cobb smoked this brand. He said it'll make you mentally
and physically alert."

"Always liked Babe Ruth," Sam said.

"He's old, worn-out. Smoked Home Runs. Terrible tobacco."

Sam shrugged. Fishback picked up another medicine ball, a heavier one, and the leather thwacked hard and fast back and forth in the men's hands. Fishback threw it over his head and started to catch it at his hip, rotating his waist.

"I don't believe what you said in court," Sam said.

"About what?"

"About Roscoe wanting to peep in on the Bathing Beauties."

"He's a pervert. A big, fat, lousy pervert. The man would stick his willie in a sewer pipe."

"He thought you were his buddy."

"I had to tell the truth," Freddie said, grinning. "It's the law."

"How much are you getting?"

"What?"

"From Hearst," Sam said. "How much did he pay you to direct that little morality play? I bet it was in silver. Or maybe a deal with his picture company? That'd be worth it to an up-and-comer like you."

Fishback walked over to large rack and planted his feet in some stirrups, bringing up a long pulley system and stretching his wide, muscular torso, a new cigarette in his teeth.

"You look like Wallace Reid," Fishback said.

"No kidding," Sam said.

"I don't like Wallace Reid," he said. "He's a dope fiend."

"How much?"

"How much they pay you, Pinkerton?"

"Three dollars a day."

Fishback laughed. Sam smiled back at him.

"You heard from Al Semnacher lately?"

"Who?"

"The guy who you got to wrangle the girls," Sam said. "Hollywood agent. He was in the papers. Wears glasses. Goofy smile."

"No."

"Funny," Sam said. No one else has heard from him either. If I were you, I'd watch my back."

"What he did to that girl wasn't right," Fishback said. "He is a beast, you know."

"He didn't kill her."

"Did she crush herself?"

"She wasn't crushed."

"I didn't have a goddamn thing to do with this," Fishback said.

"You're a cog in the wheel."

"What's that?" he asked in his thick accent.

"A piece of lousy machinery," Sam said.

"Are you different?" Fishback asked.

I know them," Roscoe said. It was late and he sat in his hotel room over a bottle of bourbon with Gavin McNab.

"I don't follow," McNab said, rubbing his eyes, still buttoned tight in his boiled-and-pressed shirt and tie, black coat slung over the back of his chair.

"You know your audience."

"They're not an audience," McNab said. "They're a jury."

"What do you think an audience is?"

"They watch you sing and dance and do a little comedy. We've spoken of this before."

Roscoe shrugged and took a sip of the bourbon. Minta had packed along a few bottles for him in her suitcase, knowing they couldn't be tipping a bellboy during the trial, risking some kind of side scandal.

"What about Mrs. Nelson?"

"What about her?" McNab asked.

"She called her occupation that of a housewife."

"So?"

"She said it forcefully—like, take it or leave it. She's no-nonsense. Doesn't get wrapped up in emotion or bullshit."

"Did you see her hat?" McNab said.

"Of course," Roscoe said. "Enormous. Reminded me of something a pirate would wear. I like her. Rock-solid old broad."

"Who else do you like?" McNab said, a smug grin creeping into one cheek, indulging the fat man.

"Mr. Sayre? C.C.?"

"Clarence," McNab said. "Cement contractor."

"He smiles. Big smiles, rosy cheeks. That's a man who knows what it's like to drink a few whiskeys, do a little dance. He knows there's no harm in that. No Satan creeping in the bottle."

McNab finished off his whiskey. He leaned back into his seat. "Roscoe?"

"Hold on," Roscoe said. "Hold on. Kitty McDonald."

McNab's face was fogged out by the smoke coming from his lips, squinting across the table, genuinely intrigued now. The whole indulgence thing passed. "Go on."

"Rich woman," Roscoe said. "A fine-looking woman. Did you see her furs?"

McNab nodded.

"She doesn't want to be there. She wants this whole business to wrap up. She'll swing with the rest of 'em. Okay, who's next? Miss Whosit? The old broad?"

"Mrs. Winterburn."

"Fantastic name. Isn't it? Winterburn. Don't you love saying it? She's the prim-faced schoolteacher, the woman who'd whack your knuckles with a ruler. Sour old kisser. Didn't she say she was in one of those women's clubs?"

"She's not a Vigilant, if that's what you're asking. Do you think I'm an idiot, Roscoe? Her club is literary. She's part of the Jack London Society."

"Ha!" Roscoe said, pounding his fist on the table, the whiskey glass trembling. "A woman of the arts. And what am I?"

"You make movie pictures."

"The arts."

"If you say so."

"Okay. Okay. I'm running them down in my mind. I watch them. Not directly but slyly out of the corner of my eye. I don't want them to think I'm trying to make contact, as if I am a desperate man."

"God forbid," McNab said, waving the smoke away with his hand. His eyes squinting more at Roscoe, maybe a little less curious now. He checked his timepiece again.

"It's two minutes past."

"Past what?"

"Last time you checked," Roscoe said.

"Christ Almighty."

"August Fritze."

"Solid fellow. Brokers cotton."

"That's not why I like him," Roscoe said, pointing his index finger at McNab.

"Do tell."

"He wears spats. Spats! What kind of man wears spats in San Francisco?"

"A man who likes spats."

"A man who likes women, drinking, song," Roscoe said. "Dierks is obvious. How on earth did you get a former liquor salesman on the jury?"

"Because I can outthink and outmaneuver Brady and U'Ren in my sleep."

"What's the explosives expert's name?"

"Crane."

"I don't get a read on him. He's kind of a mystery. Same with that Reef fellow. Both poker-faced bastards."

"And we all know you like Mrs. O'Dea."

"She smiled at me."

"Stop the earth."

"And who is the big man? The one with the hangdog face?"

"Mr. Torpey."

"And Kilkenny," Roscoe said. "Candy manufacturer. I know you found him kinda grim. But he can be won. I can make a case to him."

"When is that?"

"When I testify."

"And you've decided?"

"Yes."

McNab stubbed out the cigarette. He stood and slipped into his big black coat and buttoned up the front. He checked the timepiece again before he got the final buttons, and Roscoe knew it was an effort to unnerve him.

It worked.

"Just what did Zukor say to you?"

McNab looked Roscoe in the eye. He bit a cheek and rocked back on his heels, hands in pockets. He kept the same dead-eyed stare and said, "He said you weren't quick-witted enough to keep up with those jackals."

"Brady and U'Ren."

"Mmm-hmm."

"Zukor is a fool."

"I find him quite shrewd."

"But you know me better."

"Perhaps," McNab said. "Good night, Roscoe."

"That's it?"

"We'll speak on this tomorrow. It's quite late. Thank you for the drink."

"I'll see you out."

Roscoe walked down the long hall of the Palace to the elevator, where McNab pressed the button to ring the boy. He held his fattened leather satchel in his left hand and kept quiet as the elevator groaned into motion, the pulleys taking on the great weight of it all.

"You forgot one," McNab said, the boy rolling back the cage.

"Who?"

"Mrs. Hubbard."

Roscoe snapped his fingers.

"The woman in the feathered hat. Old and pinched face. Very sour."

"She worries me, Roscoe," McNab said. "Very much."

"Give me five minutes."

"U'Ren will ring you dry."

"You ever performed before silver miners in Arizona while wearing a dress?"

"Can't say I have."

"Give me a shot."

"If they make you bleed, it could ruin my career. Make me look foolish."

"I've sat there and listened to lies about me for two weeks," Roscoe said.

McNab looked at him, up and down, from slippers up to the top of his neatly oiled hair. He slipped into the cage, placing a hat on his head and tipping the brim at Roscoe just before the cage door rolled back and the elevator disappeared below.

THE FOG WAS WET AS RAIN.

Sam moved out onto the ferry's deck to have a smoke, most of the passengers inside, nothing visible beyond the running lights cutting through the night and the thick banks of clouds. Sam lit a cigarette and clung to the railing.

A wide swath of lights shot from the military base on Alcatraz and from the north tip of the city at the Ferry Building, crossing each other every minute or so. From the city, great horns blared across the darkness, helping the seamen find their balance, their place in the black. Sam finished his cigarette. Started a new one.

He would go to the Flood Building and file a report using his Pinkerton number and not his name. You never used your name. The system didn't work that way.

He would skip coffee and some hash and go straight home. Jose would be waiting up, rocking the baby and looking down on Eddy Street, ready for him before he put the key in the door. She'd have something warm for him already, the Murphy bed laid out with clean linens, bleached white and fresh smelling.

Jose.

His face heated with shame.

Shoes clacked on the wooden deck through the fog.

Tacoma seemed years ago. She was the prettiest nurse by far, with those soft blue eyes and a hell of a body. She'd laugh at his jokes and let him follow her through her rounds at the sanitarium, helping her wheel out terminal patients onto that giant front porch on sunny days. And while the old soldiers would stare at the yellow-gray horizon with gaping mouths, they'd trade stories about Montana or about her time in London during the war. She convinced him he wasn't terminal, that he'd be fixed up before he knew it, and it'd taken him a full two weeks before she met him in town for a plate of spaghetti and to catch a moving picture. They saw *Pollyanna* with Mary Pickford, and for weeks after that that had been his nickname for Jose every time she'd talk to him about his cure, sitting outside in that same spot watching those openmouthed, shell-shocked bedraggled men staring at the skyline. Pollyanna.

She had a warmth about her, a heat. And the films grew into the rental of a little downtown flat where the passing streetcars would clang past and rumble the building, he and Jose not seeming to notice, the little metal bed they shared rocking so hard it would skip across the beaten-wood floor, traveling from wall to wall, the pair joined at the hip.

Sam flicked the cigarette into the lapping waves.

The beams crossed over each other, one from the shore, one from the island, nearly connecting but passing, and it was night and blackness again. The horns sounded. Sam lifted the collar on his suit and tucked his hands into his jacket, moving toward the front of the ferry, whistling.

A solid fist knocked him square in the gut, dropping him to the deck, him crawling.

A big black shoe came for his face and split his lip.

Another hard kick in the gut. Sam rolled to his back, trying to find just a pocket of air for his squeezed lungs. He stared up at the man and saw the face, the dark man smiling down at him and offering a hand. Sam found an inch of breath and crawled backward, trying his feet but only getting his knees, wiping his lip, a boxer just trying to make it to round's end.

The man kept his hands in a large black overcoat. A wide-brimmed black hat sat on his gray head. He just kept smiling at Sam, quickly glancing around him through the thick blankets of fog misting their faces. He kicked at Sam hard once more, and Sam landed with a giant thwack on the deck, his mouth reaching for air, nothing coming into him, and he blacked out for a moment but never lost sight, trying just to right himself, the beams crossing overhead, cutting across the man's dark skin and misshapen ear. He toed at Sam as if he were a dead fish found on the shore.

Sam tried to breathe. The bovine horns called through the fog, dueling from the islands and shore. Sam's vision scattered, rolling to his hands, the deck a patchwork of wooden planks, blindly searching, cold and wet. More horns. They were close to the Ferry Building now. Four more kicks.

No questions.

The Dark Man reached for Sam, finding the back of his suit and belt and hoisting him to his feet and pushing him to the railing, forcing him to look at the churning water, light cutting across and through the fog and darkness, and whispering something in his ear about the way of the world, repeating "the way of the world" at least twice, but Sam not getting much, his mind turned back to '17 and the wooden sidewalks of Anaconda, the cold sprays of fog and bay tasting like copper smelting in his bloodied mouth, moving into the heart of the little mining town, the beaten floorboards in a rooming house and Frank Little's empty bed. As his feet were hoisted from the creaking deck, Sam's body halved across the ferry's railing and he grabbed and reached for something to hold, finding only slick metal, the man pushing with all his weight, pushing Sam farther off the ferry and into the blackness and fog. Sam saw Little twirl from the trestle, that first light cutting across the barren, raped hills and over the sack that covered the labor leader's head, and he let go, the horns sounding loud and close, reaching into his tweed jacket and leaning back with a little heft to his legs and aiming his boots for the deck, collapsing in a crushed heap.

The Dark Man pressed against him again.

Sam turned.

He shot straight into the Dark Man's heart with his .32.

The man held his chest, a look of surprise on his lips, as Sam flat-handed him backward and lifted with everything he had, toppling the man over into the darkness and foam, catching a glimpse of an air pocket in his black coat, the rough, strong currents of the bay flushing him out toward midnight and the Golden Gate and into the great sea—the Pacific—and nothingness.

Sam dropped to his knees, pressing his back to the steel of the ship, shaking and gasping for breath. The front of his shirt was damp with sweat and sea mist. He closed his eyes and just thought about breathing.

A big, booming bovine horn called him home.

SHE MET HIM at the lunch counter of the Owl drugstore. It was midnight. A guy in a paper hat behind the counter cleaned out coffee mugs and shined forks with a dirty rag.

"You look like shit," Daisy said.

"Shucks. You're just sayin' that."

She smiled and asked the guy in the paper hat for more coffee. She lit a cigarette and blew it from the corner of her mouth. In the bright light, her eyes looked very silver.

"We busted up LaPeer's stills last night," she said. "Out toward Palo Alto, place called Logan's Roadhouse. One of our boys, De Spain, got wind of automobiles and trucks loaded up with barrels and demijohns and the like."

"How much?"

"Four thousand of mash, one-fifty of jackass brandy, and truckloads of his bonded stuff brought in on the *Sonoma*—Scotch, Old Crow, you name it. But the big thing was the stills. Two of 'em. The latest design, all electric, new, and ready to crank out thousands of gallons."

"How'd it taste?"

"Not bad," Daisy said. "Little rough. But, get this—when we got warrants for LaPeer and found him at the Somerton Hotel, he claimed—"

"He didn't own the place."

"No, better," she said, grinning. "Said the gallons of mash were actually hair tonic and he had big plans to get the stuff in the hand of every bald man in the States."

"A true innovator," Sam said. "He make a fight of it?'

"Nope," she said. "Kinda sad. I brought my twelve-gauge and dressed for the newsboys. We had boys all in the lobby of the Somerton and along the stairwell and holding the elevator. Me and De Spain knocked on his door."

"And he just walked out with you?"

"In a robe and slippers. Meek as a kitten. He smiled for the cameras. It's all a big laugh to him."

"What's gonna happen when his suppliers don't get his dough?"

"Cry me a river," she said. "They got most of it back. The Seamen's Bank has it. Makes me sick. I just hope they spell my name right. It's Simpkins. With an *s*. Sometimes they spell it without the *s* and it annoys the folks back home."

"They still haven't found the rest of it."

"They will."

"It's long gone."

Sam didn't say anything for a while, catching Daisy's profile as she tipped her head and let out some smoke. They were the only two at the counter, a dozen or so empty stools down the line.

"Was that true what you said down in Los Angeles?" he asked. "About LaPeer killing your man?"

She shrugged.

"Did I tell you LaPeer had ratted out his two partners back in September, Jack Wise and a Jap named Kukaviza?" she asked. "He went straight into Mr. F. Forrest Mitchell's office, gave him what we needed, and then took over their turf. That's some balls."

"You look shook-up."

"You need glasses." She pulled her hand away and fiddled with another cigarette. "Why are you asking me so many questions about LaPeer's dough? He's in the life. He paid out a half mil, got the booze, and now lost it all. Cry me a river."

"You said that."

"So why do you care?"

"What would you do if you had a chance to keep his coin?"

"I'd be on a slow boat to China."

"I'm serious."

"Are you gonna eat?"

"I'm not hungry."

"I want to eat."

"Then eat."

"Are you going to Australia?"

"I haven't decided," Sam said.

"It ain't up to you. I thought it was up to the Pinkertons."

"I'm not a number."

"Why so touchy?"

31

The courtroom was packed, but no one expected to hear Roscoe's name. They all thought he'd stay silent as a sphinx, all the papers commenting about the film star sticking to his talents since the arrest. What the hell was he supposed to do after both Frank Dominguez and McNab told him to shut his goddamn mouth or he'd find himself tainting the jury pool, pissing off the court, and then getting a quick trip to see the hangman? But he was ready as McNab ushered him to the stand, finding a spot on that hard wooden chair, carrying nothing with him but a pencil, and feeling sharp as hell in a nicely cut blue suit and blue tie, crisp-laundered white shirt, and silk stockings with soft leather shoes. Everything he wore was new and fresh. Early that morning, he'd been sheared and shaved by a barber off Columbus. He felt like a million bucks.

McNab, being McNab, got right to it.

"Mr. Arbuckle, where were you on September fifth, 1921?"

"At the St. Francis Hotel. I secured rooms 1219, 1220, and 1221."

The spectators looked genuinely mystified, the block of black-hatted Vigilants whispering to one another, wide-eyed and in shock that the beast could speak and had a voice and was not just some kind of spirit conjured up from a projector. That morning Roscoe had decided to speak slow and deliberate, McNab telling him don't be a goddamn actor, don't enunciate, don't project, they smell a phony and you're done for.

"Did you see Virginia Rappe that day?"

"Yes. She came into my room about noon."

"Who was present when she entered?"

"Lowell Sherman, Fred Fishback, and a nightgown salesman named Fortlouis."

"Did Miss Rappe come there at your invitation?"

Roscoe tapped the stenographer's desk with the tip of the pencil and turned his eyes to the jury. "No. And I did not invite Miss Blake, Miss Prevon, or Mrs. Delmont and her friend Mr. Semnacher either."

"They crashed your party, so to speak."

"Yes." Roscoe's eyes lingered on the jury, running down each one, face by face, name by name, cataloging each one of them.

"And a Miss Taube. May Taube?"

"She was invited. We had an appointment at three to go motoring."

"How were you dressed when the others arrived at your suite?"

"I wore pajamas, socks, slippers, and a bathrobe."

No running from it, lay it all out like McNab said. When he asks a question, tell it the way it happened. Tell the truth down to the last detail, McNab said. And as Roscoe sat there running down that day, it felt good to say it just as it happened.

McNab walked over to the defense table and brought Roscoe his blue robe, letting him feel the rough, rich texture and identify it. The old man cataloged it into evidence, showing no shame at the attire, nothing scandalous about a fat man wearing a robe at lunchtime.

"Where, previously to seeing her in 1219 taken ill, did you see Miss Rappe?"

"In room 1220. And I saw her go into room 1221."

"When did you go into 1219?"

"About three o'clock."

"Was the door leading from room 1220 to 1219 open at that time?"

Roscoe thumped the pencil on the desk. "Yes."

"Did you know Miss Rappe was in there?"

U'Ren was on his feet, objecting, sniffing the air with his feral nose, and the judge sustained the bastard. A smile crept onto U'Ren's lips, almost frothing to get hold of Roscoe. In a moving picture, he'd be rubbing his hands together. Roscoe would be on a silver platter, an apple in his mouth.

"Where in 1219 did you see Miss Rappe?"

"I found her in the bathroom."

"Now," McNab said, talking and walking. "Tell the jury, Mr. Arbuckle, just what you saw and did."

"Well," Roscoe said, smooth and slow, though not enunciating and projecting but just talking, finding it odd as hell being up on the stage with all these people and talking regular. "I went from 1220 into 1219 and locked the door, and I went right to the bathroom. I found Virginia Rappe"—saying her last name because he decided that was more appropriate and all—"lying on the floor, rolling around, moaning, and very ill. When I opened the bathroom door it stuck against her and I could only open the door a little ways and had to edge my way in. I lifted her up and I held her head. I held her head, pulling back the hair from her face, while she vomited into the commode."

"What else happened?"

"Well, after I had helped her sit up, she asked for water and she drank a glass and one half. I wiped her face with a towel. She said she wanted to lie down, so I helped her from the bathroom and assisted her to lie down on the smaller of the two beds in the room. I went back into the bathroom and closed the door."

"When you came back out of the bathroom again, what did you observe?"

"I found Virginia Rappe on the floor, between the two beds, rolling as if in great pain and moaning. I got her up and got her onto the large bed. She at once became violently ill again. I went at once to 1220, expecting to find Mrs. Delmont. I found Miss Prevost, told her what had happened, and she went right into 1219. I went back into 1219 and Virginia Rappe was tearing her clothes. She acted then as if she were in a terrible temper. She pulled up her dress and tore at her stockings. She had black lace garters on and she was tearing them, too. Then Fishback came into the room. At that time, Miss Rappe was tearing her waist. She had one sleeve almost torn off, and I said, 'All right, Virginia, if you want to get that off I'll help you.' And I did help her to tear it off."

"What did you do then?"

"Well, I went out of the room for a few moments. When I came back, Miss Rappe was nude on the bed. Mrs. Delmont was rubbing her body with ice wrapped up in a towel. I saw a piece of ice on Miss Rappe's body and I said, 'What's that doing there?,' and Mrs. Delmont said, 'Leave it there. You let us alone. I'll take care of Virginia.' She then tried to order me to leave the room. I said to Mrs. Delmont, 'Shut up or I'll throw you out of the window.'"

"What happened then?"

"Mrs. Taube came in and I told her to telephone Mr. Boyle, the hotel manager, and she did. She used the telephone in 1220. Then I went back into room 1219 and I told Mrs. Delmont to get dressed, as the manager was coming. I pulled the bedspread over the body of Miss Rappe. Then Boyle came upstairs. I took him into room 1219."

"What was done then?"

"We got Fred Fishback's bathrobe out of a closet and put it on Miss Rappe and then I picked her up and, with Mr. Boyle, started to carry her to room 1227."

"How did you leave 1219?"

"Through the door leading into the corridor."

"Was that door open?"

"Boyle opened the door."

"What next?"

"Well, I carried Miss Rappe about three-fourths of the way. She kept slipping and I asked Mr. Boyle to help me. We put her in bed in room 1227. Then I walked back down the corridor with Mr. Boyle as far as the elevator and then went to 1219."

"Was the door from 1219 into the hall unlocked on that day?"

"Yes. Fishback went out that way when he left to take my car."

"How was it opened when you removed Miss Rappe?"

"Boyle walked right up to it and opened it."

"Was the window to 1219 open?"

"Yes. It was always wide-open."

"While in 1219, did you hear Miss Rappe say, 'You hurt me' or 'He hurt me'?"

"No, I did not. She spoke to me several times, but no one could understand just what she said."

"On the next day, or at any other time, did you have any conversation with Al Semnacher with regard to the ice on Virginia Rappe's body?"

"Absolutely not."

"Did you ever, at any time, in room 1219 on September fifth, 1921, have occasion to place your hand over that of Miss Rappe's on the door of your room?"

"No, sir."

"Did you in any way come into contact with that door leading out into the corridor?"

"No, sir."

"Do you know Fred Fishback?"

"Yes, sir."

"Did you ever, on any occasion, have a conversation with him in which you are alleged to have asked him if he had the key to Virginia Rappe's room and in which he is alleged to have said yes and in which you further are alleged to have said, 'I'll give this for it,' showing him a roll of bills?"

"No such conversation ever took place."

"Now, Mr. Arbuckle, are there any other circumstances that occurred in room 1219 that you can tell this jury?"

"No, sir."

"And you have related to the jury everything that occurred there on that day as you know it?"

"Yes, sir. Everything."

"You're safe."

"What time is it?" Sam asked.

"Noon," Jose said.

"I need to get up."

"You need to rest."

"I feel fine."

"You have a fever."

"Why's it so dark?"

"I pulled the curtains," she said. "You want me to open them?"

"Please."

Sam found his feet and dropped his head into his hands. The afternoon light was white and harsh and he squinted and looked down at his skinny legs and stocking feet.

"Where's the baby?"

"In the bedroom," she said. "Asleep."

Jose softly shut the door separating the two rooms of the apartment. She walked back to Sam carrying a little bottle and spoon. "You need to take this."

"I need a cigarette. Would you mind reaching in my coat?"

"Sam?"

He looked at her, blurred in the light behind her, and he closed one eye.

"Open up."

He did. The balsamea tasted horrible.

She poured another spoonful.

"I wired my aunt," she said. "We can stay there until I get settled in Montana."

He nodded. She found his cigarettes and a book of matches.

"I can arrange to have my checks sent direct to you."

"That's good of you, Sam."

"It's not good of me," he said. "Don't ever say that."

"What's the matter?"

"The City is nowhere to raise a child. The sooner the both of you get on that train, the better."

"Whatever you say."

"But you don't understand?"

"There are other jobs."

"Not for me," he said. "I'm not strong enough to work the docks and not educated enough to work in an office."

"You could go back to school. To business college."

"And how would we make it?"

She was quiet.

"I'll take care of you," he said. "You have my word. As long as I can work a job, those checks will keep coming."

She didn't say anything.

"Oh, for Christ's sake."

"I believe you."

Sam stared at the window, his eyes adjusting, curtains skittering in a cold wind. By the kitchen table, he noticed his steamer trunk, pulled from the bedroom, open and waiting.

"Thought you might need to get packed," Jose said, catching his stare. "And I want you to take this for luck."

She smiled with her eyes and handed him the little card given to them at Mary Jane's birth. On the flip side was her hospital number and footprints stamped in ink.

He didn't say anything, only tucked the card in his jacket. He did not meet her eye as she continued to talk, only watched the curtains that brought in the cold air and the smell of the sea. The baby started to wail in the next room. Sam lit a cigarette and watched Jose go, closing the door behind her with a soft click.

"Now," MILTON U'REN SAID, pacing, smiling with those sharp teeth, his long bony fingers clasped behind his back, "you stated that you never attempted to borrow a key from Mr. Fishback during August of 1919 in Culver City? Is that correct?"

"That is correct."

"Now, where were you employed during August of 1919?"

"I had my own company."

"You had your own company, yes, but where?"

"At Culver City."

"And you had a studio there?"

"No, sir."

"Were you using a studio?"

"I was renting a studio there."

"And from whom were you renting the studio, if from anyone?"

"Mr. Lehrman."

"Yes, then during August of 1919 you did occupy the studio in conjunction with Mr. Henry Lehrman?"

"Yes, sir."

"And you do not recall whether you had a conversation about Miss Rappe with Mr. Fishback?"

"The conversation never occurred."

"Yes or no would be sufficient," U'Ren said.

U'Ren was sweating now and the sweating pleased Roscoe a great deal. Roscoe stopped tapping his pencil and leaned back into the hard chair. He crossed his legs, resting his ankle on knee.

"You knew Miss Rappe before the fifth of September, did you not?"

"Yes, sir."

"How long had you known her?"

"About five or six years."

"About five or six years?"

"Yes, sir."

"Before Miss Rappe came to your rooms on the fifth of September, did you know that she was coming there?"

"No, sir."

"Mr. Fishback didn't say anything to you about her coming there?"

"He said that he was going to phone her."

"Do you know whether or not he did phone her?"

"I didn't hear him phone."

U'Ren took a breath, his jaw twitching. He stared down at the courtroom floor as if it would provide him some kind of key, some kind of answer, to make Roscoe reverse a story he'd been telling for months and had been playing time and again in his mind.

"How long a time elapsed from the time you saw Miss Rappe go into room 1221 until you went into room 1219?"

"Couldn't tell you."

"What did you do when she got up and went into room 1221?"

"I got up. I don't know what I did, went to the Victrola or something, or danced. I don't know. I don't remember that time."

"Well, how long a time would you say elapsed from the time you saw Miss Rappe go into room 1221 until you went into room 1219?"

"Couldn't tell you."

"Well, was it a half hour?"

"No, I don't think it was that long."

"Well, fifteen minutes?"

"I wouldn't say what time it was. It was—"

"Isn't it a fact that when you saw Miss Rappe going into 1221 that within two or three minutes thereafter you went into room 1219?"

"No, I don't think so."

"You don't think so?"

"No."

"And nothing you have heard during this trial refreshes your memory upon that subject?"

"When Miss Rappe went into 1221, I fooled around."

"It was more than two or three minutes after Miss Rappe went into room 1221 that you went into room 1219?"

"Oh, yes."

"Well, how much longer than two or three minutes?"

"Well, probably five or ten minutes."

"Probably five or ten minutes," U'Ren said, parroting it back, throwing up his hand carelessly. "All right, what were you doing in that five or ten minutes?"

"Just fooling around in that room."

"Just tell the jury what you were doing the next five or ten minutes."

"All right, I suppose I danced with Miss Blake."

"Not that you *supposed*. Tell the jury what you *remember* doing."

"I don't remember what I did in the room," Roscoe said, looking to the jury, wanting to tell them that he'd been drunk out of his mind. He leaned into his left arm, resting on the stenographer's desk.

"What time did Miss Rappe go into room 1221?"

"I couldn't tell you."

"What time did Miss Rappe go into room 1219?"

"Like I said, I never saw her go into 1219."

"What time did Mr. Fishback leave your room?"

"Between one-thirty and a quarter to two, I guess."

"To go motoring and view some seals for a motion picture?"

"Yes."

"Between one-thirty and a quarter to two," U'Ren said, repeating for the jury. "Did Miss Rappe go into room 1219 before or after Fishback left your room?"

Roscoe looked to McNab, who sat behind the defense table stifling a yawn.

"I went into 1219 after Miss Blake had come back from Tait's Café for rehearsal, sometime between two-thirty and three o'clock. I don't know when Virginia Rappe entered."

"Do you recall doing anything from the time that Miss Rappe went into room 1221 until you went into room 1219?"

"Yes, certainly."

"What did you do?"

"I put . . . changed a record on the phonograph. I think I danced with Miss Blake. I am not sure what I did."

"Then you don't recall what you did. You don't recall doing anything?"

"I was around the room. I don't just exactly know what I was doing."

"As a matter of fact, when you arose on the fifth of September and went into the bathroom to clean up it was your intention then to get ready to go out riding in your Pierce-Arrow limousine with Mrs. Taube?"

"Yes."

"But you did not get dressed at that time?"

"No, these people kept coming in and I was trying to be sociable."

"With whom?"

"With them."

"They were not your guests?"

"No. I didn't want to insult them."

"You didn't invite them there, did you?"

"No, sir."

"With the exception of Miss Rappe, you didn't know anybody that was coming there at that time, any of these young ladies?"

"No."

"You did not invite them?"

"No."

And you didn't tell anyone else to invite them?"

"No."

"And they were not your guests?"

"No."

"They just appeared as if by magic?"

"They appeared."

"And you don't know how long a time elapsed from the time that Miss Rappe went into room 1221 until you went into 1219?"

McNab stood. It was the first time that he'd objected in the two hours of grilling by U'Ren. He smiled at the jury, letting them know he understood this silly weasel-faced little man, and then smiled at Louderback. "If the court pleases, we are supposed to end this trial sometime. I object to the same question being asked more than ten times."

The courtroom laughed. Louderback did not.

"Proceed with the examination," he said.

"Very well," U'Ren said. "Answer the question."

Roscoe scratched the back of his neck and looked at the jury. "What was it?"

Two of the jury, Fritze and Sayre, smiled.

He had 'em.

32

The baby cried for two hours straight. Sam finished his coffee, took a shower, and changed into some fresh clothes, tugging on his cap and walking down to the first floor and out on Eddy Street. Newsboys shouted from corners that the jury was out on the Arbuckle case, yelling, "Will Fatty Fall?" and "Fatty's Last Stand" and the like. Sam walked with no direction in mind, absently smoking cigarettes and trudging forward, just keeping his feet moving, and suddenly found himself at Powell. A cable car idled in front of him and he got on, winded, taking a seat on an empty bench, listening to his rasping lungs as the bell clanged and the cable caught and the whole damn box made its creaky way up Nob Hill.

He could still hear the baby. See Jose's face.

The cable car passed the St. Francis and limousines and women in long furs, jewelry shops, solid restaurants with waiters and white tablecloths, tobacconists and men's clothing shops. Sam absently felt at his tweeds, tearing out a loose thread, and sat back on the hard seat, just letting the cable car do all the work on the ascension as he smoked and watched, feeling good about not having to hoof it anymore, not caring where the damn thing ended up.

The car crested at Nob Hill and, for the hell of it, he got off. He liked being able to do that. He looked at the four corners and spotted the California line that intersected at the top of the hill. He waited a beat and caught the car as it rattled past, full of businessmen and ladies on their way to teas, and held tight to the brass fitting during the rickety descent, the brakemen catching the cable, letting go, and catching the cable again during the jerky ride.

A few stops and they were at Fillmore, the street opening up to him in early night, iron buttresses arcing the street, lit up with a million small white bulbs, reminding Sam of the midways he worked back east. There were flivvers and trucks parked all along the street. Three- and four-story buildings and jutting turrets and hand-painted signs for fish merchants and pawnshops and Italian barbers.

He dodged a streetcar and another heading the opposite direction and wandered into a nickelodeon. He popped a coin in a machine and watched the pages flip, showing the devastation of the big Quake, the flattened city, smoke rising from the ashes, the tent city built on the rubble.

Men boiled crabs on the street. Big wheels of cheese and fresh fruit were displayed from market windows, long dried sausages and peppers. There were dope pushers with dark-ringed eyes and prostitutes with sagging stockings. Sam smoked and caught all of them, starting up the night like the first strings of a symphony.

He turned and walked backward, heading out from the little district, his eye on a young man in a black hat holding two black satchels, one in each hand, as if they both contained a tremendous weight. The man's head was down; slump-shouldered, he walked across the tracks.

There was music from a high window, opera with the soaring voice of Carmen, and a man in a tattered undershirt looked down at Sam, listening to his private songs. The man scratched his chest and his dirty chin and closed the window.

The steel buttresses of light ended and there was no music. The hard soles of his feet kept Sam company. He saw the Dark Man in his mind, seeing him spin and twirl, caught in the current, heading through the Golden Gate and far out into the ocean.

He heard the clang of a cable car behind him. He kept walking downhill.

He stepped off the curb to cross the street. And for some reason he would never understand, he simply stepped back, to check his pockets for change or perhaps a cigarette. He could not recall.

There was a tremendous pop and the earth rumbled beneath him and for a moment he thought it was a tremor, but then the entire raging, rattling box of a cable car crossed an inch from his nose, a wind crossing his face like a giant breath, and skittered and screamed downhill toward the bay, roaring with great yells and shrieks from the passengers, until there was a tremendous crash into an electric pole, the pole breaking in two as the cable car finally came to rest in the dead center of a house's front porch.

Sam had not moved his feet since stepping back on the curb.

He could not move.

He was still yet his heart jackhammered in his chest. He could still feel the cut of wind across his nose. More screams and people yelling came from below and Sam ran downhill to the corner of Green, where a crowd had formed, as black snakes of electric cable jumped and zapped against the street, showering the night in bright sparks. He helped an old woman and the conductor from the heap. Four others had been helped into the street. They had been cut and bruised. One man walked in a circle, still in shock.

Sam walked back up Fillmore to where the car had gone loose. In the street, the cable continued to whirl and flow in the narrow gash, never stopping, never noticing the weight was gone.

THE JURY WAS OUT, the closings wrapped up, and at eight o'clock Roscoe returned to the courtroom with Minta. The big room was empty and quiet. A few newspapermen lay on benches smoking and reading back through their notebooks; other newsmen sat on staircases and occupied phone booths, waiting for the latest. McNab said it would be tomorrow at best. Told the boys from his firm to ring him at home if there was something brewing. Roscoe walked over to the jury box. Minta was restless, not wanting to have to dodge reporters. Half of them were out on the streets covering a visit by Marshal Foch, the French war hero, and that goddamn cat show at the St. Francis. Roscoe was officially banned from the hotel, but a stray tom called Mr. Whiskers and even a little bastard called Charlie Chaplin—on account of a black smudge under its nose—were welcome. A bunch of smelly cats purring and scratching at the furniture, taking dumps in the place, even if they did cost a few thousand like the papers said.

"Let's go, Roscoe," Minta said.

The little heads of a few newsboys popped up from where they slept on the benches, looking like gophers back in Kansas. His dad used to shoot at 'em with a .22 when they popped those heads up.

"Would you pay ten grand for a cat?" Roscoe asked.

"What?"

"Didn't you read about the show at the St. Francis, crazy old women showing off ten-grand cats?"

"I read about Charlie Chaplin," she said. "He was pretty cute."

Roscoe opened the swinging door and sat down in the seat of Mrs. Hubbard, thinking that maybe if he warmed her seat he'd send her some positive thoughts. But all he could think about when he closed his eyes was the sharp little remarks made by U'Ren in the closing. U'Ren relished it, using the whole width of the box as his stage, pointing, enunciating, pulling from his whole bag of tricks, while Roscoe had to stay silent again.

"Come on, Roscoe."

"Another minute."

"They're not coming back tonight," said a newsman. "I got a tip."

Roscoe ignored him. He leaned back into Mrs. Hubbard's seat and tossed his big black shoes atop the seat in front of him. He lit a cigarette and looked at the ceiling.

The callous man—the man who laughs in the face of misery, who plays jokes on suffering women—whose only thought is to hurry a dying girl out of his room. Why didn't Arbuckle tell that story in the first place? Why his silence? Why did he not tell a soul? Why did he not speak when yet in Los Angeles, before he had even seen a lawyer who might silence him? Why remain mute?

Goddamn bastard. Roscoe let out the smoke and watched it trail up to the tin stamped ceiling, a ceiling that looked for all the world like that of any crummy saloon. U'Ren's words rattled around in his head, between his ears, and settled down in his gut.

And we shall shatter their theory of injury by immersion in cold water or by paroxysms of coughing or of nausea. And we have shattered the theory contained in Arbuckle's statement to the effect that the girl fell from the bed.

U'Ren painted a picture for them of the fat beast throwing open the hotel door, ushering in the gash, pouring the drinks, turning up the jazz, and setting a trap for Virginia. He must've mentioned that Roscoe had worn pajamas and a robe at least thirty times, as if his dress was a crime in itself. Why can't a man wear a goddamn robe and slippers in his own hotel room? Roscoe smoked some more and narrowed his eyes at where Louderback sat, trying to get a sense of the scene from a different point of view, get to see the whole drama from all angles and which ones worked best to tell the story.

And yet this defendant, who makes his living by acting—who has learned to disguise his thoughts—wants to make you believe that he did not see her go into that room.

U'Ren paused, reciting the testimony of the showgirls, that they saw him follow Virginia into 1219, then, just at the right moment, stopping to let the men and women picture the fat man locking the door behind him. His hand reaching over the poor girl's as she tried to escape. The silence lasted long enough for all to envision Fatty crawling, sloppy drunk and bloated, on top of the girl, sticking his willy inside her and riding her like a dog until he squished her.

There is no doubt that at that time she was suffering from the injury inflicted by Arbuckle—the injury that caused her death. And Arbuckle cannot explain it. The only things he has seemed to remember in this trial are the things alleged to have occurred when no one else was there to see. Why should this man, famous throughout the world, allow himself to be damned without protest if all that had happened was that Virginia Rappe had become ill and had fallen off a bed?

"Because I was directed."

"What's that?" Minta asked.

"Nothing."

"You said something," she said. "It's late. Please?"

Roscoe checked his watch, smoking the cigarette down to a nub. The newspapermen were up now, maybe eight or so of them, and they were watching him, the way children watch a polar bear in a zoo, just waiting for any little movement to bring them joy. But Roscoe's mind reeled off, and McNab was before them all now, the projector rolling.

He began with a short, solemn prayer for Miss Irene Morgan, the war nurse who had braved the battlefields of Europe beside such men at Marshal Foch, coming to the city only to share her knowledge, and facing such danger.

The prosecution did nothing but try and besmirch her character when she could not appear. Have medical experts not shown—as Miss Morgan's statement read into the record—that the girl suffered from many acute ailments? Still they want you to picture Miss Rappe as in perfect health, a giantess in strength, if you please. Would it have been possible in that little room for a man to have attacked a woman of that sort without everybody in the neighborhood knowing it or hearing it? And they try to tell you what a monster he was, this man who picked the girl up in his arms and yet could not carry her weight to another room a short distance without being assisted.

McNab walked, clad as always in a black suit with a vest, white shirt, and black tie. His balding gray head always with the same short stubble. He did not smile. He did not yell. He did not show emotion. He walked and talked to the jury as if working on things in his own mind, the way they should be thinking, too. So many questions. So many holes.

Throughout the length and breadth of this trial there has been hawked the name of Bambina Maude Delmont. Why was she not put on the stand? Why has she not been produced, this complaining witness of theirs? Why has the prosecution resorted to the spook evidence of dimly marked doors summoning their spirits of evil out of the woodwork, or through the manipulation of an expert holding a microscope to the floor, instead of producing human beings in flesh and blood who could have shed light upon this case? There has been more processing of witnesses than process of law. The district attorney has maintained his witnesses in private prisons—a thing I had believed to be abolished at the time of Little Dorrit.

Roscoe started to laugh. Minta shushed him.

And I would like to know why a witness who perhaps is believed to be so untruthful that he or she has be to kept in custody is then brought before a jury to imperil the liberty of any man? Miss Prevon was kept in this so-called Hall of Justice all night without food or drink or time for a quiet smoke. She was harassed and threatened with jail unless she was willing to sign a declaration for the grand jury that Virginia Rappe, moaning upon the bed, had explained, "I am dying. I am dying. He killed me."

McNab smiled.

All that Zey Prevost heard Virginia Rappe say was "I am dying"—he shouted this to the jury. *And they finally compromised with her and let her alone after she signed a statement that Virgina Rappe had explained, "I am dying. He hurt me."*

U'Ren protested that this was not based on a shred of testimony and that by morning he would produce reams showing that . . . McNab let him finish and continued.

I will show you, therefore, why it was that Mr. Arbuckle was wise in not making any statement. They would have processed the witnesses. Mr. Heinrich, the fingerprint expert, would have suddenly discovered that he and Salome had been under the carpet while Mr. Arbuckle and Virginia Rappe were alone in room 1219 and they would have produced a horde of chambermaids, with their eyes at every crack, their ears in every keyhole, to substantiate him.

Roscoe stood. He smiled. He straightened his tie, rubbing his hands together.

"Better?" Minta asked. She placed her black hat, the one with the veil of beads, back on her head, half of her face shielded.

"Yes."

"Can you sleep now?" Minta asked.

He nodded. "Better."

"I COULDN'T SLEEP," Sam said. "I walked. I've walked for a while."

Daisy opened the door to her apartment. Her kimono hung open past her breasts and clear down to her navel. She smiled when she caught his gaze. "Why don't you come in."

"Nice flat."

"It's cozy, on a gal's pay."

"How sure are you that the stash is LaPeer's?"

"F. Forrest Mitchell doesn't make mistakes."

"You make him sound like God."

"He's more sure of himself."

"Can I take a seat?"

"Kick your shoes off."

Sam found an old leather chair, a craned reading lamp. A window overlooking Turk Street.

"Didn't mean to ambush you like this."

"I'm not ambushed," she said, sitting on top of a coffee table, holding the front of her silk robe. She wore no paint on her face, white blond hair brushed flat back and behind her ears, looking fresh and clean. She smelled like good soap.

"I found it. The money."

She smiled. "Well, I guess I should be pleased, but I'm not. Just make sure they spell your name right. Did I tell you about that?"

"I didn't tell 'em."

"The newsboys?"

"Nobody," Sam said. "I didn't tell a soul. I left it where it lay. In the shaft of an engine-room duct, snaked through the guts of the *Sonoma* in a fire hose."

Daisy dropped her head into her hands and pushed her hair back over her ears, combing it back, her face hidden in profile. "I need a smoke. You want coffee?"

"We can leave. You can leave."

"What about the money?"

"We can decide when we're at sea," Sam said. "Don't you understand? It's a fresh start. And if it's on LaPeer's filthy dime, no tears from me. My bum lungs can heal up in Australia. You can get the city grime off you and tell Mr. F. Forrest Mitchell to take a flying leap. You know what I mean?"

"Kinda."

"Sometimes it's that way. It can come at you like a sucker punch and it's all so clear that life's a sham. It's a long con and you walk through it like asleep, halfway in a dream, and it takes something big to make you wise up and see the world for what it is. Let's get the hell out of here."

"What about your family?"

"The girls are better off without me," he said. "I'll disappoint them in the end."

"But you won't disappoint me?"

"I'll disappoint you, too. But let's have some fun first."

"What time does she sail?"

"Tomorrow. At midnight."

Daisy raised her head and smiled at him. "Aren't you gonna kiss me or something?"

"Or something."

33

Roscoe knew, could feel it, even before the judge assembled all the lawyers and the jurists, what the word was going to be. They'd been in there forty-four hours, taking breaks only to eat and to sleep back at the Hotel Manx, filing past him each time, no one looking him in the eye except for a couple boys, riding off in that little ivory bus and returning for two days straight. It was about noon on Sunday and with the doors to the Hall open you could hear the church bells ringing across the city. Roscoe had been sitting with Minta and Ma in the first row behind the defense table. McNab, who was in the judge's chambers, looked at Roscoe, crooking his finger at him to come back to the table. The bailiffs spread out, doors were open, the jury being ushered back into the box. McNab leaned in and whispered, "Louderback is shaking them loose."

"What'd we get?"

"Ten to two," McNab said. "The second one gave in because they couldn't stand the pressure anymore."

"Who was the holdout?"

"Mrs. Hubbard," McNab said, whispering again. "Hadn't changed her vote since Friday."

Roscoe didn't say a thing, but there was a rock in his stomach, a feeling of being on a long, loose slope, trying to find ground with your feet but only getting mud. He smiled, straightened his tie. He folded his hands across each other, catching Fritze's eye, the foreman, who Roscoe knew had been a good egg since the start, and Fritze shook his head sadly and opened his palms.

The titian-haired Amazon, Mrs. Hubbard, kept her head dropped, an enormous black hat on her head. Her chin down to her chest, refusing to look at anyone, as Louderback asked Roscoe to rise and explained that the jury was hung and that he saw no other course of action but to let them loose and call a new one.

"Perhaps we should look to the first of the year," Louderback said, lean and well-oiled in a blue suit. "We would hate to spoil anyone's Christmas holiday."

Roscoe shook his head. He turned back to Minta and Minta grabbed his hand and held it very tightly, and then she did something that Roscoe would always remember. She winked at him, holding on tight, and he had such pride that he almost felt like walking right over to Mrs. Hubbard and spitting in her eye.

The gavel sounded.

There was talking and murmuring in the courtroom, like any Sunday service being broken up, and newspapermen and photographers surged forth. McNab caught them all and gruffly said that he would let the facts speak for themselves and he looked forward to getting another jury in there devoid of any prejudices against his client.

Roscoe walked out with Minta and Ma, the dogs trailing him, shouting questions, flashbulbs popping and exploding. Head held high, he walked, Minta's arm in his, Ma alongside. The great doors to the Hall were open and he followed the stairs down onto the street, looking out to the greenery of Portsmouth Square.

More questions. More of the same.

"I'm very grateful to those who recognized the truth," Roscoe said. "I've only tried to bring joy and laughter to millions and only the Lord himself knows why this has befallen me. I only tried to help that poor woman. That, my friends, is my only sin."

A little girl toddled over to Roscoe and, in the click and whir of cameras, handed Roscoe a tin cup. She smiled and curtsied and said, "Better luck next time."

The newsboys roared with laughter, and he saw one of them jangle out some coin into the little girl's hand. Roscoe lit a smoke and stood there. Most of the newsmen scattered to catch Mrs. Hubbard on the steps, as she was saying that a jury was absolutely no place for a woman and that at one point the men complained of the amount of food she had consumed.

Roscoe watched the large woman brushing away the men with tablets and cameras who followed her down the street. The black-hat Vigilants soon swallowed her in their mass and walked off with her in a dark swarm toward the park.

Roscoe met McNab's eye and the big man gritted his teeth and nodded, seeing the chorus, before finding Roscoe's elbow and steering him toward the machine.

The Pierce-Arrow was kept back at the Palace.

They piled into McNab's touring car. Roscoe doffed his hat for the crowd and they moved away, down the hills and back to the hotel. There was a deep silence in the car, the silence creating some kind of shame in him. Roscoe rested his head on his knuckles, watching the city pass, thinking back to a year ago when he'd stepped off a train in Paris and received nothing short of a hero's welcome.

He wondered where they'd all gone.

SAM FOUND HIS STATEROOM, steamer trunk arriving soon after, a negro porter unloading it from his back. Sam tipped the man and sat on the small bunk, wishing for a pint of Scotch but settling for a glass of water, watching the clock on the wall, knowing the ship would sail at midnight, hearing the lot of people coming and going, screaming and yelling, excited for the big send-off.

At seven, he called the porter and ordered a bottle.

He had three stiff drinks and found himself walking the deck, crowds gathering on the railing facing the dock, waving to their families. There was champagne being chilled by barmen, ready to uncork at sea, cigarettes being smoked by women in long dresses and men in tuxedos. Chinese women handed everyone stingers and confetti, gold dust to toss into the air at send-off.

Sam checked his watch. He watched a man light another man's cigar with the crisp burning end of some currency. They laughed and blew smoke into the air.

The wind was brisk, deafening Sam's ears as he stared in disbelief.

He returned down below for a drink.

He had three more.

He walked back to the deck and searched for Daisy, checking a half dozen times with members of the crew. He found a spot on the railing and smoked several cigarettes until the pack was empty. He noted the time again, watching the length of Pier 35 until it came upon half past eleven, the gangplanks gone empty, men in overalls ready by the taut lines stretching down to the dock.

Sam returned below, the ship's horns blaring, porters roaming the halls calling for all those going ashore. He checked his timepiece, feeling a gentle hum vibrating the steel of the big ship. He drank down the last of the bottle, not even bothering with the glass.

Sam reached into the pocket of his tweeds, finding not a handkerchief but a rough card. He wiped his lips with the back of his hand and stared down into his palm at the small, insignificant card with numbers hammered into the type and the ink prints of two small feet.

He staggered to his feet, searching for the hall, instead finding a dressing mirror. "Goddamn son of a bitch."

When he opened the door, people were running crazy down the halls, throwing streamers and confetti, and champagne had already been uncorked while they were still moored. Sam staggered the hallways, using the walls for balance, getting lost, running into people, women kissing him full on the lips, until he finally found the porter and gave him a silver dollar and begged him to please unload his trunk before they sailed.

"Just set it on the pier," Sam said. "I'll find it. It's been with me for some time."

The man looked confused, black face wise and weathered, but pocketed the money. Sam wavered on his feet.

He followed the hall and then another and twisted down into the guts of the ship and down a staircase into the clanging engine room. Men in white coveralls shoveled coal into the red-hot furnace, stoking the fire, wiping their brows, getting the steamer prepped for the journey.

Sam could not breathe, the heat and grit of the place wrenching his lungs.

Two crewmen passed, not giving him a second glance, and Sam rounded the short staircase up to the steel deck overlooking the workers. With his pocketknife, he again unscrewed the vent and pulled away the grille, reaching his arm far into the air duct, fingers fanning as far as they could for the hidden fire hose but only feeling the heat in the shaft and an endless void. He stretched in with all of his shoulder, finding the short curve where he pushed the nozzle, spreading out the length of his fingers, but he knew the gold was gone.

He pulled out his hand, wiping the coal dust on his pants, replaced the grille, and screwed the vent back in place.

Sam felt a hand on his shoulder.

He turned into the face of the first officer, the same man he'd met the first day on the ship. McManus. Sam gave him his best sober stare, his legs feeling unsteady.

"Already working?" the first officer asked.

"You?" Sam asked.

The first officer shook his head. "You're the second person givin' the engine room a good thorough look today."

"And the other was a nice-looking gal with silver eyes."

"How'd you know?"

Sam shrugged in the sloppy manner of a drunk.

"One last thing," Sam asked. "Which way is up?"

FOR THE NEW YEAR'S PARTY, Hearst had a carousel delivered to the great dock at San Simeon. The guests had arrived by boat and stayed in tents all along the beach and were given rides up to the top of the hill where the castle was just beginning to take shape. Nearing midnight, Hearst finally gained his favorite carousel horse, a violent black mare with a fearsome carved face and golden saddle, and he delighted in his whirl around the sights, the dock, the tents, the vast hills. He laughed at it all, clowning for a little crowd waiting for their turn. Hearst made a big show of riding with no hands and, on another pass, sidesaddle, but what really got them was when he rode backward, waving to them all and laughing. Marion was alongside him and then behind him and then on the opposite side of the carousel, and after a few rotations, the night filled with the gay-piped calliope music, he walked in the opposite direction, the very axis tilting under him, until he made it nearly around and saw her sitting astride the giant white filly with the pink hair and the gay mouth, and she was laughing uproariously, holding a batch of cotton candy. And Hearst just stood there, seeing the enjoyment, taking pleasure in bringing it to her, very self-satisfied. He took another step forward with his giant black boots and removed his plantation hat, a stupid grin on his face, and then saw the Englishman there, holding the reigns of the false horse in his hands and performing dog tricks for his girl, pantomiming and laughing, jumping from one horse to the next.

The beach was dark, the loping hills nothing but rough-cut shadows, and the only warmth on the shore coming from the kaleidoscope of lights from the carousel and the little fires clicking along the beach where the Chinese would cook the fish and sweets in a giant party Hearst had organized to see 1922 meet its first dawn.

Hearst watched the Englishman, finding nothing attractive or charming or funny about him, wondering why the world would so adore a man like Charlie Chaplin.

Chaplin held on to the golden rod of the horse, pumping up and down, Marion laughing, and made his way onto Marion's great white horse, the one Hearst had picked out especially for her. He shrugged and smiled with so much vanity, tipping the end of a delicate champagne glass to her mouth, drinking it, spilling on the dress, a great, horrendous laugh to follow.

Hearst walked into the turn of the carousel, hands upon his back, to much laughter and praise and thanks from his guests. Men dressed as women and women as men. There were harlequins and harlots and tigers and knights. He smiled and pleasantly told them all they were welcome and returned to his great black horse, hugging its neck, the carousel pumping and twirling twice until it slowed, the calliope music gently stopping to a single note.

"You s-silly man," Marion said.

Hearst looked up from the horse's neck. She took off his hat and kissed him on the head. She cocked her hip in a sexy way and tipped a bottle of champagne by the neck into her mouth and throat. She kissed him again.

"H-how 'bout another turn, W.R.?"

"Whatever the lady wishes."

"You silly man."

He smiled at her, tasting the champagne on her lips and smelling another man's cologne on the nape of her flowered dress.

She smiled back.

THE SECOND TRIAL was well under way in January when Sam shadowed Fred Fishback to a Chinatown opium den, Fishback having been called by McNab but not showing up to the Hall. The joint was a Hip Sing Tong place, the tongs finally settling their latest turf battle in the colony, and the owner of the place offered a little cup of ny ka pa before taking Sam into the back room, where whites and Chinese had settled themselves along bunks and relaxed against silk cushions. A little Chinese boy with a pigtail worked to attach scrolls in the cracks of the hovel, a brisk January wind snaking through the cracks and dimming the candles in the room. The owner pointed to Fishback, who rested in a lower bunk with two women clutched to his chest, his own loose hand on his forehead, a great smile on his face when he saw Sam. One woman turned her head, awaking from her dream, and clawed her hand up at the wavering image of Sam.

It was Alice Blake, her face a mess of paint, a sloppy red smile on her lips.

The other woman, the girl from the Manchu, settled into Fishback's chest.

"Boom, chisel, chisel," Sam said. "Boom, chisel."

The girl said, "Yes, of course."

Fishback's face looked as if it were made of parched paper, dark circles under his eyes, a lazy, go-to-hell look. He'd grown a clipped mustache, the rest of his face stubbled and unshaven.

On the top bunk, a Chinese man in traditional silk getup stroked a white cat as he sucked on a pipe.

"Have you ever danced on a table?" Fishback asked, disheveled but still handsome.

Sam didn't say anything.

"We all danced," Fishback said, as if the words called for great effort. "For two days straight. With my beauties." He kissed them and looked to Sam. "And now I'm no longer afraid of death. I'm so rude. Would you like a smoke?"

"I'll stick to Scotch."

"You show 'em."

Fishback laughed and rocked back into the bed. The girls snuggled into him.

"I just finished a film," Fishback said. "And I couldn't stop thinking. My body was exhausted and my mind was still going. Do you have any idea what that's like?"

"I have something for you," Sam said, pulling the subpoena from his coat.

"I like to do something I fear," Fishback said. "I like to set up obstacles and defeat them. I like to be afraid of the project. I always am. When I get into something, really into something, I always believe I shouldn't have the job. But you know what? I fooled them again. I can't do it. I don't know how to do it. The anxiety works for me."

"You're wanted in court tomorrow."

"You can't save him."

"Tomorrow," Sam said, tossing the subpoena into his lap.

Alice Blake picked it from his chest and opened it with thick fingers. She squinted one eye at Sam and made a gun from a thumb and forefinger and just said, "Kennedy," before leaning over and kissing the Oriental gal and resting her head on Fishback's chest.

"Doesn't he look like Wallace Reid?" Fishback asked.

Two days later, Fishback testified. McNab slung arrows. Fishback repeated the same tale from the first trial.

Five days later, a masseuse showed up at his hotel room. She found him naked, cold, and dead on the floor. His body was shipped back to Los Angeles on the same train that had brought Virginia and buried not ten paces from her.

34

Roscoe stood trial for killing Virginia Rappe three times. The third jury acquitted him after deliberating for five minutes, calling the case an insult to their intelligence and even posing for pictures with him after the whole thing wrapped. They wrote him a letter of apology that all the newspapers ran, except the Hearst papers, Roscoe noted, and by April the movie houses had dusted off their reels of *Crazy to Marry* and *Gasoline Gus*. He could now drive down to the airfields and picnic as the zeppelins would take off and land and was welcomed on picture sets with his old buddy Buster, who asked him if he'd like to direct a couple comedies he'd written during all this mess. Minta stayed on with him, Ma taking a room downstairs by the bowling alley, and all through those first days in April he'd join his ex-wife at the piano and they'd remember old songs from when they were teenagers performing at the Byde-A-While, and sometimes Roscoe would accompany her on kazoo, bringing Luke to his feet with a great howl.

It was two days after Easter, not even a week since returning home, that Al Zukor showed up at the West Adams house, refusing to hand over his coat to the butler, saying he didn't want to interrupt, only to offer the congratulations of everyone at the picture company.

Roscoe offered him a tea, coffee, a cigar perhaps? But Zukor said he really must be going.

"I have some ideas," Roscoe said. "Some of the pictures we had set, I think

I like *Thirty Days* best. A rich playboy who can only escape his woman's rival by ducking into prison. I make fun of the situation, that's the only way."

Zukor nodded.

"Would you like to hear a song?" Roscoe asked.

"I really must be going."

"Dine with us, Musso and Frank's. Like the old days."

"That's what I wanted to talk to you about."

Roscoe looked at him.

"The Hays Commission, Will Hays, has banned you."

"Banned me?" Roscoe said, laughing. "From what?"

"Making pictures."

"I was acquitted."

"There was a deal," Zukor said, his eyes finding the floor. "You are doing the industry a great service. Be patient, *mein Kind*. If it wasn't for the commission, every goddamn picture would be sliced up by every two-bit censor and religious nut."

"I've lost a chunk of change during this mess," Roscoe said. "They say they could take my home."

"You'll be back," Zukor said. "I just wanted you to hear from me and not those goddamn newspapermen. They should be knocking on your door anytime. I suggest you get out while you can. Ask for a private table. They'll understand."

Roscoe felt a palsy in his cheeks. Minta rose from the piano. Roscoe held the edge of the piano. Luke sniffed at Zukor's leg and began a low growl.

"How can they do this?"

"We voted," Zukor said. "All of us did. It was best with the trial and all, and a few other things. The average Joe thinks Hollywood is the devil's garden. See? We have to show them different. Listen, I tried my best to stop Hays, but he was intent that you were taught a lesson."

"I was acquitted."

"He said it sends the wrong message, that we can't be tough enough on our own people. We must show toughness now." Zukor shrugged. "In a year? Maybe another story."

Roscoe just stared at him, feeling his heart drop, wanting a drink very badly.

"Maybe we can get a deal for Luke," Zukor said. "How'd you like that?"

Luke continued to growl, Minta walking by Roscoe and grabbing the dog's collar. Teeth now bared.

Zukor had a fine camel coat laid across his arm and a beaver hat in his fingers that he nearly dropped while trying to shake Roscoe's hand again. Roscoe took his hand but didn't hold it. Zukor patted his shoulder and called him his child again, and just walked away, up the little landing and across the great hallway of marble checkerboard.

Roscoe did not move.

"Why has God done this to me?"

Minta didn't answer, only sat back at the piano and started to play a song that they sang together in all those saloons and mining towns, and he turned to her, resting his hand upon her shoulder, and joined in, taking the time for a solo on the old kazoo.

He sang louder and louder, the windows of the mansion shaking, one song breaking into the next, while the front door chimed and the telephone rang. Minta's gentle voice warming his heart until tears ran down his face and hit the keys.

He would not star in another picture for a dozen years, the very same year he died.

IT WAS FALL OF 1924 and Hearst decided on a party, quickly settling on the theme, the birthday of his good friend Tom Ince. He cobbled together a group of thirteen, including Miss Davies, and they all sailed from Wilmington on his sturdy little *Oneida*. That first night there was a spectacular dinner party, lobster cocktails and roast turkey and the endless uncorking of champagne for his guests. At sunset, the crew strung red Japanese lanterns along the rigging and the whole yacht took on a mystical glow in the balmy night, the thirteen gathering on deck for song and dessert, coffee, and more champagne. A giant birthday cake was brought out for Ince, baked in the shape of a horse since the man was famous for directing all those westerns—or what Hearst loved to call "horse operas."

Ince blew out the candles and there was applause, and singing, and Marion announced after drinking more than she'd promised that everyone was to find a costume.

"But we brought no costumes," Hearst said to the gathering.

"Here lies the challenge," Marion announced, grasping a champagne bottle from a crewman and pouring another drink. Before long, the deck was filled, with one couple saying they were Indians but really just covering themselves with blankets as shawls, another couple simply exchanging clothing, George dressed himself in an old bathrobe and said he was a monk. But, as always, Chaplin stole the show, borrowing a negligee and parading around, patting his long dark curls and asking everyone in that maddening accent, "Don't I look pretty?"

Even Hearst had to laugh.

There was a scavenger hunt and more song, and Hearst drank his coffee, speaking to the captain in the wheelhouse. It was there, through the glass, that he saw his guests standing on the bow staring up at the great ship's mast as Chaplin, still in women's silks, shimmied up the cables like some kind of ape, finding his footing high above them all, screaming and shouting. Hearst watched his enraptured guests, staring up at the drunken idiot.

Chaplin had found footing high in a crow's nest and began to recite Shakespeare.

"Marion," Hearst said. "We must—"

"Shush," she said.

He stared at her. Her head tilted back, eyes up at the starred sky, hands clutched to her breasts.

". . . slings and arrows of outrageous fortune, / Or to take arms against a sea of troubles, / And by opposing end them? / To die; to sleep; / No more; and by a sleep to say we end / The heart-ache and the thousand natural shocks / That flesh is heir to, 'tis a consummation / Devoutly to be wish'd. To die, to sleep; / To sleep: perchance to dream"—Chaplin stretched out his arm before him in contemplation—"ay, there's the rub."

Chaplin finished, thank God, and upended the bottle of Hearst champagne and tossed it deep into the Pacific. In the red glow of the lanterns, there was great applause, yet what mattered to Hearst was that there was also silence. The goddamn silence of awe for the funny little man.

Hearst put his hand on Marion's shoulder. But she did not feel it.

Hearst, in his great black boots, turned and stormed below, shutting and locking the door. He took two aspirin, filled a glass with fresh water, undressed, and turned out the lights, the party sounds echoing around him as the guests rocked and spun on the ship.

He awoke at three with a tremendous headache, sliding into his silk robe and slippers, unlocking his door and wandering to the galley, where he found two Chinese crewmen playing fan-tan.

They stood at attention, but he paid them no mind, taking the steps up to the deck and searching for Marion. He would ask her to come back to bed, as he felt much better now, the heat and embarrassment of it all cooled away.

The deck of the *Oneida* was empty.

Empty bottles of champagne and half-eaten trays of food sat on linen-covered tables, the cloths flapping in a cold wind, an approaching storm heading east.

Many of the candles in the lanterns had burned out and the gaiety of it all had grown dim. The stars gone.

Hearst went below, checking Marion's quarters, the quarters she kept during such trips with guests, only to find an unmade bed. Her night garments, laid out by George, untouched.

He walked the hallway. He heard laughter and thumping.

He stopped at a door, having to stoop a bit to get his ear to wood.

A woman's laughter. A man's laughter. A horrendous thumping sound.

Hearst reached for the doorknob, his mouth gone dry.

The room was dark, but a single oil candle on a bed table burned brightly enough that Hearst could see Marion's marbled body riding a man who lay flat on his back. The man's chest was bony, with a thin path of hair. He was sweating and smiling. Marion turned her head and, even in that moment,

Hearst noted the beauty of her shoulder blades, the milk of her skin, the golden curls against the nape of her neck.

Hearst screamed. Even to him, he sounded like a woman.

He covered his mouth with a hand for the shame.

Chaplin unlatched himself from Marion and twirled a giant red satin sheet around him, holding up a hand and sliding a smile in surrender. He backed away from Hearst, who moved toward him with some kind of lethargic curiosity. Chaplin found another door, a back door, and bolted from the room as quick as a jackrabbit.

Marion was nude. Not a bit of shame on her.

He looked at the smallness of her, the moist patch of hair between her legs, and he felt a great sadness in him. The sadness broke apart as his right hand balled into a fist, and Marion saw a change coming across Hearst's face, in the scattered light, as he turned and ran from the room.

Hearst ran to the wheelhouse, robe opened, exposing his aged flesh and sagging stomach, but taking great strides, feeling virile and tall, gray and hard. He reached above the instruments and found a 12-gauge mounted on brass hooks and broke apart the gun, checking the load, and snapping it together with a hard clack.

He was on deck, the robe flowing behind him, the storm's wind blowing across his hair and eyes and him squinting as the first tapping of rain hit the polished deck, the Japanese lanterns shuttering on the lines, some of them catching in the storm and breaking apart, scattering out to sea.

Hearst yelled for Chaplin.

The coward hid.

He moved aft, around the wheelhouse.

A shadow moved behind a lifeboat.

"Come out," Hearst said. "Face me."

The figure moved, hooded in the great sheet he'd wrapped himself in, face shadowed, trying to back away. In Hearst's mind, a faint memory of calliope music played.

Hearst pulled the trigger.

Blam.

He pulled the second trigger.

Blam.

A design of blood and flesh was visible even in the darkness.

Marion screamed. The wheelhouse came awake with light. Lights switched on in tripping patterns across the deck.

Marion knelt by her lover, pulling away his stained shroud.

The face changed.

It was Tom Ince, his friend.

Marion screamed again.

The deck was cluttered with crewman and the rest of the thirteen. They circled Ince's body, and one man who worked for Hearst, a physician, pronounced him dead right away. George brought Hearst a whiskey and took him back down below, Hearst talking and babbling but not making a bit of sense to either of them. If only his mother were alive.

Hearst tied the belt around his robe. "George, call the office, have our men assembled."

"Shall they clean this up?"

"Yes, whatever it may cost," Hearst said. "It's all such an awful mess and such a beautiful boat."

The body was taken ashore; the yacht sailed on. The headline read HOL-LYWOOD DIRECTOR DIES OF HEART ATTACK.

SAM QUIT THE PINKERTONS before Roscoe's third trial, everything known to have happened at that goddamn party already recorded. He sold his .32, used the money to buy a beautiful, somewhat used L. C. Smith. The typewriter had an honored place on the kitchen table that had become his office since the TB had grown worse, he and Jose living off a smattering of government checks and the odd short story that was published in a snotty rag called *The Smart Set.*

He got paid a penny a word.

He got a really nice response to a little piece called "Confessions of a Detective."

He wrote about how all the mystery hacks got it wrong, making the business of killing into some kind of parlor game. One of the editors suggested he write for a new magazine of theirs, something called *Black Mask*.

"What do you think?"

"What does it pay?" Jose asked. Always the skeptic.

"Not much," Sam said. "But I can write longer if I want."

"By all means make the detective handsome."

"I'm gonna make him short and fat."

"You're kidding."

"And he'll be ruthless."

"What will you call him?"

"Nobody," Sam said. "Names are for suckers."

Jose adjusted Mary Jane in her arms. She'd been bathed and dressed for bed. Sam already had the Scotch out. It had helped with the fog and cold summer nights that made him wake up with coughing fits.

"You think I can write literature?"

"For something called *Black Mask*?"

"Why the hell not," he said. "If I have to read another goddamn story about English lords and little old ladies tracking down killers, I'm gonna shoot myself."

"So what do you write?"

"The truth," Sam said. "Write about sweaty, greedy sonsabitches who'd kill their own mothers for some loot."

Jose nodded. She tucked Mary Jane in her crib and closed the door behind her in the safe room, clean of his coughs.

Sam poured a drink and loaded the typewriter with a fresh white page.

"I unpacked," Jose said. "The trunk. I hope you don't mind."

"Burn the thing."

"So this works?"

"For now."

"That's all we're promised."

"Amen, sister."

"Sam?"

"Yeah?" he said. He wore an undershirt and dress pants. No shoes.

"We'll get through this," she said. "You'll get well."

"This works," Sam said. "For now."

Jose went to bed. Sam lit a cigarette and poured a drink. The long steel arms of the typewriter hammered out that first story, the first story he thought he'd ever told straight and true. When he finished, he poured some Scotch he'd bought from the old woman downstairs.

He was sweating with the sickness.

Sam opened a window and crawled out onto the fire escape, looking down at Eddy Street, watching the pimps and hustlers and sonsabitches, listening to all the music, screams, and machine horns and stray gunfire, of a place he felt he belonged. The City.

ACKNOWLEDGMENTS

Background information provided by: *The Day the Laughter Stopped*, David Yallop; *The Forgotten Films of Roscoe "Fatty" Arbuckle*, Mackinac Media; *Frame-Up!*, Andy Edmonds; *Hammett: A Life at the Edge*, William F. Nolan; *Dashiell Hammett: A Life*, Diane Johnson; *Shadow Man* and *Discovering The Maltese Falcon and Sam Spade*, Richard Layman; *Selected Letters of Dashiell Hammett*, edited by Richard Layman and Julie M. Rivett; *The Dashiell Hammett Tour*, Don Herron; the complete works of Dashiell Hammett; *American Masters*, "Dashiell Hammett: Detective, Writer"; *Citizen Hearst*, W. A. Swanberg; and *The Chief*, David Nasaw. My thanks to librarians at the University of Mississippi and the great reporters of '21 for their coverage of the Arbuckle case in the *San Francisco Chronicle* and *San Francisco Examiner*.

To David Fechheimer for sharing his personal stories of meeting Jose Hammett and Phil Haultain and shadowing Hammett while working as a private detective in San Francisco. Another Southerner made good in Frisco.

And to Don Herron, my guide to Hammett's San Francisco, who provided the color and soul to this book. Anyone with any interest in Hammett's life should make the pilgrimage and take his tour, which has been going strong for more than thirty years.

As always, this book wouldn't exist without the guidance of my friends Neil and Esther. My great thanks to both of you for everything. And to Doris and Charlie, Tim Green, and my entire family for their unshakable support.

Also to Art Copeland for his endless trips up and down the Frisco hills with me to find some dive bar or back alley and countless journeys to Chinatown. You're a great egg. See you on the next adventure.

And to Andrea Grimes and Tom Carey at the San Francisco Public Library for digging up forgotten files on the Rappe case, Ed Komara and the folks at the Louisiana Music Factory for helping me with the soundtrack, Joe Atkins for keeping me plied with bourbon and great noir, Rick Layman for patient answers to my nagging Hammett questions, Marc Harrold for being paid in cigars for legal questions, Bill Arney for his personal tour of the Hammett apartment, and Carl Kickery for serving us up a free round at the Ha-Ra.

The big thanks go to my wife, Angela—tough-as-nails former crime reporter and hard-boiled sister to Daisy Simpkins. You produced your best work yet this year with Billy. I can't wait to introduce him to The City, the way my father did for me years ago.

800
−300 Bianca
―――――
500

Meds 152
GE 12
Aldi 45

770 check

9/8

1126

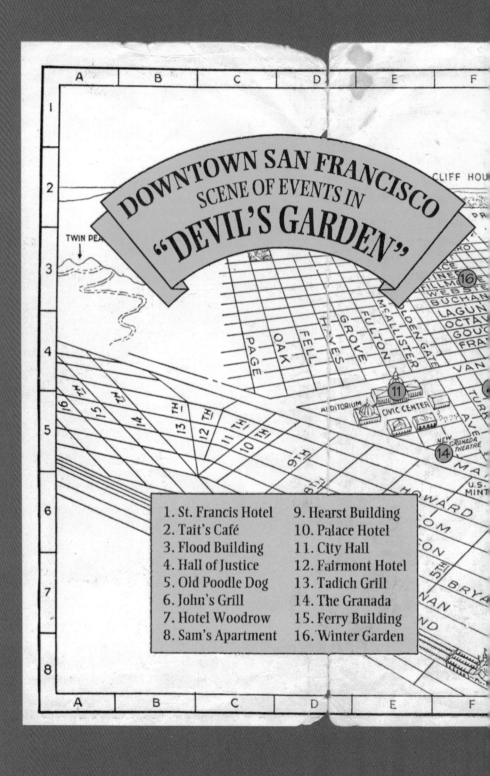